MY INNER STRANGER

Paul Devereaux

ISBN: 9798832383033

Cover design by: Mary Se
Library of Congress Control Number: 2018675309
Printed in the United States of America

CONTENTS

..1..

Charlie's voice pierced the stuffy silence of a dimly lit office, interrupting its owner's habitual post-lunch alcohol-infused nap. The door cracked open, and a beam of light that came through the gap illuminated a part of the wall decorated with discolored boxing match posters. Above them hung an old championship belt. The belt was so grimy and dusty that it was almost impossible to tell the win in which championship it was awarded for.

Some of the light also fell on the face of an old and extremely raddled man reclining in a big chair. The large executive desk in front of him featured several pieces of paper, an almost finished bottle of bourbon, a smudged glass with some golden liquid left on the bottom, and a desk nameplate that said, "Gerard McKee. CEO, One-Two Boxing." McKee screwed up his face and tried to turn away from the light, ignoring the words of his assistant who now stood in the doorway.

"Hey, Pops!" Charlie raised his voice and took a step forward. "There's some dude looking for you. All businesslike. With a tie and everything. You'd better go talk to him."

"Kid, how many times did I ask you not to bother me after lunch when I'm dealing with paperwork?" McKee asked hoarsely.

Charlie sneered.

"Paperwork? You mean these two papers? They've been on your table for a month! I bet you already forgot what these papers are."

"No one asked for your opinion, smartass."

With an effort, McKee moved closer to the desk and assumed a vertical position. The chair squeaked pitifully. McKee glanced at the swarthy, skinny boy standing in the doorway, shook his head disapprovingly, and picked up the glass.

"What if it's from the bank, or the tax office, or some sanitary inspector? Go talk to him. They won't be tiptoeing around you, you know that. Next time, they will show up with the cops and seal the gym."

McKee sent the remaining bourbon from the glass down his throat, and then stared at the bottle, wondering if he should finish it off completely. Finally, he heaved a deep sigh and looked up at Charlie.

"Fine, I'll come out. Tell him to wait."

The boy didn't move. McKee tried his best to give him the evil eye, but quickly gave up—Charlie wouldn't leave him alone until he got up from the chair. The boy knew all too well the profound gravitational effect exerted on his boss by his favorite chair and bottle. McKee heaved another sigh, leaned on the desk with his enormous calloused hands, and rose to his feet. As if mimicking his cousin the armchair, the desk, too, made a sorrowful noise under the 300-pound weight of its owner.

Despite nearing the age of retirement and being overweight, the six-foot-nine former heavyweight champion still looked imposing and sometimes downright formidable. Especially when he was about to meet someone he had no desire to see. And lately, that was the majority of visitors at One-Two Boxing. In these cases, McKee would square his broad shoulders, pull in his stomach, and proudly raise his eternally unshaven chin.

The transformation never ceased to amaze Charlie. It was only at those moments that the old man turned back into the Gerard McKee who was Charlie's childhood hero. The person whose fights, home-recorded on VHS tapes, were constantly played by Charlie's father back when they still lived in Guadalajara.

"So what are you waiting for?" McKee's hoarse voice pulled Charlie out of his daze. "Go on, show me that suit of yours."

The boy turned around and hurried to lead the way to the main entrance—past old punching bags, sadly hanging from the ceiling, past hopelessly worn-out speed bags and a couple of body opponent bags, whose faces over the years lost their menacing features and gained a depressive aspect, so characteristic now of all the furnishings of the formerly renowned One-Two Boxing.

A man in his mid-30s was standing at the entrance to the club. His appearance sharply contrasted the surroundings: he was short and lean, if not to say skinny, with a cleanly shaven, well-groomed face and a stylish haircut straight out of a fashion magazine. He was dressed in a bespoke and undoubtedly expensive formal three-piece.

The man could have easily been taken for a banker, a broker, or a large company business executive if not for one detail. His appearance lacked that relaxed disdainful arrogance so common among successful white-collars. In contrast, the stranger looked very tense. As if he himself believed that he didn't belong not only in that old and dingy, yet basking in its former glory, boxing club, but also in his own high-end suit, and maybe even in his own skin.

"Hey, Mister," MacKee shouted from a distance, addressing the stranger. "I was talking to your guys at the bank two days ago. We have agreed on a delay until the end of the month. Just don't tell me you've changed your mind. I have it all on paper, you won't be able to take my gym so easily!"

Charlie thought that the visitor flinched slightly, scared by McKee's threatening appearance and the speed with which he was approaching. But when the old man stood right in front of him, looming like a cliff over the stranger who was a full foot shorter than him, he stretched out his hand to McKee without missing a beat.

"Mr. MacKee?" the stranger was clearly trying to make his voice sound more masculine than it really was.

"Yes, it's me," answered the old man and automatically shook the outstretched hand, continuing to glare at the visitor.

The stranger's palm, almost child-like in size, drowned in McKee's giant hand.

"Jack Sullivan, nice to meet you. Don't worry, I'm not from a bank or any other organization that might threaten your gym."

"Threaten? Me?" McKee roared, reflexively attacking even before he could figure out the situation.

Unconsciously, McKee emphasized his words by squishing Sullivan's hand. Noticing that the visitor clenched his teeth in pain, Charlie hastened to intervene.

"Pops, he didn't talk about you! He said "threaten the gym" and that he's not one of those who can do it!"

"Yeah, right," McKee released Sullivan's hand and took a step back. "Sorry, Mister. My bad."

"It's okay," the guest responded, rubbing his palm, almost crushed by the hot-tempered old man.

"So how can I help you, Mr. Sullivan?"

"I want to train with you."

"No problem, the price list is hanging over there by the locker room entrance. Punching bags, barbells, dumbbells, and everything else is included in the price. There are gym membership options and group discounts. Charlie will show and tell you everything."

After giving his assistant a slight push forward, McKee was about to turn around and go back to the armchair and bottle he loved so much when Sullivan stopped him.

"No, you didn't understand. I don't want to train in your gym, I want to be trained personally by you, Mr. McKee."

With a quick glance, the old man examined Sullivan's puny physique, his pricey suit, well-groomed face, and delicate hands.

"Listen, buddy, I understand that a healthy lifestyle is a

thing now and everyone in your world is doing some kind of aerobics or Pilates. So you decided to show off in front of your golf-club buddies and instead of some faggy gym join an old-school boxing club. It's one thing to play around with pink girly barbells that won't serve even to prop a door open in the summer or take a bunch of selfies next to a punching bag, but it's something completely different to box. Trust me, that's not for you."

Charlie noticed that McKee's tone, as rough as his hands, made the visitor's cheek muscles flex. The boy almost opened his mouth to intervene again, but Sullivan didn't need his help.

"Mr. McKee, I understand very well what boxing is. I don't go to the golf club. I already have a faggy gym membership. I don't take selfies, and I don't have friends to brag to. I want to become a fighter. A real one. I want you to teach me. And I will pay as much as you ask."

Sullivan's words sounded unexpectedly harsh, even though there still was a touch of insecurity and even fear in them. That odd stranger had probably never had to confront anyone half as formidable as McKee.

At the mention of the money the gym was in desperate need of, the old man paused to think. He took a step back and, once again, examined the man in front of him from head to foot.

"How old are you?"

"Thirty-five."

"How much do you weigh?"

"One hundred and twenty pounds."

"Have you ever boxed, wrestled, maybe did some karate shit in school?"

Sullivan shook his head.

"Any sports at all?"

Sullivan shook his head again.

"Were you at least a boy scout as a kid?" chuckled McKee.

Sullivan didn't bother to reply to what was obviously a mockery. The old man scratched his chin and added, "Got picked on by a bully? Or struggling to stand up to your boss at work? Or maybe your wife dumped you for some hunk?"

Sullivan shook his head three times.

"So what do you need boxing for? Was there a re-run of *Fight Club* last night?"

"I want to become the IPBU World Champion," Salivan replied in all seriousness.

The old man gave out a cry of surprise that was a mix of a cough and a sob, and then the gym turned silent for a second. It wasn't long, however, before McKee rejoined.

"So you like the International Professional Boxing Union?" the old man barely stifled a laugh. "Neither WBA, nor WBC, nor IBF, nor WBO suit you, only IPBU?"

Again, Sullivan ignored McKee's mockery. McKee waited for a couple of seconds and added, "To hell with the IPBU. Let's train you to be a fairy godmother."

McKee found his own remark so incredibly funny that he couldn't hold his laughter anymore. The booming sound traveled through the entire gym, peeking into the farthest corners that Charlie had been overlooking when washing the floor at night for more than a year.

The boy peered at the visitor's face, expecting him to burst out in anger or maybe burst into tears under the avalanche of the old man's derisive laughter. Surprisingly, Sullivan didn't respond at all. Charlie even thought that he became calmer than he was at the beginning of his conversation with McKee.

When the old man's guffaw started to die out, Sullivan spoke in a calm, neutral, and this time quite confident voice,

"Mr. McKee, your club's official website states that you provide services to prepare boxers for professional fights. I want to purchase these services. Why I need these services and what the chances of my endeavor being successful are is none of your business."

McKee finally stopped laughing, exhaled loudly, and wiped away the tear that appeared on his seemingly long dried out eyes. Sullivan continued in the same unperturbed voice,

"I need your professional services as a coach, and your opinion on the potential success of my endeavor interests me no more than the opinion of a supermarket clerk on how well I can make a frozen key lime pie from the ingredients I purchased from him."

Charlie chuckled at the clever jibe.

"Mister McKee, do you provide coach services or not?"

The man's scoff, his calm tone, and especially Charlie's reaction brought McKee's legendary short temper to life. He made a menacing step toward Sullivan and roared, "Listen to me, you faggot-haired piece of shit! This gym is the holy temple of boxing! Of the greatest sport in the history of humanity! Of the sport built with the hundreds of thousands of gallons of real men's sweat and blood. And you are defiling it with your mere presence at the doorstep of my gym. There is no way in hell I would coach such a sleazy bastard even in a dirty craphouse, let alone in my ring. I would teach you a boxing lesson right here and right now if I weren't worried I'd kill you with one punch. But I can still change my mind, so hurry up and get your thousand-dollar suit and your shiny heels out of here."

A shiver went down Charlie's spine even though McKee's angry outburst had nothing to do with him. But to both Charlie's and the old man's surprise, Sullivan didn't back down, even though his voice betrayed his fear.

"Again, I'm ready to pay any amount you name."

"Get out of my gym!" muttered McKee through gritted teeth. "I'm counting to three."

"Call me if you change your mind," Sullivan took out a business card from the inside pocket of his jacket and handed it to the old man. "I pay forward. Any amount."

McKee sharply slapped Sullivan's outstretched hand, sending the business card down on the dirty floor. Sullivan's face contorted in pain. Rubbing his injured hand, he turned around and headed for the exit, saying as he went,

"I will be waiting for your call."

Standing in the doorway, he turned around and added, "By the way, my suit is worth three thousand dollars."

Sullivan stepped outside, slamming the old rusty door behind him.

As McKee dashed after him, Charlie grabbed his boss by the shoulder with all his strength. "Hey, Pops! Take it easy! You know there are cameras on every building around here. If you mess him up, you won't get away with it. I bet he has a big-time lawyer on standby."

The old man let out an angry breath, like a fighting bull, spat loudly on the floor, aiming at Sullivan's business card, then turned around, and, without a word to Charlie, headed back to his office. As the door closed behind his boss, the boy bent down to pick up the card and, happy that McKee had missed, stuck it in the back pocket of his shorts.

..2..

Friday was the busiest day at One-Two Boxing, with a whopping seven men hitting punching bags, lifting barbells, or exercising with jump ropes. Two of them, however, were local coaches, and another three were their relatives or friends, who paid a symbolic price for access to the gym.

Not more than five or six years earlier, however, the gym was packed every day of the week. Back then, One-Two Boxing was known as the most prestigious boxing club in the city and even in the state. The boss's office at the time looked much more presentable and featured two executive desks instead of one.

In all fairness, there was never a need there for the second desk—McKee occupied it only for the sake of status; all important decisions were made by Johnny Sifaretto. Johnny was Gerard's oldest and probably the only real friend. The Irish American and the Italian American met in first grade and quickly bonded over being bullied by their "pure-blood" schoolmates.

However strange it sounded now when you saw McKee's enormous frame and his championship belt, it was Johnny who protected Gerard for the first five years of school. He was losing almost every fight against an overwhelming number of opponents, but at least that way Gerard wasn't getting as pummeled as when he was ambushed alone by their schoolmates. It all changed in sixth grade when Gerard came back after summer vacation almost a foot taller and ten pounds heavier.

That's when he got back at all of his bullies, dishing out

punches left and right both for himself and for Johnny. It was Sifaretto who first saw McKee's potential as a big fighter and practically dragged him to a local boxing school cooped up in a damp cellar underneath a butcher's shop. Though being a decent boxer himself, Johnny chose the role of his friend's first and only manager over his own professional career.

Sports media often argued whether McKee owed his championship to his innate talent, his enormous fists that always reacted faster and more accurately than his brain or Johny Sifaretto. McKee himself never had any doubt that it was the latter. Sifaretto organized all his fights, picked his coaches, found doctors to treat his multiple injuries, and smoothed things over with federation officials.

But most importantly, only Sifaretto knew how to control McKee's hot temper that caused him so many problems. Dozens, maybe even hundreds of times, Johny stopped his friend a mere second before he did something that could cost him big money, his professional career, and maybe even freedom.

When McKee had to retire because of his injuries, Sifaretto decided to quit boxing with him, even though numerous promoters were eager to sign such a capable manager. There were even rumors that he was offered a top position in the federation. But Johnny didn't want, or rather was afraid to leave his best friend alone. So he suggested the two of them open One-Two Boxing. McKee became its face and head coach, while Sifaretto took everything else upon himself.

Johnny showed himself just as talented a businessman as a manager. The gym thrived, but what's even more important, each of the co-founders was doing what he loved most side by side with his best friend. Every working day ended with them sitting in hammocks on the rooftop of their boxing club, sipping beer, reminiscing about their boxing past, and making plans for the future. Those were the years when McKee hardly ever finished even a single bottle and never so much as glanced at anything stronger than beer.

One-Two Boxing was doing so well that soon Johny and Gerard opened a second and then a third club. For the company's tenth anniversary, Sifaretto developed a global franchising plan meant to unite around twenty different clubs in the US, Canada, the UK, and Ireland. Everything was lined up perfectly, but then a wrench was thrown in the works in the form of a subarachnoid hemorrhage.

Johny Sifaretto suddenly passed away at the age of 55. At the end of another day's work in the club, he said goodbye to Gerard, drove home, parked his car, but never got out from behind the wheel. Sifaretto's death was a bigger tragedy to McKee than even to Johnny's wife and 15-year-old son. At least they had each other, while McKee, raised by his grandmother who was now long dead, had only two things since he was 17: boxing and Johnny.

Ten years earlier, Gerard had to quit boxing, and now fate also took away his best friend. Without them, McKee was left only with one thing—his hot temper. That and his newly-developed fondness for strong spirits scared away first the investors seeking to put their money into the One-Two Boxing franchise, then most of the clubs' employees, and then also the clients.

Once the downfall of the company became apparent even to McKee, he did one last noble thing. Gerard collected all the remaining money left from his past fights and clubs' earnings in the previous years and bought out the second half of One-Two Boxing from Sifaretto's widow. The amount of money Gerard paid corresponded to the price of the company back before he drove it into the ground.

But noble gestures don't pay rent, utilities, or any other bills, so soon Gerard was forced to close two of the three clubs. He kept only the first one, the one he and Sifaretto built from scratch. McKee simply couldn't afford to give it up as well. He was in his sixties. He had no wife, no kids, no friends. All he had was a worthless 30-year-old championship title, which no one would even remember now. Take One-Two Boxing from

McKee, and what will be left of him? Nothing but an old alcoholic, filled with regret, waiting to die alone.

Trying to chase away the dark thoughts, McKee put the glass with bourbon to his lips, but before he could empty it, someone knocked on the door and, not bothering to wait for a reply, opened it.

"Pops, my last training session is over. Here's the keys, just like we agreed."

A tall young man in his early twenties, with thick dark hair and a sly smile, stood on the doorstep. He had already changed from his club uniform into regular clothes and was clearly desperate to get out of One-Two Boxing as soon as possible. His left hand in his pocket, he stretched out his right hand holding a set of keys.

"Should I put them here?" asked the young man pointing at the filing cabinet at the door.

"Hold on a moment, let's at least have a proper goodbye," answered McKee and with some difficulty climbed out of his chair.

"So it's decided then? You won't change your mind?" asked Gerard approaching the young man.

"Nah, Pops, I won't. Sorry, but you know how it is. Here I have no future, but in Dog Bite I'll have more training hours and, most importantly, I'll be able to try myself as a manager. I've already made an arrangement with an aspiring but very promising fighter. If things go well, next year we might have a go at a championship."

"All right then, Mikey. Good luck," said McKee offering a handshake. "Just so you know, you're always welcome here."

Mikey shook the hand he was offered and made an awkward attempt at hugging the old man. In response, McKee patted him on the back. As the embrace ended, Mikey handed the keys to Gerard, nodded goodbye, and left the office of his now-former boss. McKee sighed, walked up to the wall decorated with framed photos, took one of them down, and held it to his eyes.

It wasn't that he really needed Mikey as a trainer, but with him, One-Two Boxing lost the last remaining part of its glorious past. The picture showed McKee, Johnny Sifaretto with his big, never-fading smile, and little Mikey, his only son. The boy literally grew up in One-Two Boxing, visiting his father almost every day. With a grin, McKee remembered that in that time it was Mikey who usually occupied the second executive desk, and not him.

Back then Gerard was spending all his time in the gym training aspiring fighters as Johnny's son sat next to his father, absorbed in painting or doing his homework. As a child, Mikey Sifaretto was a shy and quiet boy, a straight-A student who always did as his parents told him. But he changed with his father's death, which happened at the hardest stage of his puberty. Mikey fell in with the wrong crowd, took on drinking, started experimenting with drugs and squandering away the money he inherited from his father.

Soaked in his grief and alcohol, McKee soon stopped paying visits to his friend's widow and son. The first time he learned about Mikey's problems was only a couple of years earlier, when he was first arrested for drunk driving. It was Janice who came to McKee and asked him to set her son on the right track. Using his fists, among other things, Gerard drove Mikey's low-life friends away and knocked some sense into the boy. To prevent any relapsing, the old man hired Mikey, first as his assistant, and then as a coach.

Mikey never drank alcohol, took drugs, or broke the law again, but he also never became the same kind and warm-hearted boy. The dark hole ripped deep in his heart by his father's death, was still visible to Gerard. It is possible that if McKee tried harder, the boy could have healed completely, but Gerard was too old, too tired, and too broken to be helping anyone. The only thing he could hope for at that point was to one day, ideally in the immediate future, die in the same quick and easy manner as his best friend Johnny Sifaretto.

The door opened, this time without a warning knock,

and nearly hit McKee who was standing next to it.

"Oh, sorry, Pops," said Charlie, who entered the office. "What are you standing here for?"

Gerard stared at the photo for another second, hung it back in place, and only then turned to look at his assistant.

"What do you want?" McKee answered with a question.

"Here, you've got mail."

Charlie handed a bunch of envelopes to the old man. McKee took it reluctantly and skimmed through correspondence as he headed back to his desk. Once there, the old man sat in his chair, chucked the letters onto the desk, heaved a sigh, and started rubbing his temples.

"Is it that bad?" asked Charlie, approaching the table.

"As if you didn't notice the 'past due' stamps on the envelopes while bringing them here."

"I did, but you said that you took care of the bank. That they gave you an extension."

"And so I did. But that was just the bank. Apart from that, there are also electricity bills, water bills, rent, and a bunch of other unpleasant stuff."

An uneasy silence hung in the air.

"I'll be honest, Kid, feel free to look for a new job," McKee added with a gloomy indifference in his voice. "We will, of course, hold out for a while. We can sell some of the equipment. Nobody uses it anyway. But you won't get much out of it. We may be able to cover one bill, but not more."

"Pops, is there really no way to save our gym?"

McKee shook his head.

"No one will give us a loan now. Not even the greediest loan shark. And even if they did, I have no idea how money can change anything. You're seeing for yourself the number of clients we have. And the ad we took out was no good either. Our days are in the past. One-Two Boxing is obsolete and outdated, which means nobody gives a damn about it."

McKee heaved another sigh, slumped back in his chair, and closed his eyes wearily. Oppressive silence once again gripped the office. Charlie opened his mouth to say something but quickly changed his mind. He raised his arm, hoping to enhance his words with a gesture, but changed his mind again, not knowing the right way to approach the old man.

"Kid," McKee said without opening his eyes. "The fact that I don't see you doesn't mean that I don't hear you nervously shifting your feet. Spill it out."

Charlie lingered for a couple of seconds before speaking. "Just don't get all riled up, Pops. The thing is... Basically..."

"Come on, Charlie, gather up your courage already. Think of some great Mexican hero. Speedy Gonzales, for example," added the old man with a grin.

"Okay. Look... Remember that suit who came here a week ago?"

"The semi-faggot who wanted to become an IPBU champion?" interrupted McKee.

"Well... I guess you could put it like that," answered Charlie in a lower voice. "But yeah, the guy who wanted you to train him."

McKee opened his eyes and gave Charlie a disapproving look. The boy became even more embarrassed.

"Pops, but he said he'd be willing to pay any money. You could ask him double, triple, hell, five times the price!"

The old man silently glared at Charlie. The boy lowered his eyes, but didn't back down and continued to speak staring at his own feet, "What do you have to lose? If the club gets closed, you don't think it will be defiled by some strip club or McDonald's that will open in its place? Charge him the amount that will allow us to stay afloat for another couple of months—who knows, maybe in that time we'll figure out how to attract normal customers. Why follow the ship to the bottom when there's a chance to save it?"

McKee kept glaring at Charlie, but at least he hadn't lost his temper yet, which was the boy's main concern.

"Please, Pops! I'm begging you! Do it for One-two! You owe this club! You must do everything you can to save it!"

Despite Charlie's emotional speech, the expression on the old man's face remained impervious. And so the boy resorted to a sucker punch,

"Pops, what would Mr. Sifaretto do?"

In the best traditions of One-Two combos, as he uttered those words, Charlie threw out his hand, pointing at the wall with the photographs, most of which featured smiling Johnny Sifaretto.

"Low blow, Kid. Didn't expect this from you," McKee said with a sad smile.

The old man didn't want to show it, but the mention of his old friend touched him more than Charlie could imagine. It was Sifaretto who built One-Two Boxing, while McKee was more of a hindrance to him than any real help. The club was the project of Johnny's life, and all Gerard achieved after his friend's death was to drive the company into the ground. McKee did owe a lot—only not to the club, as Charlie put it, but to Johnny Sifaretto.

Noticing that his words had finally produced an effect and eager to seize the opportunity, Charlie fumbled in the back pocket of his jeans and fished out a crumpled business card that said, "Jack Sullivan, Information Security Consultant." The boy had been fiddling with it all week until it barely held together, working up the nerve to approach the old man.

"All right, fine. You got it," spoke McKee, trying to make his voice sound as indifferent as possible. "You can call that weirdo. Tell him to come tomorrow morning."

Encouraged by this success, Charlie handed the business card to the old man and boldly, almost defiantly answered, "Oh no, Pops. After that rant of yours… No way! It has to be you. Especially since he said he'd be waiting for *your* call."

McKee chuckled.

"Look who's being brave! So you finally remembered Speedy Gonzales?"

The old man reached for the business card.

"And I also think you'd better apologize to him."

"Don't stretch your luck, Kid!" answered McKee and made as if to throw a boxing glove lying on the desk at the boy.

Charlie made as if he got scared and hurried out of his boss's office. As the door closed, the boy felt a nice and warm feeling spreading in his chest. It was probably the first win in his life, so short, but so full of misery and sorrow.

..3..

A battered pick-up truck pulled over next to a single-story industrial-looking building with a similarly battered One-Two Boxing sign. Stretched along the entire wall was a discolored and daubed with tags banner featuring Gerard McKee, still young and full of energy. His hands in boxing gloves were proudly resting on his waist adorned with a brand-new championship belt, the same belt whose stained and dusty ghost was now hanging on the wall in the club director's office.

Sitting behind the wheel of the pick-up truck, McKee grabbed a large plastic cup of coffee from the cupholder with his right hand and stuck his left hand into the inside pocket of his jacket. A flat metal flask appeared then and nearly half of its contents was poured into the coffee. McKee called it Irish breakfast, sometimes also adding with a grin, "Breakfast is the most important meal of the day."

The reason behind that was very simple: during the day the old man mostly drank the cheapest and quite disgusting bourbon, while his morning coffee was only ever spiced with genuine Irish whiskey straight from County Cork. The local club of boxing aficionados still remembered the achievements of Gerard McKee, who, even twenty years later, was known there as "the greatest Irish boxer of his generation." And so, once a month, a package with a bottle of Jameson and a postcard with a few kind words of encouragement in Irish appeared on the old man's doorstep.

McKee took a big gulp of his Irish breakfast, got out of the car, and headed for the entrance of One-Two Boxing. In the distance, far behind the club's roof, the sun had just started climbing up from beyond the horizon. The old man always came here at dawn. Insomnia made staying in bed pointless anyway. Besides, it was the only time when McKee could enjoy his solitude in the club and sometimes even climb into the ring and indulge himself in shadowboxing, trying to re-enact the most glorious fights of his past.

"Mr. McKee," came from somewhere behind the old man.

Gerard was so startled by encountering someone here at this time that he almost dropped his cup of Irish breakfast.

"God damn it!" croaked McKee, his voice still full of morning hoarseness. "Who has too many teeth to sneak up on me like that?"

The old man turned around and saw a man in a formal suit stepping out from behind the wheel of a bright red Tesla and walking towards him.

"Ah, it's you, Sullivan," added McKee. "What on earth brings you here at this hour?"

"You said in the morning. So I arrived in the morning," said Jack.

"For normal people, the morning starts no earlier than seven."

"But you're here," Sullivan retorted.

He stopped a couple of steps away from the old man, his eyes drawn to an unusual sight: staring at Sullivan were two Gerard McKee's, the real one and the champion depicted on the banner dating back 30 years. Though the features hadn't changed much over time, those two looked not more like each other than the Ghost of Christmas Past and the Ghost of Christmas Yet to Come.

"Sure, what the hell—stay since you're already here."

The old man took a sip of his coffee and whiskey and reached into his pocket for the keys to the club door.

"Electric?" McKee asked and nodded towards Sullivan's car.

"Yes."

"If you ask me, that's just faggoty crap. A real car should be running on gas, it should be roaring. And this? Nothing but a vibrator on wheels."

Sullivan chose not to comment on the coach's remark.

"Did you at least bring some sportswear? Or are you gonna be jumping around in your suit?"

Sullivan silently nodded at the duffel bag slung over his shoulder.

"Well, come on in then."

The old man turned the key in the lock, opened the squeaky iron door, and let the visitor in. The gym was enveloped in the darkness that was pierced here and there with the dim light coming from a dozen or so skylights. McKee flipped the switch on the distribution board next to the entrance, and the lights went on—not all of them, just several lamps over the ring and around the punching bags.

Sullivan looked around. Despite its overall shabbiness, this lighting made the undisturbed gym look somewhat solemn, like a crumbling and abandoned, yet still retaining its holiness, temple.

"The locker room is over there," McKee pointed the direction with his hand. "The session starts the moment you step into my gym. So no need to hurry," added the old man with a chuckle.

As Sullivan hurried in the direction pointed to him, McKee yelled to his back, "Once you're changed, start working on a punching bag. I'll get to you in a couple of minutes."

The old man slowly walked to his office, mumbling under his breath, "This is your life now, Gerard. Training some crazy faggoty broker. All because of money..."

Sullivan stepped out of the locker room just as the old man closed the office door behind him. The locker room was right next to the area designated to punch practice, which was equipped with punching bags, speed bags, and body opponent bags. Jack stopped at a loss, not knowing which equipment to start with. As he had no desire to hit something with a face and was completely clueless as to the purpose of the speed bag, he settled on one of the sturdier-looking punching bags and started awkwardly beating it with his fists.

Jack was surprised to find out that hitting a punching bag was quite unpleasant, even though he barely put any force into his punches. But he came here to become a boxer and he wouldn't give up because of some minor discomfort. The entrance door screeched behind his back.

"Ouch!" exclaimed Sullivan involuntarily.

He looked at his left fist and saw blood trickling where the skin broke on one of his knuckles.

"You need to wrap your hands," came a voice from the darkness.

Looking back at the sound, Sullivan saw a lanky boy of about seventeen walking towards him.

"Charlie, right?"

Charlie nodded.

"You're McKee's assistant, aren't you?"

"Well, if the one who washes the floors and unclogs shower drains can be called an assistant, then yes, it's me," Charlie said ironically.

"I'm sure you're actually more important to this gym than you think," Sullivan replied and held out his hand. "Jack Sullivan, nice to meet you."

Charlie shook his hand, trying to remember a single One-Two Boxing visitor who would have honored him with a formal introduction. Having failed to do that, the boy repeated his original suggestion.

"You need to wrap your hands. Otherwise, you'll be bleeding all over the place in no time. The old man probably didn't realize that you are a complete newbie and don't know how to tape your hands."

"Yeah, I'm a 100-percent boxing virgin," Sullivan replied with a friendly smile.

"Let me help you."

Charlie went to the locker room and returned with a

couple of boxing hand wraps.

"You should get your own set. What we have here is so old, it's embarrassing," said Charlie wrapping Sullivan's right hand.

"Thanks. I'll definitely follow your advice."

Charlie tried to remember a single instance of anyone following his advice or at least thanking him for something. Again, he failed.

"Here you go," said Charlie, fastening the Velcro on Sullivan's other hand. "Next time you'll try yourself, and I'll give you tips if needed."

"Thank you, Charlie, I appreciate your help."

Charlie had probably never experienced as much politeness and gratitude in his life as he did in the last three minutes. Not knowing how to respond to that kind of treatment, the boy only nodded and added,

"Well, now you can practice punches without worrying that you'll damage your fists. I guess I'll go and check how the old man is doing."

Sullivan gave Charlie another friendly smile and returned to the punching bag, now hitting it with a little more confidence. McKee, who was watching his new pupil through a gap in his office's blinds all this time, shook his head disapprovingly and mumbled under his breath, "The idiot doesn't know the first thing about boxing. Hell, he doesn't know the first thing about punching!" The old man's musings were interrupted by the sound of the door opening.

"Pops, did you really tell a newbie to work on his punches without even wrapping his fists?" Charlie's voice rang with unconcealed outrage.

"Punches? You call *that* punches?" answered the old man, not bothering to face the boy who entered his office. "No, no, wait. You call *that* fists?"

McKee made an impression of Sullivan clenching his fists while sticking out his thumbs. The old man found his own act quite amusing.

"Pops, have you forgotten why we're doing this?" Charlie's voice now sounded even more indignant. "To get money! To save our gym! If he hurts his knuckles or, god forbid, breaks a couple of fingers, how much do you think he'll pay us? If anything, he's going to sue you! Pops, do you want to save One-Two Boxing or not?"

"Oh, come on," replied the old man. "Don't get all riled up. He's gonna be fine. But tell me this, Charlie, is he wearing tights underneath his shorts?"

"These are special men's workout tights, Pops. They provide compression. Everyone wears them now. Professional athletes too. You're just behind the times."

"Well, if the times mean men are now sporting pantyhose, I'm glad I'm behind them. The gayness of this world!"

"Shouldn't you start training him already?"

"Fine, I'm going. Just stop being a smart-ass, or else I'll sic the Immigration Services on you."

The old man grinned waspishly and left the office for the punch practice area where Sullivan kept going at the punching bag with the same awkwardness. Charlie followed his boss. With every step toward his new pupil, McKee was focusing less on Charlie's words about money and saving the club and more on Sullivan's absurd and unmanly look. What the old man found especially annoying was Jack's leg-hugging snow-white tights.

In the end, as was almost always the case, his annoyance took precedence over his common sense, and once he approached Sullivan, McKee spoke in a derisive and contemptuous manner, "So, do you still wanna box? Haven't you changed your mind?"

Sullivan paused, turned to face McKee, and answered, slightly out of breath,

"No, I haven't."

"And you wanna do it professionally?"

Sullivan nodded.

"Wanna fight for IPBU title?"

McKee's tone grew more derisive with each next phrase.

"And you wanna become a champion?"

Sullivan nodded again.

"Okay, whatever you say, buddy," the old man chuckled contemptuously and turned to Charlie who was standing behind him. "Kid, get some hand wraps and two pairs of gloves."

Charlie stared at the boss, confused.

"Bring the hand wraps and two pairs of gloves," McKee repeated in an unexpectedly harsh tone.

Charlie quickly complied with the order. The old man took the gloves from his assistant and added, "Wrap your hands."

Charlie's eyes widened even more in surprise.

"Do I have to repeat every word to you twice today?" the old man's voice grew more authoritative.

Charlie quickly wrapped his hands. McKee handed the boy one pair of gloves and nodded at Sullivan. Charlie put the gloves on Jack, still not fully understanding why the old man was doing that. Unlike the boy, Sullivan looked completely calm. McKee helped Charlie put on his gloves and took a few steps back.

"Fight", said the old man in a matter-of-fact voice.

"What?" Charlie asked in surprise. "What for?"

"Our guest wants to become a professional boxer. We should give him the opportunity to find out what real professional boxing is."

"Pops, but you haven't given him a single session yet! He can't even clench his fist correctly!"

"Mr. Sullivan," McKee said to his new pupil. "Do you understand that usually boxers start training at the age of fourteen at the latest, and they become professional fighters only five or even ten years later? Do you wanna make your debut at forty-five?"

Sullivan shook his head and added, "I want to make my

debut before the end of this year."

The old man barely restrained himself from bursting out in laughter.

"Wonderful, Mr. Sullivan. Just wonderful. In this case, I believe you would agree with me that it makes no sense to train you in the same way as a regular snotty-nosed greenhorn who hasn't even started growing pubic hair."

Sullivan nodded as calmly as before.

"You are not afraid to face a 17-year-old who is barely a flyweight, are you? I assure you that Charlie, same as you, has never done any professional training. Whatever he knows about boxing, he learned by hanging around real fighters, never letting a bucket and a mop out of his hands."

Even though the old man's words were true, Charlie was still hurt by the way they were spoken.

"I'm not afraid," replied Sullivan. "But I will not force Charlie to do something that he's not okay with."

"Don't worry about that," McKee shifted his gaze to his assistant. "You don't mind, Charlie, do you? This whole thing was your idea. Or should I remind you of your little speech about the responsibilities before our gym?"

Charlie exhaled sharply, expressing indignation, and, without answering the old man, went into the locker room. McKee thought for a second that he had gone too far, but the boy immediately came back, carrying two head guards with him. He put on one of them and reached out to give the other one to Sullivan. But the old man caught his hand.

"No, no. Mr. Sullivan isn't preparing for the Olympics, is he? Head guards aren't used in professional boxing. You know that very well, Charlie."

The boy started to take off his head guard too, but the old man stopped him again, putting his hand on his shoulder. "You should keep it on. You are not the one preparing for professional fights. It would only be fair."

Charlie, who stopped at first, shook off the coach's hand, took off his head guard, and angrily threw it aside.

"Save your fury for the fight," chuckled McKee.

Charlie opened his mouth to answer the old man, but he cut him off.

"Ready?" McKee turned to Sullivan.

Sullivan nodded.

"Shouldn't we at least get into the ring?" said Charlie before the old man could ask him the same question.

"The right to get into the ring has to be earned," answered McKee sharply and cut Charlie's further objections short by commanding, "That's it. Go!"

Charlie's gloves, as if on their own will, jumped to his chin, while his feet instantly assumed a proper boxing stance. Sullivan tried to imitate the boy's movements, but his gloves were positioned too low, his torso remained almost perpendicular to that of his opponent, instead of a 45-degree angle, and his elbows completely failed to protect the lower part of his rib cage.

Even the youngest and most inexperienced boxer would have no problem beating Sullivan, having about a hundred different strategies at his disposal. Neither his chin, nor his liver, his solar plexus, or any of the other vulnerable spots were protected in any way. But unlike McKee, Charlie didn't want to hurt the newbie, let alone knock him out.

And so instead of launching a proper attack, the boy started circling around his opponent, only occasionally attempting a half-hearted punch. All of them hit nothing but Sullivan's gloves, forearms, or shoulders. Not because Jack was any good at blocking or dodging, but because that's where Charlie aimed. Sullivan didn't put any force into his punches either, afraid to hurt the boy even by accident, but did his best to match his opponent's footwork and number of attacks. Still, all of Jack's punches were so sloppy that it took Charlie no effort to parry them.

McKee instantly saw through his assistant's strategy, which only aggravated him more.

"Charlie, quit dancing around! Hit!"

The boy ignored his boss's command. McKee raised his voice, "He's open from above and below! Why the hell are you punching his gloves?"

Charlie responded to the old man with a reproving glance.

"I bet your Mexican cousins are better at hitting a piñata with their eyes closed," McKee was almost yelling.

Charlie threw the coach another reproving glance and instead of hitting his opponent's gloves or forearms, started missing on purpose.

"God damn it, Charlie!" roared the old man. "If you don't stop screwing around, I will take your place!"

The boy glanced at McKee over his shoulder. The coach's face was red, his hands clenched into giant fists. "It wouldn't be past him to get into a fight with a newbie," a thought rushed through Charlie's head. "He'll knock him out with one punch. And that would mean goodbye money, goodbye gym, and hello aiding-and-abetting murder charges. There's no way out, except for hitting."

Charlie threw his opponent a sympathetic look and mouthed "I'm sorry." Sullivan gave a slight nod of understanding and instantly received a punch to the nose, not too strong, but very accurate.

"There! Much better! Keep working!" McKee went on to encourage his assistant.

For a second, everything went dark before Sullivan's eyes. His ears started ringing slightly, but instead of backing down he fearlessly rushed forward only to get punched again, this time to the chin. Charlie didn't want to hurt Jack, but he was familiar enough with McKee's hot temper to know that if he continued to imitate fighting, the old man would lose it completely and definitely keep his earlier threat.

"Good, good!" it's been a while since Charlie heard this kind of excitement in McKee's voice. "Come on now, make those punches count! Hit harder!"

Charlie landed two punches on Sullivan's torso, aiming

for the ribs, however, and not for the liver. All these blows started taking their toll on Sullivan. His own attacks, mediocre as they were at the start, grew even less accurate. Seeing Sullivan losing ground, McKee only became more impatient. "Come on, get him! What is this faggotry?! Hit like a man! Make Mexico proud of you! Mi casa, su casa!" shouted the old man derisively, remembering the only phrase he knew in Spanish.

McKee's screaming made the boy angry. He was just so sick of hearing his jibes and racist comments! For a second, he let his anger get the better of him and landed four blows on Sullivan, one after another, this time putting all he had into them. Sullivan went limp but then forced himself to attack again, even though his fists, now heavy as lead, couldn't rise above his chest anymore.

"That's right, amigo! Hit! Hit! Finish him!" the old man was now screaming at the top of his lungs.

McKee's bloodthirsty cries, Charlie's anger towards him, and, most importantly, the fact that for the first time in his life the boy managed not just to land a punch, but to actually overpower someone bigger than him, suddenly awoke his fighting instinct. Charlie dodged another one of Sullivan's weak attacks, hit him in the liver with his left, followed it with a right hook to the head, and then another left punch straight to the opponent's unprotected face.

Splashes of blood from the injured nose traced an arc in the air and landed on Charlie's gloves and face. Sullivan's head swung backwards until it faced the ceiling. Everything went dark before his eyes, and his legs became unresponsive. Jack would have dropped on the concrete floor like a brick, but thanks to the punching bag hanging behind him, he kind of crouched down first and only then fell on his back. By the time Sullivan came to, the blood coming from his nose covered half his face.

The excitement of a fight in Charlie's eyes gave way to utter horror. He rushed to Sullivan's side, struggling to remove his gloves. "Hey, hey, buddy! How are you? Are you okay?"

Charlie addressed his fallen opponent in a concerned voice.

The gloves finally off, he slid his hand carefully to raise Sullivan's head, just as his nosebleed started overflowing into his eyes.

"I'm okay," Sullivan replied, still not fully recovered.

"He's fine," barked McKee with contempt. "Don't be so full of yourself, Charlie. You're no Tyson. You hit like a kitten."

Paying the old man no attention, Charlie stayed at Sullivan's side. "Can you stand up? How many fingers do you see?"

Instead of replying, Sullivan raised himself on his elbows and then attempted to get to his feet. His knees were still trembling, but with Charlie's help, he managed to stand up straight.

"He got more scared than actually hurt. That's why he plopped down on his butt," said the old man.

"Pops, go sit in your office. I'll take care of this," said Charlie to McKee, helping Sullivan to remove his gloves.

The old man found Charlie's sternness adorable.

"Hey, Sullivan, you were knocked over by a boy who gets blown away from the street on a windy day," managed to say McKee through his own laughter. "What will you be doing with real men in a ring? Huh, Sullivan?"

"Pops!" no longer able to resist, Charlie yelled at his boss. "Go, now! Let me deal with this!"

McKee twisted his lips into a smile, waved his arm in resign, and slowly started walking toward his office. Holding Sullivan by his elbow, Charlie took him to the locker room.

"Are you sure you are okay? You're not blacking out? No double vision? No nausea? No dizziness? Should I maybe call an ambulance? You know, it's very easy to get a concussion."

"No, everything's good," answered Sullivan in his normal, calm voice.

Feeling once again confident on his feet, Jack even tried to get rid of the support he no longer needed, but Charlie didn't let him. Once in the locker room, Charlie seated Sullivan on a bench, wetted a towel in cold water, and put it on Jack's nose bridge to stop the bleeding.

"Seriously, I'm fine, Charlie," said Sullivan, wiping blood from the lower part of his face with a corner of the towel. "The bleeding almost stopped. I'll just rest here for a bit, and I'll be back to normal."

"Right," answered Charlie and froze with indecision, not knowing what other help to offer his "victim" or how to repay the damage inflicted on him.

"If you don't mind, I would rather have some time alone."

"Right," said Charlie again, but kept standing there for a couple of seconds before realizing that he was asked to leave.

"Charlie," Sullivan stopped the boy on his way out.

Charlie turned around.

"You did everything right. No hard feelings. Good fight, man, good fight."

Sullivan gave him a thumbs up.

"Yeah, thanks," said Charlie and added. "You fought well too."

"No, I didn't," Sullivan replied and laughed a surprisingly kind and calm laugh. "But it's fine. This is just the beginning."

Sullivan rested his back on the wall, removed the towel from the bridge of his nose, smoothed it out, and put it on his head, completely covering his face.

"He's one weird dude," thought Charlie to himself. "But I like him!"

The boy walked out of the locker room, quietly closing the door behind himself, stood there for a minute, thinking what to do next, and then walked resolutely to his boss's office.

McKee was considerably surprised when the door to his office swung open hitting the adjacent wall. There was only one man ever daring to treat the door that way, and it was McKee himself. Oh yes, in the years of One-Two Boxing's existence, this door had seen it all. Because of its owner's quick temper, the shattered glass had to be replaced seven times, the broken handle five times, and twice it came down to putting in a completely new door.

"Pops, what the hell are you doing?!" screamed Charlie bursting into the office. "Did you forget what we talked about? We need money! We need this guy's money! You have almost killed him before giving him a single session! You saw the way he collapsed! If it wasn't for the bag, he would have hit concrete with the back of his head! Concrete, Pops! I suggested we go into the ring, but no, the ring has to be earned! You know better than me how dangerous it is when an unconscious man hits the ground with the back of his head!"

"Kid," McKee tried to stop the assistant's monologue, but Charlie only grew more irritated.

"I mean, what if he actually had hit his head! If he had gotten as much as a simple concussion, it would have been enough to sue the hell out of you! He would have taken your last pair of underwear! What am I saying? He still can sue you! What if he had died? WHAT WOULD HAVE HAPPENED THEN? That's a felony! I would have gone to prison for manslaughter and you for aiding and abetting! Actually, no. *You* would've gone to prison for manslaughter, and I for aiding and abetting!"

"Kid," the old man tried to stop Charlie again, but he didn't seem to hear McKee's words.

"I didn't sign up for this! What is your problem with him anyway? What did he do to you? He's a little fruity, so what? You want to kill everyone who has a screw loose? You'll have to pile all the streets of the city with dead bodies!"

At first, the boy's outburst amused the old man, but it wouldn't have been Gerard McKee if he could swallow even several minutes of rebuking. As his third interruption went unnoticed, the smile disappeared from the old man's face. He rose from his chair and headed toward Charlie. The boy was still talking, nervously pacing from one corner to another. McKee stopped him with an iron grip of his hand, turned him around so they faced each other, and spoke loudly, barely holding back his fury, "Listen to me, Kid. You're not my son, my friend, and definitely not my boss. I'm your boss. You're here because of the goodness of my heart, not because of your exceptional and indispensable mopping skills. Next time you storm into my office, or raise your voice to me, or dare to chew me out, you will end up back in your Mexican shithole faster than your half-faggoty friend pulls on tights in the morning."

Charlie felt a lump forming in his throat, just as his eyes welled up with water. But whenever the old man saw red, he stopped noticing anything around him. And so he just pushed on, adding in an even more fearful voice, "Have I made myself clear, you goddamn Jose Canseco?"

Charlie simply nodded in response, afraid that anything he said would inevitably be followed by tears. He couldn't afford to start crying in front of McKee. Not after this. Charlie turned around and opened the door, desperate to get away from the old man as soon as possible. But as the boy took a step forward, he almost ran into Jack Sullivan, who was standing on the other side of the door.

"I'm ready, coach," he said to the old man in a completely calm voice.

"For what?" McKee replied, surprised.

"For our first training session."

Charlie turned to look at the old man and was very pleased to find the utter confusion on McKee's face. "I definitely love this crazy gringo!" the boy thought to himself and smiled.

..4..

"Oh no, no! Not in my gym!" were McKee's first words when Sullivan walked out of the locker room at the beginning of their second training session.

Jack gave his coach a questioning look.

"No tights! NO MORE TIGHTS! I don't give a shit that all cool kids wear them! Now turn around and march back into the locker room. And if I see you in tights one more time, our deal is off!" said the old man and took a sip of his usual Irish breakfast.

Sullivan silently went back to the locker room and returned a couple of moments later wearing only shorts and a muscle tee.

"Okay, Rich boy," McKee said, sitting down in a folding chair. "Let's see what you remember from our training yesterday. Show me your boxing stance."

Sullivan stood sideways to the coach, raised his fists, and slightly bent his knees.

"Wow! I guess Charlie did mess you up yesterday!" the old man chuckled habitually. "You don't remember shit! What's a boxing stance? All those stance rules I tried to drum into your head yesterday were invented for a reason! The boxing stance enables a boxer to effectively move in the ring, and to both attack and defend while constantly remaining in a balanced position. Forget Charlie. With your stance, his seven-year-old sister Rosita will be able to knock you over! Your feet are too wide. This hinders rapid movement. Both your heels are flat. This hinders fluent movement. You are standing up straight, thus creating a bigger target. Not to mention that you lift your chin upward. This way you increase your chances of getting hit in it. Do you even remember why you need to protect your chin?

"Because a chin is a knock-out point," replied Sullivan, while correcting the mistakes pointed out by the coach.

"Great, you do remember something!" McKee clapped his hands mockingly a couple of times, imitating applause. Now show me your boxing steps.

Sullivan took several steps forward and then just as many steps backward.

"Wow, Rich Boy! I didn't think there could be anything worse than your boxing stance. But great job for proving me wrong! Your steps are absolute crap. Watch and learn."

The old man took another sip of his coffee and whiskey, put the cup on the floor, and got to his feet.

"Lift your lead foot very slightly," McKee began to explain and demonstrate the correct technique at the same time. "Push your body forward with your rear foot. After the toes of your lead foot touch the floor, slide your rear foot forward. This is the only correct way, not the way you're doing it where each of your legs lives a life of its own. And don't forget to keep your feet shoulder-width apart and your weight evenly distributed between both legs. The same logic applies when you're moving backward, only now the movement starts with the rear foot, and your lead foot is pushing your body. Same thing with side steps. If you're moving to the left, start with your lead foot and push yourself with your rear foot. If you're moving to the right, lift your rear foot and push your body to the right side with your lead foot."

The old man moved left and right, back and forth several more times, and then nodded at Sullivan to repeat after him.

"All right. Still crap, but it's getting better. Now the punches. I hope you remember how they are called."

"A jab, a cross, an uppercut, and a hook," replied Sullivan.

McKee gave him another mocking round of applause.

"Come on, show me the jab."

Sullivan threw a short and quick punch with his lead arm.

"Wow! Compared to what you were giving Charlie yesterday, this is a real piece of art. But still complete crap, of course. First, you forgot to rotate your body toward the rear side. Secondly, you forgot to keep your chin down. Thirdly, you forgot to rotate your fist during the punch—knuckles up, palm down!"

Without rising from his chair, McKee showed the correct rotation of the fist during a punch.

"In your rendition, the jab lost half its power, and more importantly, any boxer who's even a tiny bit less lame than you would have definitely managed to counter-attack you to the chin. And the chin is what?"

"A knock-out point," responded Sullivan, perfectly aware of another scorn coming his way.

"Great! You're a fast learner, Rich Boy! Are you that smart because you went to college?"

Sullivan didn't bother to reply.

"Show me your cross," commanded McKee after another sip from his cup of Irish breakfast.

Sullivan threw a rear-arm straight punch, trying to avoid his previous mistakes.

"Wow! This one is 10% less shitty than your jab! Congratulations, Mr. Rich Boy. At this rate of progress, the IPBU championship belt is as good as yours already."

The coach made to applaud again, but Sullivan couldn't take it anymore.

"Mr. McKee, I would be extremely grateful if you could just name my mistakes. Excessive comments reduce the effectiveness of our training."

"You think so?" responded the old man with a sneer.

"I'm just as sure about that as you are about my punches being complete shit."

Sullivan's reply amused McKee even further, and that was the sole reason he resisted another clever retort and spoke to the point.

"You didn't forget to rotate your body, kept your chin down, and even rotated your fist, but you totally forgot about your lead hand. When you throw a cross, you need to always keep your lead hand so that the glove protects your head and your elbow protects your body. Plus, you didn't retract your rear arm quickly enough, after hitting the target. If you throw a cross like that in a real fight, your opponent will first whack you with a right hook, then deliver a jab to your chin, and finally, finish you off with his own cross. Although what am I saying? You'll go down at the first punch."

McKee's last words were interrupted by the creak of the front door. Sullivan turned to see Charlie entering the room. Jack waved his hand at him.

And here's another fatal mistake that will end up in your knockout—never take your eyes away from your opponent. Whatever is happening around you, the only thing that should exist for you is your opponent! I don't care if Pamela Anderson enters the room in her birthday suit—you always look only at your opponent!"

"Pamela Anderson?" flashed through Sullivan's head. "Hasn't the old man updated his Playboy collection since the 90s?"

"That's another no-no!" bellowed McKee.

"What is?"

"Thinking!"

"Thinking?" repeated Sullivan, a sneer now twisting his mouth for the first time. "I'm not allowed to think?"

"You are not allowed to think about irrelevant things!" answered the coach in a raised voice. "Actually, scratch that. What I said first: No thinking at all. Boxing is not chess. Here, you rely on your senses. You need to feel everything: yourself, your opponent, your hands, your legs, his hands, his legs, how your punch affected him. Everything has to be felt, not thought. You pause to think, you miss a window for a punch. You pause to think again, you take a punch yourself! Boxing is not for smart-asses like you! Boxing is for real men who have fighting in their blood! Who are ready to fight, ready to kill, and ready to die for what they believe in!

"You mean a six-figure check and a piece of metal attached to the belt? That's what real men are ready to die and kill for?" Sullivan's voice—composed, calm, and detached—was a complete opposite of McKee's.

Already on edge, McKee got up from his chair and was about to unload a barrage of either blows or at least elaborate insults on Sullivan when Charlie, sensing a conflict about to blow up, hurried to Jack's rescue.

"Hey, Pops, there are some junkies hanging around at the back door again. Why don't you go kick them out?"

As was usual in these situations, McKee didn't hear his assistant's words, fully engulfed by his own fury, but Charlie grabbed the old man by the arm and repeated, "The junkies that punctured your tires last week—I think they are back."

McKee would've ignored these words as well if it wasn't for one thing: the old man hated junkies even more than gays, illegal immigrants, and liberal democrats.

"Where?" he bellowed, turning to face Charlie.

"At the back door," answered the boy and pointed the direction with his hand, as if the owner of the club didn't know where the back door was.

McKee gave Sullivan a fierce stare, exhaled even fiercer, turned around, and started walking toward the back entrance. Charlie looked at Jack. "Man, are you suicidal or something?"

"Not today," replied Sullivan, and it was hard to tell whether he was joking or being serious.

"Um... Okay..." said Charlie awkwardly. "Well, try not to talk to him like that again. It doesn't take much for him to lose his shit. Didn't you see him blowing a fuse yesterday? He was this close to attacking you!"

"Of course, I did. But you can't live your whole life in fear," Sullivan's last words sounded inappropriately serious and even dark.

"How are you doing after yesterday anyway?" asked Charlie.

"Fine. I'll live."

"Sorry about that. I didn't mean to get at you like that…"

Sullivan cut Charlie off, "It's okay. You did everything right. Don't worry about this anymore."

"Ok, whatever you say."

Jack gave the boy a friendly pat on the shoulder. From the direction of the back entrance came the sound of the old man's heavy footsteps.

"I didn't see any junkies out there."

"They must have scampered, Pops. You gave them quite a scare last time."

"Or maybe they got scared of you? Huh, Charlie? I bet you made sure that everyone in the neighborhood knows what an amazing fighter you are, knocking everyone off left and right!"

McKee chortled and ruffled up the hair on the back of the boy's head.

"Well, don't just stand there. The toilets won't clean themselves."

The old man gave Charlie a push in the back, but then immediately tugged at his T-shirt.

"Although wait. First, help our much-esteemed friend Mr. Tights wrap up and put on gloves."

The boy nodded in acknowledgment and headed for the locker room.

"Charlie," called Sullivan. "Check my bag, please. I followed your advice and bought new wraps."

Charlie smiled faintly. He was extremely pleased that someone actually followed his advice. Not to mention he only ever heard the word "please" at One-Two Boxing from Kate, who was coming over twice a month to help the old man with his bills and taxes.

"Oh, so our local wraps are not good enough for Your Highness?" McKee addressed Sullivan while pretending to curtsy.

"No, that's not it," answered Jack. "I just don't want to sully your wraps, soaked with the sweat and blood of real fighters, with my unmanly hands."

"Smartass," grumbled McKee, picking up the cup from the floor to finish his Irish breakfast.

While the old man was finishing his coffee and whiskey, Charlie managed to wrap Jack's hands and put gloves on him. McKee gestured the boy to return to his main job.

"Start with a punching bag," the coach said to Sullivan. "Perhaps, once you get a feel of punches, they will become a little bit less shitty."

Jack approached the punching bag and assumed a boxing stance.

"Let's start with a left hook to the head. Since the chances of you doing it right yourself are nil, or rather negative, listen to me first. Listen very carefully. And watch me do it."

The old man got into a boxing stance and began to explain and demonstrate at the same time,

"Your body slightly rotates to the lead side. Weight shifts to lead leg. Keep your rear hand up and close to chin and rigid. Swing your lead arm to the target without extending the arm straight. When swinging your arm, keep the elbow bent in close to 90 degrees. Now, remember the important points that you yourself would certainly have missed. Keep your eyes on the opponent. Watch above your arm, not below! Knuckles should never point upward or downward—only straight ahead! And the last thing that is true not only for hooks but also for all other punches—after hitting the target, retract your arm as quickly along the shortest path as possible. Newbies often mistakenly believe that the punch is the most important thing, that it's the final destination. Hell, no! You know how many fights end in a knockout? Less than 13%! I mean real knockouts, not the technical bullshit when the referee starts butting in. Only then the punch is the end. In the rest of the cases, the punch is only the beginning. What actually matters is putting your defense back up as quickly as possible or proceeding to another blow. Otherwise, even the best punch could be followed with an even better counterpunch."

For the first time, Sullivan noticed a warm note in the old man's voice instead of the usual mockery. The warm feelings clearly had nothing to do with the new pupil the coach still despised. He just enjoyed his beloved craft. Apparently, the change in McKee's voice didn't go unnoticed by Charlie either, as he had approached the coach with interest, no longer busy with a bucket and a mop somewhere in the background.

"Are you getting any of this or am I just gabbing away for nothing, and you will only show me more of your craptastic punches?" McKee's voice once again was ringing with contempt.

"I'm getting all of it," answered Sullivan. "But I'm absolutely sure you will call my punches craptastic anyway."

"Ha! When you're right, you're right," chuckled the old man again, adding, "Now hit it already, smartass."

Sullivan delivered several left hooks to the "head" of the punching bag. The old man heaved a deep sigh and started rubbing his eyes and forehead with his giant hand, showing in every way how much it hurt him to watch that.

"God damn it, what is this half-faggoty crap?! Okay, right arm now."

Sullivan demonstrated a couple of right hooks.

"Also half-faggoty. Give me a jab."

For the next ten minutes, McKee was yelling out various punches and their combinations. Sullivan worked hard to avoid previous mistakes and make his punches strong, but nevertheless, the old man was calling his every other punch half-faggoty, occasionally throwing in other insulting remarks about him, his punches, his stance, and even his mother.

After a few more punches, which were yet again called half-faggoty, Jack mumbled under his breath through gritted teeth, "They are not half-faggoty…"

"What? What did you say?" asked McKee, sensing a perfect opening for a new and more powerful downpour of insults.

Jack stopped practicing punches, turned to the coach, and answered in a calm voice,

"I said that my punches are not half-faggoty."

McKee opened his mouth to deliver a fresh jibe, but Sullivan spoke first, "They are completely faggoty."

"What?" asked the coach in confusion, utterly thrown by Sullivan's insulting his own punches.

"I'm gay, or a faggot, as you prefer to call it. Which means that my punches are not half, but completely faggoty."

Shocked either by Sullivan's words or by the hardness with which they were said, McKee froze, confused, which almost never happened to the trigger-happy old man. Sullivan stared at him defiantly for a second, then turned back to the punching bag, as if nothing had happened, and continued to practice his punches.

Charlie, who was standing behind McKee's back all this time, almost dropped his mop. "Holy shit!" a thought went through his head. "What's going to happen now?!" Charlie knew perfectly well how much the old man despised gays and that he wasn't exactly fond of Sullivan in the first place. The boy considered yelling "Run!" and spilling the water from the bucket under McKee's feet to give Sullivan a chance to escape before the old man jumped on him. But then Jack, for the second time that day, was saved by the old squeaky entrance door, or rather the person who opened it.

As the squeak didn't draw anyone's eyes, it was followed by a melodic high-pitched voice that echoed under the club's roof. "Hey, anybody home?"

A tall and slim woman in her mid-twenties entered the room, making click-clack sounds with her heels. Charlie didn't even need to turn around to recognize Kate. Not that he knew her voice that well, but in the three years he'd been working at One-Two Boxing, the boy only ever saw two women there:

McKee's finance assistant Kate and Mrs. Sifaretto, the club's cofounder's widow. Since the latter was well into her fifties, it was quite impossible to confuse her voice with Kate's.

"Gerard, can I have a moment with you?" asked Kate and continued to the old man's office, winking Charlie hello as she walked.

Among the mandatory attributes of the old guard and Gerard McKee, who could easily have been appointed its ambassador, were not only homophobia and racism but also a code of honor prescribing a particular way to treat women. Naturally, the old man didn't see women as equal to men, but at the same time, he never permitted himself the slightest show of rudeness with the fairer sex.

And so despite all the fury and outrage that were boiling his insides because of Sullivan's blatant and provocative coming-out, McKee only waited for a few seconds before following Kate. Still, unable to leave things just like that, he pointedly spitted on the floor first. "Whether you like gays or hate them, why would spit on the floor?" thought Charlie and cleaned up McKee's mess with a sweep of his mop.

Once in his office, the old man slammed the door shut with such force that it barely managed to avoid glass replacement number eight. Being quite familiar with McKee's short temper, like any other employee of One-Two Boxing, Kate didn't pay any attention to its latest display.

"Who's the new guy?" she asked, peeking into the gym through the open blinds.

"Just this guy..." grunted McKee through gritted teeth.

"He's cute," Kate added.

The old man chuckled, "Don't bother. He's a bumhole engineer. Besides, he won't be here for long."

"I assume in your dated and completely inappropriate lingo it means that he's a member of the LGBT community?" asked Kate, turning away from the window. "Yeah, a bona fide CEO of that community," answered McKee, barely restraining himself from spitting on the floor again.

"Oooh... I can imagine how much that's bugging you," Kate smiled wryly with just the corners of her mouth. "I told you, Pops, you should drop your antiquated and offensive views. Make your gym gay friendly, sign up to Instagram and Tik Tok, and you'll have people flocking here without any advertisement."

"Right! I'll just paint my ass in rainbow colors first!" The old man checked himself. "Sorry for the language."

It wasn't only the corners of Kate's mouth now that showed her smile.

"Man, you're funny, Pops. So saying profanities with a woman present is something bad, but hating people for their sexual orientation is the definition of being a gentleman."

"Let's get down to business already," answered McKee grimly.

"As you wish. Here's the business," said Kate and reached for her purse. "I've just deposited the check you brought me yesterday and paid some of our bills with that money. Just the most pressing ones for now. When are you going to start accepting card payments, by the way? That would allow me to take care of half of your affairs without leaving home."

Kate held out several receipts.

"You'll be the first one to know. You told me that, like, fifty times already!" replied McKee, accepting the receipts. "So, how long is it gonna last us?"

"Well, we can definitely survive for a month or two. Where did you get that check, by the way? I haven't seen amounts that big here in two years."

"That princess over there," the old man nodded toward the window, through which he could see Sullivan working hard on his punches. "I charged him triple my rate and made him pay for fifty hours of training in advance."

McKee's face stretched into a cunning smile—he was clearly proud of the way he duped Sullivan. And then he added, "Only I won't be training him anymore. Not gonna happen.

Boxing is a sport for real men, not for your LGBT characters."

"Pops, you can't do that," Kate replied in a serious tone.

"Why is that? Because he's gay? Because the goddamn liberals would immediately pounce at me? No one will be telling me what I can or can't do. My gym, my rules. Why should I be training someone I can't stand? What kind of twisted democracy is that?! So now queens have more rights than real men?"

Kate shook her head.

"No, it's not that. I mean, that too, but that's not what matters right now. What matters is that he paid for fifty hours in advance, and I already spent all that money on bills. You can still turn him down, of course. It will be very wrong, but only from a moral standpoint. Only you will have to give him back the money for the training sessions that haven't been delivered. That's the law, Pops. Not the moral law, but real law committed to paper. Do you have five grand to spare? Because if not, you will have to train him until all fifty hours are over, whether you like it or not."

"I knew I shouldn't have gotten into this," muttered the old man through gritted teeth. "I told him to get lost at first, but then Charlie talked me into it, god damn him. He does that all the time."

Kate interrupted McKee, "Talking about Charlie. That's the second reason I came here today. Can I borrow him for a couple of hours? I need some work done at home, and I can't do it alone. That is if he doesn't mind, of course."

The old man waved her away.

"Just take him. Don't bother asking for his opinion. He does more harm than good anyway."

"Pops," said Kate, staring at the old man disapprovingly. "I hope you don't say this kind of nonsense with him present. You know perfectly well that Charlie works harder than everyone else in this gym put together. Including you!"

McKee waved her away again and slumped back in his chair lost in thought. Kate took a compact mirror out of her purse, fixed her hair and makeup, checked her phone for new messages, and was about to leave when the old man finally spoke, "Kate, what will happen if that princess refuses to use up the hours he paid for? Will I still have to return him the money?"

Kate turned around.

"No. If he decides to terminate the contract for his own reasons that have nothing to do with you or the gym, the party providing services has no obligation to return the money that's already been paid."

Kate glanced at McKee suspiciously.

"Pops, what are you up to now?"

"Nothing, never mind. You can go now."

The old man started moving papers on his desk in a theatrical imitation of someone being busy working. Kate shook her head disapprovingly and left the director's office, closing the door behind her carefully and almost noiselessly.

..5..

It was already evening when Charlie finally finished helping Kate to move, but he decided to drop by the gym anyway, hoping to catch McKee and find out how the rest of the session with Sullivan went after he so suddenly came out of the closet. "Please don't be pools of blood! Please don't be pools of blood!" the boy kept muttering as he walked from the bus stop to the One-Two Boxing building.

As he turned the corner, he saw Sullivan's scarlet Tesla parked next to the club and legs sticking out from underneath it. "Did the old man kill the newbie and drop his body right at the car?" an absurd thought went through Charlie's mind before he pushed it out. The boy rounded the car and realized that the legs were not sticking out from underneath it, but were attached to Sullivan who was sitting right on the sidewalk, his back against the driver's door.

"Hey Mr. Sullivan, are you all right?" asked Charlie, approaching the car.

Jack opened his eyes and turned towards the sound. Charlie noticed that a simple turn of the head took the man a lot of effort.

"Call me Jack," Sullivan replied in a low, lifeless voice and closed his eyes again.

"Okay. Are you all right, Jack? The old man didn't beat you, did he?" added Charlie in a slightly frightened voice.

Sullivan smiled faintly.

"No, no... Nothing like that..." Jack spoke slowly, with long pauses between words. "I just don't feel my arms or legs. I need to go home but I cannot drive."

Sullivan raised his hand with an effort and demonstrated how much it trembled and how badly his fingers flexed.

"Hey, doesn't this thing have autopilot in it?"

Charlie nodded towards the car.

"Mine doesn't. I'm an information security consultant. Being paranoid about that type of stuff is an occupational hazard."

Charlie nodded in understanding, thought for a moment, and added, "Wait, so you've been training all this time? Since morning?!?"

Jack nodded faintly.

"That's more than eight hours! Training for that long can kill Mike Tyson! Working out even for two hours is not a good idea for beginners, and nobody ever does it for eight straight hours! Did the old man completely lose his mind? I'll go talk to him!"

"Don't," Sullivan stopped him. "Besides, he's not there anyway. He left about five minutes ago."

"I'll talk to him first thing in the morning then!"

"Don't, Charlie. I appreciate your concern, but you know perfectly well that nothing good can come out of that. McKee is trying to break me, and complaining will only make him try harder. Besides, I heard the way he talked to you in his office after our fight. I don't want you to lose your job because of me."

"You can't expect me to just stand there and watch him run you into the ground!"

"You have to try, Charlie. Please try. I really need that!"

"But why? Why do you need that? Why do you need professional boxing? Clearly not for money," said Charlie, pointing at the car and thinking of Sullivan's three-thousand-dollar suit.

"No, not for money..." replied Jack in a quiet voice.

"For fame then?"

Sullivan smiled slightly.

"No, fame interests me even less than money."

"For the sport itself? You've been a boxing fan since you were a kid?" Charlie kept guessing.

The smile on Sullivan's lips gave way to a short chuckle.

"God, no! I do not care for any professional sport, and I hate boxing since childhood!"

Sullivan's words left Charlie seriously baffled. "How can you hate boxing but pay insane money to learn it while letting the old man treat you like crap?" thought the boy but only said out loud, "What's the point then? Why are you doing this?"

"I have my reasons," answered Jack and tried to change the subject. "You know, I have three friends by the name of Charlie, and all of them are from England. Or rather, two from England and one from Scotland."

"You don't know any Mexican Charlies?" asked Charlie with a grin.

Sullivan shook his head.

"Well, my name's not really Charlie."

Sullivan gave the boy a questioning look.

"Yeah. I'm Manuel Enrique Fuentes."

"What's with Charlie then?"

"When I first came to One-Two Boxing looking for any kind of job, the old man said that I could stay and mop the floor on two conditions. First, no Spanish within the club's walls. And second, I'd have to answer to Charlie."

Sullivan furrowed his brows.

"You're surprised that the old man is not just a homophobe but also a racist?" chuckled Charlie and then added. "Isn't that a package deal?"

Sullivan smiled in response. "I think from now on I'm going to call you Manuel."

"Nah, thanks. I'm used to Charlie. And to be honest, I never liked the name Manuel. It reminds me of my father."

"Bad relationship?"

Charlie hesitated for a second.

"Just bad memories. He was deported when I was fifteen. And I managed to give ICE the slip. My aunt and uncle were deported as well, so I had nowhere to go. I was wandering the streets not knowing what to do, and then I came across this place. I saw Gerard," Charlie nodded at the banner covering the entire One-Two Boxing wall that featured McKee, still young, boasting a champion's belt. "My father always loved boxing, and the old man was his favorite fighter despite not being Mexican. Back in Guadalajara, we had an old VCR and a bunch of tapes with McKee's fights that my father recorded from TV. My earliest memories of myself already have those recordings in them. So in a sense Gerard is like family to me."

Charlie paused in nostalgic contemplation. Sullivan tapped the sidewalk beside him inviting the boy to sit down, which he did.

"My father always liked boxing too," said Sullivan, staring at his still trembling fists. "That's why I've hated it ever since I was a child."

Jack heaved a sigh, ran his hand through his hair, and spoke again.

"So McKee wasn't always the dick he is now, considering that he gave you a job and I assume a roof over your head?"

"Hehe," was Charlie's reply. "No, actually he's always been a dick. But he's not a bad guy. Sure, he has a horrible temper. He's racist, homophobic, sexist—you name it. But he's not a bad person. Yes, he gave me a job and let me stay in the club for a while. And later on, when I saved enough money, he co-signed the lease with me so I could have my own place. Whenever someone in the club tried to pick a fight with me, he always took my side. Once, he even broke a guy's nose because he didn't get the message the nice way. Bam!" Charlie punched the air with his left hand. "The dude's on the floor, and the old man just keeps walking like nothing happened."

"You know, up until that conversation in his office after our fight, I thought that you and McKee are friends rather than just people who work together."

"Yeah, I guess we are. I'm probably his only friend. The rest are his boxing buddies who are only good for watching fights and drinking beer with them. But the old man will never admit that we're friends. You know, I think he never admits to anything good. It's as if he's ashamed of being nice. So every time he does something nice for me, he makes sure to spice it up with another one of his racist jokes. To him, niceness is gay. Something a real man should be ashamed of." Charlie turned to Sullivan and added, "No offense. That's what McKee believes, not me! I mean, that what I think he believes anyway."

"None taken," replied Jack with a kind smile. "I know perfectly well what you're talking about. Toxic masculinity in all its glory…"

"Toxic what?" asked Charlie.

"Never mind," Jack dismissed the question. "That's a long conversation for some other time. And right now I really have to go home. I think I can feel my arms again. I'll just drive slower."

Sullivan tried to get to his feet, but after the exhausting practice and sitting in an uncomfortable position for a long time, he couldn't. Noticing that Jack needs help, Charlie leapt up and offered his new friend a hand.

"Thank you, Charlie."

Sullivan stood up and started walking back and forth next to the car, stretching his stiff legs.

"You need a ride?" he asked Charlie. "I promise not to kill us on the road."

Charlie smiled in reply. "No, thanks. I live really close."

The boy waved his hand in no particular direction.

"Charlie, could you maybe train me sometime? When you have time, without McKee. Naturally, I'll pay the price that you find fair."

The boy stared at Sullivan in surprise. That Jack listened to his advice and thanked him on a dozen occasions was already more than enough for Charlie who always felt underappreciated. Being asked to act as a coach and offered to get paid for that—that was beyond anything the boy ever dreamed about.

"Err... I mean, it's not that I don't want to, money or no money." Charlie struggled to find the right words. "You do understand that I'm not a professional coach? Hell, the old man was right when he said that all I know about boxing is whatever I saw while mopping the floor around real boxers and trainers. If you needed to be taught how to scrub off ten years' worth of mold in a shower or how to wash sweat-soaked tape so that it doesn't stink like a hobo, then I'd be your guy. But teaching boxing..."

"Charlie, you underestimate yourself. Don't forget that you knocked me down that time!"

"Again, no offense, but anyone could've done that. We had tougher bullies in elementary school."

Jack smiled, making it clear that he didn't find that offensive, and said, "It's not that. Charlie, you and only you understand what it's like to start from zero and try to learn something when nobody believes in you. I'm no idiot. I know McKee is just giving me a hard time instead of teaching me. He wants to break me, and so my main and only goal right now is not to learn boxing, but to show him that I won't break. Only then McKee will start taking me seriously, and only then he will start teaching me for real. I thought I could handle that on my own, but now I understand that even if he fails to break me mentally, I will definitely fall to pieces physically before I prove anything to the old man. I need your help, Charlie. Yours and only yours!" And as a final argument, Jack added, "You have a big heart and a clear head. You've got a big future ahead of you, but first you need to believe in yourself."

Sullivan held out his hand, which had finally stopped shaking. Encouraged by the words of his new friend, Charlie shook it firmly. Jack opened the door of his car, climbed inside, then out, and turned around with a card in his hand.

"Here, call me when you find some free time."

Charlie took the card.

"Just not today," added Jack with a smile. "I've had enough training for today."

Charlie smiled back.

"And you know what?" continued Sullivan. "It doesn't have to be just training. You can call me about anything. If you ever need help, call me anytime, day or night."

"Thanks," Charlie said happily. "I really appreciate that."

"Anytime, Charlie. Anytime!" Sullivan repeated, giving Charlie a friendly pat on the shoulder.

Jack got behind the wheel. Charlie waved at the Tesla as it drove away and then put the card in his back pocket. "Crazy or not, he's definitely a great guy!" he thought to himself and headed home.

..6..

Upon arriving at One-Two Boxing the next morning, Sullivan was surprised to see the gym crowded. At least twenty people were working out with weights or hitting punching bags, and there even were two men boxing in the ring under the guidance of a tall black guy in a club T-shirt that said "Coach" on the back.

McKee was walking among the visitors, dishing out jokes and pieces of advice. The old man was in a good mood. As he noticed Sullivan standing in the doorway, he cried out happily, his booming voice traveling across the room, "As I live and breathe! My favorite client!" The old man spread his arms in a welcoming gesture. "Well, don't just stand there! Go get changed and let's start!"

"Hey, Pops," the tall black coach leaned over the ropes to talk to McKee. "Is that the future IPBU champion you've talked so much about?"

"Yes, Derrick, that's the one!" confirmed McKee happily. "The man who will return One-Two Boxing its former glory! Give him a warm welcome!"

Everyone in the gym turned to look at the newcomer, except for those panting on a bench under a barbell. Sullivan just kept standing in the doorway, not knowing how to react to that greeting. He searched for Charlie with his eyes, but the boy wasn't there yet. Finally, feeling too uncomfortable to take any more of that staring, Jack waved his hand awkwardly and hurried toward the locker room.

When he stepped back out, McKee was standing right next to the door.

"Derrick," he called out in the direction of the ring, "help Jack wrap up."

Sullivan raised his fist, showing that he had already done that himself.

"Forget the wraps, just bring gloves," McKee changed his order.

The young coach climbed down from the ring and brought over a pair of black gloves. As he helped Sullivan to secure them on his hands, he said, "Sorry, we don't have them in pink."

Sullivan looked up and saw Derrick grinning ear to ear. Evidently, the man found his own joke absolutely hilarious. Jack, as usual, didn't say anything. The young coach gave him a pat on the shoulder, which was supposed to look friendly but in reality, was unnecessarily hard. McKee, unsurprisingly, pretended that he didn't see or hear any of that.

"Ready?" he asked Sullivan. "Let's go to a bag. Guys, make room—VIP client coming through," he added, addressing the men standing in the punch-practicing area.

As he approached the newest, barely battered punching bag, McKee patted it in a fatherly gesture and stepped aside.

"Come on, show me a jab," he said to Sullivan in a calm, almost friendly voice.

Jack threw a couple of jabs, trying to keep in mind all the rules that he spent the entire previous evening memorizing. Even though to him the punches felt almost perfect, he braced himself for an avalanche of criticism and insults. But not this time. McKee said only one word, "Good," then asked him to do several crosses, then uppercuts and hooks.

After every punch, the coach only said, "Good" or "Great." Sullivan was perfectly aware that those were not real compliments—the old man just decided to give him a break today. But he was still happy to be able for the first time to practice punches without the need to restrain himself and swallow insults.

Despite the pain in his arms and legs after the previous

marathon training, Sullivan soon surrendered himself to the rhythm. For a second he even thought that he started enjoying the process. There was something stress-relieving and almost meditative in punching the bag. Sullivan wasn't just hitting it willy-nilly. He was consciously performing movements with his arms, legs, and torso to produce real jabs, crosses, uppercuts, and hooks, just the way they were described in boxing textbooks.

But Sullivan's boxing meditation didn't last long. His focus on punching was broken by someone's muted laughter. Out of the corner of his eye, Jack saw a man pointing his finger at him. He shifted sideways to see what was going on without stopping his practice. There was a group of five young guys standing on his right, behind McKee's back.

One of them, who was pointing his finger at Sullivan before, was now apparently doing an impression of Sullivan's punches and moves. Only he wasn't showing them awkward, slow, or sloppy. No, he was trying hard to portray Jack as a caricature effeminate gay, the way only homophobes do.

Sullivan knew perfectly well that such gays simply didn't exist. Just like there are no such African Americans as they are portrayed by amateur blackface enthusiasts. And Sullivan also knew that there was nothing in his movements and habits that could give him away as a gay because his numerous gay friends repeatedly told him that his behavior was even too straight. But bullying by dim-witted individuals has never been accurate, much less fair – otherwise, it would be called constructive criticism.

Another gay punch by an impersonator caused a furor among his friends, whose laughter spread to the entire gym at that point. Sullivan swallowed the insult again and shifted to the side so that he could no longer see the bullies.

"Good," McKee said yet again. "Enough with the bag for now. Let's get down to defense. Derrick, make room for us," the old man added, shouting towards the ring.

"Doesn't the right to get into the ring have to be earned?"

Sullivan uttered with a bitter smile.

But McKee pretended that he didn't hear Jack's remark. As they approached the ring, Derrick pulled the ropes apart to make it easier for the old man to step onto the canvas. Sullivan, who had never been in the ring before, hesitated for a moment, but the young coach nodded obligingly and spread the ropes even wider for him. But just as Jack put one foot on the canvas, Derrick's hand slipped "accidentally", and the heavy rope charged down, hitting Sullivan on the back.

Startled, Jack almost fell, but at the last moment, he got hold of another rope and managed to maintain his footing. In order not to give Derrick an additional opportunity to gloat, Jack didn't turn around in his direction and pretended that he took what had happened for a real accident. Of course, that time McKee also didn't notice anything.

"So, let's start with some classics," the old man said, turning to Sullivan. "Double Arm Block."

McKee demonstrated the move, covering his face with his hands.

"The technique goes as follows…," McKee broke off. "Get into the stance!" for the first time that day, the old man's voice rang with irritation, so familiar to Sullivan. "Assume the stance as soon as you enter the ring! The ring is a place for serious work! You cannot just walk around here! Now, when a punch is coming at you, bring your arms together, turning the palms inwards towards your face and raising your fists to only about the level of your eyebrows. Keep your chin down! Keep your arms rigid!"

The old man demonstrated the move once again and then moved his head as a signal for Sullivan to repeat it. When Jack did a double arm block, McKee launched a few light punches without applying any force only to show how they are being stopped by the block.

"Now as for the general rule for any defense – for this one as well as for all that will follow. The defense, it's just like the punch, the main thing here is not only to exercise a move but what else?" McKee addressed the question to his mentee.

"Return to the boxing stance as quickly as possible," Sullivan answered.

"That's right! There you go – now you are beginning to understand some things by yourself rather than only listen to others. And why is it so important to return to the boxing stance?" This time the coach answered his question himself. "Because once you block you can't punch and you can't see clearly what your opponent is up to. That won't do. After all, if your opponent is not a complete idiot, immediately after a straight punch that bumps into your double arm block he will send a hook or a body shot. And what good is it then that you covered your face and protected yourself from a straight punch if the very next moment you will be knocked out by another punch? Go ahead and try a double arm block combined with a fast return."

McKee started throwing straight punches, and Sullivan blocked them and immediately returned to the boxing stance.

"Good. Now do it with the steps. Double arm block, return to the boxing stance, and at the same time take a step backward."

Sullivan carried out the coach's instructions.

"Excellent. Now combine it with a sidestep – first to the left, then to the right."

Sullivan did this exercise as well.

"Floats like a butterfly, in high heels," uttered Derrick, who was standing by the ropes that whole time.

He said it as if to himself but made sure that his words reached Sullivan's ears. Jack, of course, heard the taunt, and McKee pretended once again that nothing had happened. That time around though, Sullivan was willing to bet that for a hundredth of a second the old man's lips twisted into a snide smirk.

"Good. Let's move on." McKee continued lecturing and at the same time demonstrating. "The next defensive move is a catch. Open the palm of your rear hand and move it forward to place it just in front of chin level to catch the following punch. Keep your rear arm rigid so that the glove is not forced back into your face. Catch the opponent's punch. And, of course, return to the boxing stance. Go on now, try it yourself."

Sullivan repeated the technique in the exact same way as it was demonstrated by the coach.

"Excellent. Remember, this defense works against the lead arm straight punch to the head, lead arm uppercut to the head, and rear arm uppercut to the head. Like we did the last time, let's practice a quick return to the boxing stance on the spot, then do it with a backward step and some sidesteps."

Several times Sullivan diligently did every exercise, suggested by the coach.

"Wonderful," the old man said. "Now let's combine it with a counter punch. Let's first do a catch, return to the boxing stance and strike back with a jab as quickly as possible."

Sullivan started practicing the defense followed by the attack. In his opinion, he was doing quite well, especially considering that the fatigue after yesterday's training was becoming more and more noticeable by the minute. However, Derrick, who was standing in the corner, came up with something to spoil Jack's mood once again.

"Stings like Queen Bey!" he threw a remark in Sullivan's direction and checked himself as he realized how to make the next insult even more caustic.

In an incredibly fake voice, Derrick started singing, "All the single ladies! All the single ladies!" Out of the corner of his eye, Sullivan saw the young coach pacing along the ring ropes, trying to mimic the famous arm movement that Beyoncé used to accompany that song. Apparently, according to Derrick, the mention of the song so beloved by many gay people and the word "ladies" should have made Jack run away from the ring in tears.

When the young coach moved on to "Whoa, oh, oh, oh, oh-oh, oh, oh, oh, oh, oh, oh, oh, oh," Sullivan couldn't help but smile. Jack laughed inwardly, "As a proud gay man, I'm definitely offended by how incompetently this idiot performs both the song and dance." Still, the amount of effort, energy, and imagination Derrick expended trying to insult him couldn't but make Sullivan uncomfortable.

Just as Derrick finished singing and dancing, Charlie appeared at the ring.

"Okay, that's enough," McKee commanded. "The third defensive technique is a rear arm block. It works against the lead arm hook to the head. Watch and repeat after me," the old man began to demonstrate and describe the technique at the same time. "Rotate your body slightly to the lead side. Raise your rear forearm up and rigid, placing the fist at the temple, near the ear. Imagine that you are answering a call. It is such a call that if you don't answer it immediately, the consequences will be disastrous," the coach chuckled slightly and continued the lesson. "Keep your lead arm rigid and up. Don't take your eyes off your opponent. And, of course, return to the boxing stance as quickly as possible."

Several times Sullivan diligently repeated the technique that had been demonstrated by the coach.

"Good. Now with the steps." McKee said.

Charlie, who was standing by the ring, noticed with surprise and great pleasure that the old man was actually training Jack and not just tormenting him. The last time he saw McKee like that was when he just started working at One-two Boxing. The old man has always had a lousy temper, but he really liked to coach. At that time, two years ago, McKee was standing in the ring with Derrick. By that time, the twenty-year-old boxer had already had two dozen fights as an amateur, all but one of which ended in his victory by a knockout.

Derrick came to McKee with a dream to make it to the pros with his help. The old man saw in him his most favorite traits of a fighter's character – determination, toughness, and complete lack of fear – and therefore gladly took it upon himself to train the guy. McKee was not even bothered by the newcomer's black skin color. In the old man's twisted code of honor, "real men" like himself and Derrick stood above race, nationality, and social status.

McKee considered "real men" to be the pinnacle of human development. Straight after them came the Irish, among whom, in his opinion, there was the largest percentage of "real men", then all other white men, then Latino men and black men. At the end of the male part of the list were, in the old man's opinion, the least masculine of all men – Asians. Next came women, and finally, at the very bottom, there were homosexuals, drug addicts, pedophiles, and all the others that the old man tried not to think about at all.

Interestingly enough, all women, as McKee saw it, belonged to one single category – no matter whether they were white, black, or lesbian. Except that the old man especially didn't like female boxers, as he believed that they insulted the ring, which was sacred to him, by their presence on it in the role of anyone other than a ring girl. Throughout McKee's entire life, only one woman had ever been assigned to a higher category than the seventh in his list. Her name was Mary McKee and she was Gerard's grandmother. When he was a baby, Mary took him away from his alcoholic mother, who was left alone after the boy's father, Mary's son, was stabbed with a knife during a pub brawl.

Mary McKee could be easily included in the highest category of "real men" because, with her severity, determination, and fearlessness, she could challenge Gerard himself. And, being almost as big as her grandson now, this woman had such a heavy hand that baby Gerard repeatedly found himself knocked down after just a simple slap. If McKee had ever been afraid of anyone, it was his grandmother.

Even local gangsters avoided Mary McKee's shop after she had used nothing but her bare hands to almost beat to death a thug who had come to her to extort money. From then until Mary's death that thug came every week to help her unload a van with the goods. Rumors had it that it was he, who soon rose to the highest ranks of the local Irish mafia and opened the doors to big-time boxing for Gerard.

"Good. That's enough with rear arm block," McKee commanded. "Let's talk about the defense against punches to the body. Elbow block."

The old man demonstrated the elbow block on both sides and even showed several combinations with punches and a quick transition to defense. Charlie, who was still watching the training, gave a smile. It had been a long time since he saw the old man being so nimble.

"Listen and memorize the technique," the old man said to Sullivan. "Rotate your body to the preferred side: to the rear to block with the lead arm elbow, to the lead to block with the rear arm elbow. Block the punch with your forearm. And of course, return to the boxing stance as quickly as possible. Remember – don't lower your forearm too much – that way you will leave your head open for the enemy, but also don't keep the glove glued to your face – the block lifted up high isn't an obstacle for an accurate and powerful punch to the liver."

Sullivan nodded and without further instructions proceeded to practice the elbow block, both standing on the spot and moving. Charlie smiled again, happy that Jack could really practice for the first time, not just being a Punching bag taking the old man's insults, and reluctantly trudged off to perform his basic duties.

"All right, that's enough," McKee commanded and turned to Derrick, who was still standing by the ropes. "Take my place. Practice the defense. Just don't overdo it. It should be purely symbolic. The main thing is that Mr. Sullivan feels how rigid he needs to hold his arms so that the opponent can't break through his block. If anything, I'm in my office."

The young coach nodded and climbed over the ropes, obligingly continuing to hold them so that the old man could leave the ring.

"Well, are you ready?" Derrick asked Sullivan.

Jack shook up his hands, which already felt like lead, and nodded.

"Let's practice the double arm block," the young coach commanded and began throwing light, but still measurable straight punches at Sullivan – exactly the kind that were needed to practice the defense technique.

But the training lasted in that way exactly until the moment the sound of the closing door to McKee's office reached the ring. After that Derrick's punches immediately became significantly stronger. But at the same time, the coach invested just enough strength so that the training could still not be called a beating.

"So, how's your double arm block working out?" Derrick asked mockingly and immediately threw a particularly strong jab, almost breaking through Sullivan's defense.

Jack chose to remain silent, concentrating all his strength on holding his defense, which was getting harder and harder for him with each passing second.

"Go on, try the catch now," the coach commanded and threw another punch quicker than Sullivan could assume a proper position. Derrick's glove burned the skin on Sullivan's cheekbone and painfully hit the corner of his jaw at the end of its trajectory. But Sullivan decided not to pay attention to it and only opened the palm of his rear hand and moved it forward to timely catch the opponent's next punch.

"Now elbow block," Derrick's words came out later than his punch sank into Jack's solar plexus. The force of the punch was not enough to cause Jack a serious injury, but it was more than enough to knock the wind out of him. Sullivan stepped back and started gasping for air like a stranded fish.

"Come on, buddy, you need to react faster!" Derrick replied with a chuckle, but still refrained from throwing another punch.

Sullivan regained his breath and bravely returned to the boxing stance. Meanwhile, the crowd had already begun to gather around the ring.

"Ready?" Derrick asked, keeping an eye on the spectators. "Or maybe you need to fix your tampon?"

The audience roared with laughter. Sullivan raised his fists, clenched his teeth, and muttered, "What's next?"

"Whoa, looks like someone's got PMS anger!"

The spectators greeted just another Derrick's joke with a wave of laughter. The noise prompted Charlie out of the locker room.

"I asked, what's next?" repeated Jack, trying to keep his last bits of composure.

"Ok, big guy," Derrick made it look like a slip of the tongue and added. "Sorry, I meant big girl."

The new joke cracked the gym up and drew everybody who had been working out with punching bags to the ring.

"Come on, rear arm block," the coach commanded and, as before, without waiting threw a punch, and this time not one, but a whole pack of them.

But Sullivan was prepared for such a twist and effectively parried all the attacks of his opponent.

"Whoo, we have a fighter here!" Derrick laughed, addressing the spectators.

The audience supported the coach with a friendly chuckle.

"Calm your tits, Claressa Shields! We're just training, don't we?"

The spectators burst into laughter once again. Sullivan had never heard of the name Claressa Shields and so he had no idea that she was one of only seven boxers in history to hold four major world titles, but he caught that he had been called a woman again. Though it could hardly be qualified as an insult, because in a fair fight Shields could have beaten Derrick and everybody who was now laughing at Jack, all put together. But in One-Two Boxing nobody considered female boxers neither equal to men, nor being capable of putting up a "real" fight.

"Since you are such a tough guy, let's try a combo," Derrick said with a grin. "Double arm block with a fast switch to elbow block."

Sullivan blocked the first two punches successfully, but

it was important to Derrick to show off in front of his friends, so afterwards instead of a straight punch, against which double arm block is intended, he sent a left hook to the opponent's head. The blow made Sullivan a little wobbly, which opened an opportunity for Derrick to successfully deliver a straight punch to the body as well.

Only after having missed that combo Jack realized that Charlie's punches that had knocked him out last time had been quite weak. This time Sullivan remained standing only because Derrick didn't build on his success.

"Hey, is your hubby as good at giving head as you are or..."

Another one of Derrick's jokes ended abruptly in mid-sentence. The audience, who had already begun to chuckle, fell silent as if on cue when they saw Sullivan's fist bump straight into the coach's face. Derrick's words became the last straw for Jack, and for the first time in his life, he decided to respond to the insult with a punch. The coach, who hadn't expected such a development, froze, as if unable to comprehend what had just happened.

But it was not long until one of the spectators shouted, "You Go Girl!" The burst of laughter that followed quickly brought Derrick to his senses. The look of utter surprise on his face immediately changed to rage, and the coach dashed forward, completely oblivious to the fact that Sullivan was not only a rookie but also a whole foot shorter and three weight classes lighter than him.

Even to his own surprise, Sullivan managed to block the first few Derrick's punches and sprang aside timely, so that the opponent hit the ropes by inertia. The crowd of spectators began to laugh and jeer cheerfully. Charlie tried to make a dash for McKee's office to tell the old man to stop the fight before it turned into a massacre, but a couple of "guards" stood in his way. Eager to enjoy the execution of the stranger, they grabbed the boy roughly, pushed him in the opposite direction, and strongly recommended that he mind his own business.

Meanwhile, Sullivan began to miss the punches, but, nonetheless, didn't give up and even somehow made attacks in response. Jack managed to hit Derrick twice more in the face and land three good punches to the body. Still, in the meantime, Sullivan himself missed at least two dozen punches of all kinds that gave him a split lip and a cut above the eyebrow. But things would have been much worse for Jack if he hadn't been able to move around the ring so fast and deftly that Derrick spent more time chasing Jack than hitting him.

But truth be told, by that time Sullivan had run and fought on nothing but adrenaline and rage. His already utterly overworked muscles began to falter. When Charlie noticed that several times Jack almost stumbled for no reason, he knew there was no waiting any longer. If Jack slowed down even a little or lowered his arm, Derrick would tear him to pieces. But Charlie was also well aware that, his weight being almost two times less than that of the young coach, there was no way he could stop the furious fighter.

So the boy decided to use the items at hand. Charlie literally dived under the ropes, taking with him his ever-present companion – a bucket in which he dampened a mop. He spilled most of the water on his way, but one-third of the bucket that he tipped onto Derrick's back was still enough to stop him.

"What the fuck!" Derrick yelled, turning to Charlie.

Just in case, the boy didn't lower the bucket.

"Leave him alone, Derrick," Charlie spoke, his voice trembling with fear. "He's a head shorter than you and he doesn't know anything about boxing!"

Panting, Derrick stared at his new opponent with hatred. Only one thought circulated in his mind, "Should I knock him out or just push him out of the way?" Derrick would have preferred the first option, but he was too afraid to face the wrath of the old man, who always defended the boy.

"Mr. Sullivan, Jack," Charlie addressed his friend, his voice still trembling. "Go to the locker room. Please…"

Sullivan was still standing in a boxing stance with his arms held high.

"Please," Charlie begged, and at the same time, a treacherous tear ran down his cheek.

"Listen, you...," started Derrick.

"Leave him alone!!! LEAVE HIM!!! FUCK OFF!!!" in a frenzy Charlie yelled hysterically at the top of his voice and targeted the bucket at Derrick.

The boy's face flushed, his eyes became bloodshot and foam came out to his lips. Charlie looked like a rabid dog, like a small and weak one, but still capable of causing considerable damage.

"Charlie," Jack talked to him in a calming voice. "It's all right. Put the bucked down. Come with me..."

"No, Jack, go to the locker room. And I'll stand here for a while."

"Charlie," Sullivan took a step forward, holding out his hands to the boy.

"Jack, come on, please, go away!" Charlie begged once again and tears started running from both of his eyes.

Realizing that it was useless to argue with him now, Jack nodded and headed for the ropes. Once in the locker room, Sullivan used his teeth to undo the Velcro that fastened his boxing gloves, tossed the gloves on the floor, got rid of his handwraps, shoes, and finally clothes. A shiver ran through Jack's whole body as his bare foot stepped on the cold tile of the shower room. Sullivan stood under the showerhead and turned the shower on full blast.

At first, the water painfully hit his face, which was already beginning to swell because of the missed punches, but soon the pain started to recede slowly under the stream of the elastic and hot jets that pleasantly massaged his body. Jack stood for a few minutes with his head thrown back, allowing the water to wash away the blood from his split lip and the cut above his eyebrow. He turned around, pressed his back against the wall, and slid down slowly, eventually ending up on the floor.

Sullivan drew his knees up to his chest, leaned on them with his elbows and buried his forehead in his palms. He hadn't cried for a whole year already. Jack knew this for sure, because the day before it was June 23 – exactly a year had passed since he received a notification from the court informing him of the rejection of his claim. Sitting under the jets of water, Jack didn't notice the moment when the first tear dropped from the corner of his eye. But the tears were followed by movements of the face, and then of the shoulders, and then his whole body began to shake with violent, uncontrollable sobs.

Sullivan didn't know why exactly he was crying. Was it because of the terrifying experience he had just had in the ring? Was it because the day before it was June 23? Was it because of all the bullying? Was it because of the physical pain from the missed punches? Or was it maybe because of the physical and mental exhaustion of the last few days? All of these reasons definitely did their bit. But Sullivan broke down not because of all that, but because of the fact that Charlie saved him from the onslaught. He was just a boy who was half Jack's age, skinny and without any support, with tears in his eyes and a voice that trembled with fear.

He gathered his strength and rushed to the rescue of a near stranger, who, on top of that, picked a fight himself. Just a boy. But he could. He managed to find the courage to stand up for a fellow human being. Charlie could. But Jack could not...

..7..

"Hey, Pops, I think your rainbow buddy isn't coming tomorrow," Derrick said as he walked into McKee's office.

The old man glanced questioningly at him.

"He's now sitting in the shower naked, crying like a seven-year-old girl."

Derrick's face twisted into a broad smile. The old man smiled back.

"You didn't hurt him, did you?" McKee asked. "I did warn you, no GBH that later can't be explained by a training accident."

"No, nothing like that," Derrick lied. "Well, he got his ass kicked a little bit, of course, but within reason, just like you asked."

"Well done. You can take the rest of the day off."

"Thanks, Pops. By the way, there's another thing – can I let the guys in the coach's shower? I'm asking because that one's probably still wailing there."

"Go ahead," the old man said, and added with a sneer. "I hope he gets done with wailing before tonight. I don't really wanna drive a naked fag out of my shower. I won't even touch him with a mop."

McKee and Derrick both laughed at what they thought was a very good joke. Having finished laughing, the young coach waved goodbye to the old man and left the office, bumping into Charlie on the other side of the door. After their clash in the ring, when Sullivan had gone to the locker room, the boy had quickly vanished through the back exit, depriving Derrick of the opportunity to get even. But the young coach certainly couldn't afford to do it right at the doorway of the old man's office. So Derrick only gave Charlie the most furious look possible and a shoulder shove that nearly knocked the frail boy off his feet.

But Charlie didn't pay any attention to that. He was too busy comprehending the conversation, which he had heard distinctly through the door. The boy stepped inside the office and closed the door behind him.

"So that's what it is?" he spoke in a calm but extremely disappointed voice. "You couldn't break Sullivan down yourself, so you decided to bring in your buddies?" You know, when I first came to the club today, I immediately felt that something was wrong. We haven't had that many people in a year. And so many of your friends gather at our place all at once only when you watch another fight and get drunk. But then I saw you with Jack in the ring. You really trained him, you didn't just bully him. I even thought you liked it yourself..."

McKee had no idea what Charlie was getting at. He was sitting in his favorite chair, holding an almost empty glass of whiskey in his hand, and just waiting for the kid to finish his monologue. But Charlie kept on, "I should have guessed it was a trick... But I was naive to have still believed that you were a good guy. A racist – yes, a homophobe – yes, but still a good guy, as strange as it may sound."

The old man liked Charlie's monologue less and less with each word he uttered, but he still had no idea what the boy was getting at, so he continued to stare at him silently. McKee's indignation was only expressed in a menacing frown.

"What kind of a person could send his sidekick to beat up a man whose only crime is being gay? Pops, you tell me, why do you hate them so much? What did they do to you personally?"

McKee opened his mouth to reply, but Charlie continued, "Did a gay seduce you as a child? Is that what it is? Look, you Irish are Catholic, right? When you were a child, did a priest touch you where he shouldn't have? Or maybe he even made *you* touch something? Is that why you hate gays so much?"

The mention of the Irish, and the suggestion that someone might once have done something homosexual with McKee himself instantly ignited the fuse of the old man's legendary explosive temper. McKee put the glass down on the table with such force that he almost smashed it.

"Well, Charlie, you took it too far this time!" The old man roared, jumping to his feet.

"No!" Charlie shouted back with a treacherous tremor in his voice. "You won't scare me this time! You will listen to me to the end!"

McKee went around the table and dashed to Charlie. If a chair or other obstacle had gotten in his way right then, the old man would have probably shattered it to pieces.

"Are you gonna tell me what to do, brat!?!"

McKee's voice sounded so threatening that Charlie felt a shiver of panic run down his spine. But the boy didn't back down.

"Or what?" he shouted already with tears in his voice. "Are you going to hit me? Or are you maybe going to set your sidekick on me, just like you did it to Sullivan?"

McKee stopped a footstep away from the boy, panting and clenching his fists. In another instant, he would have hit Charlie. No matter what. Just because anger had once again clouded his eyes and awakened in the old man the very beast that neither he nor anyone else, except the late Johnny Sifaretto, had ever been able to contain. But Charlie's next words caught the old man off guard and instantly got him paralyzed.

"You know what, Gerard." Charlie had never called his boss by his first name before. "You should definitely hit me – BECAUSE I'M GAY, TOO!" the boy shouted at the top of his voice.

Tears and a smile of relief appeared on Charlie's face at the same time. For the first time in his life, he came out aloud.

For a few seconds, the boy stood and silently enjoyed the look of shock on the old man's face.

"And here's another piece of news for you – I'm not an illegal immigrant, as you like to call me! My parents and I, we all became citizens five years ago! And this story I told you about how they were expelled to Mexico – it's all bullshit! In fact, my father kicked me out of the house when he caught me kissing a guy! That's what it was! And when I went to my aunt and uncle's house, they wouldn't let me in, because my father had already called them and said he would curse them if they took me in. My aunt might have let me stay, but her husband, he's just like you and my father – he just slammed the door in my face.

The old man stood spellbound, looking at Charlie, not knowing what he should say or do at the moment.

"Don't worry," the boy went on. "I remember perfectly well that the last time I tried to talk to you about Sullivan, you promised to fire me if I ever raised my voice at you again. Don't bother yourself!"

Charlie reached into the pocket of his jeans, took out a bunch of keys to the club, tossed them on the floor, and yelled at the top of his voice, "I FUCKING QUIT!!!"

Charlie wheeled around and yanked the door open, almost ripping the handle off. Having already crossed the threshold, the boy stopped, turned around again, and added, "Think about it, Pops, I have worked here for two years, and over these two years, you spent more time with me than with anyone else, including your so-strongly-marked heterosexual cronies who can only shout at boxing on the TV and soak up beer. Did my homosexuality bother you until you knew about it? Huh, Pops? Was it the reason for me to have scrubbed the floors less diligently? Did it keep me from fixing the equipment, handing out our flyers, and doing other things for One-two Boxing, which, by the way, you never paid me extra for? What harm did my homosexuality do to you? Huh, Pops?"

The old man was still standing in the same spot, his face

still expressing utter confusion. Except that McKee no longer clenched his fists. Charlie took one last look at the office, the old dusty championship belt on the wall, and McKee himself.

"Take care of yourself, Pops..." Charlie added with a heavy sigh and closed the door behind him.

..8..

Boom! Boom! Boom! The drumming in McKee's ears was immediately followed by a terrible headache. Without lifting his forehead from the surface of the table, the old man covered his ears with his hands and made a sound similar to something between a moan and a growl of an animal. Two empty bottles of whiskey lay on their sides near his head.

Gerard McKee had never been known for his ability to deal with his own feelings or at least interpret them correctly. Charlie's loud confessions and his emotional resignation the day before had stirred up a whole storm of different feelings in the old man, but the only thing he could understand was that these feelings were unpleasant to him. And McKee knew only one way of dealing with unpleasant feelings – saturating them thoroughly with alcohol.

So he couldn't think of anything better to do than locking himself in his office and drinking all night long until fatigue and alcohol fumes wore him out in his favorite chair. Boom! Boom! Boom! – the drumming in his head repeated again. McKee cursed. The loud sound of his own voice caused a new bout of headache. Not without effort, the old man unstuck his face from the table and sat up straight in his chair. The headache got coupled with the pain in the back and neck, which had become stiff after sleeping in an uncomfortable position.

McKee cursed again – this time in a whisper. A new portion of "Boom! Boom! Boom!" made him squeeze his eyes shut and clutch his head. It seemed to the old man that his skull was starting to grow in size under the pressure of the brain trying to explode. McKee clutched his head tighter trying to get it back to its original size. The pressure helped to ease the pain slightly, and the old man was finally able to realize that the next drum solo "Boom! Boom! Boom!" actually came from the outside, and not from inside his head.

Still bleary-eyed, McKee looked around but couldn't detect the source of the terrible noise. He leaned back in his chair and began massaging his temples, but a new wave of "Boom! Boom! Boom!" negated the entire therapeutic effect of this procedure. The old man uttered a hushed and very sad sound which almost resembled weeping. Having looked around the office one more time, McKee guessed that the noise was coming from somewhere behind his office door. The old man had absolutely no desire to get up from his chair, but the incessant peals of "Boom! Boom! Boom!" left him no choice.

Grunting and groaning, McKee rose to his feet, feeling the increase of the pain in his head and back, as well as new unpleasant sensations in his legs. "I hope it's robbers with a shotgun, and they'll shoot my head off right away," the old man muttered under his breath, realizing that the sound was coming from the metal door of the main entrance. Leaving the office, he tried to shout that he was on his way to make the intruders stop drumming, but his voice only made his headache worse again.

When McKee finally trudged up to the entrance, he turned the key in the tight lock, its creak piercing his brain like a hot needle, forcing him to close his eyes. As if that wasn't enough, the creak of the lock was followed by an even louder and more disgusting creak of the door itself, and then a bright light from the outside that caused the old man such terrible pain that for a moment, he felt as if he went blind and deaf at the same time.

McKee managed to make out the words of the intruder, who had been drumming on the door, only after he repeated them for the fourth time.

"Hey, are you all right?"

The old man was finally able to see who was speaking. It was Jack Sullivan. For a moment, though, McKee didn't recognize him. A cut lip with traces of dried blood, a Band-Aid over his eyebrow, a few bruises on his chin, cheekbones, and forehead, and his entire once-well-groomed face now looked swollen and asymmetrical. If it wasn't for the same three-thousand-dollar suit, Sullivan could have been easily mistaken for a simple workman after a heavy drinking session followed by a fight.

"Fuck!" McKee blurted out. "Not you again!"

The old man sounded so miserable that Sullivan even felt pity for him. But it was only for a moment because the distinct smell of alcohol immediately explained to him the reasons for McKee's misery. And Sullivan hadn't felt sorry for drinkers since he was a little kid.

"Coach, are you all right?" Jack repeated again, this time raising his voice intentionally. He couldn't miss an opportunity to get back at McKee even a little for all his previous insults and bullying.

McKee suddenly grabbed Sullivan by the lapels of his jacket, pulled him inside, and closed the front door behind him. Jack thought that the old man had finally decided to kick his ass, but McKee quickly explained his actions. "The sun hurts my eyes."

Sullivan nodded understandingly, straightening his jacket and waiting for McKee to say something else, but the old man just trudged sullenly away from the door – to the nearest chair. Flopping down onto it, McKee heaved a sigh of relief. Resting his elbows on his knees, he buried his face in his hands and closed his eyes. Afraid that the old man could fall asleep immediately, Sullivan took a step toward him. "Mr. McKee, what's our training plan for today? Body punches? Defense? Maybe combos?"

"No, no, no..." the old man spoke fast. "Not today... No, no, no..."

On the one hand, Sullivan was well aware that the

hungover McKee would be of little use, on the other – in a sober, well, almost sober state, the old man didn't put a lot of effort into his training either. Sullivan's inward dispute was put to an end with an argument that he couldn't and didn't want to resist – every minute of today's training would definitely cause McKee a lot of pain.

"Mr. McKee," Sullivan said, deliberately raising his voice again. "We signed a contract, and you yourself insisted that we train every weekday..."

Every word Sullivan said gave the old man a new bout of headache. To stop it he interrupted the speaker, "All right, all right. Just stop shouting. You'll have your training!" The old man leaned back in his chair and started massaging his temples. "Just let me think for a while in silence."

Sullivan couldn't help but smile and turned away so that McKee wouldn't notice it. The old man spoke again only about three minutes later, "Rich boy, do you live in an apartment or your own house?"

"In a house," Sullivan replied and knitted his brows, surprised by the question.

"Do you have a swimming pool?"

"I do," Jack answered, even more surprised.

"Then let's go to your place. Today we'll be training in a pool."

Spotting the expression of misunderstanding on Sullivan's face, the old man added, "It's a real thing. Believe me. Floyd Mayweather, Manny Pacquiao, Miguel Cotto – all cool kids do it."

Whether it was because this type of training seemed to Sullivan to be a hastily concocted invention of the coach, or he simply didn't want to take McKee to his place, in any case, Jack continued to look at the old man distrustfully. Fearing that Sullivan would start arguing again and his words would cause another bout of headache, McKee hastened to add, "Tell me honestly, Sullivan, I'm sure your muscles are aching from yesterday and the day before. And your mug doesn't look as good as it used to. You're definitely not gonna be on the cover of Gayboy anymore," the old man chuckled at the clever joke, but immediately regretted it as the chuckle was followed by a stab of headache. "What I mean is that the usual training is gonna ruin you even more. And in the pool, it's all different. The water doesn't allow you to move quickly, it is almost impossible to get injured in it. Plus, it kinda massages your muscles. Some say that after a workout in a pool they feel even better than before."

The muscle pain was indeed killing Sullivan, and he even considered canceling the workout himself or at least stealing a couple of Oxycodone pills from his medicine cabinet. But in the end, the stubbornness and desire to prove something at least to himself got the better of him, and Jack went to training at six in the morning, adding only an aspirin pill to his breakfast. However, McKee's words about the therapeutic effect of swim training sounded extremely tempting.

"Okay, the pool it is," Sullivan said and headed for the exit.

"Hey, hey! Wait a bit," the old man stopped him. "Scoot to my office first. There's my shades in the desk drawer to the left. Fetch them, 'cause the sun's just killing me right now."

"Saying 'please' once in a while won't kill you," Sullivan thought to himself but decided not to argue with the old man. The director's office greeted Jack with a smell of alcoholic fumes, which instantly brought back the unpleasant memories from his childhood. Sullivan looked around curiously, noticing the yellowed posters of boxing matches and the wall with framed photographs of McKee and a lot of people Jack didn't know.

Judging by the autographs, many of them were celebrities of the boxing world. But only two pictures caught Sullivan's attention. The first one featured Derrick with his gloved hand raised triumphantly by the referee, and the second, modestly placed at the very bottom, showed McKee standing with Charlie and putting a fatherly arm around the boy's shoulder. Tapped bottles of whiskey weren't lost on Sullivan either. But most of all, Jack was interested in the old championship belt hanging above the director's chair.

The belt was so dirty and dusty that Jack had to come close to the wall to make out its inscription. "IPBU HEAVYWEIGHT WORLD CHAMPION," Sullivan read to himself. Of course, Jack should have already known what organization gave McKee his title, but initially, Sullivan was only interested in the old man's coaching career, so he didn't even bother to read the first part of the Wikipedia page about Gerard McKee as a boxer.

But now Jack understood why the old man had lost his temper so quickly after Sullivan had mentioned that he wanted to become the IPBU champion. "Why is his championship belt so dirty? Is it really so hard to clean it?" Sullivan thought to himself.

"Hey, what's taking you so long?" McKee's voice came from the hall. "On the left, it's the first or maybe the second drawer."

Sullivan took his eyes off the belt and hurried to find the old man's sunglasses.

The way from One-two Boxing to Jack's house took about forty minutes. When the gate opened automatically to let Sullivan's car in, McKee whistled, looking around. "Wow, Rich boy, you're even richer than I thought!"

McKee saw a two-story house that looked like it was made entirely of glass. The glass was of three different types: almost the entire first floor consisted of transparent glass that revealed all its interiors; the bedrooms on the second floor were completely hidden from prying eyes behind mirror glass with a golden tint; and the second living room, the studies, and the library, located on the same floor, were separated from the outside world by the smoked glass, which allowed you to see only the outlines of separate objects. The house was surrounded by a neat and well-kept garden that combined both Eastern and Western traditions.

"Are your parents rich?" McKee asked, getting out of the car.

"Do I look like I can't earn enough to buy a house like this myself?"

Sullivan answered louder than necessary, but to his regret, McKee had partially recovered during the ride, and the sounds no longer caused him such a severe headache as they did before.

"Don't be a smartass, just answer the question," the old man said, still wincing slightly.

Sullivan noted that the hangover definitely made McKee a lot less angry than usual.

"No, I was raised by a single mother from the age of ten. And she was a schoolteacher. But just to please you a little bit, I can say that I earned money for this house together with my husband."

Whether it was the mention of the husband or just a new phase of the hangover, but McKee felt a tiny wave of nausea at Sullivan's last words.

"The way to the pool is through the house," Sullivan said, reaching for the front door handle, which, like everything else there, was made of nothing but glass.

"Don't you usually lock the door?" McKee uttered, noticing Sullivan open the door without using keys.

"The locks are automatic. They are part of the home security system. We have facial-recognition CCTV cameras everywhere here. And the door handle also has a built-in fingerprint scanner. I took part in the development of the algorithm for this system. That's where half of the money for this house came from."

Sullivan didn't know why he had suddenly opened up and started telling the old man details of his life that the latter hadn't even asked about. Or, rather, he knew, but he didn't want to admit to himself that he still had problems with self-esteem and that he still had to prove to rough men like McKee that he, too, was worth something.

"Fancy," the old man whistled. "I'm an old-school guy and I don't like all this gimmickry, but if some algorithm for something I don't understand can bring more money than I've made in fifteen years getting punched in the mug, then why not."

Sullivan smiled, thinking to himself, "I guess if I wasn't a pathetic faggot, he could have even expressed his thought as a real compliment."

"And where does the other half of the money come from?" McKee asked.

"My husband was a successful plastic surgeon," Sullivan answered, opening the door that led to the backyard. "And answering your next question – no, he didn't only do fake boobs and noses for the real housewives. This too, of course, but Jacob's main field was reconstructive surgery. He performed the most complex surgeries, literally piecing together the faces of those who had gotten in terrible accidents."

McKee nodded in response and followed Sullivan out into the backyard.

"What, no smart remarks? Don't you want to tell me that you thought my husband worked as Liza Minnelli's double or tailored panties for Lady Gaga?"

The old man winced as he stepped into the bright sunlight.

"Some other time, Rich boy," McKee responded calmly.

"You know, when you're hungover, I like you better," Sullivan said with a grin.

In his own home, Jack felt much more confident than in One-two Boxing and therefore could talk to the old man way more freely. McKee quickly spotted a lounger with an umbrella, where he could hide from the sun, and hurried up to it, skirting the oblong pool. Having flopped down onto the lounger, the old man shouted to Sullivan, "Well, what are you waiting for? Come on, go change. Just watch it – no thongs!"

"And he's back," Jack said under his breath and headed

back into the house.

Carefully selecting the most masculine – just black – Speedo, Sullivan changed and returned to the pool. McKee had already thrown off his shoes and socks. At the moment he was sprawling out on the lounger, his hands behind his head, his bare feet exposed to the sun.

"Come on, jump in the water!" the old man commanded. "Do you even know how to swim?"

"Yes I do," Sullivan answered.

"There you go. Go ahead and do a dozen laps around the pool. Just don't rush it. It's a warm-up to stretch the muscles and relieve tension."

Sullivan prepared to dive into the water, but the old man stopped him. "Wait a sec. Tell me, is there a bar in your cool glass house? I could use a drink," McKee said, scratching the stubble on his chin.

Jack rolled his eyes disapprovingly but answered anyway, "It's to the right from the entrance. Take whatever you want, we don't throw any more parties anyway."

The old man got up from the lounger with unexpected agility and hurried into the house. Being already in the water, Sullivan heard his voice again, "Hey, Sullivan, what about your security system? Won't it fire a laser at me?"

"Don't worry, it won't," Jack said and added with a smile. "If you behave yourself."

Sullivan pulled the swimming goggles over his eyes and dived in. McKee walked into the house and looked around.

"Wow, not a single dildo in sight. Some strange gays live here," he said under his breath and laughed at his own joke.

As promised, there was a bar on the right. The old man whistled at the variety of bottles displayed there – from vodka with Cyrillic inscriptions on the label to 20-year-old whiskey. McKee's mouth watered at the sight of a bottle of Dalmore adorned with a dear head. The old man's mind immediately flashed back to the time when he and Johnny Sifaretto had once celebrated the opening of One-two Boxing with a similar bottle.

McKee almost reached for it, remembering what Sullivan had said about taking whatever he wanted, but then checked himself. The gentleman's code of honor didn't allow him to simply take advantage of someone else's hospitality and open the new bottle, which cost several thousand dollars. If the owner had poured it for him, that would have been a different story. So, instead, McKee chose to settle for Jack Daniel's.

McKee poured the whiskey into a glass and swallowed the first shot quickly as if it were a medicine. Having felt the warmth of alcohol spread through his body and bring relief, the old man could now allow himself to relax and truly enjoy the noble taste of his favorite drink. Sipping his second portion of whiskey, McKee ran his eyes through the row of bottles once more, this time looking at them like an art connoisseur, and not like a man dying of thirst.

"WhistlePig, Philadelphia. Mmm, Japanese stuff. I've tried Hibiki once, but Hakushu is worth giving a shot someday," the old man started to list out loud. "Berkshire Botanical... What's this? Gin? Not bad, not bad. The good old Scottish Glengoyne. Rumbullion, pirate's best friend. Wines – I'm not interested in that. Blavod. Haven't heard about it. Absinthe. Sketchy stuff. Metaxa, Sambuca, Tequila... Everything's like in decent houses. You might even think that normal men live here."

McKee chuckled, took a sip, smacked his lips with pleasure, and continued, "It's obviously not Sullivan who's in charge of all this, except probably for this section with some colorful shit for cocktails. His hubby's must be running the bar. Maybe he's the one who's less gay in their couple. What do they call it... Gay officer?"

The old man laughed again at his own joke. Turning his head away from the bar, McKee came across a small room divider with photographs that looked like a piece of modern art made of polished metal and color glass.

"And here it must be him, Mr. gay hubby!"

McKee stared at the picture of Sullivan and Jacob looking back at him, smiling.

"Yep, definitely the hubby," the old man repeated, shifting his gaze at the next photograph, which showed the two men at the wedding altar, and then another one featuring the newlyweds feeding each other cake decorated with the figures of the two grooms, instead of a traditional set of the bride and groom.

Jacob was slightly taller than Sullivan but just as trim and toned. He was most likely a couple of years older than Sullivan. Or maybe he just looked more imposing. Swarthy and with a head of magnificent dark brown hair, Jacob looked more like a Greek or Italian playboy – a yacht owner – rather than an American plastic surgeon.

McKee quickly ran his eyes over the rest of the photographs, recognizing in some of them Paris, London, Moscow, Rome, and other notable places. The old man noticed that in all these photographs Sullivan looked happy and smiled all the time, while he knew Jack as the owner of one of the most lifeless and sad faces that he had ever seen in his life. However, in comparison to his husband, even the old Sullivan looked rather dull.

Jacob literally scintillated with positive energy. His photographs even seemed to radiate warmth, like a light bulb.

"Enjoying himself as if he has a villa on the Canary Islands, a yacht on the Hudson, a Ferrari in the garage, and a knee-deep cock."

The old man took another sip and added, "Maybe that's why Sullivan looks like he's got a stick up his ass?"

McKee was even a little ashamed of how loudly he laughed that time. The old man flicked his fingernail at Sullivan's face in the photo, took the last sip of whiskey, put the glass on the counter, and went back to the pool. As he stepped outside, he whistled loudly, "All right, that's it, stop cruising around! Come on, get out!"

Jack swam to the edge of the pool and got out of the

water.

"How's the water? Not too cold?" McKee asked.

"Why? Do you want to dive?" Sullivan said with a grin.

"And give you the pleasure to enjoy all of this masculine splendor," McKee said, running his hands along his body. "No way."

Sullivan responded with a slight smile and thought to himself, "I definitely like him better when he's hungover. Still the same homophobe, but at least funny, not just mean as a snake."

"Run a couple of laps around the pool," McKee said. "Running is the foundation of the boxer's cardio training. Floyd Mayweather ran 6 miles a day when he was preparing for a fight."

Sullivan started running, and the old man headed back to the lounger. But as soon as McKee settled comfortably and stretched his legs under the warm beams of the sun, his stomach reminded him of its existence with an unpleasant rumble. Over three hundred pounds of the old man's live weight couldn't possibly subsist on alcohol alone for more than ten hours.

"Hey, Usain Bolt in Speedo, do you have anything to eat in your house?" he called out to Sullivan as he ran past.

"The kitchen's right next to the bar, first door to the left," Jack said without stopping.

The old man got up from the lounger and went to the house. The kitchen looked like that piece of modern art, which was decorated with the photographs of the house owners. Everything there was made of polished metal and multicolor glass, except for the seats of chairs, which were complemented with pillows of silver-gray color to match the metal elements. A large French door refrigerator with a big touch screen was exactly the same color.

McKee grabbed its handle, fearing that the refrigerator might speak in a human voice and demand his fingerprints. But the refrigerator was quite ordinary. Except that the variety of food inside was unimaginable to the old man. His old fridge rarely had anything but beer, steaks, and sausages.

There, on the contrary, entire shelves were used exclusively for various vegetables and fruits, a separate container was filled with fish and seafood, not to mention two shelves of all sorts of vegan delicacies. McKee recognized four types of milk substitutes alone: rice, almond, coconut, and soy. However, there also were both meat and regular milk.

"Thank God only one of these bumhole engineers is crazy about greens," McKee said, his huge hands raking up several sorts of ham at once, a large chunk of one of which he had already managed to stuff into his mouth.

Having closed the refrigerator door, which completely blocked his view of the hallway leading to the front entrance, McKee was surprised to find a young woman staring at him with saucer eyes. The old man stared back at her. It took McKee a few seconds to realize that a huge, unshaven, swollen from the previous night's drinking, and also barefoot man didn't fit into the sophisticated interior of the house, which seemed to come right off the pages of Architectural Digest.

"No, no, no, no," McKee said quickly, holding up his hands and trying hard to show the woman that she had nothing to fear. "I'm not some bum, I just look like one. Bad hair day, you know."

A poor attempt at a joke didn't remedy the situation. Nor did the pieces of unchewed ham that flew out of the old man's mouth as he spoke. McKee noticed the woman glance toward the table on which stood a block of kitchen knives.

"I'm with Mr. Sullivan. He's running around the pool right now. He allowed me to raid the fridge. I'm his coach."

The old man tried to put on a friendly smile.

"Gerard McKee," The coach extended his hand to the woman. "Nice to meet you."

The sight of the old man's paw feared the woman even more. But she dared to speak after all – perhaps, in order to distract the potential rapist and killer and make a dash for a knife.

"A coach? And what happened to Alberto?"

"Who's Alberto?" McKee responded blankly.

"Mr. Sullivan's Pilates coach," the woman said, her voice growing more suspicious.

"Pilates? No, no. I'm a boxing coach. We just started last week."

"Boxing?" the woman replied as her right eyebrow went up. "I didn't know Jack took up boxing."

The woman stood still for a few more seconds, looking intently into the old man's face.

"That explains a lot, though," she added, reaching into the back pocket of her jeans for her smartphone. "Gerard McKee, you say?"

"Yeah," the old man replied.

The woman quickly googled the old man's name and immediately came across an article on Wikipedia. She tapped on the photo and placed the smartphone in her extended hand at the level of McKee's face. Gerard smiled awkwardly. Surely, the present-day McKee no longer looked much like himself at the dawn of his boxing career, but a quick comparison of the moles and a scar above his eyebrow did convince the woman that the strange barefoot giant was telling the truth.

"Justine Heller," the woman said, extending her hand.

McKee shook the small and delicate hand very gently.

"Nice to meet you, ma'am," the old man said. "I'm sorry I scared you."

"Don't mention it. Go on with your meal," Justine replied and even smiled slightly. "Although, could you maybe help me with some small job first. It requires just a strong man like you."

"Yes, ma'am, of course," the old man replied gladly, hoping to redeem himself in the eyes of his new acquaintance.

"Follow me. The ramp got jammed halfway through and it moves neither forward nor backward."

Justine led McKee to the main entrance and then to the

driveway, where the family minivan was now parked next to Sullivan's red Tesla. The folding ramp protruded only halfway from the opened sliding door. Having walked around the car, McKee saw who it was meant for. Inside the minivan, a man was sitting in a wheelchair.

The old man couldn't immediately identify him as Jacob, whom he had seen in the photos. Although it was still the same swarthy and fit man with gorgeous dark brown hair, there was no trace left of his scintillating personality. This Jacob looked tired and confused as if he didn't quite understand where he was or what was happening to him.

Noticing the surprised expression on the old man's face, Justine asked, "Haven't you met Jacob yet?"

"No, I haven't. I mean, I know Jack has a husband, Jacob, but we haven't met in person."

The old man hesitated for a moment. The sight of Jacob's limp head tilted to the side and his eyes wandering aimlessly somewhere about the level of McKee's knees evoked in the old man unpleasant memories of his youth. When McKee was just starting his boxing career, his grandmother developed Alzheimer's disease.

Once so dignified, determined, and formidable, Mary McKee was becoming less and less herself with each passing day, until she finally turned into a living corpse, sitting all day in a chair in front of a TV and watching children's cartoons. McKee's relationship with his grandmother, who had raised him, wasn't exactly warm, but the way she was fading away before his eyes was killing Gerard.

"Nice to meet you, Mr. Jacob," the old man said, shaking off the memories. "Sorry, I don't know your last name. It's not Sullivan, I guess."

McKee extended his hand inside the minivan, but Jacob looked at it as if it was something completely alien. McKee might as well have given him a stick instead of his hand.

"Jacob is very tired because of the physiotherapy today, that's why we came back earlier," Justine said and put her hand on McKee's shoulder, making it clear that he shouldn't expect Jacob to shake his hand.

McKee took his hand away and, to hide his embarrassment, began to examine and feel the jammed ramp with superfluous attention.

"See, it's buzzing, but nothing happens," Justine said, pressing a button.

"Yeah, let me see," McKee replied and began pressing on various sections of the ramp, hoping to get the device working.

After a few minutes of fruitless attempts, the old man turned to Justine. "Ma'am, I can try to press harder, but there's a big chance that I'll just wreck the hell out of everything in here," McKee said.

"Okay, I think I'd better take the car to a repair shop later and leave this job to professionals," Justine replied. "Can you help me get Jacob out of the car?"

The old man nodded.

"We need to go around," the woman added.

Having opened the opposite door of the car, Justine pulled Jacob's wheelchair to the edge.

"In this situation, Mr. Sullivan usually takes Jacob in his arms, and I take out the wheelchair."

"All right, let's do it this way," McKee said.

Justine unbuckled the belt that fastened Jacob to the wheelchair, and McKee slipped his hands very carefully under the man's knees and shoulders.

"There you go," McKee said. "Is everything all right, Mr. Jacob?"

"Everything's all right," Justine answered for him. "Oh no! What a freaking day!" she added in disappointment, taking the wheelchair out of the car.

McKee followed the woman's glance and noticed that one of the front wheels was skewed.

"Let me carry him, and we'll deal with the wheelchair later," the old man suggested.

"If it's not too much trouble, Jacob and I will be very

grateful," Justine said and smiled slightly at McKee.

"No problem, ma'am, I'm happy to help!" the old man replied and headed in the direction of the house.

Jacob raised his arms and wrapped them around McKee's powerful neck. If anyone had ever told the old man that one day he would not only talk to a gay and train him but also carry one of them in his arms, McKee would have laughed at the top of his lungs. Laughed, and then slammed his fist forcefully into the face of anyone who had dared to suggest such a thing. But right then, the old man didn't feel any negative emotions about it.

McKee's twisted code of honor placed disability above sexual orientation, race, and everything else. Anyone who disrespected a physically challenged person immediately found themselves at the very bottom of the old man's personal social ladder – just below gays and drug addicts, at the same level as rapists and pedophiles.

"What do you think you are doing?" McKee was faced with Sullivan's question as soon as he entered the house.

Jack had already slipped into his robe to go search for the coach, who hadn't come back from the kitchen for too long. The harsh and even threatening tone of Sullivan's voice and the same look in his eyes surprised McKee. He could have never imagined that Jack could be so tough. The old man thought that Sullivan, like all gays, was a weak and cowardly creature and that his persistence during training was nothing more than arrogance that should soon wear off.

"I asked you what you were doing," Sullivan repeated even more sternly since no answer followed.

"Mr. McKee is helping me." Justine, who had lingered at the car trying to fix the wheelchair, came to the old man's aid. "The ramp got jammed, and then one of the wheelchair's wheels broke. So your coach helped me out."

Sullivan came up to McKee resolutely.

"I'll take it from here," he spoke to the old man as if giving him an order.

The latter silently handed Jacob over to Jack, surprised at how Sullivan didn't bend under the weight of his husband, who certainly weighed not less than Sullivan himself.

"Mr. McKee, wait for me by the pool," Sullivan's voice still sounded harsh and peremptory. "Or you can go to the kitchen if you haven't had a chance to satisfy your hunger yet."

"I'll wait by the pool," McKee responded and headed for the back exit.

After leaving the house, the old man took his former place in the lounger, but before lying down, he preferred to put on his socks and shoes. Through the glass walls, McKee watched as Sullivan carried his husband into the kitchen, sat him down on a chair, and squatted down to unlace and took off his shoes.

When Sullivan got up again, Jacob got active for the first time – he stretched out his hands to his husband like a child who wants to be held by their mother. Jack bent down, hugged Jacob tightly, and began to gently stroke his back. Despite the discomfort of his position, Sullivan stopped only when Jacob unlocked his arms and lowered them. After that Jack straightened up, pressed his husband's head to his chest, ruffled his hair, and kissed him gently on the forehead.

McKee wouldn't have admitted it even to himself, but at that moment, somewhere deep inside, in the very center of his soul, he realized that it was true love. And it didn't matter that it was shared by the two people of the same sex.

"You know, I've been working as a rehabilitologist for seven years now," Justine spoke, coming up to the old man and following his gaze. "But I've seen such loyalty as Jack shows only once before. It was a retired couple who had lived together for fifty years. And I haven't even heard of such a thing happening among young people. He takes care of Jacob more than I do, even though I work full-time."

"Stop me if I'm violating the patient confidentiality or if it's none of my business," McKee talked to Justine as he sat down on a lounger. "But what does he have? He's still too young to have dementia."

Noticing the question in Justine's eyes the old man added, "My grandmother had Alzheimer's disease. She looked at me with exactly the same eyes."

"It's not a disease. Jacob had a head injury. Very serious one. He barely survived. He was in a coma, and when he came around, it turned out that some areas of his brain had sustained irreparable damage. We are now trying to restore those functions of the brain that were partially impaired, but, unfortunately, I cannot say that we are making much progress."

McKee nodded understandingly.

"Again, stop me if it's none of my business, but what happened to him? Skiing accident or something like that?"

"No, he was attacked," Justine answered and immediately got embarrassed. "But please don't talk to Jack about it. It's an extremely painful topic for him. I shouldn't have told you that…"

"Don't worry, I won't let it slip," the old man said.

There was a long, heavy pause.

"You said you were teaching Jack boxing? Did I get it right?" Justine finally asked. "That doesn't sound like him. Although, it explains the bruises on his face."

"Yes, you got it right. We started just recently…"

McKee's answer was cut short by Sullivan's words as he appeared in the back exit, "McKee, let's go, I'll take you back. Training is over for today," he said to the old man in a less harsh, but still unfriendly tone and added, "If you want, you can count it as full 6 hours."

Sullivan had already put on his usual suit and was now standing and impatiently fiddling with his car keys.

"I ain't gonna count nothing," the old man muttered, getting up from the lounger.

Turning to Justine, McKee politely said goodbye and followed Sullivan, who had already gone to the car. When the red Tesla reversed, and the second floor of the house became visible through the windshield, McKee noticed the figure of Jacob, who raised his hand and waved slightly. The old man didn't know if Jacob was waving at him or Sullivan, or if he was just raising his hand for no apparent reason, but McKee waved back anyway.

..9..

"Pops!!! Help me!!! Where are you?!?" Kate's ear-shredding scream shattered the silence of the empty gym, making McKee spill the whiskey he had just started pouring into a glass to celebrate the end of another workday and at the same time kill the blues left by Charlie's resignation.

"What the hell?" the old man grunted and got to his feet.

By the time McKee made his way around the desk, Kate had already managed to run across the gym and literally flew into the old man's office.

"Pops, hurry up!" she panted, grabbing the old man's hand and pulling him along.

"What's the matter?!?" McKee asked, breaking into a run, so uncustomary for him.

"They are killing him! Go faster!" Kate blurted out indistinctly, forcing the old man to speed up.

When they ran out of the One-two Boxing building, McKee turned around as he heard the sound of a car speeding off. It was only for a brief moment that the old man caught a glimpse of a red car that resembled Sullivan's Tesla going away at high speed. But Kate dragged the old man in the opposite direction.

"Kate, where are we running to?" McKee shouted, starting to lose his breath already.

But no answer was needed. As they went around the corner, they almost bumped into a man standing on all fours on the ground.

"Jack, you okay?" Without waiting for the answer, Kate immediately rushed to help Sullivan to his feet. "Pops, call an ambulance!" she added, turning to the old man.

"No need for an ambulance," Jack said indistinctly, and spat a substantial amount of blood onto the asphalt, "It's just a couple of scratches."

Kate began to feel Sullivan cautiously, afraid that she could find a stab wound or a bullet hole.

"Are you dizzy? Feeling sick? Let's hope you don't have a concussion," Kate spoke hastily and turned to McKee. "Pops, why are you standing around? Come on, grab his arm – let's take him inside!"

McKee hurried to carry out the woman's order.

"It's the blood I swallowed that's making me sick, not the concussion," Jack answered, while the coach hooked his strong arm through Sullivan's. "I'll be fine."

"Can someone tell me already what happened here?" the old man demanded.

Kate tried to take Jack by his other arm, but it turned out that McKee was doing just fine on his own.

"My car broke down," Kate spoke. "I had to take a bus. I was walking from the bus stop, and then some scumbags leeched onto me. I started screaming. Jack heard it and came to the rescue. There were three of them, and all of them hefty! Well, they ganged up on him, and I ran for help."

"Kate, how many times have I told you not to hang around here at night?" McKee said in a patronizing way. "This isn't Green Hills! They can off you over a freezer pop around here! You should've called me – I would've met you at the bus stop. And it would've been even better if you'd told me right away that the car had broken down – I would've picked you up myself!"

"But I called!" Kate resented. "You probably left your phone at home again or forgot to charge it!"

McKee slapped his pocket and was vexed to find that he had indeed forgotten his phone. At that moment, the three of them turned around the corner and walked along the facade to the main entrance of One-two Boxing.

"Fuck!" Sullivan cursed. "They stole my car. That's why they backed off as soon as they searched my pockets…"

McKee could not help but chuckle as he heard Jack saying a swear word for the first time.

"Did you manage to punch anybody at least once? How many sessions have we had already? Seven or eight? You should've learned at least something."

Kate gave the old man a reproachful look and interrupted Sullivan as he started to answer, "Jack is a real hero! He attacked the three scumbags without even thinking about his own safety! And, actually, when I was running away, Jack started to get the better of them! Maybe if I'd stayed and at least kicked one of them in the balls, then right now all three of them would be lying there on the pavement!"

McKee just grinned back. The three of them stepped inside One-two Boxing.

"Take him right there," Kate commanded the old man, pointing to the chair at the entrance. "Where's your first-aid kit?"

"It's in the locker room, on top of the lockers," McKee answered, getting rid of his burden.

"OK, I'll be right back. Are you sure you're not dizzy? Maybe we should call an ambulance after all?" Kate said, carefully examining Sullivan's face and paying special attention to his newly split lip.

"No, I've been through worse here," Jack replied, exchanging glances with McKee.

The old man grinned again. Kate threw a withering look at him and added indignantly. "What are you waiting for? Go, call the police! Maybe they'll be able to catch these bastards while the trail is still hot."

"By the time they get to us those scums'll be in Mexico already," the old man said on his way to the office.

Once there, McKee reluctantly called 911, then decided to go back to the thing he was doing before he got distracted by Kate's intrusion – pouring whiskey into his glass. Taking a quick sip, McKee went up to the indoor window of his office and continued to drink leisurely, watching Kate fuss over Sullivan.

Subconsciously, McKee appreciated what Jack had done. After all, in his own code of honor, defending a woman against an assault, especially the one made by outnumbering opponents, was the main and most noble duty of a true gentleman. And it did not matter that Sullivan was eventually beaten up and spared the need to drive home. What mattered was that he unhesitatingly rushed to her rescue. Although, of course, if he had won such a fight, it would have added additional points to his masculinity.

But in any case, McKee had extremely tense relationship with his subconsciousness, especially in a situation like this, when apart from the homophobia, acknowledging Sullivan's achievement was also hindered by the sense of his own guilt. After all, if the old man had not forgotten his phone, Kate would have escaped the danger, and Sullivan would not have needed to come to her rescue. It seemed that this time some bit of the subconscious still managed to break through to the surface. The old man came up to the table, poured new portion of whiskey into a glass, and left the office.

"Here, this will help you to calm down after the fight," McKee said, handing the glass to Sullivan.

Jack could not stand alcohol and was about to refuse, but then he looked at the old man's face and for the first time saw something in it that at least remotely resembled a good attitude toward him.

"Thank you," Sullivan said, accepting the glass.

"That's the last thing we need right now!" Kate uttered, snatching the glass from Jack's hand. "The cops are coming, and he's going to smell of alcohol!"

"But he's a victim, not a criminal!" McKee resented.

"It won't hurt to be careful with our police. Or else they may say that he was drunk and attacked innocent civilians who were walking around quietly," Kate responded, handing the old man the glass of whiskey.

"Yeah, and did he also give them his car away to have a nice ride?" McKee chuckled.

Kate gave the old man another reproachful look. At that moment, as if attracted by the mentioning of their name, the police came in. What followed was the tedious taking of Kate and Sullivan's statements, during which McKee chose to retire to his office. After they had dealt with the police and the brave lawmen left the walls of One-two Boxing, the old man suggested that he drive Kate and Sullivan home in his old pickup truck.

At first Kate did not want to ride with someone who had already taken the traditional evening shot of whiskey, but McKee convinced her that because of his size, two fingers of whiskey wouldn't even be enough to fail a breathalyzer test. Besides, Kate knew that McKee was a surprisingly careful driver, never exceeding the speed limit.

The ride for the three of them sitting side-by-side in the cab of the battered pickup truck turned out to be rather quiet, the silence being interrupted only by occasional awkward attempts at conversation. But after McKee dropped off Kate who lived closer to the club, dead silence settled in the car. It was not until the pickup truck stopped at Sullivan's house gate, which did not automatically open for him that time, that McKee looked at Jack for the first time.

Sullivan's normally far-from-cheerful expression was downright funereal this time. McKee turned away, hoping that Jack would get out of the car quickly and save him the trouble of acting like a normal human and asking if he was okay. But Sullivan was so lost in his own sad thoughts that he did not even notice that they had stopped.

"Hey," McKee spoke very reluctantly at last. "Is it the car you're so upset about? You probably have cool insurance. You'll get the money tomorrow already and then you'll be able to buy a new one which would be even better."

Sullivan did not answer.

"Hey, Sullivan," the old man repeated louder this time.

"Huh? What?"Jack finally replied.

"I said, was it the stolen car that'd made you so upset?"

"No," Sullivan said softly and rubbed the fingers on his left hand.

"Are you upset that you got beaten up? But there were three of them. It could've happened to me too!"

Sullivan chuckled wistfully. "It certainly couldn't've happened to you. But that's not even the point."

"So, what is it then?"

"My wedding ring was there. I always leave it in the glove compartment when I go training."

"Is it expensive? With diamonds?"

"No, it's the cheapest we could find. It cost about ten bucks. We got married right after university and could barely scrape up enough money for the rings and two large pizzas to celebrate the wedding with our friends."

Sullivan's voice faltered at the last words, but Jack still managed to hold back tears.

"Wait a minute," McKee said. "I saw it in the photos on that thing next to the bar. You had a gorgeous wedding with tailcoats, a multi-story cake, the works."

"It was Jacob's idea to celebrate Obergefell v. Hodges that way because we haven't even got any photos from the real wedding. These rings were all we've got left...," Sullivan said, and looked down.

Deep inside McKee was filled with a mess of conflicting emotions he could not understand. On the one hand, he still seemed to dislike Sullivan, and the mention of a gay wedding did not work in his favor. On the other hand, the attachment to a commemorative item associated with a loved one was perfectly understandable to him. Especially since at that point the old man already knew about Jacob's current condition.

McKee himself also cherished the souvenir mouthguard that Johnny Sifaretto had given him at his fiftieth birthday dinner. Sifaretto gold-plated the very mouthguard that had protected McKee's teeth during his title fight. But the old man did not care that the souvenir was made of gold and that it represented his championship title. The only thing that mattered to McKee was that his best friend had picked up that mouthguard after the fight and had been keeping it for all the years ever since.

"Okay, we'll figure it out!" McKee said and reversed.

"Where are you going? Here's my gate, right in front of us!" Sullivan said in surprise.

"Do you wanna get your ring back?" the old man asked, pulling the pickup truck around.

"I do," Jack replied, his voice still marked with incomprehension.

"So we're gonna go and figure it out," McKee said firmly and pressed the gas pedal.

For the next half-hour, the two men rode in silence, although Sullivan glanced at the old man several times, thinking of asking him once again about their destination. But McKee looked so focused and even threatening that Jack never dared to do it. Finally, the pickup truck pulled up near a half-abandoned building with a tilted sign that read "Bar". Sullivan figured out that they were approximately in the same part of the city where One-two Boxing was located.

McKee put his handbrake on and turned to Jack. "All the dregs of the neighborhood gather in this bar. If you're lucky your car thieves are here now celebrating the successful job. Professionals wouldn't have assaulted a lady on the street first, and outsiders don't visit our parts. So we stand a chance."

"Great, let's call the police!" Sullivan said enthusiastically.

The old man grinned in response, "First of all, the cops aren't gonna come not only to this bar, but even to this alley. Secondly, apart from your words, they have nothing against these guys. Even if they arrest them, they'll be released in a couple of hours, and you'll never see neither your car nor the stuff from it."

"What are we going to do then?"

"I'll go and talk to the guys myself if they're there. They'll keep the car, of course, because it's too good a prize. You have insurance anyway, don't you? But I can probably beat the ring out of them. Don't worry, I'll have a good talk with them," the old man added, cracking his knuckles.

Sullivan nodded back.

"Did they have any distinguishing features? Scars, tattoos? How do I identify them?"

Jack shook his head, "I don't think so. The usual kind of goons. Two of them were young, one in his late thirties. Heads shaved, criminal-looking."

McKee scratched his chin thoughtfully.

"Then you'll have to come with me. If you're not scared, of course. Just be honest, it's not the time to pose a hero."

"I'm not scared," Sullivan said and then added. "With you, I'm not scared."

"That's the right answer," McKee said and gave Jack an almost friendly smile. "This is how we do it: we go in, look around, you identify and point them out to me. But not with your hand, use words, and don't stare at them when you see them. It's important they don't smell a rat beforehand. You point them out to me and leave right away. Get in the car and close the doors. Better lie down so that no one can see you from the outside. Do you understand me? Go straight to the exit in a flash. Otherwise, I won't be able to work at full power if I also have to protect you. You got that?" the old man repeated once again.

Sullivan nodded. The two men got out of the car and resolutely walked to the bar entrance. Once inside, they were met by dim light and the smell of cheap beer and sweat, laced here and there with tart tinges of vomit. Sullivan swallowed nervously, realizing that in a place like this, somebody like him would not last even three minutes without somebody like McKee escorting him. Throwing a cursory glance at the customers, Jack thought to himself, "Even the faces in Netflix prison documentaries look more welcoming than they do here."

"There," he whispered, leaning toward the old man. "To the right, by the wall at the back of the room, behind the standing tables. Seven men. The one in the leather jacket is the older one. To his left is one of the younger ones. I don't see the second young one."

"Got it, now get out of here. Just don't run. Don't draw any attention," McKee whispered back and stepped forward.

Pushing past the regulars, the old man approached the table. With a mastery gesture, he pushed aside a couple of men, who were talking lively, to make room for himself.

"Gentlemen, how's your pleasant evening going?" McKee's powerful voice rose above the surrounding noise as he spoke directly to the older one of the car thieves.

"Not bad, not bad," the latter answered with suspicion.

"Do you know who I am?" the old man went on, placing his huge fists on the table.

The young henchman whispered something in the older man's ear.

"Yes, yes, I think I remember," said the older man. "You have a boxing club a couple of blocks away, right?"

"That's right. Gerard McKee, nice to meet you," the old man replied, extending his hand to him.

The man shook it suspiciously, feeling the bones of his wrist start crumbling under the pressure of McKee's handshake.

"You guys," the old man spoke again. "First scared my assistant a couple of hours ago, then bruised the kid, who trains at my boxing club, and took his car from him. It's the electric, red one. I'm not asking you to return the car, you need to pay the bills somehow too, I get it, but the things that were in the car should be given back."

"Mister," the senior car thief started speaking. "I have no idea what assistant, what kid, and what red car you're talking about. The guys and I've been hanging here since lunch. Ask anybody."

At the last words, the man nodded subtly, at the same time glancing somewhere behind the old man's back. McKee, who still remembered his boxing years, noted this movement and immediately turned around, simultaneously assuming the boxing stance. As a result, a beer bottle, intended for the back of his head, ran into a classic defensive technique called the catch. Just like McKee had taught Sullivan recently, he opened the palm of his rear hand and moved it forward to place it just in front of the chin level to catch the following punch. Only in that case, instead of the opponent's glove, the old man caught the bottle.

McKee's second hand instantly executed a powerful uppercut, sending the attacker on the spittle-covered floor. The attacker turned out to be the second young henchman of the scumbags' leader, who had previously gone to fetch a new portion of beer. Even before the first attacker found himself on the floor, his friends ganged up on McKee from both sides.

One of them even managed to hit the old man in the temple, but due to poor execution and McKee's thick skull, the punch had no effect at all. The old man immediately hit the second attacker in the chin with his elbow and then sent his fist further in an arc until it sank into the nose of the attacker by his other side. At that moment, someone whom McKee had not even noticed pushed the old man in the back, and the latter found himself in the center of the room. By that time the original group, three members of which were already lying on the floor, was joined by other customers.

Jab, cross, jab, hook, cross, uppercut, and four more people found themselves on the floor. But then the two of the first batch of the attackers were already on their feet again. Bottles, beer mugs, glasses, and even chairs were brought into play. McKee was still proudly holding the center of the room, knocking down and knocking out one wave of attackers after another. But the old man also got hurt. There was a cut on his left cheekbone, and the right sleeve of his shirt was stained with blood after one of the attackers slashed him with a broken bottle.

Just another scumbag rushed at the old man, swinging a chair over his head, but McKee dodged it and tripped the attacker up so that the latter flew into the window at full speed together with the chair and landed already on the street. After that, McKee knocked out another two men.

"Knife!!!" the voice came from behind the old man.

McKee turned at the shout and saw the leader of the car thieves behind him, holding a knife with a long narrow blade. The old man had not yet returned to the boxing stance to effectively parry the stab, and now it would have taken the blade no more than four inches to stick right into his liver. But right then a lightning-quick punch flashed through the air, and the knife flew aside together with its owner.

McKee looked up – in front of him stood Sullivan, his fist returning as quickly to its place to protect his chin. Jack immediately assumed the boxing stance and once again threw a hook with lightning speed. The old man, who was taken aback by such a development, thought for a hundredth of a second that Sullivan was aiming at him, but Jack's punch had already landed in the mug of the next attacker who was trying to pounce at McKee from the side.

McKee gave an angry and at the same time joyful cry and barked, "Cover me!" He bent down, picked up the fallen car thieves' leader, threw him over his shoulder, and rushed to the exit. Sullivan raised his fists again and turned around, looking out for the next attacker. But all the customers were either already lying on the floor or hugging the walls, apprehensively gazing at the angry old man, who now got himself his own Robin.

McKee and Sullivan darted for the exit. The old man threw the still unconscious car thief into the trunk of his pickup truck and shouted to his partner, "Get behind the wheel! Drive as fast as you can to One-two!" Jack jumped into the cabin, started the engine, and pressed the gas pedal to the floor. A couple of minutes later they were at the door of the boxing club.

"Now we're going to call the police, aren't we?" Sullivan asked, turning to the old man who had already opened the door and was getting out of the passenger seat.

McKee laughed resonantly, "Good one!" Looking at the face of Sullivan, who had also gotten out of the car, the old man added, "Oh, it wasn't a joke..."

Jack shook his head.

"Kid, do you really wanna call the police after we'd trashed that bar and kidnapped that jerk?" McKee replied, taking his "trophy" out of the trunk and throwing him over his shoulder.

"But it was them who attacked you! And this one had earlier assaulted Kate and me, and stole my car. Everything's as clear as day!" Sullivan turned to the old man with sincere incomprehension.

"You're a funny man, Sullivan. We don't have any evidence that this guy attacked anyone. But he," the old man loudly slapped the car thief's bottom, which was dangling from his shoulder, "he has about twenty cronies in that bar who'd swear on the Confederate flag that it was you and I who broke into a civilized establishment and started working people over in a row."

The old man took the keys to the front door of the club out of his pocket, threw them to Sullivan, and motioned his head to open it.

"I'm gonna tell you a big secret, Rich boy," McKee went on. "In our part of the city, the cops arrest not the one who committed a crime, but the one who is easier to tie to a case. Why do you think they like it so much to catch black guys? Racism is at play too, of course, though most of the times it's not about the skin color, but about the fact that by searching a black guy you can often find a gun or a joint, and he probably already has a couple of police records. And now try tying to a case a white man, who doesn't carry anything illegal and in the past got nothing bigger than a speeding ticket. Racism is a thing of course, but the banal human desire to cheat instead of working hard should never be discounted."

Sullivan had already opened the door and both of them stepped inside One-Two Boxing. McKee dropped his still lifeless burden on the floor and started stretching his back and shoulders, bruised in the fight.

"There's only one question now," the old man spoke to his partner again. "Are you with me or not? If you don't wanna get involved in something that is now one hundred percent illegal, you know where the exit is. I'm not gonna judge. You've already done more than I asked of you. Just go a couple of blocks away from One-Two before calling Uber – so that if anything, the police wouldn't be able to connect you with this place."

"I can't call Uber," Sullivan responded. "I left my phone in the glove compartment too."

"Well, then go three blocks down the street and turn left – usually there're old-school taxi drivers hanging around near the "Wildcat" bar. It'll be even better this way – you won't leave any digital traces. Here you go," the old man added, taking a twenty-dollar bill out of his back pocket and handing it to Jack. "Your wallet's also gone, isn't it?"

Sullivan shook his head, refusing to take the banknote. It was either the memories of how he got beaten and robbed that changed Jack's mind, or the fact that the car thief regained his senses and burst into curses and threats against his kidnappers.

"Do you have a rope?" he asked McKee in a stern voice.

"That's my boy!" the old man smiled and clapped Sullivan on the shoulder. "Look over there, there should be zip ties in the back office."

Together, they tied the hands of the car thief, who actively resisted and continued to spew powerful streams of curses. Afterward, with the help of another zip tie, they hung him to one of the punching bags.

"What's your name, pretty boy?" McKee asked the car thief, looking with pleasure at his eyebrow that was split by Sullivan's punch.

"Fuck you! I'll fucking have both of you…"

Another stream of curses was abruptly cut off by a jab to the body.

"I won't repeat twice," the old man added with a bloodthirsty smile.

"Martin," the car thief gasped.

"That's better, Martin. There's just one tiny thing we want from you – tell us where to find my friend's car that you stole this afternoon, and we'll let you go."

"I don't know no…"

McKee did not even let the car thief utter the word "car", simply slapping him in the face instead of awarding him with a blow. However, given the size and strength of the old man's palm, the slap was probably much more painful than his previous punch.

"Martin, do I look like a patient person to you? Do you really think I'm gonna let you lie to my face and get away with it?"

The car thief swallowed nervously, but, apparently, the car that cost 100,000 dollars was too valuable a prize to give up after just a couple of punches.

"Where's the car, Martin?" the old man repeated.

As soon as the car thief uttered "I don't", McKee started screaming like a madman right in the car thief's face and pummeling the punching bag behind the thief's back with long hooks. Martin screamed too, but in horror.

"Listen," McKee stopped as suddenly as he had started and turned to Sullivan. "Why am I dealing with him? It's your car, so it's up to you to beat the truth out of him!"

Jack looked at the coach in fright. "Me? I can't…"

"Why? You could do it before, couldn't you? You did it on the street when they assaulted Kate and in the bar afterward. What's the difference?"

"That was something else... it was in the heat of the fight... in the heat of passion, so to speak... And now he's already tied up."

"You are right about that, it really isn't fair this way," McKee replied and with a light movement tore the zip ties that held the car thief's hands together and chained him to the punching bag.

Martin fell to his knees but quickly got up and began to look around nervously.

"Don't worry, Martin," McKee told him. "There is only one exit here, and I locked it with a key. Or do you think you can take the key out of my pocket? I'm warning you right away," the old man added with a grin. "I won't give you more than one try. Go ahead, ask him where the car is," McKee said, turning to Sullivan. "What if he's as noble as you're and immediately fess up to everything to you?"

Martin looked at Sullivan and just grinned. "Well, come on, sweetheart, let's dance," he blurted with hatred and spat forcefully at Sullivan's feet.

"Don't tell me you're gonna let him insult you and, most importantly, my gym like that," McKee told Jack with harsh notes in his voice.

Sullivan's only answer was raising his fists. Martin just laughed in response and rushed at his opponent. Jack's boxing stance was much more solid than it was during his first sparring with Charlie, but, as it turned out, the boxing skills he had learned over that time were completely useless in a dirty street fight.

Martin feigned a punch with his right hand and immediately kicked Sullivan in the groin. Jack managed to block the wicked blow with his hands, but, as a result, his head was left completely unprotected. The second time, the car thief did not miss his chance and hit Sullivan in the chin with his elbow. Jack remembered perfectly well all the defensive techniques that McKee had shown him, but none of them could be applied against kicks and elbow strikes.

Sullivan's vision went dark for a second, and he fell to the floor. Martin immediately sat on him and started showering him with a hail of blows. Boxing textbooks also did not say anything about defending oneself while lying on the floor, but Jack figured out by himself how to adapt the standard blocks for that situation. Of course, they did not work perfectly in a horizontal position, but Sullivan still managed to parry most of the car thief's blows.

"Come on, man, don't be shy!" McKee shouted. "He's just a street scumbag who can only assault women! You just need to get angry and that's it!"

The coach's words hardly reached Sullivan through the hail of his opponent's blows.

"Jack! You need to get angry!" the old man repeated, raising his voice.

The fact that McKee addressed him by his first name for the first time caught Sullivan's attention.

"Why did you take up boxing? You were angry with someone! I know it for sure! It doesn't matter whether it was your father, your boss, or a bully who beat you at school! Now you can fight him back! Imagine that this bastard is the one you were so angry with that you came to train and endured all my insults! It's him! Fight him back! Show me what you're worth! Show me you're not afraid of him!!!" McKee was already yelling in a frenzy.

And it worked... Although not quite the way the old man expected it to. Sullivan suddenly screamed, grabbed the car thief's fist that was flying at him, pulled it to himself, and sank his teeth into it. Martin was so surprised by such a turn of events that Sullivan was able to fell him on his side and then get on top of him, swapping places with him. As soon as Jack got astride of his enemy, he started pummeling him with such ferocity that McKee could only remember to have had himself. And Sullivan's punches were much more accurate and much faster than the ones of his opponent. So all of Martin's street experience was not helping him anymore.

Not a second had passed until the blood gushed out of the car thief's broken nose, and a couple of seconds later, his entire face began to turn into a homogeneous bloody mess. If McKee had not rushed forward and dragged angry Sullivan off, he would have possibly had to figure out how to drag the dead body into the back of the pickup truck in such a way so as not to attract too much attention and not leave a bloody trail behind him.

"Jeez, son, who is it that you hate so much!?!" McKee said, pinning still-furious-and-eager-to-continue-the-fight Sullivan to the floor to calm him down.

"Come on, come on, Jack, breathe, just breathe. It's over now!" the old man was saying repeatedly, getting to his feet but still not letting go of the enraged mentee.

Short and thin, Sullivan was literally drowning in the old man's arms. Seen from the outside, it must have looked like a mother calming a child. To their right came an obscure gurgling sound, followed by the words, "Near the junction of Walnut and Calume." Martin spoke, literally pushing the words through his mouth, full of blood, "An old wooden shed… Your car's there… And everything else too… We just took the money, we haven't touched other shit yet. We thought we'd deal with it tomorrow."

The red Tesla was exactly where Martin said it would be. The car was guarded only by an old padlock, which McKee got rid of with a single blow of a stone found nearby. Looking into the car, with a big relief Sullivan found both his wedding ring and even his wallet with a photo of Jacob in it. Naturally, there was no money in the wallet anymore.

For reasons unknown to Sullivan, McKee did not part with him there but offered to "accompany" him home, following Tesla in his old pickup truck, which had taken them to the shed. When he got home, Jack parked in the driveway and got out to thank McKee, whose pickup truck stopped right behind the Tesla. But the old man stopped him short, "Wait, Jack. I need to tell you something first. Do you have a bench here? Because I'm not good at expressing my thoughts briefly and clearly, and my legs are so tired today that I wouldn't wanna stand for any extra minute until tomorrow morning, or maybe even evening. The age, you know, is already beginning to take its toll."

McKee looked around, but couldn't find a place to sit down.

"Let's go inside, there are plenty of places to sit there," Sullivan said. "Or, if you want, we can sit by the pool."

"No, thanks, I'd rather stay here. You know what, follow me."

McKee led Sullivan to the back of his pickup truck, opened the tailboard, and, patting it with his hand, invited him to sit down, "Don't be afraid, my old Betty can even withstand two men like me."

Sullivan was not at all afraid for the safety of the tailboard, it was just that he had never sat on such things in his life. He was hesitant but did it anyway. The old man sat next to him.

"So, here's the thing, Jack... You'll be amazed, but I'm not a big expert on apologies."

Sullivan responded with a slight smile.

"Insults are more like my thing," McKee continued. "Well, you've already figured that out yourself... That's exactly what I wanted to talk to you about. Today, first with Kate, then at the bar... You probably saved both her honor and my life as well... Although it's unlikely that an extra hole in my body would've really killed me... But alright, that's not the point... So, here's what I wanted to say. Today you acted like a real man. And if earlier I thought that only a real man could be a real man... Well, you know ... straight, in short... You proved to me today that whoever one sleeps with doesn't make one less of a man... Take, for example, those bastards who assaulted Kate... they're probably all straight, but they're not men at all... You see, just a day ago I would've called them by the word that I often used around you. The one by which they call people like you... You know... And now I'll tell you what – now, should I call them by that word, it'd be a compliment for them... So, you are the man, Jack Sullivan, the real man!"

McKee got up from the tailboard, turned to Jack, and extended his huge hand to him. Sullivan got up too and shook the proffered hand firmly. "Thank you, Mr. McKee."

"And you know what – call me Pops, like everybody else does!" the old man said with a tenderness in his voice, unexpected even to him.

"Thank you, but Pops is not really my cup of tea. How about Gerard?" Sullivan replied and smiled amiably at the old man.

"Fine by me, Jack, fine by me," McKee repeated and covered Sullivan's palm with his other hand.

The old man shook Jack's hand in his palms for another second, but then, ashamed of his influx of emotions, hurried to let it go.

"So long, Jack, Take care of yourself."

Saying that, McKee closed the tailboard of the pickup truck and hurried to get behind the wheel. After clearing the way for the truck, Sullivan waved his hand and added, "See you tomorrow, Gerard!"

The old man nodded in response and also waved his palm as he drove away.

.. 10 ..

"Yes, yes, come in," McKee replied to a knock on the door of his office.

The door had opened and Sullivan appeared at the threshold. He had already taken a shower and changed into his traditional formal suit. He was holding a gym bag in his hand.

"I'm not distracting you, am I?" Jack asked, stepping inside.

McKee glanced at the glass he was just about to fill with whiskey, sighed, and looked at the visitor. "No, come on in." Pointing to a chair at the opposite side of the table, the old man added, "Take a seat."

Jack took the indicated place.

"Gerard, are you aware that out of the fifty hours of training I originally paid for, there're only five left?"

The old man chuckled, "After forty-five hours together, Jack, you should've already realized that I'm not the kind of person who keeps track of such things."

Jack responded with a slight smile. "Yes, that's what I thought. I'd like to continue training in One-Two Boxing, but first I need to have a serious talk with you…"

"So serious that it calls for prelubricating the gears of our brains?" McKee interrupted and with a surprisingly quick and deft movement took a second glass out of the desk drawer.

"No, thanks, I don't drink," Jack replied.

"Whatever you say, but I'm gonna throw back a shot or two."

McKee poured two fingers of whiskey into his glass.

"Go ahead, start your serious talk," McKee said, sending the portion of whiskey into his mouth in one go.

"The last three training sessions, the ones that took place after our adventure of returning my car, they were, so to speak, not as effective as I'd like them to have been."

Noticing the surprise on the old man's face, Jack hurried to explain, "No, don't get me wrong. I'm very glad that we are friends now, and you've stopped bullying me and using the f-word, but at the same time you've begun to train me too gently, as it were, too correctly, by the book. Such training would be perfect for a teenager or someone who goes boxing purely for himself. But I was serious when I said I wanted to compete in the professional ring, and I wasn't joking about the IPBU title either."

McKee could not help but smile.

"Yes, Gerard, I understand that the mention of the champion title, especially combined with the word "serious", sounds like a joke to you. But you know, you don't need to believe that I can become a champion to train me as someone who's really capable of achieving it. Those first training sessions were, of course, just terrible, both physically and mentally. No, no, I'm not asking for another apology," Jack said, noticing that McKee wanted to say something. "I mean that, no matter what, those training sessions were more useful for me than the current politically correct and respectful ones. I'm not crazy, despite what you all thought when you heard about my wish of becoming a champion. I understand perfectly well how difficult, almost impossible it's going to be to achieve that. That's why I need hard, laborious, exhausting, at-the-limit-of-human-capabilities training sessions. If I can't endure such training, then I certainly can't endure the professional ring."

"Wait a minute, Kid, let's get one thing straight," McKee finally spoke. "Do you want me to start bullying you again? To humiliate and insult you?"

"No, of course not. I value our friendship." Sullivan thought about something for a moment. "You know, when I first started training with you, you reminded me very much of my father."

"Was he also an incredibly handsome son of a bitch?" McKee replied with a smile and leaned back in his chair.

"No, he was also a malevolent alcoholic bastard."

Gerard laughed resonantly.

"I'd probably get along with your old man."

"Yeah. Until the first disagreement, and then you'd kill each other."

McKee responded with a grin.

"Like I said," Sullivan tried to get the conversation back on track. "I don't want you to bully, humiliate and insult me, but I want you to treat me as one of your former mentees, those whom you trained for the professional ring. I want you to not spare me, to push every training session to the limit. I want you to prepare me as if for a real life-and-death fight. Gerard, I found some old recordings of your training sessions on the Internet. I saw how you raced your fighters to the point where they could barely drag their feet at the end of a session. And I saw how it paid off in the ring. I want the same for myself!"

"Kid," McKee replied. "I've already got it that you're as stubborn as I am. So I'm not gonna waste my breath trying to get a very simple idea across to you – NO FUCKING WAY a thirty-five-year-old computer tech who's never in his life took any kind of sports can become a professional boxer! No, no, I'm not gonna explain it to you. I'd rather have you look at it from a different angle. You want to become an IPBU champion, right?"

Sullivan nodded.

"Now, as a former IPBU champion, I'm telling you – you can't just get there from the street. It's business, Kid! The IPBU selects fighters who can throw a show, those who attract viewers to the stands and TV screens. They don't care about your sports achievements; they only want to make money! Even leading amateur boxers with Olympic medals couldn't get there. The IPBU accepts either real world-beaters, like Pacquiao, or guys who have a lot of money behind them, those whose sponsors are willing to spend millions on their promotion, so that the Union can then reap benefits from it. Well, being well-connected won't hurt either. I myself didn't get into the IPBU from the street, the doors were opened for me. And then I started throwing shows myself, for which I was granted a championship fight. Did you know that I was the most bloodthirsty heavyweight in the world? None of my opponents left the ring without spilling at least a drop of blood. The guys from The Ring said that was a unique achievement. Nobody can boast it, neither Ali, nor Tyson," The old man stopped talking, looked intently at Sullivan, and spoke again. "Jack, with all my current respect for you, you won't be accepted to the IPBU, it just won't happen!"

"Don't you worry about it, Gerard," Jack leaned slightly in the old man's direction. "I took care of the IPBU first thing, even before I came to you."

"Kid, I don't know who promised you what," McKee interrupted. "But you won't get to the championship fight through simple bribes. Or rather, you might get there, but you surely don't have enough money for such bribery."

"No, it has nothing to do with bribes," Sullivan answered. "I won't go into details, but it's connected with my work as an information security specialist. I covered for a guy with great connections in the IPBU, and now he owes me big time. He's going to get me access to the championship fight. I only need to win eight fights with those opponents that he's going to pick for me."

The old man leaned back in his chair and roared with laughter, "Oh, Kid, you've been conned like a dummy! That job you did for him was prolly worth a couple of million, and he gave you only his word! Of course, he promised you that he'd get you access to the championship after eight fights. You won't even last through the first one! On such conditions, I can promise anyone anything! I'd promise to blow you, if you win at least five, let alone eight fights!!!"

At the last words, McKee laughed so hard that tears showed in the old man's eyes.

"Okay, I was expecting something like this," Sullivan replied calmly and picked up the gym bag that was standing on the floor next to his chair. "I have another argument."

Jack took an inch thick wad of banknotes out of his bag and placed them on the table in front of McKee.

"What's this?" the old man asked, looking at the money.

"This is exactly how much your boxing club needs to not be closed before the end of this year. You can be sure the amount is right, I consulted with Kate."

"And?" McKee asked again, not understanding what Sullivan was getting at.

"The money is yours."

"Kid, I'd rather burn this place to hell myself than borrow from a friend. Banks and loans are one thing, but never in my life have I borrowed a single dollar from friends and I'm not gonna break my principles in my old age. Besides, I don't like this club so much anymore, you know. I was going to retire anyway. Maybe I'll start a podcast about boxing. If I find out what a podcast is."

The old man grinned, but this time rather sadly.

"But I'm not asking you to borrow from me. This money is yours, right here and right now, you don't have to pay it back."

"What's the catch then?" the old man asked suspiciously.

"No catch. Only one condition – from tomorrow on you're going to train me as if you are preparing me for the professional ring, as if someday I'm going to be able to have a shot at the championship title."

"Jack, you're killing me," the old man laughed again. "How can I possibly promise you something that I'm completely unable to provide? NO FUCKING WAY you gonna become a professional boxer and even more so a champion!"

"Gerard, I didn't ask you to promise me that I'd be able to get in the ring, I didn't ask you to promise me the victories. I didn't ask you to provide any guarantees, and I didn't offer you to sign a contract with obligations. Isn't that right?"

McKee nodded reluctantly.

"All I ask of you," Sullivan went on, "is to train me the same way you trained those in whose success in the ring you believed. You know the difference, don't you? Just do everything you did with others. Make me go all out, help me reach my own limits, doesn't matter that in your opinion these limits are still too far from what a real fighter needs. If you don't believe in me – that's fine. You have every right to. Moreover, I myself wouldn't train with someone who'd now believe in me. Such a coach is clearly crazy! I ask of you only one thing – help me become the best version of myself in the ring."

The old man's face softened, but he clearly still had serious doubts about the idea proposed by Sullivan. Jack leaned back in his chair, wondering how else he could influence McKee. His gaze fell on the championship belt hanging on the wall above the coach's head. An old, dusty IPBU Heavyweight Champion belt.

"Gerard, have you ever wondered why I came to train to you of all people?"

"If we're friends now, can I still joke about your homosexuality? In a friendly way, just like guys make fun of each other, like I slept with your mother or sister, stuff like that?"

"Sure, go ahead," Sullivan said, rolling his eyes slightly.

"Then ask me again. Just do it, ask me."

"Have you ever wondered why I came to train to you of all people?"

"Because I'm sexy as hell?" without waiting for a proper reaction, the old man added. "Got it? It's because you're gay, and you came to train to me just because of my handsomeness."

"Yeah, I got it. Thanks for the explanation," Sullivan replied with a sour smile. "Yes, your raw tough guy sexuality played its role, of course, but it's not the main thing. I came to train to you because you're the best coach in the country."

McKee leaned back in his chair, laughing.

"Yeah, Kid, your joke's even funnier than mine!"

"It's not a joke, I'm being completely serious," Sullivan replied calmly.

"You really serious?" the old man answered still with a laugh in his voice. "Then I don't know what kind of shit source you looked up for the information about my coaching career. Let me tell you how good I'm at coaching. Since the very opening of One-Two Boxing, I've had twelve mentees... no, wait, thirteen... no, that's right – twelve. The thing is, only one of 'em got to the title fight. He got there and lost. Split decision, but still lost. Two more stopped a few steps away from the title fight, and, well, I can name three people at most that you could call at least somewhat remarkable. They won at least five or seven fights and knocked out a couple of opponents. The others couldn't do even that much. So here's my track record as a coach – one contender, two on their way to contenders, and three half-losers. Yeah, I'm just like Angelo Dundee!" The old man thought for a moment but then continued, "Some things could work out with Derrick. He had five fights and all five won by knockout no later than the seventh round, but then he got that injury and everything went down the drain..."

Sullivan distracted the old man from his reflection, "Have you ever wondered how your fighters did before you started training them and after they left you for other coaches?" Jack said and, after a bit of thinking, added. "I think your sparkling personality pushed them to that step."

McKee grinned back once again.

"And I did wonder," Sullivan continued. "Both before and after you, they performed much worse than with you. Do you remember, for example, Rick Cruise? Before you, he had five fights in the professional ring. Only two victories and both on points. You gave him six victories, including four by knockout. Then he left you for a more famous and prominent coach – Sid Carlsson. He won the first fight with him, but in that fight he got knocked down twice. But then he lost four fights in a row and after that never returned to the ring."

"You remember the stats for all of my fighters by heart just like that?" McKee asked incredulously.

"I deal with information security. Most of my work consists in analyzing huge amounts of data, so yes – I easily remember the information I need. And Rick Cruise is just one of the examples. Ted Dempsey, Nick Peterson, Will Warrington – they all performed much better when you trained them. And I'm not just speaking about victories. Even when they lost, they fought better. With you, they threw more punches, hit the opponents more often, missed fewer punches, knocked their opponents down more often, and found themselves on the canvas less often. I analyzed each of your fighters and each of their fights with you, and then each of their fights before and after you. And I did it with other coaches as well. Carlsson, Jefferson, Atlas, Mateen, Pacheco – all these coaches whose mentees won titles can't boast such a contribution to their victories as you made. You do understand that even a mediocre coach could make a star out of such people as Mayweather, Sugar Ray Robinson, Ali, Hopkins, De La Hoya. They are natural-born boxers and that says it all. You didn't have any fighters with such qualities. On the contrary, you got such mentees, with whom even Cus D'Amato or Freddie Roach couldn't have done more than you did. Don't you believe it? Let's go to my house – I'll show you all my calculations for each of the currently working coaches. All the fighters, all the fights, punches, points. I even wrote a special damn program to collect data and analyze it!"

McKee moved a little closer to the table, clearly interested in Sullivan's reasoning.

"I might be crazy with this idea, but I'm not an idiot. I understood that to achieve what I want, I didn't need a good coach, I needed an extraordinary coach, specifically such a coach who knows how to make real fighters out of the most unsuitable material. Yes, your guys didn't become champions, but with you, they exhibited not a hundred, or two hundred, but the whole thousand percent of their capabilities! That's the one and only reason why I came to you, agreed to your insane charge, and endured all your bullying."

The old man smiled at the mention of the insane charge he had jacked up for Sullivan while signing the training contract.

"Consider it a challenge," Sullivan continued. "Will the great Gerard McKee be able to turn a thirty-five-year-old geek into a boxer who can win at least one professional fight? For that matter, let's lower the bar even further – can you make out of me a fighter who can at least stay on his feet until the end of the first fight?"

"Seriously, Jack?" McKee grinned, getting even closer to Sullivan. "You daring me? As if I'm some sixth grader?"

"Not up to the challenge?" Sullivan also replied with a grin and extended his hand to the old man. "And don't forget that you're saving your club for good measure," Jack added, motioning with his head to the money lying on the table.

"Heh-heh," McKee laughed. "You should go into politics with such skills, rather than sit at the computer. Well, what the heck! It's a deal!"

With a resonant slap, the old man shook the extended hand.

"We should definitely drink to this! And this time there's no getting out of it! At least take a sip. I'll pour you a good one, real – Irish!" McKee said, reaching into the bottom drawer of his desk, where he kept a bottle of Jameson, which he got straight from his historical homeland from members of the local boxing club.

Sullivan nodded reluctantly, aware that refusing the old man's offer in such circumstances would be akin to spitting in his face.

"But here's the thing, Jack," McKee said, pouring whiskey into glasses. "Now, of course, I'm not gonna rip you off at triple rate as it was before, but if you wanna train as a professional, you're gonna need a team, not just me alone. You need a separate fitness coach, you need a sparring partner, and it won't hurt to make up a diet program so that you grow muscle. Even at friendly prices, all this is gonna cost you more than you pay now."

"Money's not a problem," Sullivan said, accepting a glass of whiskey. "But I have one condition."

"There's already been one," McKee said, raising his glass and clinking it against Sullivan's. "It'll be the second one."

"OK, the second one. I want Charlie to help you with my training. I want you to officially hire him as an assistant coach and pay him accordingly. Include his salary in my bill."

McKee tossed a shot of whiskey down his throat and spoke in a voice that was not nearly as cheerful as before.

"Yeah, I'd be happy to, but it's not gonna work. The Kid's gone. We had an argument and he left. You prolly noticed yourself he ain't been around lately."

"Have you tried calling him?"

After asking the question, Sullivan put the glass to his mouth and tilted it just enough for the liquid to barely touch his lips.

"Yes, I tried, of course. I called, and even came to his apartment. The Kid disappeared."

"And what would you say if you found him?" Sullivan took a tiny sip of whiskey and winced. "Would you apologize to him? I suppose your argument wasn't his fault, was it?"

McKee poured a second shot of whiskey and immediately sent it down his throat again in one throw.

"Somehow I didn't think about it. Well, yes, I'd prolly apologize after all. Someone has to be an example for the Kid. I apologized to you, why not apologize to him as well. Maybe I'll get into the taste and start apologizing to everyone right and left."

McKee poured another shot of whiskey into his glass and laughed.

"Well, technically, you didn't apologize to me. You didn't say "I'm sorry"," Sullivan replied, and looked at the old man through a glass of whiskey.

"Oh, come on, Jack! These are all formalities, the main thing's not the words, but the impulse of my noble soul!" The old man gave Sullivan a friendly slap on the shoulder.

"So, are you ready to apologize to Charlie?"

"Uh-hum," the old man mumbled, without taking his lips off the glass.

"Then let's go!"

"What? Where?" McKee asked in surprise.

"To my house."

"What for?"

"To apologize to Charlie."

The old man stared at Sullivan questioningly.

"He's been staying at my place ever since you had a fight with him. That's why I didn't want to take you to my house back then, so that you wouldn't run into him, but I sent him a message on the way, and he was hiding on the second floor all the time you were with me."

McKee looked at Jack questioningly for another second, digesting the words he had said, and then burst into loud and resonant laughter, "Damn, Sullivan, holy crap!"

The old man wanted to give Sullivan another friendly slap on the shoulder, but at that very moment Sullivan decided to lean back in his chair, and McKee's palm fell exactly on his glass. The glass flew out of Jack's hand, flashed across the room, and hit the wall. Surprisingly, without breaking, it fell on the floor and spun on the spot. For a moment, they both watched the glass rattling around in a circle, and then they started laughing together.

.. 11 ..

"You wanna become a professional boxer?" the old man said to Sullivan instead of greeting as he opened the door to the club. "Here's your first tip – at least start dressing like one."

Jack entered the room and shook the coach's hand.

"It's good to see you, too, Gerard."

"Oh, no, it's not Gerard to you during training! If you want me to train you as one of my own, for the time of training it's only coach or Mr. McKee. Well, Almighty God will also do," the old man added with a grin. "From now on, while we're training, I'm your father, mother, the federal government, and high power all put together. Every word I say should be the law to you! And not the usual, state law, in which you can always find a loophole or talk your way out with the help of a lawyer, but the law of nature, the breaking of which is always followed by instant payback. Think of me as gravity – you make a mistake, you slip – you get your face smacked against the ground!"

"Yes sir, Mr. McKee," Sullivan replied without the slightest trace of sarcasm.

"And, seriously, get rid of the suit. Buy yourself some normal sports clothes. If you wanna be an athlete, everything sporting should become natural to you. And be sure to hook up to ESPN!"

"Yes sir, coach," Jack replied as seriously as he did the first time.

"Mr. senior assistant coach," McKee greeted Charlie, who entered after Sullivan and put his foot over the threshold of One-Two Boxing for the first time after his resignation.

The old man extended his hand to him for the first time ever and the boy happily shook it, carefully trying to hide his delight about it.

"Well, gentlemen," McKee continued. "Go to the locker room and we'll start training."

"Hey, Charlie," the old man stopped the boy, who had already taken a step toward the locker room. "I've something for you."

McKee picked up a bag from a nearby chair and tossed it to Charlie. A few minutes later, having changed, Sullivan and Charlie were standing in front of the coach again. The boy, beaming with joy, was wearing a new uniform T-shirt with the One-Two Boxing logo at the front and the inscription "senior assistant coach" on the back.

"We'll start today's training session with a warm-up," McKee addressed both of them. "And the best warm-up for a boxer is a jump rope."

The old man glanced at Charlie, but he just smiled back.

"Charlie, what do you think the job of an assistant coach consists in?"

Charlie came to his senses, made a dash for the gear piled along the wall, and returned a moment later with a jump rope.

"Kid," McKee addressed him. "As a senior assistant, you're not only gonna bring and serve but also help me with demonstrations, so fetch the second one."

Charlie made another dash and returned with the second jump rope even quicker than he did the first time.

"By the way, Jack, pay attention to this jump rope," the coach said to him, accepting the second jump rope from Charlie. "A plastic speed rope with plastic handles and 90-degree connection. This is the best option. Spins easily and perfectly for a typical boxer's rhythm. The thin plastic handles are effortless to hold which lets you concentrate on the rope and doing tricks. The 90-degree connection helps the rope spin easier and avoid kinks. If you wanna become a real professional, you should pay attention to details, even if they seem as small as the design of a jump rope. I'm telling you this now 'cause after today's training session, all three of us are going shopping. We are gonna buy a jump rope, handwraps, gloves, a punching bag and everything of that kind for you to take home. If you really wanna become a professional, your every day should start with boxing and end with it, you need to keep it going outside the walls of the gym. Do you understand me?"

"Yes sir," Sullivan said.

"So, why do we need to work with a jump rope at all?" the old man went on with his instructions. "Working with a jump rope gives you better endurance, better footwork, increased stamina for throwing combinations, improved breathing efficiency, and ability to stay calm. In terms of cost-effectiveness, there's nothing more useful and impactful in my entire gym than a jump rope."

McKee handed the jump rope to Charlie. "Come on, Kid, you show, and I'm gonna explain. I'm getting a little old to be jumping around."

Charlie started jumping.

"I don't need to teach you how to basically jump rope, do I?" McKee asked Sullivan.

Jack shook his head.

"That's great. Then just add a few notes to your knowledge on this subject. Land on the balls of your feet with your knees slightly bent. Breathe only through your nose. Spin the rope using your arms, not your shoulders. That's the basics. Don't you stand still. Start jumping! Try to get in sync with Charlie's movements. The way you're jumping now, we call it Basic Jump or single 2-footed bounce. Actually, there are more than a dozen different exercises with a jump rope. We'll start with the classics – Fast Regular Bounce. For this move, you do jump rope regular bounce, but focus on spinning the rope really fast. Make sure to keep your elbows in and your hands jutting out to the sides of your hips. Your feet should only come about 1 to 2 inches off the ground."

Charlie started demonstrating Fast Regular Bounce. Sullivan began to repeat after him and turned out to be jumping even faster than the assistant coach. McKee grinned at them, "Oh, guys, if I still was that old politically incorrect Gerard McKee, I'd definitely joke about the fact that you're so great at jumping rope because you spent your entire childhood jumping rope along with your girl friends, all done up in beautiful dresses."

"It's so great that you're not a homophobe anymore, otherwise you would've told us this joke," Sullivan replied sarcastically without stopping to jump.

"No side talk while training!" the old man responded in a deliberately serious voice, but still with a smile on his lips. "Try switching between Basic Jump and Fast Regular Bounce. In a fight, it's very important to be able to switch over from an explosive attack to resting in defense, followed by a new explosive attack. Remember, the professional fight is 12 rounds of 3 minutes each, that is, 36 minutes in total. Not a single boxer in the world, even the hardiest one, can fight all this time at the maximum of his capabilities, so you need to learn how to switch between modes. With other exercises, be it push-ups or punch practice, the rest is always passive – you do something or you do nothing, but with a jump rope you rest during Basic Jump, yet still continue doing something. Just like in a fight – even when you are in a clinch with your opponent, you can rest, even though you still carry on working. Okay, we're done with it. Good job. Stop for a second. Now we'll try Side Swing."

McKee's speech was interrupted by the creaking of the front door. All three of them turned around and saw Kate coming in.

"Hey, boys!" she greeted them, complementing her words with a wave of her hand.

Instead of the usual dress and high-heeled shoes, the woman was wearing leggings, a bra top, and sneakers – each one of the items was the same pale pink color. Previously having been hidden under rather loose clothing, the outlines of Kate's body were now very advantageously emphasized by the tight sportswear.

"I know! I look stunning!" the woman added with a smile on her lips, responding to the mute glances of the three men.

"Kate," McKee said, slightly taken aback by her new looks. "What are you doing here at this time? Are there any problems with the finances?"

"Does it look like I came to talk business?" Kate replied, pointing at her clothes and smiling even wider. "No, Pops, everything's fine with our finances. Thank you once again, Mr. Sullivan," she glanced at Jack, giving him a wink. "It's just that after that incident with the scumbags that Jack saved me from... Again, thank you once more, Mr. Sullivan. I thought I could use some self-defense lessons. And who should I take them from if not from my own boss, who pays me so little that he absolutely must provide me with free boxing lessons."

Kate put her hands on her hips and gave McKee an intent stare.

"Any objections? Suggestions?" without waiting for an answer, Kate immediately added. "Great! Pops, have you already made coffee today?"

With her eyes, Kate pointed to McKee's office, the most valuable item in which was not the old man's championship belt, but the fancy Swiss coffee machine, which the coach gave as a gift to his best friend and co-founder of the club Johnny Sifaretto in honor of the opening of One-Two Boxing. After receiving this gift, Johnny would repeat humorously that more than boxing and Gerard himself he liked only one thing – well-brewed fresh coffee.

The old man answered Kate's question with a mere nod of his head.

"Then I'll have some now to put a pep in my step and join you, boys, a bit later."

Kate hurried to the director's office, almost skipping. McKee could not help but watch her go all the way to the door.

As soon as the door closed behind Kate, the old man turned back to Jack and Charlie.

"Wooow," the coach drawled. "Did you see that?" Not getting the expected response, the old man added, "Oh, yeah, sure, sure. I don't understand you gay guys. No, no, don't get me wrong. I'm not being offensive. I mean, I can still somehow understand in theory how you have sex with each other, but how can you not want such a stunningly juicy..." the old man hesitated for a moment, "lower part of the back. It's something unreal, all right! I'm damn older than both of you put together, and I still can't take my eyes off such a beauty! You know, if you were straight, I'd never allow her to train with us. With such distractions during training sessions," McKee imitated woman's breasts with the help of his palms, "even Rocky Marciano would lose every fight."

"What are you talking about?" Kate asked, unexpectedly emerging behind the old man's back with a mug of coffee in her hands.

Being caught off guard, McKee was still "holding" imaginary breasts in front of him. He quickly clenched his palms into fists.

"Nothing much, just showing the guys how to throw a combination correctly."

The coach awkwardly demonstrated a jab-cross combo. Jack could barely contain himself, and Charlie still let out a short laugh. McKee gave them a glare, "Now, I see you two ain't warmed up enough yet, since you wanna laugh so much. Off you go outside. Run ten laps around the block and come back."

"I'm going to finish my coffee and join you too!" Kate said to Jack and Charlie, who were already leaving the gym, chuckling as they walked.

Sullivan and Charlie ran the first lap in silence, but at the second one, Jack turned to his young companion.

"Was it my imagination, or did the old man really address both of us as gays twice?" Sullivan threw a questioning look at Charlie. "Is there anything you want to tell me?"

Charlie just looked down in response.

"You fell out with McKee and left not only because he was bullying me, didn't you?"

Charlie did not answer this time either, continuing to look intently at the asphalt under his feet.

"Did you tell him you were gay?" when there was no answer once again, Jack added. "Is that true? Charlie, you do understand that I'm literally the very person with whom you can come clean?"

"I don't know!" Charlie shouted and suddenly sped up.

Jack also picked up speed and soon caught up with Charlie.

"You don't know what you said to the old man back then?"

"No, not that!" the boy answered emotionally. "That I know. Yes, I told the old man I was gay, but I don't know if it's true or not!"

Charlie sped up again, and this time so much that it took Sullivan almost half a circle to catch up with the boy.

"Charlie, wait!" panting, he grabbed the running boy by the arm and stopped him. "Stop! Talk to me. I know how difficult it is. I've been through it all!"

"Oh, yes?!" Charlie answered, pulling his hand out of Jack's, but yet stopping. "Did your father also kick you out of the house when he found out that you were gay?"

Sullivan stared at him in surprise. "In fact, my father kicked me out of the house along with my mother. But it happened long before both he and I found out that I was gay. Although, he must've always known about it, since from the age of five he called me faggot every time he saw me throwing a ball or when he found out that I once again failed to fight back against school bullies."

Jack smiled sadly and sat down on the sidewalk. Turning to Charlie, he added, "So your father wasn't expelled from the country by the Immigration Service?"

"No! I lied to you! I first lied to McKee when I came to

him for the first time asking for a job, and then I started telling everyone else the same story. My father is a US citizen and nobody was expelled from anywhere. He kicked me out of the house when he caught me kissing Héctor Mendez."

"I hope Héctor is your classmate and not some forty-year-old dude with a ponytail?"

"Yes, he's a classmate," Charlie replied, sitting down on the sidewalk next to Jack.

"So you're gay?"

"I told you I don't know!" Charlie answered, flinging up his hands.

"Relax, Charlie, it's all right. I don't care if you're gay or not. Just talk to me. I know how hard it is. I want to help you."

"Seriously, I don't know. I kissed Héctor only once. We made out and that was it, there was nothing more to it. Does that count as being gay?"

"It depends on what you think about it yourself. Despite what all sorts of narrow-minded homophobes say, it doesn't work that way. Kissing a guy once doesn't automatically make you gay. You know, listening to "Bad Romance" on one occasion doesn't make you a Lady Gaga fan. But if after that you listened to "Alejandro", "The Edge of Glory", "Applause" and "Born This Way" and you liked them all very much – then you are definitely a fan of Lady Gaga... and maybe a little bit gay."

Charlie smiled at Sullivan's joke.

"So, Charlie, what do you think about it yourself? What did you feel back then with Héctor?"

"I don't know. It happened spontaneously. I don't even remember why we suddenly started kissing. He and I were best friends back in Guadalajara. Our fathers worked together as engineers at a local branch of an American chemical company. And then they were transferred together to a new facility in the US, so we ended up here. But I don't remember ever thinking of him as anything other than a friend. But I can't say I didn't like it then. You know, that was my first kiss. It was strange. Wet, but probably not bad."

"Did you later talk about it with Héctor?"

Charlie shook his head.

"When my father caught us, he sent Héctor home, and yelled at me for two hours, and then kicked me out of the house and told me never to come close to home again. Héctor's family lived across the street, so I couldn't go to him after that. And then, the next day, when I tried to find him at school, Héctor wasn't there. Later I found out that he'd been sent back to Mexico to live with his aunt. I guess my father told his father everything, and he decided that in Mexico Héctor would get rid of his gay demons. I remember his aunt, she was super religious. She had crosses and icons all over her house. And she was angry as hell."

"I'm sorry about that, Charlie. I really am sorry that it happened to you. It's terrible and you absolutely don't deserve such treatment." Jack put a friendly arm around Charlie's shoulders and added, "When was that? Two years ago, am I right?"

Charlie nodded.

"Did you have anything besides the kiss with Héctor?"

Charlie shook his head. "Since then, I've only been thinking about survival. I spend almost all of my time in One-Two. And when I'm not in the gym, I just sit at home alone, playing my old PlayStation. At first, I tried to keep in touch with my old friends. But in fact, Héctor was the only real friend to me, and all the others were just classmates. Besides, rumors about me and Héctor started spreading around the school, and that didn't add to my popularity in any way. Some immediately turned away from me, others just spoke less with me. As a result, all the school contacts came to nothing. Although you know, one weird kid with whom we had several classes together, but never really talked, on the contrary, kept coming up to me and even called a couple of times. I have no idea where he got my number from. He's probably gay and decided, since they say about me that I'm gay, that we should stick together.

But he's weird... Or is it bad that I don't want to be friends with him?"

"It's only bad if you don't want to be friends with him because of something like his skin color or sexual orientation," Jack answered.

"No, he's also a Latino, and the fact that he's gay doesn't bother me. But he's weird, that's why I don't want to be friends with him. He likes weird music, talks weirdly. Well, he's weird!"

"Charlie, you have every right not to be friends with someone you don't like. You can't bully anyone for being weird, but you don't have to be friends with them."

Charlie nodded several times, then stretched out his legs and stared at the toes of his old, battered sneakers.

"And what about girls?" Jack asked.

"Huh?" Charlie gave him a look of misunderstanding.

"Have you ever liked girls? Classmates or maybe some especially hot teacher?" Sullivan added with a smile.

"I don't know. I didn't really like anyone. Well, I mean, in the way you're asking about. Neither girls, no boys. I had friends of both genders, but somehow I didn't think about anything extra. Well, you know... I liked computer games or playing ball in the yard. You know, the game that you Americans absolutely insanely call soccer, when all over the world it's called football. Do you even realize that the word "football" comes from "foot" and "ball", and in your "football", you use hands and the thing you carry in these hands is nowhere near the damned ball!?"

"You chose the wrong person to complain about it, Charlie," Sullivan laughed shortly. "I think both American and international football are equally meaningless activities. As, by the way, all other sports. Figure skating, synchronized swimming, or, let's say, gymnastics – at least they're nice to watch, but when a bunch of men run around the field back and forth – as for me it's utter idiocy. And also I'll immediately point out that, contrary to the popular stereotype about gays, I'm not a fan of figure skating either. Although, my husband likes it very much… Liked it very much…"

Sullivan stopped short, but quickly tried to get the conversation back on track, "So, there was nothing with girls?"

"Well…," Charlie drawled. "Taylor McBride once kissed me on the cheek, probably in the sixth grade."

"Sounds hot," Sullivan joked. "Let's try to sum it up – you had nothing with girls, and you kissed a boy once, but that's about it. Did you feel something then… well, you know, there," Jack pointed to the area below the waist with his eyes.

"No," Charlie said, backing the words up with a shake of his head. "And it probably lasted less than a minute, then my father came in and all hell broke loose…"

"But you've never had any romantic feelings for either girls or boys?"

Charlie thought about it, shook his head again, but then added, "I once really liked Captain America and Star-Lord. Does that count?" Charlie thought a bit more. "Although I've always liked Jennifer Lopez, just as long as I can remember, and Lara Croft in "Shadow of the Tomb Raider" is very cool."

"Jennifer Lopez is a National treasure, and I also like Star-Lord, since the days of comics, rather than just in the movie. I even have Marvel Preview #4, in which he first appeared."

Sullivan got to his feet and continued, "I'll tell you what, Charlie – whether you're gay or not is up to you to decide. You know, a couple of years ago, even among gays themselves, there was drawn a strict line between those who were one of them and all others. Those who called themselves bisexual were bullied by gays even more than by straight people. It was believed that bisexuals are gays who are ashamed to fully admit their own homosexuality. I've personally always thought it was complete bullshit. I also had experience with women at the time, and I can't say it was disgusting to me. As for me, if it weren't for the idiotic public puritan morality, the absolute majority of people would be bisexuals, some'd gravitate more to the opposite sex, others – to their own, but in general, almost everyone would at least try both. Times've changed, Charlie. That's where you're lucky. Nowadays there is Pansexuality, Polysexuality, Queer, and a whole bunch of other terms that no one understands except those who invented them and those who want to attack others on Twitter, accusing everybody of narrow-mindedness, that is, everybody who's not into this mess. For me, all of it is also nonsense – the opposite end of the same idiocy as homophobia. There's no need to invent a billion terms, you just need to do what you want with the one you want to do it who also wouldn't mind doing it with you. That's all there is to it, everything else is unneeded fiction for hypocritically appearing smarter, more advanced, and more important than you really are."

Charlie also got up from the sidewalk. Sullivan put his hands on his shoulders and added, "So here's my advice, Charlie, don't think about whether you're gay or not. If you see a boy you like – meet with him and see where it'll lead you. If you see a girl, meet with her. The main thing is not to fill your head with unnecessary thoughts. Don't think that you should by all means engage yourself in anything with a boy since you've already kissed one once. And don't think that you're bound to try it with a girl only to check whether you're certainly gay or actually straight or maybe bi. Follow your heart and don't listen to any bullshit that homophobes or belligerent gays say on TV. You know, I've been repeatedly attacked by other gays, because in their opinion, I don't behave gay enough, because I'm allegedly ashamed of my sexual orientation. But my husband's always loved me for who I am. He never asked me to watch figure skating with him or wear chaps and drag myself along to a pride parade with a whistle in my teeth and a feather boa around my neck. He loved me for who I am, not 'cause I'm gay. Well, did I help you with this talk, or did I just confuse you even more?"

"You helped... I guess," Charlie said and presented Jack with a smile.

"Well, then let's run! We still have eight laps to go!"

Without waiting for Charlie's response, Sullivan darted forward.

"Wait for me!" Charlie shouted, rushing after his older buddy.

..12..

Just like the previous three training sessions, Sullivan started yet another one, with a jump rope warm-up and a jog around the block. However, for some reason this time the old man sent him running alone, without Charlie. After running the required ten laps and getting back to One-Two Boxing, Jack understood why McKee needed his senior assistant.

The interior of the boxing club had undergone significant changes since Sullivan left it less than twenty minutes ago. Now it looked like an obstacle course. However, the obstacles did not form a straight line, but rather two parallel lines. And at the far end of these lines stood Derrick, who had not been in the gym when Sullivan had left it.

"Greetings, Jack Sullivan," Kate said festively, standing in the middle of the gym with Charlie.

"Welcome to the Boxing Ninja Warrior show!" Charlie went on after her, trying to mimic the voice of a TV host.

Sullivan looked around blankly and noticed McKee standing at some distance.

"Don't look at me," the coach responded. "It was all their idea. I needed to check your fitness and basic skills to move on to the second stage of our training sessions, and these two here," McKee waved his hand in the direction of Kate and Charlie, who were smiling happily, "decided to make a freaking TV show out of it."

"Attention, contender!" Charlie announced as loudly and festively as he could. "Take your place at the start line!"

Sullivan looked around again and guessed that the strip of duck tape on the floor a foot away from him was the start line. Jack stopped in front of the marked line.

"Contender." It was now Kate's turn to pretend to be a TV host. "You will have to go through a series of most difficult obstacles; honor and glory await you upon the completion!"

"Well," Charlie added, this time less festively. "We don't have much space here to set up a long line, so you'll have to run in circles."

Meanwhile, McKee went over to Jack and started wrapping his hands. "Don't mind me, keep listening. They invented such a jumble there it's easy to get confused."

Kate began to list the trials, "First you have to do ten push-ups, get up, practice shadowboxing, execute the combination of punches that will be announced by our dear Mr. McKee, then do ten jumping jacks, run through our "wall of death..."

Sullivan guessed that the "wall of death" had something to do with the three punching bags that were hung in a line in the front.

"...Stop," Kate continued. "Do ten squats, approach our dear Mr. Everson..."

Sullivan guessed again that Everson was the last name of Derrick, who was standing nearby behind the "wall of death". On his hands, Jack noticed punch mitts.

"And throw the combination that our dear Mr. McKee will announce for you once again."

Charlie went on after Kate. "After that, you have to dodge the same sequence of punches thrown by dear Mr. Everson, as well as one bonus secret punch that dear Mr. Everson will choose by himself."

"Then, the contender has to turn around and move on to the second part of our series of obstacles," Kate intercepted Charlie's speech and continued. "Here you need to do five burpees, and at the end of each rep you also need to catch a med ball, which can fly to you from both the front and any of the sides."

"Next, the contender is up to the test called "trinity of

horror"." Charlie's turn came again.

Apparently, such a poetic name was given to the three body opponent bags, placed in a row in the second line of obstacles facing Derrick.

"There's only one way you can cope with this hair-raising trial," Charlie continued. "Jab – cross, a swift sidestep, another jab – cross, another sidestep, the final jab – cross, then turn immediately in the opposite direction, but this time each of the opponents must get a jab – uppercut, otherwise their souls will remain in the world of the living and continue tormenting us at night with their ghosts!"

"And last but not least," Kate spoke again. "The Ducking alley."

Sullivan didn't need Kate's explanations to get an idea of the final trial. Seeing a pair of stands, between which an elastic rope was stretched at shoulder level, Jack immediately recognized the familiar exercise for practicing a defense technique when a boxer ducks under the opponent's blow, passing over his head. All that was needed here was to go forward, with each step diving under the rope so that it took turns being on one or the other side of the head.

"One important thing," Charlie announced. "If the contender fails any of the trials, he has to return to the start line and repeat everything from the beginning. And do so until all the trials are passed impeccably."

"Good luck to you, man," McKee said to Jack, slapping him on the shoulder. "I personally am already confused starting from the third one. I've no idea why the hell they invented this entire jumble. Like you're gonna have the "wall of death" in the ring."

It came as a surprise for Sullivan when the gym got suddenly filled with loud noise. Jack turned around and saw a small but very loud wireless speaker sitting on a stool behind him, which, apparently, Kate had just turned on with her smartphone. It took Sullivan a couple of moments to realize that all this noise was typical sounds of the crowd gathering before a boxing match.

"Now that's actually not a bad idea," the coach said. "During a real fight, it's gonna be even noisier, and at the same time you're gonna be pummeled, but you'll still need to listen to the coach's shouts from your corner all the time."

"Contender, are you ready?" Charlie and Kate announced together this time.

Sullivan nodded in response.

"GO!!!" the couple of hosts shouted and hurried out of Jack's way.

Sullivan did ten push-ups and assumed the boxing stance waiting for McKee's command.

"Jab, jab, hook, cross," the old man shouted out.

Sullivan executed it and immediately started doing jumping jacks. Meanwhile, Charlie and Kate prepared the "wall of death" by swinging the punching bags so that they moved in opposite directions, forming a passage between them. With this trial, Sullivan got off to a rocky start. The very first punching bag hit him in the shoulder.

"Whooo," Charlie drawled. "Too bad! You'll have to start all over again!"

Sullivan got back to the start line. Without waiting for the hosts' signal, Jack started pushing up. The push-ups were followed by the combination of jab, uppercut, jab, uppercut, and another jumping jack rep. This time, Sullivan managed to run past the first punching bag only to be hit on the head by the second one.

"That's better!" Kate supported the contender. "But anyway, you have to start all over again."

Sullivan returned to the start line for the second time and immediately began doing push-ups. Left hook, right hook, left hook, right hook. Jumping jacks. On the third attempt, Jack almost passed the "wall of death", but the last punching bag still rubbed him slightly on the back and the hosts had the contender start from the beginning again.

As before Sullivan passed push-ups, shadowboxing, and

jumping jacks flawlessly, but the "wall of death" got him again.

"For God's sake," McKee called out, "You just can't swing 'em properly, that's why he fails!"

For the fourth attempt, the old man rocked the punching bags himself and Sullivan managed to make his way through the "wall of death" for the first time. But he was so focused on this obstacle that he forgot what he had to do after the "wall of death". The hosts clued him in that the next trial would be ten squats but still sent the contender to the start line.

Already the fifth set of push-ups, shadowboxing, and jumping jacks began to tell on Sullivan. Large beads of sweat appeared on his forehead, and his breathing became shakier. But he still managed to slip through the "wall of death" and then do ten squats. After that, Derrick was waiting for him with punch mitts. The young coach stood at the ready and competently positioned the mitts for the jab, jab, cross, shouted out by McKee. Then Derrick himself tried to throw the same punches at Sullivan.

Jack dodged twice and blocked once. Up next, it was time to deal with the secret punch. And that was where Derrick got creative. With his right hand, he threw a hook to the head, and at the same time lead a straight body shot with his left hand. And it did not matter that no one had ever done this in the ring – after all, by throwing both hands forward you remain completely open to a counterattack. But here Sullivan was not meant to counterattack and therefore Derrick could do whatever he wanted.

Jack managed to dodge the blow to the head, but the body shot hit the target. Of course, the young coach was wearing punch mitts, and so the blow was not particularly strong, but it was still not a pleasant experience. Especially considering the trial was thus failed and Sullivan had to start all over again for the sixth time.

Despite the fatigue, which was already taking hold, Jack swiftly coped with the first five tests and appeared before Derrick again. This time the combination was a set of cross, uppercut, and hook. Sullivan coped with both throwing punches and parrying Derrick's "mirrored" combo. All that remained was to parry the secret punch. The young coach went overboard again, this time accompanying the punches with a grin.

To take his opponent aback, Derrick led not one, but two deceptive swings, showing first the jab, then the cross, and only then throwing a real uppercut. Again, Derrick would never do such a thing in the ring, because after two deceptive swings, he would almost certainly face a powerful counterattack from the opponent. But Sullivan could not counterattack, so the coach's punch mitts very unpleasantly cut into his chin, leaving a bloody scratch on the skin.

"See you next time. I'll be looking forward to it," Derrick whispered softly, so that only Jack could hear it, and backed up the words with a mocking laugh.

"Is it because of our clash in the ring back then?" Sullivan thought to himself, returning to the start line. "Or is it because I'm gay? Or maybe he just hates me so much the same old way, for no apparent reason."

The first five trials of the seventh attempt were as successful as the previous time, and Sullivan approached Derrick fully determined not to fail this one as well. This time the old man suggested a long combination of jab, jab, cross, uppercut, jab, hook. Jack executed it perfectly – by the book. And he also impeccably coped with the mirrored attack. Now Derrick had decided to throw a regular jab as the secret punch. Very strong, almost breaking through Sullivan's double arm block, but still a regular jab.

Only the third time Jack saw through the trick. He was initially ready for some sucker punch and was not surprised that instead of one blow, as it was supposed to be according to the rules of this trial, without the slightest delay after the jab Derrick sent an even more powerful cross. If Sullivan had decided to use a block against it, he would have earned a big bruise, to say the least, but Jack guessed to make a turn followed by a sidestep as quickly as came the opponent's blow.

Taken off balance by the force of his own blow, Derrick flew forward after his fist and almost tripped, which caused him to take a couple of awkward steps forward.

"Finally, the sixth trial has bent before our magnificent contender!" Charlie shouted triumphantly.

But Sullivan chose not to get distracted by celebrating the victory over Derrick. He turned around and got down to the second part of the trials. Next came burpees, each rep of which had to be followed by catching a med ball, alternately thrown from different sides by either Kate or Charlie. Sullivan also coped with it with flying colors, although, unlike as it was at the beginning of the training session, the exercises were no longer smooth sailing.

The burpees were followed by the "trinity of horror" trial, represented by the three body opponent bags set in a row. Sullivan approached the first one, threw a jab – cross, took a sidestep, did the same with the second, and finally with the third body opponent bag. Now it was the time to go in the opposite direction, which Jack did almost at the same pace.

Sullivan had already started the last trial of the ducking alley when he suddenly heard Charlie's voice, "Whoo, what a pity! In the opposite direction, the "trinity of horror" had to be passed by throwing a jab – uppercut, not a jab – cross. I'm sorry, but you'll have to start all over again."

Sullivan clenched his teeth tightly not to show his irritation at the failed trial and silently went to the start line. Push-ups, shadowboxing, jumping jacks, "wall of death" and squats – it seemed like Jack could already pass this part of the obstacle course with his eyes closed.

Sullivan also coped perfectly with practicing punches to punch mitts, as well as with the parrying of the same combo from Derrick. When it got to the secret punch, Sullivan noticed the opponent bend his knees and rotate the upper body to the rear side. Jack figured out it was going to be the rear arm uppercut to the body.

Sullivan remembered that the best defense against such a blow was the elbow block. Jack rotated the body to the lead side lightning-fast and positioned his forearm to block the punch. Except that Derrick was not going to hit the liver, which Sullivan managed to cover just as well as a real professional boxer would have done. His punch flew lower – just to the area that was forbidden to hit not only in boxing but also in any other sport as well.

Even though the blow softened by the punch mitts did not knock Sullivan out, but still forced him to fall on one knee. In a scorching wave, the pain shot from the genitals up to his whole body. Bewildered Charlie and Kate eyed Jack, who at that moment looked as if he was going to propose to Derrick; and only McKee immediately realized what was going on.

He walked over to Sullivan, helped him to his feet, and led him to the nearest chair. Then the old man came up to Derrick and first shoved him in the chest with his hand, after which grabbed his T-shirt and pulled him back to himself. McKee whispered something in the young coach's ear. Judging by the menacing expression on the old man's face, it was far from a compliment. Derrick wanted to say something in response, but McKee gave him such a furious look that the subordinate only silently took off the punch mitts and handed them to the old man, then headed toward the back exit.

"Cut it out, enough with your games! Turn off that noise!" McKee shouted to Charlie and Kate.

The sound of the back door open and then close announced that Derrick left the gym. Turning to Sullivan, the old man added, "Consider you've passed everything! Tomorrow we'll get down to the second stage of the training. In the meantime, you can go to my office and lie down on the sofa."

Without looking up, Sullivan answered, "No, I want to finish."

McKee grinned, once again marveling at the

stubbornness of his pupil. "Okay, whatever you say, tough guy. Then I'll take Derrick's place."

"I'm gonna sit for a couple of minutes and start from the beginning," Jack added.

"Take your time," the old man said, putting on punch mitts.

As promised, after a couple of minutes Sullivan got to his feet and got back to the start line.

"Please turn on the noise again," Jack turned to Kate with a tired smile on his lips and gave Charlie a thumbs-up.

Kate tapped on the smartphone screen a couple of times and the gym got filled with the noise of the crowd once again. It was the eighth time that Sullivan started doing push-ups, which took him considerable effort. Shadowboxing went better, but jumping jacks took Sullivan twice as much time as it did at first. When it was time for the "wall of death", Jack successfully got past the first punching bag, but as he tried to pass the second one the muscles of his tired legs failed him.

A cramp ran down his left calf, which made Sullivan seem to stumble out of the blue, and the second punching bag hit him right in the ear, forcing him to fall on one knee again.

"It's just us, we didn't swing the punching bags properly again!" Charlie called out, running up to Jack and trying to help him to his feet. "It doesn't count! You can move on!"

Politely but resolutely Sullivan rejected the help of his young friend and got to his feet on his own. "Damn! That kid has giant balls!" McKee thought to himself, watching Jack, who, contrary to Charlie's suggestion, was returning to the start line.

Ten push-ups, shadowboxing, jumping jacks, the "wall of death", ten squats. Now not only his legs, but Sullivan's whole body was already exhausted from the overwork, but he continued, ignoring the pain. Jab, cross, jab, cross to the punch mitts, which this time were held by the old man himself. Out of respect for the pupil's perseverance, McKee did not cut him any slack and sent a long and swift hook as the secret punch, which

Sullivan barely managed to dodge, ducking under the coach's arm.

Burpees with a med ball and the "trinity of horror". This time Sullivan did not forget anything: jab – cross for the first go and jab – uppercut while passing along the body opponent bags in the opposite direction. And finally, the ducking alley. Step, duck, step, duck from the other side, step again. The last step, the last duck, and the sounds of the crowd from the speaker suddenly changed to a fanfare. Charlie and Kate hurried to hug and congratulate Sullivan. Even McKee, who had already gotten rid of the punch mitts, congratulated his pupil with a strong handshake.

"Thank you," Jack said, and added. "Now I'm ready to take you up on your offer to lie down on the couch in the office."

The old man laughed in response, "Come on, let's go. I need to go there too on very urgent matters."

Once in the director's office, Sullivan hurried to lie down, and McKee bent in front of his desk to take out a traditional bottle of bourbon and a glass. How could he possibly not celebrate such a glorious victory of his pupil?

"Gerard," Sullivan said.

"Yeah, what?" the old man replied, pouring a shot of bourbon.

"Remember, you said it'd be nice to make up a diet to build muscle?"

"Yeah, I remember," McKee said, and immediately threw the first portion of the burning liquid into his mouth.

"Is Derrick into that?"

"All of my coaches are into that."

"Can you please send him to my place tomorrow morning so that he can tell and show me how to eat properly?"

"You wanna Home-Alone him? Wanna beat the hell out of him with a can of paint and set his ass on fire?" the old man replied and immediately laughed at his own joke.

"Don't worry, he'll be back safe and sound. I just want to

talk to him in private."

"Sounds promising," McKee chuckled again and added. "Whatever you say, Jack. If it's necessary, so be it. I'll tell him, and if he's not at your doorstep by nine in the morning, I'll freaking fire him. Either way, he's gotten way too cocky lately."

"By the way, what happened to him? You said he left his career because of an injury."

"Yeah," McKee said, automatically slowly sipping his second portion of bourbon. "He got into a car accident. He's got pins and bolts all over his back. Could've become a wheelchair user, but got lucky to have good doctors. He can surely show off in front of you, but nobody's gonna let him in the professional ring anymore. There's too much risk. It's a shame, of course, the kid showed great promise."

The old man exhaled sadly and took another sip of bourbon.

"What kind of accident?" Sullivan asked.

"I don't know. I wasn't there. At the time, we had a long break between fights, and I decided to go on vacation to my homeland. I came back only to find him lying in a hospital bed all covered in wires. Says it was a drunk driver. But you know what, Jack, I think it was him who was that drunk driver..."

Having said the last words, McKee looked into his glass somewhat hesitantly but still took another sip.

..13..

"Damn, that's a pretty nice shack you've got here. Seems like you're doing just fine, right?" Derrick said when Sullivan opened the gate for him.

"How did he manage to make these words sound so offensive?" Jack thought to himself, letting the guest in.

"Here," Derrick said, handing Sullivan a heavy bag. "I put myself out enough already when I went to the store for all this and brought it to you. I believe you can carry it to the door yourself. Or maybe you have help for this?"

Jack silently took the package and went to the house.

"Eh, Sullivan? Do you have a house nigga? You know, the one in a jacket like a penguin and with white gloves."

Instead of answering, Jack opened the front door of the house and motioned for the guest to come in first.

Once inside the house and having quickly examined the interior, Derrick whistled, "Yeah, it's not bad to be white."

Sullivan ignored this remark too. "The kitchen is that way."

"You meant, one of the kitchens, right, white boy?" Derrick asked mockingly.

"No, I meant the kitchen is that way," Sullivan answered coldly.

After entering the kitchen, Jack put the bag on the table and began taking out its contents: eggs, lean chicken, milk curd, nuts, avocado, beans.

"Those are proteins, they're for muscle mass," Derrick started "teaching", pointing his finger in an indefinite direction. "These are healthy fats. These are carbs for energy."

"Do you like steak?"

"What steak? There's no steak in there!" Derrick responded, throwing a blank look at the owner of the house.

"That doesn't answer my question," Sullivan said calmly. "Do you like steak or not?"

"Why, I do," Derrick uttered suspiciously. "Only if it's normal, and not made from some old dog."

Sullivan took two large pieces of meat out of the fridge.

"A ribeye steak. The best I could find. I usually eat simpler things myself, but I picked the fanciest one specially for you."

"Specially for me?" Derrick replied with even more suspicion in his voice. "Is it poisoned?"

"I'll try it before serving, so you can be sure it's safe."

"Is this some kind of a white man thing? Or some kind of a gay thing? Why are you gonna feed me steak all of a sudden?"

"Never heard of such a thing. Although, if you want, I'll make sure to check with both whites and gays as well."

Derrick grimaced something in between a grin and an expression of disgust.

"I just want to talk to you. And cooking steak is a great conversation starter."

"Talk to me? No, thanks, white boy, I'm getting outta here!"

Derrick turned around and walked to the exit.

"Are you seriously going to walk away from a hundred dollar steak?" Sullivan called after him.

"A hundred bucks?" Derrick replied, immediately turning around. "For a steak?!? White people are crazy!" He thought to himself for a moment. "You're not gonna try to turn me into a gay, are you?"

Sullivan shook his head.

"Or agitate for the Republicans?"

Jack shook his head again.

"Okay, the hell with it, white boy, I can bear with your chatter for a hundred-dollar steak. Just don't you think you're buying me with this piece of meat. If you start selling me some bullshit – I'll slap you on the mug with this steak and make off with it."

"You seriously could assume that I was going to bribe you with food?" Sullivan responded with irony in his voice.

"I don't know man. You're kinda crazy."

Jack smiled back.

"Have a seat," he said, motioning Derrick to a chair on the opposite side of the kitchen island that separated them.

Derrick sat down.

"You know, just a week ago, I would've never talked to you," Sullivan began as he pat both sides of the steak with paper towels. "I don't mean you personally, but just somebody like you. And don't even try to play the black card," Jack quickly reacted to Derrick's opening his mouth. "By 'somebody like you', I mean somebody to whom I personally have done nothing wrong, but for some reason, they still can't stand me. Whether because I'm gay, white, or because of the way I tie my shoelaces – it doesn't matter. I've met a lot of people like you. Take McKee, for example. Compared to him not long after we met, you are just nothing short of my best friend. Only a week ago, I would've just ignored you and your dislike for me. Why should I spend my energy trying to prove to someone that I'm better than they think of me? Hand me salt and pepper, please. They're over there, to your left."

Derrick handed Sullivan salt and pepper shakers. Jack continued, "But it was McKee who got me to switch gears. At first, the old man downright hated me. I think you know a lot more about this than I do."

Derrick responded with a grin.

"And now some may even say McKee and I are friends. Yes, of course, I saved his life…"

"You saved the old man's life?" Derrick asked in surprise.

"I'll tell you later. So, I recently talked to the old man about it. Of course, I'm very glad that he changed his attitude towards me, but even to me, it was surprising how quickly it happened. So I dropped by his office one night to ask him about it. Sure enough, I took a bottle of good whiskey along."

Derrick smiled, quite genially this time.

"After drinking about three glasses, the old man was finally able to answer me. Yes, the fact that I saved his life made its bit of course, but that was not the main thing. You know what McKee told me?" Sullivan asked the question that did not require any answer and took out a cast iron skillet from the shelf under the countertop. "He told me there were two things that affected him first of all. Firstly, it was Charlie or rather the thing he told him. The boy asked McKee whether gays had done to him anything bad personally. And the old man was lost for an answer. He told me that this thought had been lingering in his mind for days on end and he'd never found an answer. And secondly, he was affected by getting to know me as a person. As someone who has a job, a house, a husband, who's got problems, and that there are things that trouble me, things that upset me. Goes without saying, the old man didn't tell me that the way I'm telling you right now, you know him. He's not very good with words. But the gist is the same. He changed his attitude toward me when he found out that I've got the same problems, the same fears and reasons for frustration as 'normal' men have," Sullivan said, accompanying the last words with air quotes.

By that time, the skillet had already become almost red-hot, so Jack hurried to add canola oil and place the steak in the middle of it.

"You'll be surprised," Jack continued. "But, it turns out, the old man's never interacted with gays before. Shocking news, isn't it?"

Derrick answered with a smile again.

"It turns out that sometimes in order to change an old inveterate homophobe, it's enough just to show them that gays are the most ordinary people, rather than some aliens from other planets hunting for such rough men as McKee and raping them in dark alleys."

Sullivan turned the steaks over.

"Would you like something to drink in the meantime? There's beer in the fridge."

"I don't drink alcohol," Derrick answered.

"Good for you," Jack said. "Me too. There's also juice, milk, tonic if you want. And maybe something else liquid."

Derrick got up from his chair and went over to the fridge.

"So as for why I'm telling you about the old man," Sullivan continued. "After he'd changed his way of thinking, I thought that I had to at least try to change your opinion as well. You're not a bad guy, and neither is the old man. We just had problems with communication."

Derrick returned to his seat, holding a bottle of tonic in his hand. "So what, now you gonna tell me how wonderful you are?"

"No, I'm not an idiot, after all," Sullivan answered. "I'm just going to tell you that I'm human too. That's all. I'll do it once, without excessive details, without going soppy. If it doesn't change your mind, that's on you. I won't try again, I promise. In this case, my conscience will be clear."

"Okay, go ahead, tell me," Derrick said and took a sip of tonic.

"You know, I prepared for this conversation properly," Sullivan said and turned the steaks over again. "Not only did I buy steaks, but I also called my black friend, who is in addition gay. I asked him how things are going with homophobia among you guys. And this friend of mine told me a very interesting thing – it turns out that ordinary straight black guys treat black gays almost the same way white guys do – they mostly dislike them and oftentimes despise. But black guys treat white gays differently – they don't like them, but they don't like them firstly because they are white, and the fact that they are gay is just an added bonus. Tell me honestly, is there such a thing? Do black homophobes really dislike white gays first of all because they're white, and only secondly because they are gay?"

Derrick took another sip of tonic and either nodded or shook his head, thus neither confirming nor denying those words.

"So, how about slavery?" Sullivan asked and pushed the steak to one side of the skillet.

Derrick almost choked on another sip of tonic.

"Don't worry – I'm not going to justify slavery or even make any judgment on slavery in the US. I just want to tell you that my ancestors and I personally have nothing to do with it. The thing is, Derrick, my mother is an immigrant. She's Russian. Did you know that there was also slavery in Russia?"

Derrick shook his head.

"Only in Russia, the slaves were exactly the same white people as those who owned them. It was called Serfdom. Do you know how long official slavery lasted in the US?"

"Too long!" Derrick replied with dignity.

"That's a great answer, I totally agree with you," Sullivan said, adding butter, garlic, thyme, and rosemary into the skillet. "But I'm still going to tell you the exact numbers – I've prepared not for nothing. From 1619 till 1865. That is, a little less than a quarter of a century. Do you want to know how long Serfdom existed in Russia? From the eleventh century up until 1861. Which makes it more than eight hundred years. And yes, I'll immediately add that my ancestors were poor serfs, whom their owners could buy, sell, beat and kill. And please don't get me wrong, I don't want to get into comparison of whose ancestors suffered more. No, I'm just pointing out to you that not all white people are the descendants of slave owners. On the contrary, some of them were once slaves themselves."

"Smooth talk. You're just like some politician," Derrick grinned. "What about your dad? Maybe he descended from Confederates?"

Sullivan spooned butter over steak and only then answered the question, "Ethnically, my father is mostly Polish, also a little Romanian, Czech, and Hungarian. These countries, too, have never been engaged in slavery, since, just as in Russia, there were enough native poor people who could be mercilessly exploited. Besides, there's never been a full-fledged fleet in any of those countries. And without ships, it's very difficult to engage in the slave trade. But now I'll tell you the whole truth – my father definitely abused black people. He was a policeman."

Derrick's face broke into a satisfied smirk.

"But, do you know, why exactly I'm sure that he would beat innocent black guys in his days? No, not because he was a policeman. But because he beat me and my mother almost every day. And I'm almost sure that at work he didn't limit himself to black people, it's most likely my father beat both Latinos and white people. Of course, only those who couldn't make complaints about it later. You know, I can hardly imagine that a person who beats his own wife and child would limit himself only to members of another race outside the house. Racism aside, when you're a first-class piece of shit, it's probably hard for you to resist hitting some defenseless Juan or Billy Bob from a trailer park. So, yes, Derrick, if you want, you can blame me for my father's sins."

Sullivan flipped the steaks, turned away, and opened the fridge. Jack pretended to be looking for something there, but Derrick knew perfectly well that in reality he did not want to show the guest how much he was upset by the memories of his father.

"All right, slavery seems to be out of the way now," Sullivan went on again, turning back to Derrick and closing the fridge door behind him, without taking anything out. "Now let's talk about white privilege. You may have thought I've such a house because of my rich parents or because I got a cool education thanks to the color of my skin?"

Derrick chuckled, making it clear that such an idea had crept into his head.

"Do you know three 20-story subsidized buildings on Helms Street?" Sullivan asked, turning back to the fridge.

"You think there's such brotha in the city who's not familiar with the most hardcore ghetto buildings of the entire district? As a child, my mother would often scare my brothers and me that if we behaved badly, she'd send us to live there," Derrick replied with a grin.

Sullivan took some cucumbers and tomatoes out of the fridge and began to wash them.

"I grew up in one of them," Jack said.

Derrick slapped his knee and laughed out loud, "You think I might believe that such a white dude as you could live in the Towers?"

"Turn around and you'll see. Over there by the window," Jack pointed in the direction of a room divider with photos standing in the opposite corner of the room, identical to the one in the adjacent room next to the bar. "There're my childhood photos somewhere in the middle. See for yourself."

Reluctantly, Derrick got up from his chair and went up to the room divider. In the center, he saw a photograph of a boy of about eleven years old, standing along with a beautiful tall woman with a kind face and a frightened Bambi eyes. Behind them, Derrick recognized the outlines of the infamous buildings he had seen more than once.

"Daamn," Derrick whistled. "You sure it's not photoshopped? Or maybe you and your mom just took a picture passing by?"

Instead of answering, Sullivan started chopping the vegetables he had just washed.

"And how did you end up there?" Derrick asked, returning to his seat.

"My father left us when I was ten," Sullivan said. "More precisely, he didn't leave us, he kicked us out of the house. He came home from work one day and announced that his new girlfriend would now live here, and my mother and I could go wherever the hell we wanted. Sounds terrible, but in fact, it was the happiest day of my life. At the time, of course. Living with my father was a nightmare. Hand me that big salad bowl over there, please," Jack asked, pointing with a knife in its direction.

Derrick fulfilled the request.

"We left with one suitcase and, I think, two hundred dollars," Sullivan continued his story. "Mom didn't have any relatives or friends on this side of the Atlantic, so we checked into the cheapest motel we could find. But we barely had enough money for a week, so my mother started looking for work like crazy, knocking on literally every door and begging almost on her knees. And here's another interesting fact about white privilege – no one gives a shit that you're white when you're an emigrant from a poor country, without education, without work experience, and with a heavy accent. You see, my mother came to the United States at the age of seventeen on a modeling contract. In Russia, her father, that is, my grandfather drank, her mother worked at three jobs to feed my mother and her two brothers. Plus they lived in a place that made Helms Street look like Irving Street. So my mother thought the modeling contract was a golden ticket. But, as is most often the case with immigrants, her American dream was not destined to come true."

Sullivan put the chopped vegetables in a bowl and went to check the steak, while continuing his story, "After a couple of advertising campaigns, my mother's modeling career stooped to presentations in supermarkets, which hardly paid for food and a tiny rented apartment. So the proposal from my father, who was very imposing in his police uniform, seemed most attractive to her. Especially since my father promised her he'd place her into a good college. But when she moved in with him, my father turned from a gallant gentleman into a domestic tyrant, who forbade my mother not only to work and study but also to leave the house without a good reason. And so, ten years later, my mother ended up on the street without education and any experience other than modeling work. In the end, all she could find was a janitor job at a school. Do you know Garfield High?"

"Yeah," Derrick said, "There were legends about it at our school. I heard there were a couple of shootings there and somebody was even killed."

"Um–hum, Mr. Reynolds. He threatened a seventh-grader that he would fail him, so the kid came the next day with a gun and emptied an entire clip at him," Sullivan replied and got back to preparing a salad. "That was the school where my mother got a job. As a nice bonus, she was offered a one-room apartment in a high-rise building on Helms Street for a purely nominal fee."

"Don't tell me that you studied at Garfield?!?" Derrick said and raised his fist to his mouth, preparing himself to be surprised.

Sullivan nodded in response.

"No way, Man!" Derrick shouted and slapped his knee for the second time. "And how did you manage to survive there?"

"Three broken ribs, two concussions, a broken arm, four broken fingers, and a countless number of wedgies. How else do you think the only white kid in the whole school could survive?" Sullivan replied calmly, dressing the salad with olive oil.

"So that's why you decided to become a boxer? Getting ready for the homecoming?" Derrick replied with a laugh. "Wanna knock the shit out of all those who dipped you in the toilet?"

Sullivan shook his head.

"And do you know, thanks to what, or rather whom, I became who I am now?"

"Yourself?" Derrick asked, still chuckling. "Because you're so smart and you tried so hard despite being bullied by black kids?"

Sullivan shook his head again.

"No, not myself. I became what I became thanks to Mr. Danny Martin. Can you guess what color his skin is?"

"Jewish?" Derrick replied.

"No, it's darker than yours," Sullivan said, turning the

steaks over again. "Mr. Martin was our neighbor, he lived a floor above. He had to walk around me almost every day, going down the stairs. My mother would always send me to the yard to get some fresh air. After all, it's not good when a child sits at home all the time watching TV. But, as you can guess, things were no better in my yard than at school. So instead of going to the yard, I would go up to the floor above – so that my mother wouldn't see me – and sit on the stairs with a book. For a very long time, Mr. Martin just sighed heavily passing me by. Surprisingly enough, even that no longer young black gentleman, who was born and raised in the ghetto, didn't have good feelings toward the white kid. But then one day, which I think was in the second year that we lived on Helms Street, Mr. Martin caught me reading a book on computers, which I'd taken from the school library. He asked me if I was into these things, and when I shrugged my shoulders in response, he called me to follow him. Mr. Martin had a small pawnshop nearby. Someone brought him a non-working computer there – a huge box with less memory than in any modern phone. Mr. Martin offered me two bucks if I could fix it and let me tinker with it in the back room."

"And thanks to your genius, you fixed it in five minutes?" Derrick asked, taking a final sip of his tonic.

"The trash bin's over there," Sullivan indicated the direction with a nod of his head, although Derrick did not show any desire to do anything with the empty bottle. "No, I didn't fix it. I took it apart, and then I couldn't even put it back together. It's just that one day I came to the pawnshop with a black eye and the old man must have taken pity on me. He allowed me to continue hanging out with him and trying to revive the old computer. He brought me a couple more 'test subjects', and then began tinkering with the hardware with me. As a result, after a month we managed to assemble one working computer out of three broken ones. It inspired Mr. Martin to immediately put 'computer repair' right next to the 'pawnshop' sign. Of course, there were almost no computers in our neighborhood, but that new phrase on the sign didn't trouble anybody anyway. Everybody noticed only the word 'repair' and soon the pawnshop became filled with broken TV sets, VCRs, tape recorders, and so on. At some point, I really started to get somewhere and Mr. Martin even began to pay me. It was in the pawnshop of my black neighbor that I got the skills that helped me to get a scholarship to study at a normal university, where I got to learn programming, which paid for this house in the end. Moreover, it was Mr. Martin, who through some absolutely incredible number of acquaintances, acquaintances of acquaintances, and almost strangers managed by all means possible to provide me with the opportunity to appear before the scholarship board of a white privilege charity organization, which eventually gave me an education grant."

Sullivan turned off the burner under the pan.

"The steak should rest 15 minutes before slicing."

He took a pack of juice out of the fridge and poured himself a glass. After taking a sip, Jack continued, "And when I started showing progress with my studies, got acquainted with teachers and trustees, I offered to create a charity project at my university together with Mr. Martin's repair shop, which by that time his pawnshop had finally turned into. Together, we created a training workshop where local children, instead of running around the streets dreaming of becoming gangsta rappers, could learn a really useful and promising profession. And every year the best students of this workshop can apply for the university scholarship, regardless of what grades they have at school. Because you probably understand perfectly well what level of education Garfield High School can provide."

Derrick looked at Sullivan, this time without a grin.

"Over the past fifteen years, more than two dozen guys, black guys," Jack specified, "got these scholarships and managed to graduate from the university, which previously gave that opportunity almost exclusively to white privilege kids. Three of them are now working at Google, several at

Microsoft. Four guys, who graduated three years ago, launched a startup and are now negotiating its sale to Facebook. It's going to be a multi-million dollar deal. Their photos are also over there, you can see for yourself. And next to them is the photo of Mr. Martin on the porch of his house in Florida, where he moved upon retirement. I bought him that house. When I sold my first program, I didn't keep a single cent for myself. I used the entire sum to buy houses for my mother and Mr. Martin. Nothing fancy, just nice small houses."

Sullivan stopped to take another sip of juice.

"You know, you can think that I'm trying to impress you, telling you how incredibly wonderful I am. It's up to you, I'm not going to try and convince you otherwise. I just wanted to tell you the whole truth. Just the facts. Believe it or not."

Sullivan finished his juice and reached into the cupboard for plates.

"Let's eat in the open air. We have a place for this in the patio."

Jack handed Derrick the plates, taking the glasses and the bowl of salad.

"And there's one last thing I wanted to tell you. I just saw it on the news this morning, and I remembered something. Do you know Mick Mako?"

"Here's the deal, I'll give you the answer to all such questions at once," Derrick replied, leaving the kitchen for the patio. "I know all the famous black guys and everything related to our world. Of course, I know Mick Mako. He's the most freaking famous rapper from our state! Two Grammys and three multi-platinum albums!"

"Did you know that he went to Garfield High?"

"Dude, I just told you – I know EVERYTHING!"

"Everything?" Sullivan asked with a slight smile on his lips. "Did you know that we studied together?"

"You studied together with Mick Mako?!?" Derrick, who was still holding the plates, waved his hands so hard that he almost dropped them.

"Yeah, it was him and his friends who broke two of my ribs. What a piece of shit," Sullivan said, putting a glass and the bowl of salad on the table. "I sure understand that it's not a crime to you to beat up a white kid, but believe me, it was not only me whom he treated like that. Kendrick, which was his name back then, terrorized everyone who was weaker than him. Once he and four of his friends beat up one black boy so hard he needed an ambulance."

Sullivan headed back to the kitchen for the steaks. Derrick followed him.

"But it's not about how much of a jerk he was as a child," Jack continued. "You've seen how he lives now – an estate in Los Angeles, a Lamborghini, gold chains a pound each. I'm almost a beggar compared to him. You said that you knew everything about the life of your community. Do you know what Kendrick did for his home neighborhood of Helms street?"

Derrick shook his head.

"I know, because I go there every month, visiting the repair shop. One time before his concert, Kendrick, or Mick Mako as he now likes to call himself, gave away T-shirts with his visage to local boys. That's all. That was all he did for the neighborhood he was born and grew up in."

Sullivan placed the steaks on the plates and headed out to the patio. Before putting them on the table, Jack added, "Mr. Martin and I established a program through which twenty-seven black children were able to get a prestigious and, most importantly, very useful education, which, in turn, helped them to get well-paid jobs and move their families from the ghetto to decent neighborhoods. I personally paid for the education of four more of them who tried as hard as others but didn't receive a scholarship because of their juvenile criminal records. And over all this time Mick Mako only gave out T-shirts that read 'Get Rich or Die Young'."

Sullivan put the plates with the steaks on the table and stared intently into Derrick's eyes, "And now tell me, Derrick, do you think that maybe it's time to stop dividing people into white and black and start dividing them into those who help others and those who care only about themselves?"

Derrick did not look away, but his eyes still gave away embarrassment.

"Have a seat," Sullivan said, cutting a small piece off of the steak that lay in front of his guest and putting it in his mouth. "See? It's not poisoned."

Jack sat down and began slicing his steak energetically and with great concentration. Derrick took a seat opposite to him. Only two-thirds of the steaks later, the awkward silence was broken by the words of the guest, "If you want to quickly build muscle mass, you'll also need to buy protein powder and Creatine. We can go there together after the next session at One-Two. I know a good store."

Sullivan looked up at Derrick and responded with a slight smile. Derrick smiled back awkwardly.

..14..

Upon Kate's strong request, which was more like an order, it was decided to hold the next training session on the Dutch beach in the evening. Here the way into the water was strewn with stones at least five feet deep, so this place did not enjoy popularity with the public, which made it possible for Jack, Charlie, Kate, and Derrick to safely work on the sand without the fear of tripping over sunbathers.

"Come on, take off your shoes. There ain't no reason to run on the sand in shoes!" McKee commanded, perching on a large stone that was strikingly similar in shape to a chair or even a medieval throne.

All four of his mentees quickly got rid of their shoes.

"So, let's start with running as usual," the old man continued to order around. "You run from here to those three big stones over there. You see them?"

Sullivan and the others nodded in response.

"Run in that direction at a marathon pace, when you turn back – run as fast as you can. As if a tax officer's chasing right after you."

The old man smiled and leaned back on the 'back' of his improvised stone chair. "So, why are you still standing? Run!"

It was unusual and uncomfortable to run on the sand, but on the plus side, the width of the beach allowed Charlie, Kate, Jack, and Derrick, who joined them for the first time, to form up in line.

Such a company and such formation allowed Jack to finally feel a part of the team. Both at school and later on at the university, Sullivan was always the shortest and thinnest student, so whenever it came to splitting into teams at PE lessons, he was always chosen last and never allowed to play any responsible role whatsoever. Most of the times, his classmates just shouted at him to get out of their way and stop messing up the game.

And now Charlie, Kate, Derrick, and he were not just a solid team, but the team whose main goal was to help him prepare for professional fights in the ring. Even Kate, who started training to acquire self-defense skills, was very quickly inspired by Sullivan's indomitable determination and also became part of his cheer team. If earlier the woman had dropped by One-Two Boxing no more than a couple of times a month, now she could be found at the club almost every evening.

"Keep your knees higher and your feet straight, otherwise you might twist your ankles!" Derrick commanded when the team yet again switched from jogging to sprinting.

Sullivan sped up and outran Derrick and Kate, but Charlie, who was light and filled with the energy of youth, still pulled away.

"Come on, old-timers, don't fall behind!" he shouted cheerfully and put on speed.

Ten minutes later, Derrick commanded, "Stop, stop! We're done with running!"

When all four of them caught up with McKee, who was sitting on his stone throne, the old man greeted them with a grin. "You look like a modern politically correct version of the Justice League: a gay, Mexican, Afro-American, and woman. Everyone's young, full of energy, and ready to fight the main evil of the XXI century – the white heterosexual man."

All four of them responded with smiles, although a couple of weeks ago such a joke would probably have seemed offensive to them. But now Jack, Charlie, and Kate were sure that the old man did not mean to offend anyone, it was just that his sense of humor was still quite rude.

"Okay, Fantastic Four," McKee continued. "We're done

with the warm-up, it's time to move on to serious work. The thing we're gonna start with today – the balance of your stance. And the sand's just right for this."

The old man got up from his stone throne and began to walk to and fro.

"Look, here's a more or less flat surface. Charlie, work your feet over it, level out a small site so that there's enough space for all four of you."

Charlie began to carry out the instructions of the coach, while the old man continued lecturing, "Footwork in boxing is no less important than the arm-action. And when two more or less equal opponents clash in the ring, especially if both of them prefer defensive tactics, it so often happens that the one who works better with his feet gets the victory. The better your footwork, the faster you move in the ring. A quick approach to the enemy means a quick and unexpected blow, and a quick step back allows you to avoid a counterattack. The foundation of effective footwork is the balanced stance. Incorrectly distributed weight won't allow you to move at maximum speed and will also lead to increased fatigue. Among young and ardent boxers, it's a common practice that a fighter jumps around like a madman for the first couple of rounds, but in the middle of the fight, his legs become exhausted and start to feel like wood. Experienced guys, when fighting with such youngsters, first go into deep defense, allowing the rookie to use up all his energy, and then literally smash him, throwing punches from any direction and in any sequence. Okay, Charlie, that's enough. Thanks."

Charlie raised his eyebrow slightly, hearing this word from the old man for the first time in his life.

"Come on," the coach continued. "Get to this area and take the boxing stance."

All four of them executed the old man's command.

"Now jump aside quickly. Do make sure not to wipe off the traces. That way you'll practice jumping as well."

Jack, Charlie, Kate, and Derrick jumped aside almost in

sync, with the last two nearly bumping into each other.

"Here," McKee said, approaching the footprints left on the sand by his mentees. "Look at your footprints. Derrick's both feet pressed the sand almost identically. So, his weight was distributed almost equally. That's how the balanced stance should look like. You did pretty well, too, Jack," the old man added, taking a step toward Sullivan. "Though there's a slight overweight on your front leg. Work on it."

Sullivan thought to himself that such an analysis could not be considered indicative, since the imbalance could have occurred not while practicing the stance, but at the moment of the jump itself. But Jack decided not to argue, responding to the coach only with a short nod.

"And speaking of you two," McKee said, looking at the footprints left on the sand by Charlie and Kate's feet. "It's all bad. You, kid, have a clear-cut overweight on your rear leg, and as for you, young lady, it's on the contrary, almost all your weight's on the front leg."

Having walked around his mentees, standing in line, the old man returned to his former place to be able to watch all four of them at the same time.

"Now I want you to take the boxing stance again and start shadowboxing. Focus all your attention on your legs, weight distribution, and the way you shift it when you move over from lead arm punches to rear arm punches and from attack to defense. It was really not a bad idea with sand after all. On concrete in sneakers, you definitely wouldn't be able to get such a clear feel of these moments."

"You're welcome," Kate said cheerfully.

"Yes, yes," the old man replied. "Thank you, Kate. It was a very wise suggestion. Come on, get started already. Derrick, you stand on the side and watch Jack practice. Maybe you'll notice some mistakes that I can't see from the front."

The team got down to shadowboxing. Less than a minute later, Derrick said to Sullivan, "Jack, look, I'll show you how you can increase jab power." The young coach began to demonstrate and explain at the same time, "When you jab, step forward an inch with your front foot and relax your hips to drop your body weight into the jab. Time your jab so that your fist impacts right when your weight drops into the ground."

"Yes, yes, that's a great remark, Derrick," the old man added.

Charlie's left eyebrow went up again because usually the old man only got irritated when someone dared to give a piece of advice that McKee had not hit upon himself. "Jack's company's obviously done the old man some good," Charlie thought to himself. "And Kate's hanging out in the club all the time now has also had a positive effect on his manners."

"This is also known as Jack Dempsey's 'Falling Step' principle," McKee continued. "Dempsey was a heavyweight champion in the twenties. One of the greatest fighters in history. Frenzied attack, a very aggressive style, and his punch was just crazy. I was compared to him in my time," the old man added, not without pride.

McKee nodded approvingly once more and turned to his young assistant. "Okay, Charlie. Go fetch punch mitts from the car. I took two pairs. One for you, one for Derrick."

Charlie quickly crossed the sand and grass strip that separated the beach from the parking lot, and in less than a minute he was standing in front of McKee again with two pairs of punch mitts.

"You stay here," the old man said, turning to Derrick. "And you, Charlie, run to those rocks where you turned around. Your task is the following," McKee added, shifting his gaze to Jack. "You perform combos with Derrick, then turn around and run to Charlie. But you run slowly, working with your arms. You run to Charlie, follow his commands. Then you turn back and run to Derrick, but this time as fast as possible, give it your best. In the ring, you need to be able to work rhythmically. You explode, launch an attack, throw a couple of combos, and go back to defense to catch your breath, regain your strength, and attack again. Understood?"

Sullivan nodded.

"Then do it, come on!" McKee commanded, slapping Jack on the shoulder and turning to Kate, who was standing further off. "Well, young lady, would you like to continue our self-defense lessons?"

It took Sullivan about half an hour to train with Derrick and Charlie, then McKee shared a few more tricks of the trade, and then arranged the first full-fledged instructional, rather than humiliating sparring with Derrick for Jack. At some point during the fourth hour of the One-Two Boxing team's stay on the beach, when the sky was already beginning to turn to sunset colors, the solitude of the trainees was disturbed by a minivan pulling up and parking next to Sullivan's Tesla.

McKee thought the car looked familiar, but he could not recall where exactly he had seen it.

"Guys," Sullivan said to the others as soon as he noticed the approaching minivan. "I have a little surprise for you. I've been spending more time with all of you over the past few weeks than I have at home. You've become some kind of a work-family for me. And I wanted to introduce you, my work-family, to my real family…"

As soon as the rear sliding door of the minivan opened and the folding ramp showed out of it, McKee remembered where he had seen this car. The front door opened at the very next moment and the woman that McKee also already knew stepped out. It was Justine – rehabilitologist who worked with Sullivan's husband Jacob.

"Come on, I'm going to need your help," Jack said, heading toward the parking lot.

The others followed him. When all five of them came up to the minivan, Jacob also got out of the car, only this time he managed to move out in his wheelchair by himself. Sullivan went up to him, put his hand on his shoulder, bent down, and gently kissed his husband on the forehead, "Are you all right? Aren't you tired? If you want, we can go home. Everyone will understand."

Kate and Derrick were surprised at how much tenderness and care there was in Sullivan's voice. The Jack they had known before was resolute and reserved, he rarely smiled or displayed any feelings. Jacob shook his head and smiled back at Jack.

"I decided not to tell you in advance because I didn't know if it was going to work out," Sullivan spoke to the others. "It all depended on how Jacob would feel. Are you sure everything's fine? Won't it strain him too much?" Jack asked, turning to Justine.

"Don't worry," the woman replied. "I've told you a million times. I'm a professional and if something could harm the patient, I wouldn't agree, even if you started begging me. Everything will be fine. I'm sure this will only benefit Jacob."

"Okay, whatever you say. Thank you for coming," Sullivan said and turned to the others. "Guys, this is my husband, Jacob. And this is his doctor and my savior Justine."

Sullivan bent over to his spouse and continued, "Jacob, Justine. You already know Charlie and Gerard. And these are my other two friends – Kate and Derrick."

"It's nice to meet you," Justine said and held out her hand to Kate.

"Yes, nice to meet you too," Derrick said with a bit of embarrassment and held out his hand to Jacob, immediately pulled it back and extended forward slightly again, not knowing whether to try to shake hands with a new acquaintance or not.

"Jacob," the man said and held out his hand himself.

Jacob's voice was very weak, as well as his handshake. Derrick squeezed his hand just a little bit and hurried to return his palm to its place. But Jacob's hand was still left hanging in the air. Kate instantly hurried to remedy the situation by shaking Jacob's hand and greeting him. Her example was followed by McKee, who took Jacob's hand in his huge palm in such a gentle manner as if it were a priceless artifact made of the finest glass.

The last person to greet Sullivan's husband was Charlie. During the boy's stay at Jack's house, he managed not only to get acquainted but also to make friends with Jacob, who, due to his injury, was now much closer in terms of development to a seventeen-year-old boy than to his own husband. With their hands, Charlie and Jacob performed in the air some kind of a ritual, which was only known by the two of them, and afterward they both laughed. Jacob's laugh was more like a weak cough.

"Jacob and Justine aren't the whole surprise," Sullivan spoke again. "We decided to set up a picnic on the beach for you. Can you help me unload?"

Charlie looked into the trunk of the minivan and saw a large picnic basket, a portable fridge, some folding chairs, and even a few tiki torches inside. The boy hurried to get inside the car and began to pass things to Kate and Derrick who also came to help.

"Gerard, can you help me move Jacob?" Sullivan asked the old man, already taking hold of one of the armrests of the wheelchair. "Otherwise he might get stuck in the sand."

"Of course!" McKee responded cheerfully and got hold of the second armrest.

"Let me do it," Derrick said, approaching Jack, and, noticing the questioning look on his face, immediately added. "It's not because I think you aren't strong enough. It's because you're short. You and this big guy won't be able to carry him normally – the wheelchair's gonna be skewed too much. Come on, step aside, don't argue with your coach!"

Derrick accompanied the last words with a smile, which convinced Sullivan to let go of the wheelchair. Soon all seven of them were on the sand. Charlie put up the tiki torches, Kate and Justine unfolded a large tablecloth, Sullivan set the chairs.

"Wow," McKee said, peeking into the basket. "Real plates, real glasses, even metal forks! I've never been to such a fancy picnic in my life!"

"Just wait until we start serving food!" Jack answered with a smile, covering his husband's legs with a blanket.

"Most of the dishes are from a restaurant since we didn't have much time to cook, but Jack and I prepared some things ourselves," Justine said and began to take out containers with food from the basket, simultaneously reciting the names of the dishes. "Spicy Lentil Wraps with Tahini Sauce, Fried Chicken, Tomato and Mozzarella Caprese Skewers, Broccoli and Feta Pasta Salad, and for dessert – Peanut Butter and Jelly Icebox Cookies."

"Since most of us are driving," Sullivan continued the announcement of tonight's menu. "All our drinks are non-alcoholic: ice tea, homemade lemonade, and juices – orange and grape."

Having heard that the picnic was going to be non-alcoholic, McKee became noticeably sad, but Kate managed to quickly restore his good mood by slipping a plate of spicy fried chicken under the old man's nose. Just as the plates and food were set, the drinks were poured into glasses, and everyone present settled comfortably in their chairs, the sun touched the water's edge on the horizon.

For a while, the company silently enjoyed the beauty of the sunset sky, afraid to even start eating, as if the clatter of forks and plates could scare off the sun, so it would have a second thought about going down over the horizon. Sullivan broke the silence. "Now that we aren't starving yet, I'd like to propose a toast," he said, getting up from his chair. "You know, in my life, somehow it was always only one person who supported me. In my childhood, it was my neighbor Mr. Martin, at the university I got my first real friend Sophia, then it was her who introduced me to Jacob."

Sullivan turned to his husband, who was sitting next to him. Giving him a look full of love and tenderness and taking his hand in his palm, he continued, "But, unfortunately, some time later there happened a tragedy that chained Jacob to this chair. And I was left without support, completely alone in the scariest days of my life. I had to become the same support and foundation, to be that tower of strength that Jacob had always been for me. And I did everything I could and I continue doing everything I can," Sullivan raised his husband's hand to his lips and kissed it. "But it is very difficult and very terrifying to be alone."

McKee looked down and started fiddling nervously with his glass of ice tea. He knew exactly what Jack was talking about. All his life, from the very childhood, he had Johnny Sifaretto. He was his friend, his brother, his mentor, his manager, his business partner, his everything. And then he was gone, and in an instant, Gerard was left without a friend, without a brother, without a mentor, without a partner, without everything... only with a worthless champion belt on the wall and a business he had no idea how to run.

"And right now," Sullivan continued. "As much as four people who support me suddenly appeared in my life. Yes, of course, I pay three of you," Jack added with a slight grin. "But still. I know you do it not for the money. More precisely, not only for the money. I know that you really want to help me. Even though you absolutely don't believe in my success."

Jack grinned again, glancing at the old man. Then he raised his glass of lemonade. "I want to say thank you, Charlie. You were the first to support me and even stand up for me, even though I'm twice your age, and everything should be the other way round. Thank you very much, Charlie. I'll never forget it."

Sullivan met the kid's gaze, smiled at him, and nodded. Charley, incredibly flattered by such a speech, could only smile shyly in response.

"Thank you, Gerard," Jack continued. "Even though we got off to a rough start, you were able to show humanity when it was most needed, you were able to find the strength in yourself to understand and even help another person from a world that is completely alien to you. And it's priceless. Especially when it comes to such a...," Sullivan hesitated, choosing the right word. "Such an experienced and wise person like you…"

"Call a spade a spade," McKee said. "An old, stubborn fool."

Sullivan smiled again, and the others responded with suppressed chuckles.

"Anyway, Gerard," Jack continued his interrupted speech. "I know how difficult it is to change one's views even at my age, and agewise I'm still a far cry from you. So thank you Gerard for everything. I really appreciate our friendship."

Sullivan nodded to the coach and moved on to the next participant of the picnic. "Kate. The only person here whom I don't pay for friendship."

The audience responded with short chuckles again.

"Nobody asked you to support me. You volunteered yourself to spend, apparently, all your free time in the company of the sweaty men. I certainly appreciate that, too."

The others laughed once again. Kate gave Jack a beaming smile in response.

"Thank you, Kate. And finally, Derrick," Sullivan turned to the young coach. "If we were in a bad movie right now, I'd say something like 'ma man, wazzap brother'."

Derrick let out a short laugh.

"But, fortunately, we're not in a bad movie, so I can talk to you normally. The story of the two of us is very similar to our story with Gerard, so I won't explain the same thing over again, but I'll just say thank you too for being able to step outside the negative social stereotypes and also become part of our friendly team."

Sullivan was about to announce the end of the toast but changed his mind. "These're all of the members of my new One-Two Boxing family, but I'd like to thank one more person who's also here with us. Justine," Jack said, turning to the woman sitting by the other side of Jacob's wheelchair. "I've known you for much longer than I've known these guys, but to be honest, I don't remember ever thanking you from the bottom of my heart for what you've done and are doing for me and Jacob."

Sullivan put his hand on his husband's shoulder. "Yes, I pay you too, of course, but with money I only pay for your services, not for how you treat Jacob, how you care about him, how you worry about him, sometimes even more than I do. It's all priceless. And I want you to know, Justine, how much I appreciate you and our relationship. Thank you."

Jack raised his glass and finally solemnly announced the end of the toast, "Charlie, Gerard, Kate, Derrick, Justine, and, of course, my beloved Jacob, who has always been my main support and companion. Thank you all very much. Here's to you!"

"And to you, Jack," McKee supported the toast. "I think that everyone here will agree with me. Despite that we've only known each other for a couple of months, and especially that you're the most reckless and crazy son of a bitch I and all of us have ever known, we've managed to learn a lot from you. Here's to you, Jack! And to you, Jacob!" The old man added, clanging glasses with Jack.

The others followed suit. When the formalities were out of the way, the picnickers took their places again and started to eat. The light of the already set sun was replaced by the flames of the lit tiki torches. The lack of alcohol did not prevent the company from enjoying a fun and relaxed atmosphere and soon they began to share stories from their past, joking and laughing at each other's anecdotes.

From the outside, one might have thought that it was really one big and strange family, or at least a group of close, old friends. Only McKee was less talkative than usual. All that time, Jack's words about how he was left without support and how difficult and terrifying it was to be alone lingered in Gerard's mind. He was sitting and thinking about how Jack had managed to cope with his loneliness, and he himself had not.

After Johnny Sifaretto's death, Gerard did nothing but constantly destroy the business he was left with and his own liver. A small and frail gay, who had a disabled husband on his hands, coped with everything and endured without giving up, and he – a huge, powerful, and fearless real man let things slide immediately after the death of his friend. He threw a towel and left the ring without even trying to continue the fight in the next rounds. Whereas Sullivan returned to One-Two Boxing again and again, despite all the difficult and humiliating trials of the previous days.

McKee looked round the cheerful and smiling faces of the picnickers and thought that he had last enjoyed such a company when Johnny had still been alive. Johnny liked to throw barbecue parties, to which he invited the whole neighborhood. Whole families came to those parties. Johnny's boy Mickey was running around the pool with other kids, his wife was in charge of the drinks, and Johnny himself, together with his best friend Gerard, were working magic at the grill.

Sweet and at the same time bitter memories made McKee get up from his chair and walk away from the others. The old man did not know if he still knew how to cry, but he was so sad that he was seriously afraid that a treacherous tear was about to roll out of the corner of his eye. And if it did happen, he did not want anyone other than the sea and the moon rising over the horizon to see the liquid in his eyes.

The old man had been standing at the water's edge for about ten minutes and was staring blankly into the distance, where the sea met the sky, when someone put a hand on his shoulder, and a voice came from behind his back. "Is everything all right?"

McKee turned his head and saw Sullivan. Just in case, the old man quickly ran his hand over his face, pretending to scratch his nose, but his eyes and skin turned out to be dry.

"Yes, everything's fine," he said in a surprisingly hoarse voice. "I was just thinking my own thoughts here. Thanks for the picnic. That was a great idea."

"Don't mention it. I'm glad you liked it. Some lemonade?" Sullivan added, offering a glass to the coach.

McKee refused with a wave of his hand.

"I added a drop of gin to it. I took a minibar bottle just for you," Jack said enticingly.

"Now we're talking!" McKee said, hastily snatching the glass from Sullivan's hand.

Having swallowed almost half of the liquid in one gulp, the old man looked at Jack suspiciously. "No gin whatsoever, right?"

Sullivan shook his head with a smile.

"Tricked the old man," McKee said and laughed.

But this time his laugh sounded unusually sad.

"Are you sure you're all right?" Jack asked again. "You can talk to me. I won't laugh and I won't tell others."

"No, thanks, I'm fine. I just wanted to be alone. Go to the others, they're probably already waiting for you. Jacob looks good today," the old man added after a bit of thinking.

"Okay, whatever you say. If you want to stand manfully and brutally in proud solitude – it's up to you. I won't interfere."

Sullivan slapped the old man on the back and had already taken a couple of steps in the opposite direction before adding, "Oh, yeah, here's one more thing. I'm having my first fight in three months," Jack shouted without stopping. "Everything's already decided, it can't be put off. It's all or nothing. You can also think about it in your proud solitude."

Jack winked at the old man and smiled. McKee could only respond to the unexpected news by raising his eyebrows. The look of utter surprise on the coach's face clearly amused Sullivan.

..15..

"Fuck!!!" McKee swore with feeling. "What's wrong with you, Jack? I don't fucking understand! I DON'T UNDERSTAND!"

The coach got up from his chair with such aggression that the chair flew back, its metal legs squeaking disgustingly over the concrete floor. Having walked up to Sullivan and Derrick, who were sparring in the ring, the old man continued in a raised tone, "It seems like you do everything right. You've honed the technique, you work fine with the bag, you follow all my commands. So why do you always screw everything up in the ring?!?" Not getting any answer, McKee swore even louder than the first time. "Fuck!!!"

Sullivan and Derrick both looked at the old man with shame, acknowledging the fairness of his words. And though technically Derrick had nothing to do with it, being a junior coach and Jack's sparring partner, he also felt responsible for his shortcomings.

"Kid, there's a month left until your first fucking fight, which you, son of a bitch, arranged without consulting me. A fucking MONTH," McKee raised his voice again. "Do you even realize that with the shit you're demonstrating now there's no point going in the ring?!? You won't even take down a wheelchair user!" The coach said, without even thinking that his words could badly hurt his protégé. "I don't know how the fuck it could be even possible, but now you're fighting worse than when we just started preparing for this fucking fight!"

"Maybe we should practice shuffle uppercuts or punching while slipping and weaving?" Derrick suggested in an uncertain voice.

"What's the point?" The old man replied, still in a raised tone. "He's got no strength in his punch, that's the problem. He already knows all the techniques better than you and even me. He's so big-freaking-brained that he grasps everything on the fly. Fat lot of use! His punches are shit! What's the use of the technique if there's no strength in it? After all, this is not some figure skating or gymnastics, where you get the damn points for your technical merit. This is boxing! You may have no technique at all if your fist is made of iron and your chin's like stone. Remember Butterbean? Nobody gave a shit about whatever technique he had. By the look of him, nobody'd even think he was a boxer. And so what? No one cared! His punches were like cannon fire and that's the main thing!"

After he finished talking, McKee put his hands on his hips and stared intently at Sullivan. Jack withstood that heavy stare for a minute, but then lowered his eyes. The last two months that had passed since Sullivan had announced his upcoming fight to the old man, McKee had been training him like a madman. He made him come to the gym at six in the morning and sometimes train until the very evening.

During this period, Sullivan managed to run more than a hundred miles, work for about the same number of hours in the ring and even tear a punching bag. And the old man did not just make him run like crazy, but really trained him, noticing and correcting every smallest mistake in his technique. One time the old man got so pedantic that with a ruler, protractor, and marker, he began to draw a diagram on the floor, representing the ideal footing for a combination.

Sometimes it even seemed to Jack that McKee finally believed he really stood a chance in IPBU. But now, apparently, the old man was even more sure that Jack should not step into the professional ring than when he had first heard about his crazy idea. And this time Sullivan could not blame the old man's narrow-mindedness or homophobia for that. No, now Jack knew perfectly well that it was him who had failed the coach, and not the other way round.

"I need a break!" McKee finally broke the silence.

With a wave of his hand, the coach turned around and headed for his office.

"And what should we do? Continue sparring?" Derrick said in the direction of his boss who was walking away.

"Do whatever you want! I don't give a shit anymore!" McKee replied irritably, slamming the office door behind him.

"You heard the boss," the young coach said, turning to Sullivan.

Without further ado, Jack raised his gloves and went on the attack.

"Don't take it personally," Derrick spoke already fighting off the blows of his opponent. "The old man just gets emotional when it comes to boxing. He likes you. You know that, right?"

"It's okay," Sullivan said, switching to defense. "He's right. I have a really shitty punch."

"We-e-e-ll," Derrick drawled, throwing a jab to the opponent's head.

"Come on, you don't need to spare my feelings," Jack replied, ducking under the opponent's punch and striking back to the body. "You can see it perfectly well, too."

"I wouldn't say it's straight shitty," Derrick responded, taking a side step and blocking Sullivan's blows. "But you should definitely work on it."

"All I've been doing all this time is working on my punches. Every day I get up in the morning and go to the punching bag as soon as I've brushed my teeth," Jack said, going into deep defense under a hail of the opponent's blows. "Then here, and then again at home as I return. I even punch the bag a couple of times before going to bed. It doesn't make any difference. The strength of the punch is still the same."

"Maybe you should gain more muscle mass?" Derrick asked and threw forward another uppercut.

Sullivan quickly covered his ribs with his elbow and replied, "I already weigh 146 pounds. I gained 4 pounds of pure muscle over the time I've been training. I might even need to go through a cutting phase before the weigh-in."

"Then maybe you should lower your weight class instead?" It was Derrick's turn now to defend himself from the punches to the body. "With your height, you can cut up to bantamweight."

"No, I only need welterweight," Sullivan responded and threw an unexpectedly fast cross.

Barely managing to cover up against the blow, Derrick asked in surprise, "Why? You can choose between as many as six weights below, why cling to the most competitive?"

"Because I want to become an IPBU welterweight champion," Sullivan replied and threw a combo.

"Wanna take a swing at Joe Ryan? Go ahead, it's your call," Derrick responded with a grin and almost missed a fast and tough uppercut to the body. "The guy hasn't even had a single knockdown in his entire career, including amateur fights. The second-best record in the whole history of the weight class. A couple more successful fights and he'll become the best welterweight champion of all titles. Ryan's not a person, he's a killing machine."

Even before finishing the last word, Derrick unexpectedly missed two punches to the body at once, sent to the target so quickly that the young coach did not even have time to realize that he needed to lower his elbows a bit. The mention of the reigning champion's name seemed to give Sullivan's fists an extra boost.

"That's better!" Derrick said in a slightly constrained voice, "You should've proceeded with the attack. One-two to the body, the opponent's hands involuntarily fall, and you immediately punch in the head. From a short distance, the punches won't be so strong, but if you have enough charge to throw at least a few punches in a row, then the fight can be immediately finished by a technical knockout. The main thing is to act quickly and decisively, without letting the opponent recover himself."

The coach's words were interrupted by a mobile phone ringtone coming from the locker room.

"Sorry, I have to answer it," Sullivan said. "Justine asked me to keep my phone at hand all the time. Things haven't been going well for Jacob lately."

"Yes, of course. No need to apologize," Derrick replied, helping Jack to get rid of the gloves.

Sullivan disappeared into the locker room. Soon he returned, holding a charger in one hand, and in the other a laptop for which that device was intended.

"Derrick, is there anywhere an outlet I can find? It was a call from work, I need to do one thing urgently, and, sure enough, my laptop died just in time."

"Yes, go to the old man's office. You can settle on the couch there," the coach answered. "Pops probably managed to take a shot, or even two, so he must be in a better mood already."

Sullivan nodded in response and went to the director's office.

"Gerard." After a knock, the door opened slightly, and Jack's face appeared in the gap. "Can I come in?"

As expected, McKee was clutching a glass of whiskey in his hand. As a response, he only threw a questioning look at the visitor.

"I have a very urgent matter to attend to for my work. I need to sit down with a laptop somewhere not far from an outlet."

"Go ahead," the old man replied reluctantly, but still quite friendly. "Over there, you can sit in the armchair. The outlet's in the corner," he added, indicating with a movement of his head the armchair that stood against the wall to the right of his desk.

Sullivan quickly crossed the room, placed the laptop on a small table next to the chair, plugged it into an outlet, and immediately began to tap on the keyboard. McKee looked into his glass, rolled the remaining inch of the liquid at the bottom for a couple of moments, and reluctantly threw it in his mouth.

This time the whiskey was especially disgusting because, during his last trip to a store, the old man discovered that he had forgotten his wallet at home, which caused McKee to put the usual bottle of medium disgust whiskey back in its place and take the one he could pay for with a single crumpled and battered banknote that he found in his pocket.

The old man grimaced, feeling an unpleasant taste of the hooch in his mouth, and thought to himself that this "whiskey" must have been made from technical-grade alcohol and colored with an old tea bag, which had been gathering dust on some table for a while before. With the disgusting taste, McKee felt a headache approaching, which came as a free bonus with that kind of drinks.

Meanwhile, the frequency of tapping on the keyboard accelerated and turned into a real drum-roll. Anticipating how the drumming would soon turn into a concert of a whole symphony orchestra in his head, the old man was about to get up from his chair and leave the office, but he paused for a moment. His attention was attracted by the speed of that drumming. McKee closed his eyes and listened intently.

The taps were heard with a constant rhythm and minimal breaks – as if Sullivan was pressing only two adjacent keys. To make sure that Jack was not performing some strange two-button exercise, the old man opened his eyes and turned his head in the direction of his pupil. No, Sullivan's fingers moved all over the keyboard, they just did it so quickly that pressing any two keys that were opposite to each other on the keyboard took Sullivan some thousandths of a millisecond, which could be calculated only with the help of some fancy scientific equipment.

"Hmm," McKee gave out an involuntary sound from his chest.

"Am I bothering you?" Sullivan said, turning to the old man.

At the same time, Jack's fingers continued to run

over the keyboard with the same speed. It was as if they were completely independent and needed the participation of neither the eyes nor even the brain to perform their work.

"No, no," McKee replied with a wave of his hand. "Go on, it's all right."

The old man got up from his desk and hurried out of the office.

"Hey, Derrick, come here," he closed the door behind him and called out to a young coach who was loitering at the opposite end of the gym.

"What?" Derrick responded, approaching the boss at a brisk pace.

"That time when Sullivan punched you in the nose," taking a couple of steps away from the office door and lowering his voice, the old man spoke conspiratorially. "You know, when you picked on him in the ring…"

"You mean when you ordered me to pick on him?" Derrick interrupted the old man.

McKee immediately interrupted him in response, "Yeah, yeah, let's just not argue about who ordered what to whom, and who didn't mind at all himself. It's not about that now. You better tell me something – was it a clean punch or did he use some kind of a dirty trick?"

"Well, it wasn't all that simple…"

"Give me a break. Don't try to defend your maiden honor," McKee interrupted his subordinate again. "Happens to everybody. Leave the excuses for telling your grandchildren. Was it a clean punch or not?"

"Clean," Derrick admitted reluctantly.

"Right in the nose, just by the textbook?" the old man asked.

Derrick nodded affirmatively.

"Were you remaining in the stance or did you lower your gloves?"

"Take the stance as soon as you enter the ring!" Derrick replied, quoting the words of the old man himself, which he drummed into all of his students' heads as if it was a sacred mantra.

The old man nodded approvingly and went on, "Now answer me honestly, without bullshit, and think carefully. Did you miss that punch because you got cocky and forgot to watch your opponent, or because it was too fast?"

Derrick shifted from foot to foot for a couple of seconds and then finally answered, "Because it was too fast."

It came as a surprise to Derrick when McKee smiled broadly and slapped him on the shoulder. Without saying another word, the old man looked in the direction of the office but immediately turned back.

"Give me this," McKee said, and without waiting for the reaction of his subordinate he snatched the rolled-up hand wrap from Derrick's hand, which he was shifting from palm to palm while they were talking.

Jack, who was still actively tapping on the keyboard, heard the sound of the door opening and the old man's voice pronouncing his name. Even before he had time to look up from the laptop screen and see McKee himself, Sullivan noticed with his peripheral vision something small and red rapidly approach him. As if of its own will, his right hand instantly flew into the air and caught the object thrown at him.

Jack looked in surprise at the rolled-up red hand wrap he had caught, then shifted his gaze to the old man. McKee's face was literally beaming with joy as if he was a five-year-old child who met Santa Claus for the first time at a local mall.

"What the hell?" Jack said.

"Nothing, nothing! Keep working!" the old man said with a wave of his hand. "When you're done, I'll be waiting for you in the gym."

With that, McKee hurried back out of the office.

About half an hour later, Sullivan finished his work, closed the laptop, and went out into the gym. The expression on the old man's face still retained a bit of his initial exaltation. Derrick was standing next to him, clutching a stopwatch in his hand, and in front of them, Charlie was jigging about on the spot and throwing punches into the air.

"Stop!" Derrick commanded, pressing the button on the stopwatch.

"Jack, come to us!" The old man greeted him joyfully and waved his hand.

Sullivan approached the others.

"Listen here, Jack, it's very important. Listen to me carefully. But go ahead and warm up first. Jump on the spot to get your blood going. Shake your hands. Rotate them at all the joints, as I taught you. Do it, get ready so that your body could go all out."

Sullivan began to follow the instructions of the coach, looking suspiciously at the others who were silently staring at him. After a couple of minutes, McKee waved his hand, making it clear that the warm-up could be stopped.

"The thing is, Jack," he said, putting his hand on his pupil's shoulder. – "Now you have to try to throw as many straight punches as possible. Forget about the technique, forget about the footwork, forget about the strength and accuracy of the punch. Forget about everything. Now I want you to focus on the speed and speed only. Oh! You know what – close your eyes. Close your eyes and throw punches as if your hands are whips. Don't think about anything, just throw out straight punches as quickly as possible! Do you understand me?"

Sullivan nodded affirmatively.

"Ready?" the old man asked, removing his hand from Jack's shoulder.

Sullivan nodded again, assuming the stance at the same time.

McKee glanced at Derrick. He raised the stopwatch and commanded "Go!", simultaneously pressing the button. Jack closed his eyes and started throwing his fists out in front of him, trying to make each subsequent blow go faster than the previous one. By the end of the exercise, his heart was beating so hard in his chest that when Jack opened his eyes, the first couple of seconds he saw nothing but black dots skipping in front of him.

When his vision finally cleared, Sullivan saw the old man's face in front of him, with a wide smile from ear to ear. Jack thought to himself that he had never seen McKee even half as happy as he was now. Charlie and Derrick also looked unusual. The boy's face expressed delight and impatience – as if he had learned some incredibly cool secret and could not wait for the moment when he would be allowed to share it with others. And on Derrick's face Jack managed to read something in between respect and envy.

"Let's go to the office, we need to talk," McKee exclaimed and slapped Sullivan on the shoulder.

Once at his desk, the old man immediately reached into a drawer for a bottle. At first, he took out the cheap disgusting hooch that he had been choking on earlier, but changed his mind right away and pulled out another drawer, where he kept a bottle of real Irish whiskey, which was saved only for special occasions.

"Join me?" He turned to Sullivan, who sat down across from him.

Jack shook his head.

"Well, it's up to you. I won't insist," the old man poured whiskey into his glass and added. "It's outright criminal wasting good whiskey on someone who doesn't appreciate it!"

McKee tossed a shot in his mouth and put the empty glass down on the desk with a slam.

"Kid, I wanna apologize to you," the old man said.

Sullivan's left eyebrow rose in surprise. Even when McKee "apologized" for all the bullying that he had subjected Jack to in the first weeks of his training, he never said the words of apology themselves.

"You're probably wondering why I'm suddenly apologizing now, even though I never formally apologized to you when we were sitting on the tailboard of my pickup truck after all that trouble with your car?"

"That's exactly my thoughts," Sullivan said.

The old man grinned.

"That's because then it was about my personal, so to speak, qualities. And now we are talking about my expertise. About boxing. It's a completely different matter. You know, I never rushed to become Mr. Popular in everyday life, but boxing is different. I never considered myself a great coach, but I always considered myself a pretty much worthy professional. I have my own professional integrity. I've never worked just for money or to have something to get busy with. I'd never allow myself to tarnish this gym by such behavior."

Sullivan thought to himself that initially, the old man had accepted him to train solely for the sake of money, and there had been no professional integrity in it whatsoever until after that unfortunate incident with his stolen car. But he decided to keep these thoughts to himself.

"But I screwed up with you," the old man continued in the meantime. "And I'm not talking about those first training sessions when, to be honest, I just wanted to get rid of you. And I'm sorry for that, too, okay. I'm sorry!" McKee added with great emphasis.

Jack smiled subtly. "I never even asked you for this apology. But thanks anyway. I appreciate how much you're trying to become a more cultured person now."

"Uh-huh," McKee muttered under his breath, pouring a second portion of whisky. "But that's not what I was talking about. I was talking about how I screwed everything up when I already started training you seriously. You see, Jack, I was training you as I usually trained my heavyweight guys. Strength, technique, aggression. Only this way, and only in this order. Your technique's perfectly fine. You're quick on the uptake, you grasp everything on the fly. You can still work on your aggression, but you're no coward either, that's for sure. You probably need to pump up your confidence. You don't chicken out when under attack, but you yourself don't attack as intensely as you could. But that's okay. Strength, that's your main weakness," the old man chuckled and repeated. "Strength is your main weakness. Well, that's funny."

McKee threw the second shot of whiskey down his throat and leaned back in his chair.

"You see, Jack, I've always been a slugger myself and I've always believed that the strength of the punch is the most important thing. Knockout – that's what every boxer should go for in every fight. The victory on points is for fag...," the old man checked himself and pretended to clear his throat. "You know what I mean, generally. I've always stood for strength. And you don't have one. You don't have it, and that's that. No matter how hard I tried, I couldn't find strength in you. And that's what got on my nerves. But it's my mistake. My idiotic mistake. So I decided to apologize for it. How could an old fool like me imagine that it was possible to train a man in his thirties with a cool diploma and head full of all sorts of clever things the same way I trained twenty-year-old fellas who didn't even think about anything but boxing, parties, and pussy."

"Not to mention that I'm gay," Jack added with a slight grin.

"Oh, that doesn't mean shit," the old man waved the comment away. "You've proved it to me already that sexual orientation doesn't matter. The main thing is that you want to be a real man yourself, and not some kind of chihuahua carrying type. No offense to those guys, I'm sure they're not bad people either. But they definitely have no business being in the ring."

"Gerard, I really hate to interrupt you," Sullivan spoke again. "But it seems to me that you're already starting to get confused in what you wanted to tell me initially. I'm losing track of what you're getting at."

"Speed!" the old man snapped and slammed his fist on the table. "That's what I wanted to tell you! You're a fast son of a bitch, Jack Sullivan! And shame on me for not noticing that before! I mean, I saw you beating the shit out of those scumbags at the bar that time. That was fucking fast! Do you know why I made you throw jabs just now?"

Sullivan shook his head.

"That was a speed test. First I made Derrick and Charlie do it, and I counted how many punches they managed to throw in a minute. So listen here. Derrick threw eighty punches in a minute. But he's a heavyweight. Big guys are always slower than the smaller ones. That's why I asked Charlie too. The kid, of course, tried so hard that he completely forgot about the technique. Besides, he's still just a youngster. Youngsters are fast. Their joints are flexible, and their bones don't weigh nothing yet. So his result can be safely divided into two. But still. The kid threw a hundred and two punches in a minute. And now, do you know how many punches have you thrown in a minute, Sullivan?"

Jack nodded his head questioningly.

"One hundred and twenty-seven! ONE HUNDRED AND FREAKING TWENTY-SEVEN!" the old man repeated with emphasis. "And all of them were thrown with perfect technique. Even better than Derrick did. I wouldn't be surprised if it's some fucking record. And you're fast not only in terms of punches. Why do you think I threw those hand wraps at you over there?"

"To check my reaction?"

"That's it! Good thinking! You're a smart guy, Sullivan. Smart and fast. And that's what I had to work at, and I, the old knucklehead, kept focusing on strength. But speed, it's even better than strength. Do you know such a formula as 'E' equals 'm' multiplied by 'c' squared?"

"Mass-energy equivalence," Sullivan answered.

"Well, probably. The bottom line, it was Einstein's idea. So the way it goes – energy equals strength multiplied by speed squared. Squared! That is, speed is much more important here than strength because speed is squared! Fuck the fact that you don't have strength, Jack, but you have speed! Squared! Your speed is already squared compared to an average fighter, and here it's once more squared!"

Sullivan barely managed to suppress a smile. But he chose not to disappoint the old man with his explanations that 'm' there was actually not some 'strength', but mass, 'c' was not just speed, but the speed of light, and in any case that formula from the theory of relativity was not suitable at all for being used in boxing.

Meanwhile, McKee managed to swallow the third and fourth shots of whiskey all at once.

"Kid, I'll tell you what," the old man spoke again, his voice being clearly far from sober already. "From tomorrow on and up until your first fight, we're gonna train for speed, and only speed! And you know what – this time I can tell you quite seriously – you really stand a chance! No, no," McKee immediately hastened to clarify. "I'm not so drunk yet to say that there's a chance of you becoming a champion. I'm not sure I can get that much drunk at all. No, I'm only talking about the chance in the first fight. You've got it, man. I'm telling you that for sure. And I know a thing or two about boxing."

With a nod of his head, the old man pointed somewhere back. Sullivan guessed that McKee meant to imply the championship belt hanging on the wall behind him. Old and dusty, with the letters that read "IPBU". The same very letters that, for reasons unknown to anybody, Jack Sullivan craved so strongly.

..16..

"All right, guys, leave the room for a minute. I need to be alone with Jack," McKee said, raising his voice a little so that everyone could immediately sense the seriousness of his words.

Charlie, Derrick, and Kate left obediently, gently closing the locker room door behind them. Jack was sitting on a bench with his gloved hands on his knees and his head down. His shoulders and back experienced an unusual cool sensation caused by a polyester boxing robe, its back decorated with large letters that read 'Sullivan'.

The old man squatted down next to him and put his huge hand on his pupil's shoulder.

"Kid, whatever happens there," he said in a surprisingly quiet and calm voice. "You're already a boxer. You've earned the right to enter the ring. Whether you win or lose, it doesn't change who you are, Jack Sullivan. You're the man, you're the real man. And I'm proud to be your coach. No matter how your first fight ends. But now I want you to forget about winning or losing, forget about the letters IPBU, forget about your dreams, about rounds, about minutes, about points, even about the opponent. I want you to think only about one thing right now – about your punch. Put all your skills into it, all your training, all your mind, all your talent, all your joys and disappointments, all your pain, all that made you come to me. I want all of it, all of you to concentrate right here."

McKee lifted Jack's hand and patted the front of the glove with his palm.

"Think about the punch and only the punch. Don't waste

the punches, but don't hold them back either. Make each of your punches count. Sharp, clean, fast. Just the way you can do it."

McKee straightened his legs with obvious difficulty and stood upright.

"I'm gonna leave you alone. You'll close your eyes and focus all your thoughts and feelings on the punch. When the time comes, I'll knock on the door. You'll get up and walk out of the locker room. We'll all go to the ring together and get into it. You'll listen to the referee's instructions, touch gloves with your opponent. And all this time you'll be thinking only about one thing – only about the punch. But as soon as you hear the first bell, you'll stop thinking about the punch. The punch will start doing all the thinking for you. Do you understand me, Jack?"

McKee slightly squeezed his pupil's shoulder. Sullivan replied with a nod.

"You're alright, Kid. You're alright," the old man added and hurried out of the locker room.

On the other side of the door, Kate, Derrick, and Charlie were waiting for him. Charlie was nervously clutching the handle of the bucket containing the cornerman's equipment. All three of them, as well as McKee himself, were wearing uniforms specifying that they were the members of Jack Sullivan's team. Just as Charlie opened his mouth to say something, McKee warned him, "We'd better all be quiet. It's the first fight in your life for the two of you, and Derrick and I haven't been in the ring for several years already. Pull yourself together. This is no walk in the park. You're not here to watch the fight from the best seats. We came to work. Our task is to help Jack. So it's better if you run over your duties a few more times in your head. If any of you screw up, I won't take you to the next fight. And I won't give a damn that Jack insisted on taking all of you, rather than professional assistants, as I suggested to him. Above all others, that goes for you, Charlie."

McKee threw a menacing look at the kid.

PAUL DEVEREAUX

"Gerard?" A voice came from the opposite end of the corridor.

McKee and the others turned around. A tall guy in his early twenties with dark hair and a rather sly smile was walking toward them.

"Mikey?" the old man replied, extending his hand in response.

"It's Mike now," he replied with a barely noticeable note of irritation and shook McKee's hand.

The son of the old man's former business partner and best friend, Johnny Sifaretto, looked completely different from when he worked as a junior coach at One-Two Boxing. Now he was wearing an expensive suit, and he even seemed to have grown taller an inch or two. And most importantly, now his face was beaming with a pompous sense of self-importance. Mike also shook Derrick's hand and nodded friendly to Kate, but he did not even look at Charlie. The assistant cornerman was not worthy of the attention of the newly-minted manager.

"What are you doing here?" Derrick asked.

"I'm Rick Stanton's manager now. I was assigned yesterday. Just imagine, the day before the debut fight. He had a problem with his previous manager. Picture my surprise when I found out that my guy would fight against Gerard McKee's boy! Especially considering that when I left One-Two, you didn't have a single pupil in sight. And it hasn't even been half a year since then."

"Actually, Jack came to me the very day you quit. If I remember it right," McKee replied.

"Pops, is it true what they say about him? That he's never boxed in his life and that he's some kind of accountant or something?"

"A programmer," Charlie answered for the old man and immediately specified. "Information security consultant."

Mike did not even honor the kid with a look in his direction, and, again, talked to McKee, "And he's kind of close to his forties?"

"He's thirty-five," Charlie said again.

Mike gave a smirk. The old man did not like this smirk at all.

"Okay, Mikey," McKee spoke with the emphasis on the diminutive version of his name. "It's time for us to go. It was good to see you."

The old man held out his hand and added after shaking it, "The ring takes no notice of professions and age. Only the character."

Mike smirked again, "Okay, Pops, good luck to you. Let's drop by a nearby bar after the fight? I mean, we haven't seen each other for a long time, you could tell me how the club's doing."

"Sure, Mikey, see you later."

Mike waved his hand to Derrick and Kate and hurried to the opposite end of the corridor, where his fighter's locker room was.

"Jackass," Charlie muttered under his breath.

Meanwhile, McKee knocked on the door, signaling that it was time to go. A moment later, the door swung open and Sullivan appeared at the threshold. His face was so focused that he seemed to not see anything around him.

"Good l..," Charlie started to speak, but McKee cut him off immediately.

"Shush! No talking to the fighter before the fight! We walk in silence, and everyone should think about their duties and only about them."

Charlie looked down guiltily and a little frightfully.

"Let's go!" McKee commanded.

All five of them turned around and walked toward the exit into the arena. Charlie could barely contain his excitement. Marching silently and resolutely toward the ring as a whole team together with the fighter was very cool. Just like in the movies! But the boy's excitement quickly subsided when they went out into the hall. The place was not much bigger and not much better than their old and battered One-

Two Boxing, and at the very best only half of the spectator seats were occupied.

"What did you expect, Caesars Palace?" seeing the disappointment on the boy's face, Derrick whispered to him. "It's just a night of debutants. They won't even show it on Pay-per-view. Only a free YouTube video shot from some lousy camera."

Derrick nodded in the direction of the cameraman walking along the ring, holding a video camera on his shoulder, which was clearly older than Charlie himself.

"Well, at least we have commentators," Charlie muttered, glancing at the table next to the ring, at which were sitting two men with headphones and microphones.

...

"Good evening to our dear boxing fans! Greetings from Tingley Station and our tenth anniversary night of debutants. This is truly yours Harry Roberts and my old friend, a former heavyweight boxer, and now the author of the popular podcast about boxing, Larry Girard."

"Hi, everyone!"

"Tonight we are having five fights and now the participants of the first one of them are already approaching the ring. So let's not waste our time and start with presenting the fighters. Jack Sullivan is the first to enter the ring, and I can immediately see a smile on my colleague's lips. Larry, what's so funny?"

"I don't even know where to start, Harry. I'm sorry, I do understand that it's unprofessional on the part of a commentator to laugh at a fighter, especially at a debutant, of whose capabilities we don't know anything yet, but in this case, it seems to me that it's quite appropriate to laugh. The only explanation I can think of for the appearance of this Mr. Sullivan in the ring is that he'd lost some kind of a bet."

"For you, our dear spectators, I hasten to say a few words about our first fighter, Jack Sullivan. And then you will

immediately understand what seemed so funny to my colleague, who, let me remind you, was in the past a professional boxer himself and held more than twenty fights. Jack Sullivan is thirty-five years old, which, to put it mildly, is a bit late for making a debut in boxing, and, perhaps, in any other sport."

"Indeed, Harry, I wouldn't be surprised if it's some kind of a record."

"Quite possibly, Larry. Jack Sullivan hasn't held a single amateur fight and, as far as I know, he started training only about five months ago."

"And Sullivan is a programmer by profession."

"Yes, that's right, Larry, Sullivan worked as a programmer, and now he's an independent security consultant."

"Hardly a "physical" security consultant. Sorry for my laughter, I couldn't resist."

"That's what our first fighter Jack Sullivan's like – a thirty-five-year-old programmer, without any experience in boxing and with only five months of training behind him."

"Perhaps, Sullivan's only advantage is that his coach is the legendary heavyweight, world champion Gerard McKee. The bloody Gerard, who never left the ring without causing his opponent to spill at least a couple drops of blood."

"But even this advantage is quite controversial. Surely, as a boxer, McKee was one of the best in his generation, who left the ring undefeated. But as a coach, McKee has nothing to show for himself. None of his pupils ever won a title."

"Meanwhile, the second participant of our fight today, Rick Stanton, is stepping into the ring."

"And this, let me tell you Harry, is a whole different story. Stanton is a real fighter."

"Yes, Larry, you're undoubtedly right. Rick Stanton can be called the complete opposite of Jack Sullivan. He's only twenty, but as an amateur, he's already managed to hold more than three dozen fights, all of which ended in his favor."

"It's worth mentioning that, according to rumors, Stanton was supposed to defend our flag at the Olympics, but due to the *conflict in the Federation, he was not included in the final team squad list. That's why Stanton decided to end his amateur career and go pro. And I don't even doubt that this guy has a great future ahead of him. It's quite possible, dear spectators, that today you will witness the first triumph of the future world champion."*

"And we're ready to start our today's boxing celebration! The referee's almost done with instructing the boxers, here comes the traditional wishes for a fair fight, the welcoming touching of gloves, and the boxers are going to their corners. The bell's ringing and...

- What the fuck!!!

...

The arena, which only a moment before had been filled with the sounds of voices, the creaking of chairs, and other noise, suddenly descended into complete silence. Even the elderly and experienced referee was slow to react. Rick Stanton was lying on the canvas, stretched out in a straight line with his hands lying along his body. His eyes stared blankly at the ceiling. Behind them was an endless void of absent consciousness.

Less than two seconds ago, having heard the sound of the boxing bell, Stanton rushed forward, intending to finish off the green opponent in the very first round. But even Stanton himself could not have imagined that the fight would end so quickly. Sullivan's lightning-fast whip-like right cross crashed into his chin even before the boxing bell disc stopped vibrating after being struck.

At last, the referee remembered about his duties and started to count. Already by the count of three, he realized that Stanton would not recover for a long time and declared Sullivan's victory by knockout. The silence that hung in the arena was broken by a loud and resonant cry of joy. It was Charlie who could not help himself and immediately dived under the ropes to congratulate Sullivan.

Following the shout of the assistant cornerman, there came a couple more cheers from the crowd, but the rest of the audience remained silent, some began to talk quietly to each other. Most of them were disappointed. It seemed to the audience that Sullivan's victory was just an incredibly rare fluke, and they were thereby stripped of the pleasure to watch the magnificent spectacle of the young fighter dealing away with an upstart white collar."

Gerard McKee did not want to admit to himself that he shared this opinion. Moreover, somewhere deep inside, he would have preferred Sullivan's loss to such an outcome. But only a decent loss. McKee would have preferred that his pupil remained standing courageously throughout all the twelve rounds and, even despite the loss on points, he would have proven to everyone that he was a real boxer. And such a victory was nothing but the triumph of a banana peel over someone who had slipped on it.

But the old man tried to shove those thoughts to the very back of his head and put on a happy smile, getting in the ring and congratulating Sullivan on his victory. Jack himself also did not share the enthusiasm of Charlie and Kate, who joined him. Not because he thought the victory was undeserved, but because he did not care about any of the victories except for one – the final one, for the IPBU champion title against the current belt holder Joe Ryan. The man whose laughing face came to him in nightmares at least once a week.

..17..

In celebration of Sullivan's first victory, the old man decided to cancel the next training session and arrange a get-together night of watching boxing instead. It just so happened that the reason for that was most suitable – the IPBU Welterweight champion Joe Ryan was going to defend his title for the tenth time. In case of his victory over the challenger Carlos Vargas, Ryan would set the second record in the history of IPBU for the number of defenses in his weight category.

"I take it this is how you show up for a boxing night?" Sullivan said as a greeting, crossing the threshold of One-Two Boxing and handing a pack of beer to the old man, who opened the door to him.

"Heh-heh, it looks like the first victory finally turned you into a real man," McKee responded, taking the beer with one hand and shaking the guest's outstretched palm with the other. "And will you look at that, you guessed to come in sports, after all! I was starting to fear you'd show up in your ten-thousand-dollar suit."

"I only have a three-thousand-dollar suit anyway," Jack added quietly, walking into the gym and greeting Charlie on the way.

"Cool suit. Adidas Originals?" Charlie said, shaking Jack's hand. "Come into the office. All our folks are already there. The fight is about to begin."

There was a small rearrangement in the old man's office – the TV that had been gathering dust in the corner was placed opposite the couch. There were two armchairs on either side of it. A small table appeared in front of the couch, on which there were already put at least a dozen bottles and cans of beer, as well as simple snacks. Apart from Derrick and Kate, whom Jack greeted with a nod, there were two men in the office who were not familiar to him.

"Jack, meet Chuck Duran," the old man addressed Sullivan, leading him to the first one of the strangers. "Chuck is your new cutman."

Jack gave McKee a slightly surprised look, then shook the extended hand.

"And don't you look at me like that. If you're gonna continue fighting, you can't go without a professional cutman. You can keep those two clowns in your corner if you want to," McKee nodded in the direction of Charlie and Kate. "But without a real cutman, I just won't let you into the ring anymore. You can't imagine how often some lousy cutman becomes the reason for a TKO of a fighter who, if not for a cut, might as well have won. Watch Lennox Lewis versus Vitali Klitschko sometime. Lewis took only two of the six rounds, but the fight was stopped because of Klitschko's cut. The whole stadium booed Lewis, but the victory was still awarded to him. If not for that and for the fight against Byrd, where Klitschko also led on points but tore his rotator cuff, Doctor Ironfist would remain undefeated. Both times Klitschko was defeated not by his rivals, but by his own body and the bad job of the team, which was supposed to be responsible for proper physical training and work during breaks."

"Nice to meet you, sir," Jack said to the cutman. "I'm glad you will become a part of our team."

A short man in his fifties with gray hair on his temples and a bushy mustache only nodded in response.

"Chuck talks roughly twice a year," McKee said with a grin. "For this, I like him even more than for wonders he does with cuts."

"Pops, they're starting to present the fighters already," Derrick said.

"Yeah," the old man replied and hurried to introduce the

second stranger to Jack. "Kevin Norris. Starting tomorrow, he's your new sparring partner. Sure enough, he's not as handsome as Derrick, but he's in your weight category. Enough screwing around like amateurs. Now you're officially a professional boxer and you need a professional welterweight sparring partner."

"Nice to meet you," getting up from the couch and offering his hand to Jack, said a man with a shaved head and piercing blue eyes, who was about five years younger than Sullivan.

"Likewise," Jack replied to the greeting, feeling the firmness of the new sparring partner's handshake.

"Pops, the referee's already giving the last instructions, they'll start shortly," Derrick warned again.

"Yeah, come on, Jack, have a seat. If you really wanna become a pro, then you gotta learn from the best."

Sullivan settled down on the couch next to Charlie and Kate. The woman handed Jack a bottle of mineral water kept especially for him. He responded with a grateful smile.

...

– So, there are only a few seconds left before the start of the most anticipated fight of this year. I remind for those who have just tuned in to our broadcast. Today, right now, IPBU Welterweight champion Joe Ryan will defend his title for the tenth time. He is opposed by Carlos Vargas. Both fighters have perfect records, which makes today's fight especially interesting. And now we are starting!

Ryan immediately advances on the opponent, shooting Vargas with fast punches from all sides. It's only a probing yet, Ryan doesn't invest in punches in order to be able to quickly go into defense. Vargas was clearly ready for such a start. He doesn't pay attention to the opponent's blows and, on the contrary, tries to respond with proper punches, hoping to catch Ryan with a counterblow. A good hook by Ryan. And another one in the same *spot. No wonder Ryan was dubbed 'can-opener'. This fighter can find a weak spot in any defense, even the most solid one. Wow! Vargas finds himself on the canvas. Another hook from Ryan knocks down the opponent. Less than a minute has passed since the beginning of the round, but emotions are already running high.*

...

"I told you Ryan was going to take care of this upstart in the first round!" Kevin exclaimed happily, turning to Derrick.

"Wait a bit, don't get too excited. I promise you they'll dance all twelve rounds straight. Vargas won't give up so easily."

"I also think that Ryan will win ahead of the game!" Charlie cut in. "He's been the best Welterweight since Sugar Ray Robinson!"

"Oh, like you have a clue!" McKee said and tousled the boy's hair.

Kevin and Derrick joined the old man and also began to make fun of Charlie, showering him with a hail of questions on who else of the boxers he considered the best and whether Ryan, in his opinion, could beat Rambo and the Ninja Turtles. Meanwhile, none of them noticed how intently Sullivan was looking at the screen. He literally did not take his eyes off the champion for a second, chasing him like a cat chases a laser pointer dot running about on the floor.

...

– Wow! What a splendid first round! Joe Ryan's shown himself a true champion. Already at the fifteenth second, he sent the challenger to the first knockdown in his career. But, we've got to give it to Vargas. Despite the missed punches, he managed to pull himself together, regain his breath due to the competent work in clinch and even go into the counterattack. Of course, the first round is undoubtedly taken by the champion, but its ending can be fairly given to Vargas.

And now we're moving on to the second round. Vargas rushes to the attack, intending to rehabilitate himself for the beginning of the first round. A good left hook follows, but Ryan knows how to defend himself just as well as how to attack. The referee breaks the clinch and Vargas rushes to the attack again. A great combination. Vargas doesn't give Ryan the opportunity to go into a counterattack.

...

"I told you Vargas wouldn't give up so easily!" Derrick exclaimed happily. "Now this Ryan of yours can well end up on the canvas!"

"If Vargas only attacks all the time, he won't last long," McKee stated with authority. "Ryan just allows him to work at defense, exhausting him. He acts very competently. Watch carefully, Jack. You've plenty to learn from Ryan."

Sullivan did not react to the coach's remark, only squeezing the bottle of mineral water so tightly that if not for the cap being tightly screwed, half of the liquid would have burst out like a fountain.

...

– There's less than a minute left until the end of the second round, and Vargas is still attacking. Clearly, the absolute majority of his punches landed on the defense, but still for the initiative this round will undoubtedly be scored in his favor. Whoo! Ryan performs an uppercut from defense and Vargas finds himself back on the canvas. The second round and the second knockdown! Looks like I was too quick to give this round to the challenger after all. Vargas is back on his feet. There are fifteen seconds left until the end of the round and now Ryan switches to the attack. I'm afraid this fight might end right here and right now. But Vargas is saved by the bell. The second round is over and, perhaps, here we've got a draw. Sure, Vargas dominated almost the entire round except for the last thirty seconds, but his punches had no effect on the

champion, which Ryan proved by knocking down his opponent for the second time, after which he attacked him with such a hail of punches that, if not for the gong, Vargas had every chance to lose by technical knockout.

...

"Well, I told you so," Kevin turned to Derrick. "Ryan is a real killer. There's no such Vargas to hold a candle to him. The killer!!!"

Kevin took a large gulp of beer and continued to praise the current champion in unison with the commentator, who during the break began to recite all of Joe Ryan's previous achievements and records. Charlie started repeating after him. McKee also said a few words of praise about Ryan. And even Kate joined the conversation for the first time, saying that, in her opinion, Joe Ryan was very cute.

Sullivan was the only one to sit silently, not taking his eyes off the TV screen. However, now he seemed to be looking through it. When the third round began, Ryan went on the attack again and drew first blood, cutting his opponent's eyebrow with a straight left punch. The audience met the punch with a wild delight. Kevin and Charlie started chanting the champion's name.

Finally, when Kevin shouted 'Kill him!!!' in response to another successful attack of the champion, Sullivan snapped and, muttering something about having to go to the toilet, hurried out of the office. Meanwhile, in the ring, despite Ryan's successful attacks, the challenger still remained on his feet and from time to time even managed to perform a successful counterattack.

Everyone present was so carried away by the fight that no one paid attention to the fact that Sullivan had been missing for three rounds straight. No one would possibly have noticed his absence until the very end of the fight, but McKee himself needed to release some of the contents of the six bottles of beer he drank during the first five rounds of the fight.

Going out into the gym, the old man noticed Sullivan, who had gotten rid of his sports jacket and T-shirt and was practicing on the punching bag.

"Aha, so that's where you are! Well done, Jack!" McKee said as he hurried to the toilet. "Go on, practice what Joe Ryan just taught you."

Sullivan met the coach's last words with a frantic combination that almost ripped the punching bag off the hook. But the old man did not see that, as he disappeared behind the toilet door. Only after getting rid of, probably, half a gallon of liquid, and already walking slowly around the gym, McKee finally paid attention to how exactly Jack was practicing his punches.

"Holy shit! What're you doing?!" The old man blurted in surprise and hurried toward his pupil. "Why the fuck are you punching without gloves and even hand wraps on!?! Are you crazy!?! You're gonna damage your hands, and we're having the next fight in a month!"

Sullivan did not react to the coach's words and continued to beat the punching bag furiously.

"Jack!" McKee shouted and, without waiting for his pupil's reaction, caught his hand on the fly.

Simultaneously, several drops of blood landed on the old man's face. McKee paid no attention to that, but only brought Jack's fist closer to his face. Both the knuckles and all the first phalanges of his fingers were already bleeding.

"Jack, what the fuck!" the old man snapped, shifting his gaze from the pupil's fist to his face.

The coach was surprised to find tears on Sullivan's face.

"Jack, what's happening!?!"

Sullivan left the old man's words unanswered. Instead, he pulled his hand out of McKee's palm and dashed toward the locker room.

"Jack!" The old man hurried after him. "What on earth is going on?"

Without stopping, Sullivan forcefully swung open the door to the locker room, so that it hit the wall and broke a tile with its handle.

"Jack!" the old man shouted as he entered the locker room following his pupil. "What the fuck is going on!?! Talk to me!"

Sullivan made a circle around the locker room, bypassing the long bench installed in the middle of it and, meeting the coach's eyes, finally answered, "Joe Ryan – that's what's going on!"

Sullivan's voice was trembling. Both from the tears and the rage that overwhelmed him.

"What about him?" the old man asked uncomprehendingly.

Instead of answering, Jack let out either a cry of rage or a groan of pain. He swung his bloody fist, intending to slam it into the metal door of one of the lockers, but the coach intercepted the blow timely. If McKee had not done that, Sullivan would have surely broken at least a couple of fingers.

Fearing that Jack would make a new attempt to break loose, the old man turned him around sharply and pressed his back against the very locker door with the help of which he had just intended to destroy his boxing career. The old man's huge palm covered most of his pupil's chest.

"Jack, stop it!" McKee spoke threateningly, but at the same time caringly. "You'll only harm yourself with this! What's happened with you and Joe Ryan? Why are you running mad here?"

Once again Sullivan unsuccessfully tried to escape from the old man's iron embrace, lowered his gaze, wiped his tears with his free hand while smearing blood over his face, and only then answered, "Joe Ryan killed my husband."

"What? What do you mean? Jacob's dead? I saw him only yesterday!?!" The old man spoke dumbfounded. "How's that?"

"Joe Ryan killed my husband two years ago. What you saw is not my husband. It's just a shell which retains some ragged scraps of the source code."

Shocked by his pupil's confession, McKee lowered his hands. Jack squeezed himself between the wall of lockers and the old man, moved aside, and sat down on the far end of the bench. Resting his elbows on his knees, Sullivan hid his face in his palms. For a moment, McKee thought Jack was going to start crying again, but he spoke in a surprisingly calm voice. All the rage had vacated his body, having left only quiet despair inside him.

"I take care of him, feed him, put him to bed, talk to him for hours, snuggle him in my arms all night when he can't sleep. But it's not Jacob. He doesn't even recognize me half of the time. Sometimes he won't utter a single word for a few days straight, sometimes, on the contrary, he can talk some nonsense for hours. Sometimes he remembers something from our past. Something simple, like a painting that was hanging on the wall in our first apartment. And sometimes he perceives something he saw in a movie or on TV as a memory from our life."

Jack took a deep breath, nervously ran his hand through his hair, and continued, "Once he started crying because I couldn't remember the name of our dog. We've never had a dog. Then he remembered the name himself. Lassie. Freaking Lassie. He was sobbing and shouting at me because I couldn't remember that we'd once had a damned collie."

Finally, the emotions lost their grip on Jack so that he could feel the pain in his bleeding fists. He grimaced, flexing his numb fingers. The old man noticed that and hurried to get the first-aid kit from the top of the locker.

"I love Jacob. I've always loved him and still do. I'll never stop caring for him, I'll never leave him. But it's not him anymore. I die inside every time I come home and meet his eye. It's not Jacob. Now he has only two looks on his face – an absent one, as if at the moment his brain's in a hibernation mode, or a look of the five-year-old child. The one who already knows how to talk and do something, but it's still a far cry from a fully developed person. Now I don't see Jacob in his eyes anymore. My Jacob. Cheerful, joyful, intelligent, passionate about a million occasions from having wine to a good game of chess. My Jacob died two years ago. My Jacob was killed by Joe Ryan."

McKee finally found hydrogen peroxide and cotton pads in the first-aid kit. The old man took Jack's right palm in his hands and began to carefully wipe his fingers from the already dried blood.

"Jack...," the old man spoke awkwardly, making long pauses after each word he uttered. "I don't know what to say and do in such cases. I'm awfully bad at this sort of thing. So I apologize upfront for things I'm gonna say wrong, or on the contrary for not saying something that has to be said. I don't know if I can ask you what happened to Jacob and what Joe Ryan has to do with it. If I can even mention his name or not. Jack..." McKee put aside the peroxide and the cotton pad and began to bandage his pupil's damaged fist. "I know only one thing – I'm ready to listen to whatever you'd want to tell me yourself. Or we can just sit in silence. I don't know what's gonna be best for you. Just know that I'm here, I'm not going anywhere. I've lost loved ones too. And I haven't talked to anyone about it yet. But maybe I should've after all. I don't know, Jack. It's up to you. I'm with you, whatever you decide."

After finishing speaking, the old man began to treat and bandage Sullivan's second bloody fist. Jack was silent. Having finished with the medical procedures, the old man got up from the bench, put the first-aid kit back in its place, and hesitated at the door. He did not know if he should say anything else, or maybe, on the contrary, go out and leave Sullivan alone.

McKee almost inclined to the second option when Jack suddenly broke the silence.

"Once you said that you and Mr. Sifaretto used to sit on the roof a lot," Sullivan asked, although his words did not sound like a question.

"Yes, all the time. Almost every day," the old man

answered.

"Can we go up there now?"

"Of course, I'll just fetch the keys from the office."

"Gerard," Jack called out to the old man when the he had already crossed the threshold of the locker room. "Just don't tell anyone about all this. Tell them I just had to go do something else urgently."

"Of course. I wasn't going to."

The old man turned back toward the exit, but Jack called out to him again, "And you know what, maybe take some whiskey with you as well."

McKee smiled and hurried to the office. After a couple of minutes, both were standing on the roof. It was the first time the old man had set foot here since Johnny Sifaretto passed away. And it was also the first time he was standing here with someone other than his best friend, manager, and business partner. The picture that unfolded before McKee stirred a whole storm of emotions in him – both positive and negative.

On the one hand, the old man remembered all those evenings they spent here with Johnny, recalling the glorious past, making plans for the future, laughing, and slowly sipping beer. On the other hand, the picture of desolation that appeared before McKee became another reminder that the only thing he had done since the death of his best friend was wasting his legacy.

A long time ago, when they were just starting the One-Two Boxing business, Johnny set a very cozy place here with an artificial lawn, a pair of comfortable loungers, soft lighting, and other small mercies. Being unattended for years, all of it had turned yellow and flaked, got covered with dirt, rust, and mold from the sun, rain, and wind. And now the once wonderful place for friendly gatherings looked more like a wasteland somewhere near a trailer park, where locals dump old stuff.

"Hey, are you okay?" Jack asked, noticing that the old man seemed to have frozen.

"Huh? Yeah, yeah, I'm fine," McKee replied. "I just haven't been here for a long time. Here you go."

The old man handed Jack the glasses and hurried to open the bottle of whiskey.

"Real, Irish," McKee added, pouring the golden liquid into the glasses.

After doing that, the old man put the bottle on the roof parapet and took his glass from Jack's hands. Nodding to his pupil, McKee threw the first portion of whiskey down his throat with a customary gesture. Jack tried to repeat that movement, but he did not "throw" fast enough, and the strong drink burnt his mouth and throat, which were not accustomed to such a thing. Sullivan started coughing and almost dropped his glass.

"Went smooth, right?" the old man said with a smile and patted his pupil on the back.

"I can't even imagine how you do it. It's like drinking fire," Jack replied, after having cleared his throat at last.

"That's the whole point of it," McKee added with a grin. "Let's drink the second one. Take your time now. Take small sips. The first one's burning hot, and the second one warms you down."

McKee poured a second portion of whiskey into the glasses. Jack did not refuse, but he did not hold the glass up to his lips either. Instead, he decided to walk with it along the parapet, gazing thoughtfully into the dark sky. The old man was dying to find out what happened to Jacob two years ago, and what the famous champion had to do with it, but he was too afraid that his insensitivity could make Jack fall back into that state of furious frenzy that almost cost him his future career.

It took at least fifteen minutes of awkward silence, during which the old man managed to drink three more shots before Jack finally spoke.

"We were driving home after visiting friends," Sullivan began without any preamble and took a sip of whiskey. He grimaced and continued. "While waiting at the intersection, Jacob got interested in the sign of a bar and its massive antique wooden doors. He suggested that we come in. Jacob liked to do that. He often said that the most interesting places were never found where you were heading to. We went in. The bar was half empty. Five more people, at most. We sat down at a table. I ordered coffee, Jacob asked for a glass of wine. The place turned out to be very pleasant – cozy, with vintage furniture and good music. About twenty minutes after we arrived, four men barged into the bar. They were tipsy already. They stood at the bar counter, talking loudly, laughing, swearing a lot – fuck this, fuck that, fuck everything and so on and so forth."

Sullivan took the second sip of whiskey, put the glass on the parapet, and began to run his hand over its rough concrete surface.

"Such things always get on my nerves," Sullivan continued, without going into details about the fact that drunk men had been scaring him since the very childhood, as his drunken father beat him and his mother. "Jacob noticed it right away and tried to distract me. Besides, our song, *Rocket Man*, just started playing. Yes, yes, I know how unoriginal it is for a gay couple to choose an Elton John piece as their song," Jack added, turning to McKee.

The old man pretended to understand what Sullivan was talking about, although in fact, McKee had no idea what Rocket Man was, and all he knew about Elton John was that he had something to do with show business. Music, as well as cinema, literature, and other art forms had never been included in the retired boxer's sphere of interests.

"Jacob dragged me to dance," Jack said after a pause and another sip of whiskey. "It was actually very romantic. I immediately remembered the times right after we'd first met. But it didn't last long. A group of tipsy men quickly started throwing dirty jokes in our direction. If, of course, homophobic insults could be called jokes at all. I wanted to leave immediately, but Jacob isn't like me. He always said that we'd be able to defeat homophobia only when we stopped being afraid of it ourselves. When Elton said 'And I think it's gonna be a long long time' for the last time, we went to our table. Jacob insisted that we finish our drinks before leaving. The drunken thugs wouldn't calm down. Their sharp remarks kept reaching our table. Jacob wanted to calm them, but I stopped him. Jacob was never afraid of anyone. Just when we finished our drinks and asked for the bill, a handful of peanuts flew at Jacob's back, which amused the friends of the drunken gang leader who'd thrown it. After that, I wasn't able to stop Jacob. He got up and walked boldly toward them. Jacob's always been fearless. I got distracted for a moment by a waiter who came up with the bill, and when I turned back to Jacob, I saw the scumbags leader's fist smash into my husband's face. I hurried to him, but I was too late. The blow was so strong that Jacob dropped on the spot. And hit his head on the granite floor." Jack stopped talking to take another sip of whiskey. "When I ran up to him, there was already a small pool of blood under the back of his head. I started screaming, calling for help. Someone called 911. That bastard's friends shouted that it was time for them to get out. I looked up and met the eye of their leader, the one who hit Jacob. When he noticed that I was looking directly at him, he laughed. He laughed, said 'fucking fagots', and left. He didn't even run away. He just left slowly, as if nothing had happened."

Sullivan finished the rest of the whiskey and handed the glass to McKee, making it clear that he needed another portion. The old man was so astounded by Jack's story that it took him some time to figure out what Sullivan wanted from him.

"When the ambulance arrived, my entire jacket was already covered in Jacob's blood. I tried to put pressure on the wound with it, but the blood kept coming. At the hospital, Jacob was sent straight to the OR. The injury caused brain herniation and he needed decompressive craniectomy. While Jacob was having the surgery, the cops arrived. I told them everything, described the bastard who hit him. I even remembered all of his clothes. A black Versace polo with a golden pattern on the collar, a black and red Givenchy bomber jacket, a finger-thick golden chain around his neck. I still remember it all in great detail, as if that all happened yesterday."

Sullivan took the first sip of his new portion of whiskey. Although he was not accustomed to alcohol, the whiskey he drank did not seem to have any effect on him.

"Jacob fell into a coma. I spent three days in the hospital. I drank shitty coffee and ate chocolate bars from a vending machine. On the fourth day, the medical staff literally pushed me out of the department. I had to take a shower, shave, change clothes. But instead of going home, I went to the police station first. I thought they must've caught the bastard by that time already. After all, I gave such an accurate description, and there were at least five witnesses in the bar besides myself, and even cameras inside and outside. Instead, I found that the police refused to open a case. The cops visited the bar. There was nobody there anymore, except for the bartender. He told them that Jacob had been drunk, he'd slipped, fallen, and hit his head. That's all. The cameras in the bar were allegedly hung just for show, and they didn't record anything. There were no other witnesses. At the hospital, the doctors confirmed that there was alcohol in Jacob's blood. One freaking glass of wine, but it was enough for them. Case closed. And no matter what I said about the attack, I didn't have any evidence. I came home completely devastated. I didn't understand what had happened. Why did the bartender lie? Where did the other witnesses go? At first I thought that scumbag might've been some kind of local gang member, and the bartender was scared of him. But then everything fell into place."

Jack drank the rest of the whiskey in one go and started turning the glass in his hand, looking at it so intently, as if it was a unique piece of art.

"To distract myself from all those terrible thoughts, I turned on the TV. On one of the channels there was showbiz news. There was something about an athlete who got behind the wheel drunk a couple of days ago and crashed into a lamppost. Then there was a phone recorded video, where the police questioned a guy leaning against a red Ferrari with a broken bumper and a dented hood. It was him. The same black polo with a golden pattern on the collar, the same black and red bomber jacket, and the same finger-thick golden chain around his neck. Just an hour after he attacked Jacob, that bastard crashed his Ferrari, while almost running over a couple who were crossing the street on a crosswalk. Can you guess who that athlete was?" Jack asked, turning to McKee.

"Joe Ryan," the old man replied.

"The most highly paid boxer in history, an ambassador of Adidas, TAG Heuer and Beluga vodka, the IPBU Welterweight world champion, lucky Joe Ryan," Sullivan said fiercely through his teeth and threw the glass over the roof parapet with all his might.

The glass flew at least a few dozen feet before hitting the asphalt of the alley, which was deserted at this hour, and smashing into millions of shards.

"I hope it wasn't a very important glass given to you by some famous boxer or the last thing you have left from your father?" Jack addressed McKee in a surprisingly calm voice.

"Made in China. It's 99 cents in the store next door," the old man replied.

Jack smiled sadly at the corners of his mouth and continued, "You probably think why I decided to take revenge on Joe Ryan in such an idiotic and almost impossible way, instead of suing him, contacting the media or, if nothing else, hiring a killer to bump him off?"

"Kid, you think too highly of my mental abilities," McKee answered. "I'm actually still digesting your story. Jack, it's terrible..."

With a gesture, Sullivan cut the old man short.

"Gerard, I already know that you empathize with me. Please, no condolences. I've heard so many of them over the last two years that they make me sick. I just want to tell you the rest of it, so that we'd never have to return to this conversation again."

"Sure, Jack, whatever goes best for you," the old man replied and handed his glass to his pupil. "Do you want to throw the second one? I'll put it on your tab."

Jack once again smiled sadly in response.

"Just pour me some more whiskey."

The old man happily complied with Sullivan's request, after which he himself took a couple of sips straight from the bottle.

"I tried to do it differently. I tried everything. I filed reports to police chiefs and the prosecutor's office, sent lawyers to them, filed civil claims. I hired private detectives. The first one said that he'd found one of the witnesses – the one who'd called 911, and also a recording from a street surveillance camera that showed Ryan's Ferrari coming around the corner of the building where the bar was located, just a minute after the call. But when I came to his office to get the evidence, the detective told me he hadn't said anything like that. Then I hired a second detective. He found the camera and uncovered the name of the witness. But it turned out the recording from the camera was taken by someone very similar to the first detective, the witness disappeared from the city, and the first detective himself unexpectedly came into possession of a brand new Dodge Charger. I suppose Joe Ryan offered a much higher price for the evidence, and the witness was either bribed or intimidated. The bartender the police were talking to also suddenly decided to move to Florida. I found him there, but he wouldn't talk to me, even when I offered him three thousand dollars for it. And the next day he disappeared from Florida. I tried to involve the media, but even TMZ refused to cover my story, as I had no proof."

Sullivan finished another portion of whiskey and handed the glass to McKee.

"I was thinking about a killer, too. You will be surprised,

but there's no one among my acquaintances who can put me in touch with an elite assassin ready to get a shot at an international star, who, on top of that, always walks with a whole crowd of entourage. So I couldn't think of anything better than to meet the bastard in the ring."

Sullivan turned his back to the parapet and for the first time looked McKee straight in the eye.

"Gerard, I understand that what I'm going to say now will sound insulting to you and after that you might not even want to train me anymore, but I want to come clean with you."

"Sure! Shoot," the old man replied.

"I don't give a shit about boxing, I don't give a shit about the ring, I don't give a shit about victories and I don't give a shit about the championship title. All I want is to humiliate Joe Ryan in front of everyone. I want to make him bleed, make him feel pain. I want to destroy his legacy. I want to take away from him what he loves the most. I want to take his glory. I want him to finally lose. And not just lose, but lose to fucking fagot. And I want everyone to see it."

As he spoke, Jack clenched his fists so tightly that fresh blood showed through the bandages. Sullivan and McKee looked at each other in silence for some time until the old man finally shrugged his shoulders and said, "Taking revenge for a loved one is a much more valid reason to box than just wanting to get a piece of iron glued to your belt," McKee said and added. "If there was a sport in the world which could help me get even with the intracranial aneurysm that killed Johnny, I'd put on tights right away and go get ready for a figure skating championship."

Sullivan smiled, McKee smiled too, and then they both started laughing, imagining the old man in tights spinning on ice. Having laughed heartily, McKee gave Jack a friendly slap on the shoulder with a familiar gesture and said, "Thank you for telling me the whole truth. I appreciate it, Kid. And you may not worry – your secret is safe with me."

"I know, Gerard, I know. That's why I told you

everything."

Having said that, Sullivan experienced a slight pang of guilt. After all, he had not really told the old man the whole truth. He kept to himself the most important thing – he was not going to just humiliate Joe Ryan by defeating him in a fair fight and taking away his championship title. Jack planned to kill him. Right there, in the ring. In front of thousands of spectators in the arena and millions of TV viewers around the world.

Sullivan did not tell the old man that even before he first came to One-Two Boxing, he had studied in detail several hundred deaths due to injuries sustained in boxing, about which he could find information on the Internet, and even interviewed a dozen doctors, pretending to be a journalist who was writing an article for Sports Illustrated.

Jack Sullivan knew exactly how, when, and where to hit in such a way that Joe Ryan would never be able to enter the ring again. He was never going to seriously learn how to box, he just needed someone who would make him capable of getting to the fight where he could deliver that crucial blow.

..18..

"The first participant of our fight today enters the ring – twenty-three-year-old Patrick Crawford. It's his fifth fight. In his debut fight Crawford was confidently leading on points in all the first ten rounds and the eleventh round was about to end with an early victory by technical knockout, but, surprisingly for everyone present at that fight, Crawford ran into a blindly thrown punch of his opponent Steve Joshua and found himself in knockout, which was far from technical. We've got to give it to Crawford, the first defeat only spurred the young fighter and since then not only hasn't he lost in a single fight, but also won all the next four of them by knockout no later than the fifth round.

And here we've got Patrick Crawford's opponent, Internet sensation Jack Sullivan, who also got into the ring. Sullivan has only one fight and one victory to his name. But what a victory! It took Sullivan only a second and a half to knock out Rick Stanton. And this became the fastest KO in the history of IPBU.

"I'm sorry to interrupt, Harry, but it's worth mentioning that Rick Stanton has already managed to rehabilitate himself after that defeat. Just yesterday, in the second round he knocked out a very experienced fighter, Pedro Mendez, who had under his belt twenty-three fights and only two defeats, both of which were a split decision."

"Yes, yes, Stan, I was going to say that myself. It was a splendid fight and a very nice and confident victory for Stanton. Which makes our today's fight even more interesting. Immediately after the Stanton vs. Sullivan fight, the record of the fastest knockout in the history of IPBU went viral on YouTube. Even before the end of the day, it was viewed by more than two hundred thousand people and at least several thousand of them left their comments. Opinions of the public were divided almost equally. Some praised Sullivan's speed and accuracy, while others said it was just a fluke."

"Or on the contrary – a bad break, if viewed from Stanton's perspective."

"Yes, yes, exactly. Sullivan got hugely lucky and, Stanton, perhaps, even more unlucky."

"Besides, yesterday Rick Stanton himself added fuel to the fire during a press conference after the fight with Mendez. He confirmed the opinion of many viewers that Sullivan just got lucky, and added that he acted incompetently and unprofessionally. According to Stanton, if not for pure chance, Sullivan's decision to throw a punch instead of going into defense would undoubtedly have resulted in him ending up on the canvas himself.

"Stan, blaming chance for your defeat is, unfortunately, a very common and sad tactic of many young fighters, but the chance can't be dismissed either. Even great champions sometimes lost that way. In this case, time will clear things up. And if Sullivan was indeed just lucky, then maybe now we'll see Patrick Crawford put an end to the dispute."

"And right now we're starting! Here comes the bell!"

"No way!!!"

"I can't believe it! It's incredible!"

"How could this happen?!? I've no words to describe it!"

"He did it again!"

"Perhaps, Crawford will still get back on his feet?"

"No, it's over! The referee officially declared a knockout!"

"It's just unbelievable! Ladies and gentlemen, you and I have just witnessed the rarest natural phenomenon – lightning struck the same place twice! Jack Sullivan knocked out his opponent with the first punch again!"

"Not only did he just win by a lightning-fast knockout again, but even did it the same way – with a right cross to the jaw!"

"Attention! I'm receiving a message from the judges. The first and last punch of this fight, which knocked Patrick Crawford *out, was made in the second second. Yes, this is no longer a record, but it's the second fastest knockout in the history of IPBU, which makes Jack Sullivan the holder of a unique achievement – he has both the first and second fastest knockouts in the history of IPBU on his record! Such thing's never happened before!"*

"Harry, I've also received an equally interesting message. With this victory, Jack Sullivan set a unique record in the history of not only IPBU but boxing in general. He became the only boxer who has as much as two records at once in the list of the twenty fastest knockouts in history. Plus, both of his records also got into the top five."

"Wow, Stan, I'm telling you, if the credit doesn't go to Jack Sullivan himself, then it should be black magic, to say the least!"

...

Charlie made a dash for the ring as soon as Patrick Crawford landed on the canvas, but McKee grabbed the boy by the uniform T-shirt with the "Team Sullivan" inscription on the back and jerked him back before he could grab the ropes.

"Where are you going! The fight's not finished yet!" the old man growled to the Charlie's ear in an angry whisper.

But as soon as the referee officially announced the knockout, even the huge and still very strong hand of the old man could not contain Charlie. Had McKee not let go of Charlie's T-shirt at the last moment, it would undoubtedly have stayed in his fist, and the boy would have ended up shirtless in the ring.

"YOU WON!!! YOU WON!!! YOU DID IT!!!" Running up to Jack, Charlie yelled so loudly that for a moment his still boyish ringing voice interrupted all the other sounds of the hall filled with several hundred spectators, at least half of whom jumped up from their seats and also started shouting.

Judging by the expression on Sullivan's face, Charlie's yells struck him a lot more than his own victory. Jack smiled shyly and put his hands on the boy's shoulders, trying to calm him down, but Charlie only got more worked up. He crouched down, wrapped his arms around Sullivan's hips, and lifted him into the air. The young assistant cornerman was so excited that he managed not only to lift a short, yet still adult man who weighed noticeably more than him but also to swing him in his arms until Derrick got into the ring.

The former heavyweight boxer easily took away Charlie's burden and lifted Jack even higher.

"Raise your glove, Jack!" he shouted, lifting up his head. "Greet the audience!"

Getting even more embarrassed, Sullivan complied with the request and triumphantly raised his glove above his head. Only after that did Derrick put him down – it was time for Jack to be officially declared the winner. The obligatory formalities were followed by a short interview for a local TV channel, after which Sullivan went off to the locker room to get changed.

And all that time Charlie was dying with the feelings that overwhelmed him: "Jack! Their Jack!! Their Jack has won again!!! Their Jack knocked the opponent out again!!!! Their Jack won with the first punch again!!!!!" The boy was jigging about outside the locker room door, waiting for Sullivan to finally come out.

"WE MUST GO CELEBRATE!" Charlie shouted right in Jack's face as soon as he cracked the door open.

Slightly stunned by such a greeting, Sullivan smiled at Charlie and politely but insistently moved him aside so that he could go out to the rest of his team members, who were standing at the opposite wall of the corridor.

"Guys, thank you all for your support and help today..."

"Sure thing," Derrick interrupted Jack. "We've done so much today. Getting from the locker room to the ring and back in five minutes is a very difficult job."

McKee grinned at his assistant's ironic remark.

"Yeah, sorry I once again deprived you of the opportunity to work during breaks," Jack replied in the same ironic way. "Guys, I really hate to leave you right after the fight, but I need to go home. Jacob had an episode again. It's nothing serious, everything will be fine, but I'd better be with him now."

"Of course, Jack, you should go. No need to apologize," the old man answered for everyone and slapped his pupil on the shoulder. "You did well today, kid. We are proud of you!"

"Thank you, Gerard," Jack replied, shaking the outstretched hand. "And thank you guys, too."

Sullivan also shook hands with Derrick and Charlie, and gallantly kissed Kate's gentle hand, which was the only one there that was smaller than Jack's own hand. After that, Sullivan hurried to the back exit, leaving Charlie in utter disappointment. The boy was already imagining all of them going to some posh bar together, swinging Jack in their arms, singing songs in his honor, and how maybe the old man would take pity and even let him drink at least a glass of beer.

After Sullivan had left, the boy still suggested that the others go celebrate without the winner, but Kate and Derrick said they had to go about their own business, and McKee burst into loud laughter when Charlie put forward the idea of just the two of them visiting a bar.

"Let's go, kiddo, grab your stuff. I'll give you a ride home," Derrick spoke to him when the old man was finally done laughing.

After making up with McKee, Charlie moved out from Jack's place and returned to his former tiny apartment not far from One-Two Boxing. Sullivan did not want to let him go, but the boy insisted on his decision, saying that "the real man should be independent."

So now, instead of a grand celebration of Sullivan's second victory, Charlie was met only by an old PlayStation, an even older TV, and the remains of yesterday's pizza in a box, which was sitting snugly on the floor between the TV and a bowed mattress that served Charlie as a bed.

After getting rid of his sneakers, yet not wanting to take off the T-shirt with the inscription "Team Sullivan", the boy flopped down on the mattress. The pizza was already a bit dry but it was nothing Charlie's teeth could not handle. So the boy decided to give it a second chance.

As soon as he turned on the TV, it immediately showed the title screen of his favorite game, boxing simulator 'Real Fight'. Charlie picked up his gamepad from the floor, but instead of continuing a previous game, he decided to change his character – Andy Gomez – to a new one, for the creation of which the boy went to the editor.

Charlie no longer wanted to play as a fictional best Mexican boxer in history, who won his first professional fight when he was fifteen, and by the age of seventeen had already won the title of heavyweight champion. Now the boy wanted to fight as a rookie, who had only two fights under his belt.

Charlie typed in 'Jack Sullivan' and began diligently recreating the appearance of his new most beloved boxer in the world. The options available in the old game only allowed for creating someone that looked more like a police composite sketch of Jack Sullivan, rather than a real person, but Charlie still liked it.

For the next three hours and three pieces of half-dried pizza, the boy was taking pains to repeat Sullivan's achievements and knock out his opponent with a single punch, although he knew perfectly well that in this game it was technically impossible. Weary from the intense experiences of the day and the equally intense gaming session, Charlie fell asleep without undressing and without turning off the PlayStation.

The next morning he was woken up by a phone call.

"Charlie? Did I wake you up?" Jack's voice came from the phone.

"No, no, it's fine," Charlie answered sleepily, sitting up on the mattress.

There was a cross standing out vividly on his cheek, imprinted over a night spent with a gamepad propped under his head instead of a pillow.

"Are you busy right now?" Sullivan asked.

"Me? Not really, I guess."

"Can I drive over to your place in about half an hour? I want to take you somewhere."

"In half an hour? Yeah, okay," Charlie replied and yawned deeply.

"See you then."

"Yep, see you," Charlie said, and instead of getting up, he flopped down on the mattress again, this time without forgetting to put a real pillow under his head.

When, exactly half an hour later, the phone rang again, Charlie jumped up in hot haste and, having pressed the speaker mode button, began to run chaotically around his tiny apartment, changing clothes and washing his face at the same time.

"Charlie, I'm downstairs. Will you come down?" Sullivan's voice came from the phone.

"Yeah, sure," Charlie mumbled through the foam of toothpaste. "Three minutes!"

"Okay, I'm waiting for you."

It took Charlie even less than three minutes to get it done. In the parking lot in front of the house, filled with old, battered Fords and Chevys, an unexpected "guest" was waiting for him, looking just as foreign there as Jack Sullivan did in One-Two Boxing when he had first crossed the threshold of the gym.

It was an old-style sports convertible of a make unknown to Charlie, which had gleaming black paintwork.

"Hop in, I'll take you for a spin!"

Charlie was so surprised by the car that it was only now that he noticed Jack, who was behind the wheel of the said convertible. Sullivan lifted his sunglasses, designed at around the same time as the car itself, and with a nod of his head pointed the boy to the passenger seat.

"What is this ride?" Charlie asked, carefully opening the door and getting inside. "What happened to your Tesla?"

"A 1965 Aston Martin DB5 convertible," Jack answered, starting the engine and pulling away. "Tesla stayed at home."

"Midlife crisis?"

Sullivan smiled genially.

"No. It's not mine. It's Jacob's. He bought it seven years ago. He noticed it at a car dump when we were traveling through the Midwest. It was such a huge dump, there were even planes there. That's why Jacob decided to pull off the road and take a look. He always liked finding interesting things in accidental places. The car was in such a terrible condition that no one but Jacob would've recognized it. He'd had a Goldfinger poster as a child." Noticing a look of incomprehension on Charlie's face, Jack hurried to explain. "It's one of the first James Bond movies of the sixties, featuring Sean Connery back at the time. A DB5 was the car he was driving in that movie. Jacob immediately fell in love with this car. He bought it for just a little over a thousand dollars. He then paid much more for its delivery to us across half the country. And after that, he'd been personally restoring it for five years and spent a couple tens of thousand on it."

Another gear shift was followed by an unpleasant grinding sound.

"The transmission's naughty," Jack said. "You know, Jacob was so funny while working on it. All that focused, with oily spots on his hands and face, such a car mechanic through and through. Although in fact, he didn't know anything about cars until he turned his attention to this DB5. He learned everything himself. Jacob's like that. Passionate, enthusiastic, never giving up."

Sullivan retired into himself and his memories for a minute, but the red light and the need to hit the brakes brought him back to reality.

"He had almost finished the work when it all happened. His injury. I forgot about the car. Jacob kept it in a garage on the outskirts of the city. And now I remembered. He has his birthday in four months. An anniversary. Forty years. I want to do something nice for him. I found a man who managed to finally get the car into good shape. And I decided to take it for a spin so that when I make him this present, everything should be perfect."

"Cool, great idea!" Charlie spoke for the first time since they started off. "Jack, where are we actually going?"

"Oh, shoot, I'm sorry. I was speaking too much. By the way, we're almost there."

Charlie looked around. The neighborhood they were driving through was one of the most prestigious in the whole district.

"Charlie, have you ever thought about what you want to become in the future? You're not going to work as the old man's assistant all your life, are you?"

The boy shrugged his shoulders and answered in an apologetic tone, "I don't know. A boxer?"

"I expected this answer," Sullivan smiled. "And besides that? You do understand that boxing is a very risky and unreliable business, where only few achieve success. No, no, don't think that I'm trying to talk you out of it or mean that you won't be able to succeed. It's just that the whole thing involves too many risks. Injuries and all that. Take Derrick, for example. He had every chance of succeeding big time, but it didn't work out for him. I mean, with boxing, you should always have a plan B."

"I guess," Charlie said with uncertainty.

"We've already got where we need to be," Jack said, waving hello to an attendant who had raised the barrier for him.

The campus they drove into was separated from the road by an impenetrable wall of trees, so Charlie was extremely surprised to see a courtyard in front of him, which was surrounded by ancient-looking buildings. The boy thought to himself that all of that was very similar to some Yale or even Hogwarts.

Jack parked the car in an 'employees only' parking lot

and turned off the engine.

"Charlie, I brought you here to meet someone. My old friend. There was a time when he helped me a lot to figure out myself and things I should do. And now I want him to help you too."

Charlie looked at Jack skeptically and even a bit frightenedly.

"Don't worry," Sullivan said. "There won't be anything scary or difficult for you there. He'll talk to you, let you fill out some test papers, do some exercises. Don't be afraid – there're no wrong answers. The whole process is designed to find out what inclinations and capabilities you have so that in the future you wouldn't waste your time on what you actually don't like yourself."

Jack waved to someone behind Charlie. "There he is! Let's go, I'll introduce you."

Jack and Charlie got out of the car just when a tall man in his sixties approached it. He was wearing a tweed jacket and his whole appearance literally screamed 'Professor!'

"Good to see you, Jack! You paid us a visit at last!" the man spoke happily and genially began to shake the hand extended to him.

"I'm very glad to see you too. I'm sorry I haven't come by for so long." When the handshake was finally dealt with, Jack turned to Charlie. "Meet my new friend Charlie, and this is my very old friend Nigel Ba..."

"Call me Nigel, no need for formalities," a man with a professorial appearance interrupted Jack and began to shake Charlie's hand just as genially. "I am very glad to meet you, young man. Jack has told me a lot about you."

Charlie cast Sullivan another surprised look.

"Only the good things!" Jack hastened to respond. "I didn't say anything about our crazy night in Juarez!"

Sullivan winked conspiratorially at Charlie, who clearly did not appreciate the joke.

"Well, shall we get down to business straight away?"

Nigel said, pointing in the direction of one of the buildings nearby.

"What do you say, Charlie, don't you mind?" Jack asked. "Sorry, I never got to ask you how you feel about my idea."

The boy shrugged his shoulders and answered with uncertainty, "I could give it a try."

"Glad to hear that, young man. Let's go to my office then," Nigel put his hand on the boy's back and turned him in the right direction. "And, Jack, it would be better if you wait for us in the main building. Your presence will only confuse Charlie."

"Whatever you say, Doc. But I'd rather wait in the car. The weather is too good to sit indoors."

Nigel nodded approvingly and led Charlie toward the building on the south side of the campus. Charlie cast a pleading glance at Jack, begging not to leave him alone. Jack waved his hand in response, as if answering, "You'll be fine." Then he returned to the driver's seat of the Aston Martin, took out a smartphone from his pocket, plugged headphones into it, put them into his ears, and played the new Woodkid album. As soon as the music started playing, Jack leaned back, exposing his face to the warm rays of the no longer burning, but still very warm autumn sun. He seemed to melt into this light, this music, and this car, every inch of which was literally soaked with the love and care from Jacob, who treated the DB5 as if it was his own child.

Jack knew it was impossible, but it still seemed to him that the interior of the Aston Martin smelled not of old leather and polish, but of Jacob. When his favorite 'The Great Escape' started playing in the headphones, Sullivan was surprised to realize that he was completely calm. For the first time in the last two years, there was no fear, pain, guilt, doubt, or even banal anxiety in his soul.

Surely, things had been going not too well for Jacob lately and the 'episodes' happened more frequently than before, but now for the first time, Jack had no doubt that they could overcome it. That he could overcome it. For the first time, he felt confidence and even strength in him. Not the brute, vulgar masculine strength that boxers in the ring and ordinary yahoos who put up fights in bars try against each other, but the real human strength.

The strength that does not depend on gender, age, race, nationality, social status, and income level. Jack felt the real strength in himself – the one that gives you the opportunity to do the right thing and achieve the right goals, no matter how difficult and scary it is. This realization allowed Sullivan to finally let go of billions of thoughts that were always swarming in his head, and completely dissolve into the present moment – the way he was urged by that audiobook about Zen, which Justine had recently given him.

Jack got so carried away by the music-sun-car meditation that the next hour flew by like two minutes for him, and he noticed Charlie's presence only when the boy who had already gotten into the passenger seat took out one of his headphones.

"What're you listening to?" Charlie asked.

"Just some music," shuddering slightly from surprise, Jack did not go into details. "How did it go?"

"Well, fine, I guess," Charlie answered, shrugging his shoulders.

"What did Nigel say?"

"That I have a head for writing. He suggests choosing English and literature, journalism, or even screenwriting."

"And what do *you* think?"

Charlie responded with another shrug of his shoulders.

"Have you ever tried to write anything?"

Charlie shook his head in response.

"Something secret?" Jack persisted.

"No, not really. Just some stuff about boxing. When I had a fight with the old man, I was sitting at your place, and I had nothing to do. Justine was busy with Jacob, trying to get him to write to develop fine motor skills. He didn't want to. Then she asked me to sit with him and write something so that Jacob could see it wasn't just him who had to do it. So I sat down to write. And later after that I also did it by myself a couple of times. Just out of boredom."

Charlie did not want to tell that, in fact, writing got him so engaged that since then he had already filled up two thick notebooks. And even more so, he was not going to tell that his writing was not just about boxing, but about two novice boxers – young and old, who train together under a super-old former champion, strict and even rude, but fair.

"Let's go walk around the campus," Jack suggested, getting out from the driver's seat.

Charlie followed suit, and they walked down the path along the north side of the courtyard.

"How do you like this place?" Sullivan asked.

"It's fine," Charlie said. "A bit too fancy, though."

Jack smiled slightly in response.

"That's true. But the teaching here is very good. It's one of the best schools in the whole country. Remember I told you about Mr. Martin from the repair shop and how later he and I together with my university established a charity project, which helps talented kids from underprivileged classes to get a decent education?"

Charlie nodded in response.

"The project turned out very successful and now includes ten universities already. And five years ago we decided that we should start looking for young talents even under university age. Then we had several schools that joined us, including this one. Every year, our project's council selects twenty kids who receive the right to study for free in the best schools of our district. Five of them enter this school. And as the head of the council, I personally select one of the five."

Jack stopped, turned to Charlie, and put his hand on his shoulder. "Charlie, I want you to be that one student this year."

The boy was so surprised that the only thing he managed to answer was, "But the new school year's already begun..."

"Yes, but lately I've been busy with other things and just forgot to select my candidate. So the place is still free. Besides, it's been less than a month. Not a big deal."

"But I haven't been to school for almost two years... I told you that I quit after I started working in One-Two..."

"Charlie, I've been at your place. I've seen the textbooks. I know you've been learning all this time. And I saw the browser history on the computer you used when you lived in my house. I wasn't going to pry into your personal business, it's just my professional habit to check all systems for suspicious activity. Imagine my surprise when I almost didn't see any porn there but found a lot of educational materials, including the ones that aren't yet supposed to be taught in school at your age."

Charlie blushed visibly at the mention of porn. Noticing that, Jack hurried to continue speaking about studying, "Charlie, you're a very smart and extremely independent and organized guy. I wasn't like that at your age. If I'd been kicked out of the house at fifteen, I would've definitely died under some bridge. While you managed not only to survive, but to find a job, earn a roof over your head and even continue learning on your own. These are exactly the qualities we're looking for in the participants of our program."

"Weell," Charlie drawled. "I don't know. I'm sorry, Jack, I probably should've been very happy with such an offer... Thanks, but I... I don't know. What about One-Two? The old man won't be able to handle it without me."

"Charlie, I've already settled everything with the old man. He'll hire a person to clean the floor and wash hand wraps, and from now on you will only perform the duties of an assistant coach. You'll come in the evenings, after school. I'm sure you can handle it."

Judging by the expression on his face, Charlie was still extremely skeptical about Jack's idea of putting him in a fancy school, which, most certainly, accepts only geniuses and rich folk. Right at that moment, a mobile phone started ringing in

Sullivan's pocket.

"That's the old man himself," Jack said, looking at the screen. "Now you can hear for yourself what he thinks about it."

Sullivan pressed the answer button and put the phone on the speaker mode.

"Gerard, hi. Listen, Charlie and I are now here at that school I told you about. He's not very inspired by the idea of studying here just yet."

"Is he listening?" McKee's voice came from the phone. "Kid, listen, if you're gonna act up and miss such a badass opportunity, you'll never set foot in my gym again. Such a chance is given once in a lifetime! You should kiss Jack's feet for that, how you still dare to have doubts?! Don't even think of passing up on that! Do you understand me?"

"Yes," Charlie muttered, slightly offended.

"I can't hear you," McKee said. "What are you saying there?"

"I understood! I got it!" Charlie repeated louder.

"Now that's better! Jack, are you there?"

"I'm here, Gerard, my phone's on speaker mode," Sullivan answered.

"Listen, your two super-fast victories have paid off. Now they want you in the big ring. I just got a call. The next fight's already been scheduled. Pack your bags. We're going to Vegas!"

..19..

"Listen to me carefully and don't even try to interrupt!" McKee spoke in a more serious voice than ever before when he addressed Sullivan, who was sitting on the bench. "Artur Melikov is a very serious opponent. The Russian school is extremely severe. In amateur boxing, only Cubans are tougher than communists. Though, they're also communists. Apparently, dictatorship toughens you up more than democracy. But back to Melikov! He's one of the most experienced fighters of today. Twenty-five professional fights and almost three hundred amateur ones!"

It was at least the fourth time during their preparation for his third fight that Sullivan had to hear this reasoning of the old man, and he could already predict every word McKee was about to say with 90% accuracy, but he did not interrupt the coach. Jack was pleased with how seriously the old man took that fight. It seemed that McKee had finally come to believe that Sullivan could make a real boxer.

"Only three defeats," the old man continued. "All on points, all with a minimum difference and against more advertised fighters. And as an amateur, he only won all the time. Melikov has an iron chin. No one's ever managed to at least knock him down. So don't even think that with him you might pull off something similar to what you did in your first fights. This fight will end before the last round only in one single case – if you end up on the canvas. Your goal is not to knock him out. Your goal is to get through all the twelve rounds, not take too many punches, and be active. The only weakness of Melikov is his lack of showmanship. That's why he hasn't yet been promoted for championship fights. He's downright boring to look at. Melikov doesn't move much and doesn't punch much. He doesn't show off, doesn't play with his opponent, doesn't throw punches for viewer's entertainment, but hits only when he's sure the punch won't miss the target. He's like a tank. He's slow, unwieldy, but deadly. Twenty-one knockouts out of twenty-two victories are no joke. All his three defeats followed the same pattern – the opponent moved more and threw more punches. They did little damage to him, but they looked much more active. You should act in the same way. Focus on your footwork, not your arms. Don't put too much strength in your punches, spare it, but make sure that you're all over the ring, that you come from all angles, be everywhere and all the time. Today you don't need to work on the opponent, you need to play to the crowd. If the crowd roots for you, judges will follow them."

Making sure that McKee had finally finished, Jack said, "Seems kinda unsportsmanlike."

"Yeah, you tell me about it. I'm sick of it. But there's nothing you can do. If I could have it my way, I'd get rid of rounds and judges altogether. All fights would last till the final victory. Combat sport should be as close as possible to real combat. You certainly can't win a street fight on points. But we don't get to make rules. If you wanna build a professional career – you'll have to cave in to all those bureaucrats and hucksters, for whom boxing is just a source of income, no different from selling toilet paper."

Mackie's thought process was interrupted by a knock on the door and Derrick's voice, "Pops, it's time to go!"

"Well, Jack, let's do it," the old man said, putting his hands on his pupil's shoulders. "Pull yourself together, take a deep breath, breathe out and when you do that, blow all unnecessary thoughts and doubts out of your head. Kid, you can do it! I believe in you!"

"We all believe in you!" Kate's cheerful voice came from the hallway.

McKee cast a reproachful look toward the door but said nothing. The old man only thought to himself that someday he would ultimately make Jack get rid of those bozos and hire himself only professional cornermen.

This time, Charlie was not disappointed with the arena as he entered it. The format of the Sullivan vs. Melikov fight was exactly the same as in all those fights that he had previously seen only on TV: a huge hall, thousands of spectators, stage lighting, numerous cameras. Although, none of that was meant for Jack. His fight against Artur Melikov was only an undercard. This night's main event would be a championship fight for the IPBU regular heavyweight champion title.

This fight was the reason all these spectators came here. But it did not mean that they would not root fervently for Jack. As long as he put on a real show for them. Charlie really wanted to believe it, but today, even he, Sullivan's biggest fan in the whole world, doubted the success of his idol. Over the course of the preparation for the fight, the boy watched each of Artur Melikov's fights three times and those videos inspired great respect for his friend's new opponent and even made the boy a little frightened of him.

This time on his way to the ring, Jack was accompanied not only by his usual One-Two Boxing team but also by professional cutman Chuck Duran. In this fight, McKee laid perhaps even more responsibility on him than on Sullivan himself. Melikov was shorter than Sullivan, which meant that with the same weight within the welterweight category he had more muscle mass, and thus a heavier and more dangerous fist, capable of easily cutting the opponent's face with a direct hit.

Walking down the aisle leading to the ring, Jack kept his hooded head down and looked only at his feet. He absolutely did not want to look at the spectators, even when they joyfully greeted him and shouted encouraging phrases. Sullivan did not want all of that – the ring, the stands, the spectators – to become something important to him, something real. All of that should have remained the mere problems he had to solve on his way to the main goal.

Jack thought of all that was happening as a process of code debugging – he had to find errors that prevented him from continuing to write a program, the errors that did not allow for it to work. That's all. Jack Sullivan needed a program that would allow him to destroy Joe Ryan. Rick Stanton, Patrick Crawford, and now Artur Melikov were just errors in the code. And they had to be resolved as quickly and efficiently as possible, without wasting attention on spectators and celebrating the victory.

When the ring was no more than ten steps away, all of a sudden Sullivan raised his eyes for the first time and looked at the crowd. He did it because he felt someone's gaze on him. Not just the idle gaze of curious spectators, but something more than that. Something important.

Sullivan began to run his eyes around the stands, but now the ring was already in front of him, and the boxer had to stop his search. After climbing into the ring and getting rid of the robe, Jack started skipping on the spot the way McKee taught him – to get his blood going and warm the muscles up for the fight.

Finally, the referee invited the fighters for traditional instructions. Only then did Jack take a look at his opponent for the first time. Artur Melikov was not just calm, he looked as if he was bored. Meanwhile, the referee gave the last instructions, the opponents touched gloves, the bell rang and the fight began. Sullivan perfectly remembered the old man's guidance, "Don't try to repeat the same punch you used in the previous fights! He'll be waiting for it!" So he took a quick step to the left and simultaneously threw a left hook. It worked! The quick sharp punch crushed right into the opponent's cheekbone, which was exactly the spot Jack was aiming at.

But nothing happened. Melikov did not even blink an eye. It was as if he had not even noticed the punch. Jack stayed focused, took a step back to let the opponent's counterattack punch go by, after which he jumped back again, but this time to the right side, simultaneously striking with a left jab followed immediately by a right hook. The first punch was blocked, but the second one landed where it was intended. And again, nothing. Absolutely nothing!

Once again Jack dodged the opponent's counterattack and charged forward again. A step forward, a quick one-two to the body, and a jump back. Nothing! Sullivan spent the entire first round according to the principles of Muhammad Ali, 'Float like a butterfly, sting like a bee,' and he managed to follow both the first and second part of this formula excellently. Except that Artur Melikov did not care. The opponent's punches did no more harm to him than bee stings to a tank's armor.

When the bell announced the end of the round, Jack went to his corner already a little out of breath, whereas his opponent looked as if he were still bored. Finally, the time came for what Charlie had been waiting for with such great impatience – for the first time Sullivan appeared in his corner during a break. The boy deftly moved up a chair for him, equally deftly took the mouth guard out of his mouth, and handed him a straw so that the boxer could take a couple of sips of water from the bottle.

"Kid, everything's going great!" McKee began to give Sullivan his instructions. "Pointswise, you killed him in this round. Your thrown and landed punches advantage is colossal. And he never even broke through your guard. The audience is yours. Listen to them buzzing! Now I want you to keep the same pace, but punch a little slower and not so hard. Save your energy! Remember what we've talked about!"

Sullivan nodded and put in the mouth guard. The second round almost completely repeated the first one. Sullivan was still floating around his opponent and stinging him in all kinds of ways and from all angles. And Melikov, just as before, continued to show no reaction whatsoever to the hits taken. But the spectators were thrilled. They had not seen such activity in the ring for a long time. Sullivan even heard someone in the crowd chanting his name.

"Well done, Jack," the coach greeted the fighter during the second break. "You're doing everything just as I asked. Keep up the good work."

Sullivan decided not to disappoint the old man by saying that, in fact, he did not try so hard to follow his advice. It was just that his energy level was already beginning to fade. After all, Jack had never been in a real fight before. Those few seconds he had spent in the ring previously did not even deserve mentioning. And in his training sessions, neither he punched his sparring partner with full strength, nor did his partner throw punches similar to Melikov's, which, although blocked, caused Sullivan perhaps even greater damage than his own punches that came right on target.

"Coach, there's nothing I can do against him!" This time it was Jack who spoke first, sitting down on a chair in his corner for the third time. "What should I do next?"

"Don't worry! Everything's going to plan!" McKee replied in a calm tone. "You're leading on points with a good score. The crowd is on your side. Soon they'll start booing Melikov for his passive attitude. This happened to him before. He's an excellent fighter, but painfully boring! That is, until it comes to knockout. Not to get hit by him – that's your main task, Jack! So keep it up – attack, move back, attack again, and then move back again. But make sure not to punch hard – save your energy."

Jack put his mouth guard in and, as soon as the bell rang, went on the attack again. Left, right, to the head, to the body, jab, cross, uppercut, hook, single punches, combinations – Sullivan used up the entire arsenal available to a boxer. All that remained was to bite the opponent's ear, in the best traditions of Mike Tyson. But Melikov was unbeatable. He went forward despite all the blows. Unstoppable like death or taxes. And his face was still expressing such boredom that Jack was expecting his opponent to start yawning any minute now.

It was this infinite calmness at the level of boredom that got under Sullivan's skin. It began to seem to him that no matter how hard he tried, no matter how fast and accurate his punches were, he would still never be able to beat Artur Melikov. Not being able to beat him meant not being able to move on, and without being able to move on he would never manage to get to Joe Ryan.

Artur Melikov was the one critical error that could not be resolved and because of it, the whole program, no matter how ingenious it might have been at its core, would go to pieces. Back when he was a programmer, Jack Sullivan had that one program with a critical error that he could not resolve. It was a really brilliant program that could make a lot of difference. It was a work of art. A triumph equaled only by its monumental failure.

It was Sullivan's Magnum opus, which he had been working on since university. He never told anyone about his creation. Therefore, no one ever found out that it was this very failure – the inability to resolve a single critical error – that made Jack quit his job as a programmer and retrain as an information security consultant. Even Jacob thought his husband had decided to change his career path simply because he had gotten tired of programming.

Jab, cross, a quick step forward, uppercut, and hook while jumping back. Two of the four punches hit the target, but Melikov continued to move forward safe and sound.

There came another sound of the bell, and once again Jack got a chance to recover his breath in his corner.

"So, Jack, listen to me," McKee said. "Everything's going great, your point advantage is growing. But you're starting to get tired. I can see that. And Melikov's breathing like a steam train. He can go through all twelve rounds in one breath. You need to slow down, or you'll be completely out of gas in the final rounds and that's where he catches you. It doesn't matter even if your score is ten times higher – a knockout is gonna cancel it out anyway. Come on, Jack. You've already got the upper hand, now you only need to hold the position you've gained. Do you understand me?"

Jack nodded, accepting the mouth guard from Charlie.

"Good luck, Jack!" his young assistant cornerman dared to chime in.

Sullivan smiled and winked at the boy. The fifth round started even more successfully for Jack than the previous one – Melikov missed three punches in a row. The audience roared with delight and many even jumped to their feet. Now at least a hundred people were chanting, "Sullivan! Sullivan! Sullivan!" But Melikov continued to move forward as if nothing had happened. Like a mystical creature from the horror movie "It Follows". Jack could not stand this movie, which, on the contrary, Jacob liked very much, but he often reflected on it, thinking that the main villain of that movie was a great allusion to his real life problems.

And here was another such problem right in front of him. And this time it acted exactly like in that movie – not too fast, but mercilessly approaching him, no matter how hard he tried to get rid of it. And Jack snapped. The thought of having to attack Melikov again and again for another seven rounds, while the latter would keep moving onward, became so unbearable to Sullivan that he forgot about all the instructions of his coach and rushed forward.

Jab, cross, uppercut, uppercut, cross, left hook, right hook, jab, jab. The hall broke forth into shouts of delight. Such a long and desperate combination had not been seen within the walls of this arena for a very long time. And then something happened, which McKee was so afraid of, and about which he warned his pupil so persistently. Enraged, Jack forgot about the defense for just a second, but for Melikov, who had been waiting for this moment from the very beginning of the fight, one second was enough. Not fast, but very accurate and very hard jab struck the opponent's jaw.

Jack felt his jaw joints cracked, then Melikov's face

disappeared for some reason, and bright light appeared instead. "Three, four..." Sullivan heard distant words, the meaning of which he could not understand at that moment. And suddenly he heard someone's voice. The voice was very familiar, but it did not come from his corner. Jack could not make out the words that the voice was saying, but he knew the voice was calling for him to get up.

"Five, six..." This time Sullivan understood what these words meant and got up so quickly that the referee barely had time to utter the next number.

"Are you all right?" the referee's voice broke through the ringing in his ears.

"Yes, I'm all right," Jack replied, although in fact, getting up so suddenly caused his vision to go dark for a moment.

"Can you continue the fight?" the referee asked again.

"Yes, I'm fine," Jack replied in a fairly confident voice.

The referee motioned Melikov to come closer and gave the signal to continue the fight. Melikov went at the opponent. This time Jack remembered the old man's advice and followed it to the letter. After a knockdown, you just need to wait for the bell to ring. Move a lot, punch a little, in case of any danger get into a clinch immediately, and hold on to the opponent.

"How are you, Kid?" McKee asked with genuine concern in his voice when Jack took a seat in the corner for the fifth time. "Dizziness? Ringing in your ears?"

"No, everything's all right. Now it's all right," Sullivan said.

"Jack, be careful! You have a smart head, which is probably easier to concuss than the one with only three thoughts in it. It's a serious matter. Not worth risking."

"It's fine, Gerard," Jack said, and added. "Really."

Sullivan spent the sixth and seventh rounds exactly as the coach advised him during the break – attacking a lot, but weakly, and most importantly – stepping aside or getting into a clinch at the slightest risk. The main thing was to show the spectators and the judges that the knockdown did not cause much harm and Jack was able to get the fight back on track. After all, four of the five rounds were still scored in his favor.

The judges considered both of these rounds to end in a draw. Sullivan was more active, but the number of his punches, and most importantly – their accuracy – had noticeably decreased, while Melikov, on the contrary, started pushing harder.

"Jack, you need to win at least one more round," McKee said during the break. "You won the first four rounds by a long shot. He won one, two ended in a draw. We need to win another one. And then it's gonna be no big deal. Even if you lose all the other ones, but with the smaller difference than you had scored in the first four rounds – the victory will still be yours. The crowd likes it when a rookie first goes all out and then shows what he's made of. And such a veteran as Melikov, on the contrary, will never be announced the winner if he wins only half of the rounds. Come on, Jack, give it all you've got."

"We believe in you!" Derrick and Charlie said in unison.

Despite being very tired already, Jack began the eighth round with a decent attack and an even more decent counterattack, undertaken after he managed to dodge the opponent's weighty hook. And then something happened that Jack never understood – even when he later reviewed the recording of the fight. Melikov's next hook flew as if out of nowhere and bumped into the opponent's left eyebrow. Sullivan lost his balance for a moment, but still remained standing and did not touch the canvas.

A sharp pain burned his face, and for some reason, he felt a stinging sensation in his eye. Jack shut the eye tightly and was about to rush to counterattack, but suddenly the referee appeared in front of him, stopping the fight with gestures and pointing Sullivan in the direction of the ropes. Jack obeyed uncomprehendingly. At the ropes there was a man waiting for him, who quickly cleaned his eye and, without even warning him, started picking his forehead, causing him a new bout of burning pain.

Until the very break, Jack did not get to realize that Melikov's last punch had cut his eyebrow and caused profuse bleeding. The man, who turned out to be a medic, was joined by Jack's personal cutman. Together they did something with the boxer's eyebrow, and after a few seconds the medic allowed the referee to continue the fight. But just as Sullivan was about to lunge at his opponent, there came the sound of the bell.

"Chuck, how bad is it?" McKee asked, leaning over Jack and examining his cut.

"It's bad," the cutman answered shortly and continued working on his patient's eyebrow.

"Listen up, Jack," the old man turned to his pupil. "It's very serious. If you take one more hit to this eyebrow they may stop the fight. So now take care of your left side as if it is made of glass. It's better to miss some punches to the body, but do not remove the glove from this eyebrow. Do you understand me?"

Jack nodded right at the time of the signal starting the next round. The ninth and tenth rounds were a real disaster for Sullivan. His tired legs were not of much use, and because of the need to hold his left hand near the damaged eyebrow all the time, Jack missed at once several heavy punches to the body. These rounds were clearly won by Melikov, and the difference in points between the fighters had already been cut to a minimum.

But it was not the points that worried McKee, who was watching his fighter so intently that the old man's vision was starting to get blurry. The coach understood that everything was pointing to an early victory for Melikov, if not by an honest KO, then at least by a TKO. Jack looked as if he only had enough energy in him for one more round at best, and in the last, twelfth round, he would collapse exhausted on the canvas, even if Melikov completely stopped attacking.

"Listen up, Jack. And listen carefully," the old man began his second last, or maybe the last instruction in this fight. "You can't win anymore. Don't even start to argue with me. You need to forget about pride now. You just need to survive. You need to run about for two more rounds and not let yourself be knocked out. If you lose on points – it's not the end. The fight was phenomenal. The crowd stood on their feet half the time. Promoters will never miss the opportunity to arrange a rematch. I guarantee it. But it's only if on points. If he knocks you out – that's it. That's the end. They'll write off your first two victories as luck, and that's that. Taking risks hoping for some absolutely incredible victory is much worse for you now than losing on points. Do you understand me? Run, Jack! Run and clinch! No one will consider you to be less of a man because of this. You fought like a hero!"

Jack once again responded to the coach with a nod and got to his feet for the eleventh, penultimate round. Sullivan spent it exactly as the coach asked – he ran and clinched. Jack hardly attacked, but he almost did not take hits either, preventing the opponent from aiming his punches or clinching him. The spectators did not like it at all and started to boo Sullivan. But during the break, McKee, Derrick, and Charlie vied to praise Jack and insist that he spend the last round in the same vein.

At the beginning of the twelfth round, Sullivan felt like a piece of shit. Both physically and mentally. His legs were shaky from fatigue, his whole body ached after a dozen of missed punches, and his split eyebrow was already swollen and began to obscure his vision. But on the inside, Jack felt even worse. No matter how hard he had been trying over these past six months, no matter how desperately he had trained, he still could not win in a fair fight.

And what difference would it make if, having lost on points, he would still have the chance to continue his career? If he could not beat Artur Malikov, then he would definitely never be able to even get to the fight with Joe Ryan. And this was his last chance to take revenge on the bastard who had destroyed his life and taken away from him the only person whom Jack not only loved himself, but who loved and supported him in return.

All these thoughts were swarming in Jack's head while he seemed to be automatically 'dancing' around his opponent, periodically alternating the dance with hugging him in a clinch.

"Doing great!" The coach's voice sounded from his corner. "One minute left! You almost did it! Hold it, Kid!"

The phrase 'hold it!' felt to Sullivan like a slap in the face. All his life he was weak, short, timid, cowardly, not acting manly. All his life he had to suffer and wait for something. Wait until he grew up, wait for his graduation from high school when he would not be bullied by his classmates anymore, wait for Jacob to come out of a coma, wait for him to recover.

Jack was tired of waiting. Waiting never did him any good. One problem was just replaced by another one over time. Waiting did not mean solving problems. Jack did not want to wait ever again. Jack wanted to solve problems. Right here and right now. And it did not matter if he lost. Waiting – that was the real ordeal.

When there were only thirty seconds left until the end of the round and the whole fight, Sullivan clenched the mouth guard tightly, lowered his left glove, which had seemed to be almost glued to his face earlier, and rushed into the attack. Two powerful punches to the body to leave his opponent out of breath and force him to lower his guard were immediately followed by a one-two to the head. A step aside made it impossible for the opponent to lock Sullivan in a clinch. Next was a powerful punch right to the temple. A step forward was followed by shooting several fast punches to the body from a close distance and two quick uppercuts.

For the first time in the entire fight, Sullivan managed not only to force Melikov to retreat but also pin him to the ropes. Jab, cross, jab, cross, uppercut, uppercut. Jack's punches had never been so heavy. Melikov missed so many blows in a row that his hands dropped down by themselves. Sullivan was about to shoot his head with a burst of punches, like a training speed bag, but he managed to hit only twice before the referee intervened.

That was it. The fight was finished. It was all over. Yes, Jack displayed a powerful combination at the last seconds, but it was hardly enough to score at least the last round in his favor. Even without the last one, Melikov still had five won rounds against Jack's four, not to mention the knockdown and the split eyebrow, which were scored a lot higher than just much activity in the ring.

Jack dropped his hands limply, lowered his gaze, and trudged to his corner. Before Sullivan even managed to take a couple of steps, Charlie immediately ran into him, grabbed him in his arms, and began to yell something in excitement. Jack did not understand a word. Besides, the whole arena broke into shouts. Charlie was joined by the rest of Sullivan's team. The old man personally picked up his pupil in his arms and started shaking him in the air.

It was only about twenty seconds later that Sullivan was finally able to make out Charlie's yells and understand what had happened. It turned out that the referee intervened not because the sound of the bell had announced the end of the round and the entire fight. No, the referee intervened because Artur Melikov had lost consciousness due to missed punches. Yes, he remained on his feet, but only because the ropes supported him from behind, and the opponent's punches were flying at him nonstop from the front.

As soon as the referee pulled Sullivan aside, Melikov dropped to one knee and remained in that position until his team members picked him up and sat him down on a chair. But Jack did not notice any of that, because, after the referee's signal, he lowered his gaze and trudged to his corner, thinking that everything was already lost. Both the fight and his last chance to get back at Joe Ryan.

Now, when he realized what had happened, realized that he had won, realized that he had knocked out Melikov, knocked out the most experienced fighter whom no one had ever knocked out before, Sullivan smiled. Sitting on the shoulder of the old man who had lifted him there, Jack smiled and, without Derrick's tip, triumphantly raised the glove over his head.

For the first time in his life, Jack felt like a winner. The one, whom nobody would ever be able to humiliate and intimidate.

"I guess Pops was right when he said that the Russians were the toughest guys," Derrick turned to Jack when McKee finally put him back down.

"Why?" Sullivan asked blankly. "He lost, didn't he?"

"But you won!" Derrick replied with a sly smile. "You're half Russian, right?"

"Right," Sullivan replied and laughed. Loud and resonantly. The way he had not laughed for two years already.

..20..

"Sullivan! Sullivan! Sullivan!" the sound of the crowd shouting in the arena was still audible when Jack and his team entered the locker room. Charlie continued calling out his friend's name, looking at the others and gesturing for them to join him. And they did join! McKee, Derrick, Kate, and even taciturn cutman Chuck started chanting "Sullivan! Sullivan! Sullivan!" all together and continued to do so until embarrassed but merrily laughing Jack persuaded them to stop.

Kate rushed to embrace the winner and began to kiss him loudly on the cheeks and forehead, almost grazing the hurriedly plastered cut, while Derrick and Charlie were vying to give their opinions on the best moments of the fight. Jack had been smiling intensely for a while now, so that his cheeks were already beginning to ache.

Now it was no longer the victory itself that made him happy, it was not the solution of a seemingly unresolvable critical error and not the opportunity to go further, toward the long-awaited fight with Joe Ryan. Now he was happy with all this – Kate, who was jubilant, Derrick and Charlie, who were interrupting each other like brothers do, and even Chuck, who was chuckling quietly in the far corner of the locker room. Now they were all like one big and happy family.

A sister, three brothers, a distant cousin, and, of course, the head of the family – wise, big, and mighty Gerard McKee, whose imposing figure was now occupying the entire doorway. The old man was standing with his huge arms crossed on his chest, leaning back against the door, his eyes half-closed, a subtle thoughtful smile on his lips.

Jack and Gerard locked eyes with each other. The coach nodded slightly. Sullivan nodded back. They both understood each other without words.

Kate, who was still full of excitement, finally did graze the split eyebrow. Jack squeezed his eyes shut in pain, and when he opened them again, the old man was no longer in the doorway. The cut started bleeding again and Chuck hurried to perform his professional duties. When the bleeding was stopped and Chuck was not blocking the view, Sullivan saw the coach in the doorway again. Only this time he had a smartphone in his hand, and the expression on his face was far from happily thoughtful.

"Guys," McKee said, trying to drown the stormy dialogue between Derrick and Charlie. "Guys!" he repeated at the top of his strong voice.

Derrick and Charlie fell silent and, as if on cue, turned to the coach.

"Everybody, go out for a minute, I need to talk to Jack," McKee said, lowering his voice.

"But we're one team..." Kate spoke but stopped short as she saw the old man's menacing look.

Everyone except Jack hurried to leave the locker room. The old man closed the door after them.

"Jack, I don't know how to say such things, so I'll say it right away." McKee put his hand on his pupil's shoulder. "Justine called. Jacob's in the hospital, he had a stroke."

The old man paused, waiting for Jack's reaction, but he remained silent. Except that the smile disappeared from his face. Now Sullivan looked exactly as he did the day he first came to One-Two Boxing – he looked tense as if he felt uncomfortable being not only in this room but also in his own body.

"Jack..." not getting any reaction, the old man continued. "It's very bad. The doctors said he might not survive the night. There's a chance, but not a big one."

These words did not trigger any reaction from Jack either. Only a big tear rolled out of his left eye, the one that was now half-hidden under the swollen split eyebrow. It rolled down his cheek, ran along the edge of the cheekbone down to the chin, and flew downward, landing on the still wrapped fist. The old man followed the path of the tear with his eyes and saw how much Jack's hands were shaking.

Before McKee could speak again, the phone vibrated in his palm.

"It's Justine. Jack, take it, talk to her."

The old man took Sullivan's hand and put the phone in it, having tapped the answer button in advance.

"Hello," Jack answered in a hoarse voice and after that he did not say a single word, only listening to the voice of the woman who had been caring for his husband.

At the same time, Derrick's laughter came from the corridor, joined by the others. McKee hurried out of the locker room. The laughter stopped immediately. A minute later, Jack himself appeared in the corridor.

"I... I need to get to the airport," he said in a faltering, trembling voice, not looking at anyone in particular, as if into the void.

"Jack, we're so sorry," Kate began, but the old man checked her sharply.

"Son," the coach spoke. "We just looked at the schedule. The next flight is only tomorrow. The one we were going to take back home."

"Jacob can't wait for me until tomorrow..." Jack spoke into the void again and another tear rolled down his face.

A heavy silence hung in the corridor, interrupted only by the echoes of the audience shouting in the arena, reacting to successful actions of the participants of this night's second fight, which was well underway at that moment.

"You can go by car," Kate spoke timidly. "It'll take about five hours. I have a car. I rented it in the morning when we arrived. I wanted to drive around the city after the fight."

Kate scurried into the locker room and came back a moment later, rummaging in her purse on the move.

"Here," she said, holding the keys in the palm of her hand and addressing everyone at once.

"Thanks," Jack answered in an automatic voice and took the keys.

"No way," the old man objected, and his huge palm "swallowed" Sullivan's fist, which was clutching the keys. "You can't drive now."

"That's right, we're going all together!" Charlie said.

"Not a chance," McKee replied and added, now addressing all of them. "Listen to me carefully. It's just me and Jack who's going. Charlie, pack his clothes and things quickly. Derrick, you get done with all the formalities about the fight, Chuck will help you, he knows everything. Then scoot to the hotel, get the bags from my room and Jack's, then check us out. Tomorrow, you take the first flight home, along with our stuff, just as we were going to. Is everything clear to everyone?"

Everyone started nodding in unison. Charlie ran to the locker room to pack Jack's things.

"Kate, keep an eye on the kid," McKee said. "Make him stay with you in the hotel room until the very flight. It's no good for him wandering around all by himself. What, Chuck?" the old man turned to the cutman, who approached him from the side.

"If the wound opens again," Chuck replied and handed him a tube of some ointment.

"Yeah, thanks."

Less than half an hour later, the car with McKee behind the wheel and Sullivan in the passenger seat left Las Vegas. Jack was still wearing his shorts and boxing robe. The old man took Sullivan's usual clothes along but did not gather the courage to suggest that he get changed. They drove the first hundred miles in silence, except that Jack had already called Justine twice. But even when he called, he hardly said anything.

Justine said that Jacob was under sedatives and would

recover from them by Jack's arrival at best. So there was absolutely no need for them to be in a hurry. The doctors did not say anything new either. They said the condition was serious but stable. Any new conclusions could be made not sooner than in seven to ten hours. Justine did not say it openly, but both Jack and McKee, who had heard their conversation, realized that they should not expect Jacob to ever leave the hospital room. Their trip had only one purpose now – to make it in time to say goodbye.

After another fifty miles, the old man made a stop – he had to refuel both the car and himself. McKee inserted the gas nozzle and walked to the gas station store. When he came out clutching a large bottle of coke in one hand and five bags of beef jerky in the other, there was a small crowd formed around Jack comprised of three boys about eighteen years old and two girls just about the same age, but wearing make-up so heavy that it made them look not younger than thirty-five.

The group of young people recognized Sullivan. The boys were overwhelmed with the excitement of meeting someone whose fight they saw live on TV less than two hours ago. The girls didn't watch the fight, but they were very happy to meet someone who was on TV. Jack looked silently at them, or rather through them, not reacting to the boys' questions and girls' awkward attempts at flirting.

McKee hastened to rid his pupil of the attention he absolutely did not need at the moment. There was no reaction from the teenagers to the first polite request of the old man to leave the tired boxer alone. Then McKee put his supplies on the roof of the car, grabbed a boy in each hand, and literally threw them into their pickup parked next to them. The other three teenagers chose to retreat on their own.

"You'd better get changed, Jack," McKee said. "You stand out too much like this."

Without saying a word, Sullivan followed the old man's advice and changed into the suit that had been lying on the back seat. The three thousand dollar one, in which he first appeared within the walls of One-Two Boxing. Jack was going to go to Vegas in his usual tracksuit, but Kate insisted that he dress up to the nines.

"Looking good," McKee said without knowing why he did so.

Jack did not answer, returning silently to his seat. The old man also hurried to get into the car. Five minutes after they left the gas station, an old pickup began to overtake them. As the pickup caught up with them, a boy leaned out of its window – one of those whom McKee had thrown into that very pickup earlier. He shouted, 'Old jerk!' and threw a large cup of Slurpee on the windshield of their car.

The old man had to slam on the brakes sharply, as the blue liquid covered the entire glass. Enraged, McKee jumped out from the driver's seat and burst into a thunderous barrage of curses thrown in the direction of the pickup, which was speeding away. After all the cursing and spitting on the asphalt a couple of times, the old man began to wipe the Slurpee off the glass with a handkerchief.

"Jack, push the wiper fluid button a couple of times," he said into the window and continued to mumble to himself. "Fucking kids, fucking Slurpee, fucking "pro-life" Republicans. Hell, I'd launch a state program in support of abortions so that there'd be fewer of such little bastards…"

The old man heard an odd sound from the interior of the car and turned around to see what it was. It was Jack. He was laughing. Chuckling, more precisely. McKee smiled back. After one cleaned windshield, thirty miles traveled and two packs of beef jerky eaten by the old man, Jack finally spoke, "Have you ever had such horrible thoughts in your head that they scared you? That you were afraid of the very fact you could even think like that."

A piece of beef jerky hung from the old man's mouth.

"Um… Maybe… Probably… I've had all kinds of shit in my head. And it's not just thoughts. I caused a lot of trouble in my youth. Maybe even killed somebody. We used to fight so hard.

And then there was no time to check whether the dude you knocked out was alive or not..."

The old man stopped in mid-sentence, realizing that it was not the time for the stories of his youth. Jack must have wanted to relate something himself, and the only thing he needed from McKee was a short answer, which would give him the strength to communicate what lay heavy at his heart. It was about three minutes later when Sullivan spoke again, "Have you ever felt like you wanted to confess something terrible? And not just to get it off your chest, but on the contrary, to be judged, humiliated, insulted. So that you'd get what you deserve..."

"You know, Jack, I've already told you this a number of times, but you still stubbornly continue to think that I'm your equal. I'm a simple guy. You're ten times smarter than me. Boxing and booze – that's what my head is mostly filled with. So, in fact, I can't really have such deep psychologically poetic thoughts as you just expressed. Hell, I rarely even think before I say something."

The old man was silent for a minute and then continued, "But now, when I give it some thought, I can say to you – tell me anything. I won't judge, humiliate or insult you. You're my friend, and I know you're a good man, a real man. If you have some really terrible thoughts in your head – it's just because you're all so smart. You must've been reading all sorts of thick books without pictures – that's where it creeps into your head from. So come on, spit it out, don't be afraid."

Another long pause hung in the air, but after about five minutes Sullivan finally spoke, "I wanted him to die. I wanted... I loved Jacob and I will always love him. I wouldn't care if he was paralyzed, even completely. I'd take care of him for the rest of my life and thank the universe that he'd survived, even in that shape. But when I realized that Jacob would never come back, that he'd remain this creature forever..." Jack stumbled over the last word. "It's terrible. It's unacceptable to think so. It's still Jacob... And even if not, even if there are really only some scraps of the source code left in him, only ghosts... Even if so, he's still human. He has feelings, he knows how to be happy, he still even talks. Yes, most of the time he doesn't make sense, but he still talks. He's a human, not some kind of creature. A HUMAN! HOW can you wish death on a person?!? HOW can you wish death on a person who was once your husband? The one you loved more than anything else in the world..."

Jack started gasping for air from the emotions that overwhelmed him, and the old man hurried to help him. "Jack, Jack, wait, don't get all worked up like that. I, I understand. I mean, really. I completely understand. I didn't tell you, but my grandma raised me. My father was killed in a bar fight, my mother was drunk all the time, and my grandmother took me away from her. Grandma was a very harsh woman. The whole neighborhood was afraid of her. But she was my only family. And I loved her. Yes, it was a very strange love mixed with fear, but it was still love and she was my only family. Just when I was starting my boxing career, she was diagnosed with Alzheimer's. And I started losing her. Literally every day there was less and less of her in her body. And there had been a lot of her. She was a proud and striking woman. She raised my father, and then me all by herself, set up her own business, taught herself how to play the piano, did all the men's part of the housework, she even crafted furniture. She had so much character that it would have been enough for three. You know, you remind me of her sometimes with your stubbornness," McKee glanced at Jack and smiled slightly. "And this person, the remarkable person, began to fade away, began to dissolve right before my eyes. It was killing me, Jack, seriously, it was just killing me. Just like you said about Jacob. To look and see the shell of your loved one, it's terrible. Real torture. And I also wanted it to end faster. I also did, Jack. You're not the only one. And I'll tell you something now. I'll tell you something I've never told anyone. I've done a lot of stupid things in my life, but I only really regret two of them. The second one is how I flushed my best friend's legacy down the toilet, how I brought One-Two Boxing to its current wretched state. And the first..." McKee stopped to take a deep breath. "The first one had to do with my grandmother. About three or four years after she'd got her diagnosis, there was almost nothing left of the proud and strong Mary McKee. But at the time she still came to herself sometimes. Not for long, sometimes only for five to ten minutes. One day, during one such awakening, she looked at me and said..."

It seemed to Jack that the old man's voice started trembling, which was extremely difficult for him to believe.

"... she said, 'Son, don't let me stay like this. I must die a human. I can't be a burden and pee under myself. Help me stay human!' And then she looked down as if trying to remember something else she wanted to say, but she never looked back up. After that, my grandmother had lived for almost five more years. She forgot how to talk, soiled herself and all she did was watch children's cartoons on TV. And then even that was over. She'd been a living corpse for the last couple of months. And I was looking at all that. Five years, Jack, five years. That's something I'll never forgive myself for. Grandma was the kind of person I could never have become, even if I'd tried my best, which I never really did. And she wanted to die a human. She asked me to help her do so. And I couldn't. I pussied out. I got scared, I wasn't acting like a man. And it would've been fine if I'd been afraid of taking some risk for my own sake. But no, it was for the sake of my grandmother, the one who raised me, my only family. And now, Jack, tell me, was Jacob a remarkable person? Was your husband such a person?"

"He was," Sullivan replied timidly, almost in a whisper.

"Now tell me, would Jacob like to become what he's become? Would Jacob choose to remain like that himself, or would he want to die a human?"

"Human..." Jack answered even more quietly.

"I can't hear you, speak louder!"

"Jacob would like to die a human," Sullivan replied more

confidently this time.

"Then throw all that religious and liberal crap out of your head and stop blaming yourself for thinking the same way Jacob did himself. There's life like life when you can feel joy, when you do something, when you support your family and friends, when you live. And there's life like eating, shitting, sleeping. Like animal life. Like to breathe means to live. Life like life is sacred. Life as an animal is nothing. Cockroaches, flowers, mushrooms of all fricking kinds, they also live. So what? They don't even realize that they live. What's sacred about it? We're people and we should live like people. And we should die like people. Some live through their entire lives just eating, shitting, sleeping. First, they live off their parents, then they go on welfare. I mean, is *that* life sacred? Man, such people should be composted – that way they'd be of at least some use. And Jacob was a doctor, wasn't he?"

Jack nodded.

"Which means he helped people. He served a good cause. Unlike me, who'd just been swinging fists around for half of my life. He was a real decent man. Tell me, when you were together, did you help him, support him?"

Jack nodded again.

"And when it all happened, you didn't leave him, right? Right!" McKee immediately answered himself. "You could've put him in some kind of home. You could! But you didn't! So what was the bad thing you did? Huh? What was it? Right, there wasn't any!" The old man answered himself again. "And the fact that you didn't want to watch this decent man turn into a shadow of himself – what's wrong with that? What is so shameful about it? If you didn't love him, *then* you could take it calmly. The only thing you're guilty of in this situation is that you loved Jacob. It's as simple as that."

Two hours later, McKee and Jack finally made it to the hospital. Justine was already waiting for them in the hall. She said that Jacob had passed away without regaining consciousness four hours ago – at the same time when Jack had left Las Vegas. Justine did not want Jack to find out about his husband's death over the phone while on his way to him.

..21..

"Am I the only one who thought that a funeral always comes with nasty weather?" Derrick said, putting on his sunglasses.

Charlie shrugged his shoulders in response, and McKee gave Derrick a reproachful look, although he caught himself thinking that the weather was so good that he was tempted to take off his jacket and shoes and stretch out on the grass right between the tombstones. The old man took Kate by the hand, as the sharp heels prevented her from walking steadily on the lawn, and the four of them approached a rather large group of people gathered around the casket, which was about to be lowered into the ground, a large photograph of a smiling Jacob placed next to it.

Several men respectfully made way for the One-Two Boxing team to get closer – either being gallant toward Kate or slightly frightened by the huge McKee, who for some reason looked even more threatening than usual in a strict suit and tie.

Sullivan was standing by the opposite side of the casket and did not notice his boxing friends coming. By his sides stood two equally beautiful women, who were almost opposite in appearance. The one on the left possessed a rich Mediterranean beauty – gorgeous dark curly hair, large brown eyes, olive skin. She looked about the same age as Jack.

The woman on Jack's right was in her early fifties, but she still looked like she could have stepped off a fashion magazine cover. She resembled a northern aristocrat from somewhere in Sweden: nobly pale skin, piercing blue eyes, refined facial features, and blonde hair. The only thing the newly widowed man's female companions had in common was that they were both a head taller than him.

There was no priest at Jacob's funeral, and no one gave speeches. Only some unknown to the old man, but very sublime and slightly sad music was playing. And when it was time to lower the casket into the ground, unexpectedly for everyone, there began to play 'The Imperial March', which was recognized even by McKee, who had watched no more than a dozen movies in his entire life.

At first, the sound of the completely inappropriate for the occasion Darth Vader's Theme caused confusion among the attendees, but then a dozen of carefully restrained smiles still broke out on people's faces. As it turned out later, such background music was the idea of Jacob himself, who either jokingly or seriously had left instructions in case of his death ten years ago – at the same time when he had decided to take out life insurance and make a will in the name of his husband.

It was only when Jacob's coffin was already in the ground and those present began to slowly disperse that Jack first met the gaze of McKee and the other members of his team. Kate waved humbly at him, without raising her arm, but Sullivan did not respond. He approached one of the cemetery attendants, asked him for a shovel, and continued to fill up his husband's grave himself. In unspoken agreement, the old man, Derrick, and Charlie went to help him.

When the work was done, apart from the four men, there were only Kate and Jack's two companions who were still in the cemetery. Putting the shovel aside, Sullivan silently extended his hand to the old man, Derrick, and Charlie in turn. The three firm and slightly soil-stained handshakes left nothing to be said. That simple gesture was more manly and masculine than any victory in the ring.

"Hi, Kate," Jack uttered, noticing that he had deprived the woman of attention.

"Hi," Kate greeted him very tenderly in response. "How

are you?"

Jack nodded back, making it clear that he was fine.

"Thanks for coming, guys," Sullivan took a step toward his female companions. "Let me introduce you to my mom, Ellen," Jack motioned toward the aristocratic looking woman. "And this is Sophia." Sullivan took the young woman by the elbow. "She's Jacob's cousin and my first ever friend. We went to a university together. We were inseparable. And then *she* was the one to introduce me to Jacob. And these are my new friends with whom I practice boxing: Gerard, Derrick, Charlie, and Kate."

After the exchange of mutual greetings, Jack turned to McKee and his companions, "Will you come to our house for a wake?"

"Of course, Jack," the old man answered for everyone.

"Did I send a car for you or did you come by yourself?" Sullivan asked. "Sorry, I'm a little confused."

"We took Derrick's car. Don't sweat it, everything's fine."

Jack nodded and added, "All right, then follow behind the procession."

Jack nodded once again. His mother and Sophia took him by the arms and the three of them walked toward the black limousine, which headed the line of a dozen same cars. When they retired to a distance that was safe for making such observations, Derrick said, "Is it just me, or is she smoking hot?"

"Yep," McKee replied. "A true duchess. And those eyes are really something. Just like the sky."

"The sky?" Charlie asked. "Doesn't she have brown eyes?"

"Sophia's are brown," Kate replied. "But as far as I understand, Pops is not talking about her. Is that right, Pops?"

She playfully nudged the old man in the side with her elbow.

"Sure thing I'm not talking about her. She's probably still a snot-nosed kid just like you. While Ellen is the real woman."

"Be careful checking Jack's mom out or he might kick your ass," Derrick said with a grin.

"Oh, give me a break," the old man replied irritably and picked up his pace toward the car. "Smart asses."

At Sullivan's house, guests were greeted by tables with drinks and snacks, obliging waiters, and live music performed by such a tiny pianist that her feet barely reached the pedals. Jack himself was nowhere to be seen. The event was orchestrated by his mother, who was gracefully moving from one group of guests to another.

McKee, who had separated from his companions to get another portion of the first-class whiskey offered to the guests, watched with his heart in his mouth as Ellen moved in his direction. One more couple of guests and she would definitely come up to him. The old man carefully straightened his tie and jacket, which he had not worn since Johnny Sifaretto's funeral, and ran his hand through his thinning, but still quite impressive hair, which was even combed for the occasion.

"Gerard, right?" Ellen asked, approaching the old man.

"Yes, Mrs. Sullivan, that's right," McKee blurted out as if he was approached by a general.

"I'm neither Mrs. nor Sullivan," the woman corrected him with a slight smile. "I was never officially married to Jack's father."

"Oh, I'm sorry, ma'am," the old man replied awkwardly. "I knew that. Jack told me about his childhood. Excuse me. What's your full name?"

"Actually, my name is Elena Kovalenko. I'm Russian. But you don't have to even try to pronounce it. Just call me Ellen."

The woman gracefully extended her hand to the old man. McKee took her palm in his huge hand as gently and gallantly as possible, bringing it to his lips and kissing it. The old man was doing this for the first time in his life.

"Jack said you were one of his boxing friends," Ellen continued. "Tell me, please, what does it mean?"

"Didn't he tell you? Jack is now a professional boxer. And

quite a good one."

Had Ellen taken a sip of wine at that moment, she would have definitely choked.

"Jack? A boxer? My Jack?"

"Yes, ma'am. He's already got three fights under his belt. Three fights, three victories, and three knockouts. He even managed to set a record for the fastest knockout. You should be proud of him!"

"Well, I've always been proud of him," Ellen replied with another light smile. "Jack's always been an extraordinary boy. He took after his grandfather. My dad was a scientist. A mathematician. In the USSR. He showed great promise and was going to move to Moscow to work at the Academy of Sciences. But then he had a quarrel with the chief secretary of a local party office and thereby doomed himself. Instead of the Academy, my dad had to work as a math teacher at a rural school. He could not get any other job. Dad began to drink out of frustration, and then getting back to his former position was out of the question, even after the secretary himself was removed. I'm sorry. I opened up a bit too much. It's just that you have a very welcoming face."

"It's okay. There's no need to apologize. I'm only glad," McKee spoke quickly, trying to hide the embarrassment caused by the last words of the woman. "I just wanna say, ma'am, that you did a damn good job with Jack. I've never met anyone like him before. I don't even know how so much intelligence and character could fit into such a small package."

Ellen smiled slightly again in response to the old man's words.

"I'd like to take credit for the fact that he grew up like this, but the truth be told, Jack's developed his traits all by himself. I was more of a hindrance to him."

"I'm sure that's not true, ma'am!"

"Oh, no, trust me, it's true. It's not about me trying to be nice. And please stop calling me ma'am, just Ellen."

"All right, ma'am," McKee said, and immediately

corrected himself. "Ellen."

"Even the way I look and talk now is more of Jack's achievement rather than my own. I moved to America still being a child myself, as one could say, I didn't even have time to finish school. I worked as a model, but then it so happened that the only way of not starving was to get a job washing floors in a school. But thanks to that, I was finally able to get a high school diploma. Then I was promoted to a Russian language teacher. The school was very bad, and no foreign language teacher was willing to work there, so they employed me to avoid losing funding. But I became like this, wearing an expensive Chanel dress and having no accent, only because Jack had found a place for me in his charity project. I was so ashamed that everyone else there was much smarter and more cultured than me, that I got into a college and then university when I was already in my forties. Of course, Jack paid for all of that. But it was a very useful experience – now I know all the ins and outs of the educational process like no one else. I'm sorry, I've opened up again."

"No, no, I'm extremely pleased that you are talking to me like this. I know exactly what you're talking about. What it means to be ashamed in front of others. I've always been surrounded by people much smarter and more educated than me. Take your son, for example. He forgets all the time that I'm a simple old bumpkin who used his head only to get it punched. He'd sometimes ask me some stuff, which not only don't I know how to answer, but I don't even know whether that's a question or a statement."

Ellen answered the old man with another fleeting smile, took her last sip of wine, put the empty glass on the nearest table, ran a quick look at the huge figure of McKee from head to toe, and said, "Gerard, would you care to accompany me in a stroll around the garden? I'd love to hear about how my son became a boxer. I'm sure you have a lot of fascinating stories to tell."

"That'd be a real honor for me, Ellen," the old man

replied and offered the woman his hand.

On their way to the garden, McKee and Ellen bumped into Kate, who smiled and winked slyly at the old man. The coach pretended not to notice it. Having followed the unusual couple with her eyes, Kate headed to a buffet table, where a woman was already standing, small ringlets of her brown curly hair scattered over her shoulders.

"Sophia, right?" Kate addressed her.

"Yes," the woman answered. "And you Kate?"

Kate nodded back.

"When Jack said that you were Jacob's cousin, I somehow didn't realize at first that this was a huge loss not only for him but also for you. Please accept my deepest condolences. I've only seen Jacob a couple of times and that's all... you know... when he was already sick. But he looked like a very nice guy. And Jack was so fond of him. We all love Jack very much, and I have no doubt that he could only marry an incredibly good person."

"Thank you," Sophia replied. "He was truly a very nice guy. We grew up together. He was left without parents at the age of ten. His father died when Jacob was five, and later his mother died of cancer. He was adopted by his paternal grandparents, and we're related on the maternal side. We were like a second family to him. He spent every summer with us, we were like a real brother and sister. Then he went to study first in New York, then in Chicago, and when he came back, it was the time when I introduced him to Jack. After university, I went to work in Texas and we haven't seen each other much in recent years... But he really was a very nice guy..."

Sophia lowered her gaze thoughtfully and began fiddling nervously with the ring on her left hand. "I'm sorry, do you mind if we talk about something other than Jacob? Here one should probably talk only about him, but it's hard for me..."

"Yes, of course, I completely understand. It's such a big tragedy. Of course, it's hard for you to think about him now, to remember the past that you spent together," Kate hastened to calm her.

"Thank you," Sophia looked up at Kate and smiled slightly at her.

In fact, it was hard for Sophia to talk about Jacob not because of the childhood memories and not because of the loss itself, but because she blamed herself for not seeing her cousin often enough in recent years, and especially after his injury. Over the last year of Jacob's life, Sophia had come to visit him only once – even before Jack conceived his crazy plan of becoming a boxer.

"So you've come from Texas?" Kate hastened to change the subject.

"No, from Philadelphia."

"What do you do? I'm currently finishing my studies in economics and I help with accounting at One-Two – the gym where Jack boxes."

"I do music. Writing, producing. Mostly for indie movies, nothing big and fancy, but it's enough to live on."

"Wow! Music!? Seriously?"

"And what do you think I should do?" Sophia replied with a smile.

"Judging by your legs, height, and incredibly beautiful skin and hair, I'd say you could be a model. But your face looks too serious. A woman with such a face would never engage in something like modeling. You look like a lawyer from a movie. In a formal Prada suit, you know, like in 'The Good Wife'."

"I actually *was* a lawyer," Sophia replied, smiling even more friendly. "I used to work for a big oil company in Texas. And I also had a Prada suit. Even two of them, I think."

"Wow!" Kate repeated again. "You really *are* like a movie character – an awesome lawyer who became a musician. How is that even possible?"

"Somehow it just so happened. I was offered a partnership in my firm. That's a big decision to make. More responsibility, more working hours, more sleepless nights.

And that's when I realized that not only didn't I want more of it, but I didn't want any of it, at all. You know, I lost faith in our procedural system in my first year of work. Laws, courts – all of it works not for the one who's right, but for the one who has more money for lawyers, pseudo-independent expertise, great experts, PR guys, and so on. I've been working in that field for so long only because of stereotypes – a cool job, lots of money, prestige, more prospects, plus being a woman who has achieved success in the men's world. Who'd give up on that of their own accord? It was only when that big offer was made to me that I realized I wasn't interested in it at all. I realized that the money, prestige, and the awareness of my fulfilled feminist duty didn't make me even a tiny bit happier."

"You're awesome, straight awesome! I really admire your fortitude. I could never do what you did! And why is it the music of all things?"

"Actually, Jack's the one to blame for that. I was into music at university. I played guitar in one student band, synthesizer in another; I was even a DJ at campus parties for a little while. And he always supported me in that. It was Jack who made me audition for both bands. And then when I realized I didn't want to be a lawyer anymore, I didn't know what to do next. I was headhunted by that Texas firm in my last year. Right after my graduation, I took a flight to Houston and immediately started slaving away there for sixty hours a week. I was on vacation for only ten days in the first five years. My head was filled to the brim with nothing else but corporate law. Then I called Jack. Starting from my first year in university I've always sought his advice on important matters. And he reminded me of how much I loved music, how I could spend the whole weekend without sleeping, making a new mix on my laptop, and still not feeling tired and broken, as when I was practicing law, but on the contrary, I was happy and satisfied. Certainly, it's also because I was only twenty at the time, but still. And he was right. Surely I earn ten times less doing music than lawyering, but I enjoy every minute of my work."

"Wow, Sophia! You're a dream woman! If I were gay, I'd marry you."

"Thank you," Sophia replied and ran her palm over Kate's arm. "If I were gay, I would at least let you buy me a drink."

"In that case, let me offer you this wonderful Merlot," Kate said, picking up a glass of wine from the tray of a passing waiter and handing it to her new acquaintance.

Sophia accepted the glass, making a mock curtsy. The women smiled at each other.

"Sophia, I think it's the beginning of a wonderful friendship," Kate said, raising her glass. "Even considering that we met under such tragic circumstances. I hope that didn't sound insensitive to Jacob's memory."

"No," Sophia replied. "In fact, it's very much in the spirit of Jacob. He would definitely like that. He believed that there was no such thing as an inappropriate place or time for good things, such as starting a new friendship. Jacob was always in search of an opportunity to extract something positive even from the most negative experience. You heard what he'd done in the cemetery, didn't you? Only Jacob could come up with the idea of making people laugh playing 'The Imperial March' at his own funeral."

"In that case, to Jacob! To his positive attitude and the fact that even with his death he managed to do something good, bringing you and me together."

Kate raised her glass. Sophia replied to her toast, after which she quickly wiped away a small tear that appeared in the corner of her eye.

Meanwhile, nobody had seen the owner of the house ever since the wake started. His mother began to worry. Ellen asked McKee to look for Jack on the other side of the garden while she went to look around the house. The old man found Sullivan first. He was in an opened garage, sitting in the driver's seat of the Aston Martin, which he never got a chance to give as a present to his husband. Jacob would have had to live for exactly another month and a day to see his fortieth birthday.

Jack got rid of his tie and jacket, while leaving his sunglasses on, which was completely unnecessary in the lengthening shadows of the twilight. There were headphones plugged into his ears. In the instructions regarding his own funeral, Jacob left not only the orders about the music that must be played at his burial but also a list of twenty songs that he would like Jack to remember him with. One of them was Sophia's song – her first and so far the only song she wrote for herself and not for a client.

Even though the song was telling the story of a girl's unrequited love for a guy, Jacob called it an anthem of his own love for Jack. Sophia hid this song from everyone, but Jacob, who was always neglecting other people's personal space, found it on her laptop when she stayed with him and Jack over the weekend during one of her visits. Despite the dressing-down he was given for that, Jacob was still able to get Sophia to give him a copy of the song, and since then it had been played in Sullivan's house no less frequently than 'Rocket man'.

"Can I sit here?" McKee asked as he approached the car.

Despite the fact that looking through sunglasses at dusk Jack could only make out a dark silhouette of a man against the background of dim garden lights, he immediately recognized the giant figure of the coach.

"What?" he asked, taking the headphones out of his ears.

"Can I sit with you?" the old man repeated.

Jack nodded at the passenger seat. McKee settled awkwardly in the seat designed for skinny London dandies rather than huge Irish boxers.

"You all right?" the coach asked.

Jack let out a long breath and answered, "I feel like I'd been getting pummelled by Artur Melikov not for twelve, but a good two hundred and twelve rounds."

"So you're saying that you're about to knock him out?" the old man attempted to joke.

"You know, now that he's gone, not Jacob, but his shell,

which I couldn't bear to look at... Only now do I realize how hurtful it was for me to lose him back then, in that bar. I knew he hadn't been around for those two years, but some part of me, a very stupid, very very stupid part, thought that he hadn't been dead yet. And now he's fully gone. Until this very moment, I didn't even realize that I had some absolutely idiotic hope. You know, I probably even came up with this asinine boxing plan just because I thought there was some kind of sacred magic in it. The minute I took revenge and Joe Ryan was defeated, the spell would break. Just like in 'Snow White'. Jacob would wake up and everything would be fine again. All I had to do was to beat Joe Ryan."

"Well, you still *can* beat Ryan. It won't bring Jacob back, of course, but at least it's something. Better than nothing. You can at least blow off some steam punching him in his cocky mug."

Jack gave no response to that, running his hands over the surface of the wheel. Restoring this wheel was the first thing Jacob did when he began to work on the DB5, and that was extremely unusual since the whole car was a total mess at the time.

"By the way, Jack. I got a call from IPBU. But you don't have to worry about anything. I explained everything to them. They understood. They were very respectful. They said they'd wait for you to return to the ring, no matter if it would take six months or a year. Your fight with Melikov made quite a stir. It's a pity you couldn't enjoy it. Everyone's now waiting for your comeback."

"There will be no comeback," Jack replied.

"Well, yes, of course, not yet. No question about it. They understand."

"There will be no comeback," Sullivan repeated and added. "Ever."

"Yes, sorry, it's not the right time to talk about it now. I'm such an old fool. Have nothing but boxing on my mind. You need to get over it now. Enough about boxing... later, we'll decide everything later..."

"No, Gerard, I wasn't clear enough," Jack interrupted the old man. "I'm serious. I'm not going back to it. Never. No more boxing. The money I promised you for ten victories – it's yours. You earned it rightfully. It's my decision to terminate the contract."

"What money, Jack. I don't give a shit about money. We're family, what money are you talking about!? You've achieved so much. Nobody's saying that you need to get back in the ring right now, but why give up everything in the heat of the moment?"

Sullivan took off his glasses abruptly, got out from behind the wheel, and stood up in front of the car, facing the old man.

"We're not family, Gerard," Jack said, raising his voice. "Jacob was my family. And now he's gone. I made up this surrogate boxing family for myself and made you all believe in it. WE'RE NOT FAMILY!" Sullivan finally yelled out.

"Okay, not family," the old man tried to calm Jack down. "We're friends. Call it whatever you want. The main thing is that we take care of each other..."

"Friends," Jack drawled with a grin. "What kind of a universe is that where a pussyass gay programmer can be friends with a roughneck boxer? Don't be ridiculous."

McKee understood that it was the pain of Sullivan's loss that was behind those words, but still, it was extremely unpleasant for him to hear them.

"You're not a pussyass. You're the real man. You're a boxer!"

"I hate boxers!" Jack's voice grew louder and angrier with every word he said. "I hate athletes! I despise all of you! Beating the fucking hell out of each other in the ring – is that an accomplishment or something? Any kid at the checkout at McDonald's benefits society more than the greatest athlete. You don't do anything good for others at all! You just boost your own ego and make money off of idiots like yourself, who are ready to pay for watching the thing they want but are afraid to do. You were the world champion and so what? What have you achieved? What value have you brought to those around you? Huh? Answer me, Gerard? Who the fuck needs you in this world?"

The old man did not answer.

"We're done here. Get the fuck out of my house," Sullivan threw the words at McKee like a powerful jab and spat on the ground.

The old man still remained silent and motionless. Jack turned to leave but saw Kate, Charlie, and Derrick standing behind him. And a little further away stood Ellen and Sophia. They came hearing Jack's yells, but he was so carried away that he did not notice them approaching. Neither new friends, nor the old university friend, nor even his own mother – none of them recognized Jack. His always so reserved and even distant face was now twisted with anger and rage.

For a minute they all looked at him, and he kept switching his glance from one of them to the other. Unable to stand it, Jack finally walked between Charlie and Derrick, pushing them both aside, went out through the open gate and disappeared somewhere into the night. It was not until Sullivan left that Kate glanced at McKee. Even under the poor lighting, she immediately noticed how much the coach had changed. He seemed to have become smaller as if he had shrunk and turned from an elderly but still powerful and proud figure into a pathetic old man.

An old man who had no family, no children, and who was now left without a friend and his precious business, which he was so proud of and which made him feel alive for the first time in all the years that had passed since the death of Johnny Sifaretto.

..22..

Jack got back home only in the early morning when the darkness of the night had begun to turn into morning twilight. The guests had left a long time ago and the house standing behind the open gates now looked completely uninhabited. Sullivan ran his hand along the live fence of thujas and was about to enter the property when he was called from behind, "You done wandering?"

Jack turned around and saw Sophia sitting on the sidewalk on the opposite side of the road. She was still wearing the same strict black mourning dress, but there were no shoes on her feet, and her hair no longer rested nobly on her shoulders but was drawn back into a ponytail. There were only two strands of hair dangling on both sides of her face, elegantly framing it. Sophia was clutching a bottle of beer in her hand.

Sullivan looked at her but said nothing. He turned back and took a step toward the house.

"Hey!" Sophia shouted after him and got up from the sidewalk. "I'm talking to you!"

Jack waved his hand, making it clear that he was not in the mood to answer, and took another step toward the house. Suddenly, there was a loud sound of glass breaking right behind him. Sullivan turned around to see a large beer splash on the asphalt next to him and a pile of fragments from what a second ago was the bottle Sophia was clutching in her hand.

An angry shadow ran over Sullivan's face again, and he started walking resolutely toward Sophia.

"You know," Sophia said in an inebriated voice. "You're

not the only one who lost him. He was like a brother to me. I miss him too."

Her eyes welled up with tears. Jack's face lightened up instantly. He took the last three steps to Sophia and wrapped her in a tight embrace. The woman, who was still noticeably taller than Sullivan even without heels, twined her arms around his neck, bent her head, and rested her forehead against his. Two timid tears quickly turned into a full-fledged stream as her whole body started shaking with sobs.

Sophia's tears were falling on Jack's face, mixing with his own, and soon they were both sobbing without restraint and in self-abandonment. They stopped only when the first rays of dawn sunlight fell upon the road they were standing in the middle of.

Then Jack took Sophia by the hand, and they walked to the house together. Once inside, Sullivan went to the kitchen to make some coffee, and Sophia settled in the living room on the sofa. Jack returned with two cups of fragrant coffee made just the way Sophia liked it – with thick frothed milk, cinnamon, and a spoonful of honey – only to find the woman sleeping.

At first, Sullivan wanted to take her to the guest bedroom, but then changed his mind. Instead, Jack picked up a blanket from a nearby chair and carefully covered her with it. For a few minutes he stood watching Sophia sleep nicely and peacefully, and then he sat down next to her, gently lifting her head and putting it on his lap.

Jack remembered how Sophia used to ask him to stroke her hair – it was the best way for her to calm down in a stressful situation. That was how, gently stroking his friend's head, Sullivan fell asleep himself.

...

Jack woke up around noon to find out that Sophia was no longer lying next to him on the sofa. But it was not long until he found her. A mug of fresh, steaming coffee appeared right under Sullivan's nose.

"Good morning, sleepyhead," said Sophia and kissed Jack on the top of his head.

"Morning," Jack said and took a long sip of coffee.

Sophia got enough time not only to make coffee but also to wash and change out of her black mourning dress into home pajamas. Without makeup and with her eyelids swollen from yesterday's tears, Sophia no longer looked like that gorgeous Mediterranean beauty from the cover of a fashion magazine, but that way Jack always liked her the most – real, alive, rather than embellished and retouched.

After taking a few more sips of coffee, Jack got up from the sofa and winced, feeling his back and neck aching from sleeping in an uncomfortable position.

"What time is your flight?" he asked, putting the mug on the coffee table.

"I'm not flying anywhere," Sophia replied, sitting down in an armchair next to the sofa.

"How do you mean?"

"Literally. I returned my ticket last night."

"Why? Don't you have things to do in Philly?"

"Honestly, not really. I finished my last soundtrack a week ago. But even if I had – do you seriously think that I'd leave you alone in your condition?"

"And what is this condition I'm in?"

"Don't you remember the crazy thing you did last night before going for a marathon walk until six in the morning? I thought that old giant would have a heart attack. Ellen, by the way, was also very worried when you left. I made her take some valium and go home. What came over you then? I've never seen you like that before."

"Let's not talk about it. I can handle it. I'm a big boy already, I'll figure it out somehow. So you can safely buy a ticket for the next flight."

"Yeah, good one. Your opinion is definitely very

important to me right now," Sophia replied sarcastically. "There's no doubt, of course, that you can adequately assess your psychological state at the moment. Right, I'm on it, off to pack my bags. I would've never left you alone myself, besides, Ellen asked me to look after you, and your boxing friends were worried too. They're good guys. They were very understanding, despite the crazy thing you did."

"I asked you not to talk about it..."

"All right, all right, I'll shut up. Seriously though, you've only two options – you can either put up with my presence or forcibly push me out of the house. But in that case, I'll be scratching and biting, and then I'll call your mom and you'll have to explain it to her too."

Jack was about to make some objection to Sophia, but she hastened to advance the last rock-solid argument, which would definitely make Sullivan cave. "And you're very well aware that Jacob would never forgive me if I left you now." Sophia took a sip of coffee and pointed the mug toward the large stand-up framed photo of Jack's late husband, which was left from yesterday's ceremony, still placed in the corner.

Sullivan sighed sadly and waved his hand. "Okay, whatever you say. I need to take a shower. Do whatever you want."

"When will you learn that you'll never be able to out-argue me? Next time, give up right away, that'll save you some time!" Sophia called after Jack as he headed for the bathroom.

...

After taking a long, almost meditative shower and changing into fresh clothes, Jack sat down on the bed and started staring blankly at the wall. He suddenly realized that he did not know what to do next. For the first time in his life, he had nothing to do. Sullivan started working part-time at twelve and continued to do so in parallel to his studies up until graduation.

Then he got a full-time job, and he spent all his free time with Jacob. It was Jacob who always decided for the both of them where to go, what to do, what to listen to and watch. After the assault, when Jacob could no longer make such decisions, Jack spent all his time caring for him and trying to get to Joe Ryan with the help of lawyers and private detectives. By that time, Jack had cut his work to a minimum, accepting only the most important orders from his regular customers. Then he started boxing.

And now he no longer had either a job, Jacob, or boxing. Only a huge amount of free time and complete lack of understanding of what to spend it on. Jack did not even know how to choose a movie – it was always up to Jacob, who was a huge movie fan. The last time Sullivan chose something himself and decided what to do and where to go – was during those very university years when Sophia and he were inseparable. But that was more than ten years ago.

For the first time, Jack realized how much he depended on Jacob. Of course, he always knew that Jacob was the only person he needed and that he never wanted to do anything without his husband, but only now did Jack realize that Jacob was everything to him, not only in an intimately-romantic way but in every way. Even the clothes Sullivan had just put on had been chosen by Jacob.

With this realization, the pain of losing a loved one was joined by yet a new feeling – fear. Now the banal phrase "How will I live without him?" took on a new meaning for Jack. He did not just lose the only person he had ever loved so much and who loved him just as much in return. He had lost the person who for the last ten years had defined his entire life in all its manifestations.

Which neighborhood to settle into, what their house should look like, its interior from the layout of the rooms down to the last little detail, such as towel hooks in the bathroom, where and when to go on vacation, what sights to see, what to eat, what to drink, what to watch, what to listen to, what to wear, what ride to take. Even all of Jack's personal belongings – his car, his clothes, his smartphone, his key fob – were either given to him as a present or chosen for him by Jacob.

Sullivan was horrified to realize that over the past two years, when he had to make decisions himself, he actually did not choose anything. The things he still had to buy during that period of time – the minivan for transporting Jacob or the sportswear for the One-Two Boxing – were not chosen by him. He just came to a store and told a sales assistant what he needed. And even when he was given several options to choose from, he asked sales assistants to decide for him.

And all this time he ate only the food he had eaten before with Jacob, watched only those movies and shows that they had watched together, listened only to music from his collection. Woodkid's latest album was the only new thing he listened to. But he did not make that choice either! It was Jacob who liked Woodkid and was subscribed to his updates. Jack just got a message on the screen announcing a new release, and he played it. That's it! Absolutely everything in Sullivan's life was decided by Jacob.

The dread of realizing that he was left completely helpless without Jacob made Jack start nervously cracking his knuckles – a bad habit that he seemed to have gotten rid of back in his university years. Sullivan's stupor was broken by a sudden blow. He looked up and saw Sophia standing next to him, clutching a pillow in her hand.

"Have you forgotten about our agreement?" Sophia said. "As long as you keep breaking your fingers – you'll be getting hit on the head!"

It was only after hearing these words that Jack remembered that it was Sophia, and not himself, who had him break this bad habit.

"Please don't leave me alone!" Jack said, catching the woman's free hand and squeezing it in his palms. "Let's set you up with a studio so you can work here! I'll pay for everything! Just don't leave me alone!"

"Whoa-whoa! Jack, slow down! I'm not going anywhere! Everything'll be fine!"

Sullivan drew Sophia closer to him and rested his face against her stomach. She ran her fingers through Jack's hair and began stroking his head gently and carefully as if he was her own child. But it made Sullivan even more uncomfortable – he immediately thought that even this haircut was chosen by Jacob, who extolled his husband's thick and silky hair all the time, although Jack himself always wanted to get a shorter haircut.

..23..

The first three days since Jacob's funeral, Jack and Sophia spent at home. They watched TV, listened to music, ordered in food, lay on the bed, sofa or even on the floor, and talked for hours on end. They discussed their shared memories of Jacob, told each other their own stories which he was the part of.

It was Sophia who chose music, food, and movies. Every time she asked for Jack's opinion and suggested that he choose something, he either chose from things Jacob liked or said something in the vein of "I don't care, pick something yourself." Later, various types of binge indoor activities got coupled with strolls outside. At first, they were short strolls in the neighborhood, but with each passing day, they got farther and longer.

And with each passing day, they talked less and less about Jacob and more often recalled the time of them being inseparable friends at university. Not because they had already begun to forget about the deceased, on the contrary – because it was too hard for both of them to talk about him. Over the first week of such life, Jack and Sophia's peace was disturbed only once. Ellen, despite all the reassurances given to her over the phone, still decided to personally verify her son's psychological stability.

But her visit did not last long. After having tea, which is traditional for Russians on such occasions, and a rather awkward conversation, the woman gave both of them a tight hug and went back home. Jack's relationship with his mother had always been a bit strained. He seemed uncomfortable around her. Sophia, who had noticed that back in the days of their common youth, had no luck trying to understand the reasons for Jack acting in such a way.

After all, all things considered, one could not possibly say that Sullivan treated his mother badly. He bought her a house as soon as he got his first large professional fee, and then completely took over all her expenses. And paying her bills was not the only thing to express his good attitude towards her – if Ellen had any problems, Jack immediately rushed to her aid, dropping everything else.

Sophia always liked Ellen and Ellen liked her in return, several times even calling her a daughter, which she never had. Jack's mother was a very quiet, calm, and kind woman, around whom Sophia sometimes felt even more comfortable than around her own mother. So it was completely unclear to her why Jack always felt uneasy in the presence of his mother.

Other than that visit, Jack and Sophia's pastime resembled the life of an old married couple – a lot of TV watching, simple pleasures of life, like shoulder massage, warmth, tenderness, and caring for each other with no physical intimacy whatsoever. But soon their quiet family idyll was broken by another completely unexpected guest.

In the second week of their living together, when Jack and Sophia were sitting on a bench in the front garden and drinking coffee, a shy voice called out Jack's name from the street. When Sullivan opened the gate, there was Charlie behind it, dressed in the Pembridge Academy uniform, where he had started studying a month before Jack's fight with Artur Melikov and Jacob's death.

Jack extended his hand to the boy. The handshake turned out to be rather awkward. Sullivan had not seen or heard from anyone from One-Two Boxing since the day of the funeral and that unpleasant scene with McKee, which he tried hard not to recall. Jack invited the guest inside the house and showed him into the kitchen. The boy refused both food and drinks, as well as taking a seat on a chair pulled up to him. Charlie was obviously nervous, so he decided to get straight to the point of his visit.

"Jack... You... you must come back!" the boy stammered, not looking at Sullivan.

Sullivan hesitated to answer. He took a few steps around the kitchen, picked up a mug, as if intending to pour himself some tea, but immediately changed his mind.

"Charlie," he finally spoke. "I'm sorry I haven't called you all this time and haven't visited you at the academy, even though I promised to do so." Sullivan picked up the mug again. "And I'm sorry for that... for that speech I made at the wake. You shouldn't have heard all that. And I shouldn't have used those words... But my position hasn't changed. I'm not going back to the ring. This chapter of my life is closed. But it doesn't mean that we can't stay friends. You can still call me for any matters. I'll help you anytime. And it's not only about help. We'll definitely hang out together. Now is just not the right time. Don't worry, nothing will change between you and me."

"It... It's not myself I'm worried about," the boy spoke again, stammering as before. "You need to come back... You really need to come back. For the old man's sake!"

"Did McKee send you? What did he say?"

"No. He didn't say anything. He said nothing at all. No one has seen him for a week already. One-Two is closed. We've all called him a million times – he doesn't answer. And we came over to his place – he won't answer the door. We thought he'd gone somewhere or even kicked the bucket. But no, the truck's parked outside. Kate talked to the neighbors – they say every other day they hear him rattling a bag full of bottles when he gets back home from a store."

Jack frowned but still decided to make himself some tea.

"Jack, he won't last long like that! And we tried everything we could – we left him messages, put notes under his door. Derrick once managed to waylay him in the evening when he went to a store to buy booze. The old man passed him by as if he didn't know him. Derrick tried to stop him, but the old man gave him such a scowl he didn't take any further chances. And he'd only bought booze, hadn't even taken any food. Jack, he's going to kill himself that way!"

"Charlie... I don't know how to explain it to you...," Jack spoke, fiddling with his mug. "Yes, I said too much to the old man, of course, but he's a big boy, he should've understood the circumstances himself. I'll... I'll probably call him one of these days. I'll try to reason with him. But that's all I can do. I'm not going back. I can't go back to the ring for him. Even though I like the old man. I'll apologize to him for the words I used, but I can't apologize for the way I think. I won't change it. It's my principle position, and I will continue to stick to it regardless of whether it hurts someone's feelings or not."

Charlie looked down and put his hands inside his pockets, like a child who broke something while playing ball indoors, although his parents told him a hundred times not to do it.

"Talking won't do any good," Charlie said under his breath. "Neither apologies. You don't understand, Jack, the old man needs *you*, not an apology. He needs the ring. That's all he has. You don't understand... The old man, he... he's very lonely. When he retired from boxing, there was only Mr. Sifaretto who was there for him, and then he was gone too. The old man hadn't had anything since then. Until you showed up. Damn, Jack, how hard can it be for you to understand that you've made all the difference for the old man! Just remember what he was like when you first came – homophobic, racist, alcoholic. And what a change has he undergone! It's incredible! It hadn't been half a year since he met you that he became a different person! There's a reason for that, Jack. How can't you see!?! You became his friend, his partner, you brought him back to boxing! You've restored his belief that his life's not over yet. And the same thing with boxing. It was probably only with you that he felt like a real coach for the first time! It was you who convinced him that he knows how to coach at all! You've become the new Mr. Sifaretto for him! He barely got over the death of the real Mr. Sifaretto, he won't be able to get over your leaving too! Jack, please! Do it for the old man! Please, I'm begging you!"

"Charlie, I can't..." Jack tried to answer, but Charlie immediately interrupted him.

"I'm not saying that now you have to box for the rest of your life. No, there's no need for that. Just don't leave the old man. Have at least one more fight. And then we'll figure something out. We'll say you got injured. We'll figure something out! Just don't leave like that, Jack! Please, do it for the old man!" The boy's voice started trembling noticeably. "He's good deep inside! It's just that he had a hard life, and there was no one around, no one to support him."

Charlie's pleas suddenly irritated Jack.

"And who will support me, Charlie? Who will think about me? I've been trying hard my whole life, striving, toiling away like mad, helping everyone, even started a charity, put *you* in school, and what did I get?" Sullivan spoke in a raised tone now. "I had one person, exactly one person who supported me, and not whom I had to support. One! And what did I get for all these efforts? What did I get for all this support of others?!? He's been murdered, Charlie, murdered! Do you hear me!?!"

Sullivan started turning back into that man who yelled at McKee a week ago. Charlie got quite a scare when Jack, who had always been so calm and friendly to him, suddenly switched to yelling. But then Sophia, who had been standing not far from them in the hall all this time, came to the boy's rescue.

"Hey!" she shouted in Jack's direction, resolutely entering the kitchen. "Shut it! Stop yelling at the kid! What's wrong with you?"

Sophia turned to Charlie and addressed the boy already in a different, gentle, soothing voice, "Charlie, never mind him. He's not himself now. You know that. Too little time has passed yet. You know he's not like that. It's not him, it's his pain talking."

Sophia noticed that Charlie could not take his eyes off Jack as if mesmerized by the metamorphoses that had taken place in him. Sophia turned to Sullivan and again spoke in a different voice – strict and authoritative, "Go to the bedroom! I'll talk to you later!"

Jack responded to Sophia's command with a withering look, but the woman did not lose her cool and repeated in exactly the same strict voice, "Go to the bedroom! I'll sort this out myself and talk to you later. Go!"

Jack obeyed. Not because Sophia's strictness had some effect on him, but because he himself did not want to continue this conversation. When the sound of the bedroom door slam reached the kitchen, Sophia turned back to Charlie. "He'll make it right with the old man. Everything will be fine, I promise!"

Having reassured Charlie, Sophia called an Uber for him, and only after personally getting the boy in the car she returned to the house and resolutely headed toward Jack's bedroom, from which were coming the sounds of music – the very playlist that Jacob had compiled for him.

"What's wrong with you?" Sophia shouted, almost breaking into the room. "You over there yelling at old people, children, what's next? Pregnant women? The disabled? Puppies? I've never seen you like this! You've always been the nicest guy!"

"The nicest guy...," Jack grinned bitterly in response. "And what came out of it? What did I get? Is this the reward I received for being nice? Becoming a widower at thirty-five!? Losing everything I had!? I'm done with being nice!"

"Done?" Sophia spoke back just as emotionally. "Seriously? And now what? You gonna be a dick? Seriously, Jack? Gonna give everything up to become a dick?"

Jack chose not to answer Sophia's questions.

"There are seven billion people in the world, at least six billion of them are dicks, and most of the shit falls to the lot of the remaining one billion who aren't dicks. So what of it? Let's all quit being nice and start being dicks! How about we all become dicks, Jack? People like you are the backbone of this whole world! Should you become a dick, that's it, you can shut down this project called humanity! You're not like that, Jack! It's hard for you, I get it, but you can't just give everything up and become a dick because things have been looking bad for you. My life, of course, can't come close to yours in terms of hardship, but it's far from perfect too. I lost Jacob as well! But at least you had him! Ten or twelve years, how long was it that you lived together? In perfect harmony! And I've already had two broken marriages over this time. You think I've had a time of my life? So now what? Maybe we should start being dicks together? Let's go yell at the elderly and children all over the town. And we can also poke sticks in the wheels of wheelchairs and trip pregnant women. What do you say, Jack, shall we go do that?"

Sullivan remained silent but his expression became sad rather than angry. Noticing that, Sophia spoke in a calmer voice too, "I understand how much it sucks for you now. I'm suffering too because of what happened to him. But you're strong, Jack, you can handle it. Somehow you even managed to become a boxer, and a good one. Having done that, you can handle anything!"

"I can't, Soph," Jack finally spoke. "I'm weak. I've never been strong. It was all Jacob. He made me strong. And without him, I'm nothing. You don't understand. He deserves all the credit for all of this. The house, our life, even these clothes, and this haircut – it's all him."

"You really think the haircut is what makes you strong?"

"No, of course not. The thing is, it was Jacob who always decided everything, it was him who took responsibility. That's why I could look strong. But in fact, it was all him. And now he's gone. I'm alone. And I'm weak. Always been and always will be. It's time to stop lying to myself."

"Jack, that's utter nonsense! I knew you long before Jacob. You'd never been weak."

"Come on, you don't have to console me..."

"No, I'm serious," Sophia interrupted him. "Don't you remember?"

"Remember what?"

"It's apparent that you probably don't remember anything. You've always been strong! You supported me. You *always* supported me. It was only thanks to you that I managed to graduate with such good marks, and I got big into music only at your suggestion."

"Well, that's not difficult. You don't need much strength for such support."

"But it wasn't just that! How could you forget it all? Take, for example, my second year at university. Remember, those two who mixed something into my beer at a party and already started dragging me somewhere. And you stopped them."

"Stopped them, yeah, sure," Jack grinned. "They both were almost twice as big as me. They kicked the shit out of me. You probably forgot that. You nursed me back then when my beaten guts hurt so much I couldn't get out of bed for two days."

"Exactly! Exactly, Jack! That *is* strength! You weren't afraid to stand up for me against two huge bastards! You defended me at the risk of your own life! That is strength! If it were the other way round, if you were twice as big as them – would there be something special about it? Is it strength when you don't risk anything?"

"It was more of stupidity than strength. I had to call someone for help, rather than posing a hero."

"Just don't belittle what you did! If you had gone to look for help, they would've had enough time to rape me."

"Well, thank you for trying to cheer me up, but I know what I was like before Jacob, what I was like with him, and how I feel now without him. Without him, I'm nothing."

"No, you don't know anything!" the woman's voice started trembling. "Do you know, for example, why I visited you so rarely? And why I moved to Philly and didn't come back home?"

Jack shrugged his shoulders. "You got a lot of work, and you were married. Twice. One could hardly make time in such circumstances. And Philly... I don't know. Didn't you say something about its unique atmosphere, that the city itself inspired you?"

"I said a lot of things. Only it's not true. I didn't come back because of you."

"Because of me?" Jack asked, raising his eyebrows in surprise. "What bad did I do?"

"No, you didn't do anything. It's because of what you became with Jacob."

"What did I become? Happy? And you didn't like that? Were you jealous of us or something? Is that the reason? Because we made it, and you didn't?"

"No, not happy. Well, I mean, yes, you became happier, but that's not what troubled me. You became weak."

"I became weak? With Jacob?" Jack asked with even greater surprise and started walking about the room. "Didn't you get anything wrong?"

"No, it's you who got everything wrong. Of course, you've always been insecure because of not being masculine enough, because of your height, because you didn't look tough enough, but you coped with that and not only with that. You coped in general. You tried hard, strived, went forward no matter what. You protected me, supported me, nudged me forward. Where is weakness in that? You'd achieved so much over those years. Valedictorian, the winner of all those programming competitions. And your charity project? That's something incredible! Who else besides you, being still a student himself, thinks about ways to help others? No one! Just think about it – all that you'd achieved, all the meaningful things you'd done – all of that had been before Jacob! And with him, you just kept going further down the beaten track. With him, you stopped progressing."

"I need something to drink," Jack said and left the bedroom.

The music followed him. The user movement tracking system which transmitted the sound to speakers along the way was one of Sullivan's dozen inventions. And all the proceeds from the licensing of this technology, just like almost all the other ones he had, were annually transferred to his charity fund.

"Jack," Sophia followed him. "I loved Jacob as much as you did. I don't mean to say anything bad about him. And I actually *can't* say anything bad about him. He was a great person. He loved both you and me very much. And he always wished us only the best."

Jack stopped in the middle of the kitchen and began to look around indecisively, not knowing what to choose – tea, coffee, water, or maybe something from the bar.

"He never meant ill and never did anything like that on purpose," Sophia continued. "But he had a certain power, uncontrolled. He subdued people. Unwittingly, probably even with the best of intentions in mind. But it was there. With him around, you had to obey, adapt to him. You didn't even notice it yourself. You just started doing what he told you to do and even thinking the way he wanted you to think. He was always like that, ever since he was a kid. I remember when he sometimes stayed with us for a whole summer, and then, every time after he went back home, it was like the scales fell from my eyes."

Jack never decided what he wanted to drink, but he took the mug and now was walking from one corner of the kitchen to another, holding it in his hand. In the meantime, Sophia kept going on, "With him, I listened only to the music he listened to, and I wanted to do only what he liked to do. And after him leaving, I suddenly remembered Britney Spears and Christina Aguilera, skateboarding, MTV. I even forgot about my friends when he was around! It's not his fault. There was just too much of him, he was too outstanding. He took the shine out of anyone who happened to be around. It's like turning the light on in a room on a bright sunny day. You won't even notice that the light bulb is on until you look directly at it. The light of the bulb simply dissolves in the light of the Sun. And you also dissolved in Jacob! You disappeared with him around. When the two of you were together, you weren't really there, there wasn't that old Jack, there wasn't my Jack, there wasn't my best friend. There was only Jacob's husband! Think about it – even all your friends were actually his friends!"

Sophia's words were cut short by the sound of breaking glass. Not being able to stand the accusations against his late husband any longer, Jack snapped and threw the mug on the floor.

"Stop it! Stop it! Stop it!" he pleaded, covering his ears with his hands. "Stop talking about Jacob! He's the only one who ever loved me! He didn't subdue me! He made me whole, looked out for me, he supported me! He was everything to me! Only he ever loved me!"

"It's not true!" Sophia shouted back with tears in her voice. "He wasn't the only one who loved you! Look! There! Listen to that!" The woman cried, pointing her hand toward the speaker in the corner of the kitchen, from which at that moment came the starting chords of her song – the very song that Jacob called an anthem for his love for Jack. "This song. For years, I couldn't forgive Jacob for going through my laptop and finding this song. It was mine and only mine. No one was supposed to hear it. And he took it from me."

"The Song?!?" Jack cried out. "Seriously, Soph?!? Are you mad at him because of the song? Is it because of this song that you just said all those nasty things about him? Jacob loved this song. He thought it was about me. Like it's about his love for me. What's wrong with that? What's wrong with Jacob loving this song?"

"It *is* about you!!!" Sophia blurted and stormed out of the kitchen.

"How do you mean it's about me?" Jack replied uncomprehendingly and hurried after her.

Sullivan caught up with Sophia almost at the front door

and grabbed her by the hand so that she would not leave. Sophia forcefully pulled her hand out of Jack's palms but stopped nonetheless.

"Do you know why I actually couldn't look at you and Jacob being together?" she spoke with a breaking voice, almost screaming. "I could forgive him for taking you away from me, but I could never forgive him for dissolving you. Because of him, not only did I lose the opportunity to be with you, because of him, the former you disappeared completely. I loved Jacob. I loved him very much as if he'd been my blood brother. But I've always loved you more!"

Sophia opened the door and went out into the garden. Jack followed her. He was shocked by the woman's confession and found himself at a loss for any reply.

"You know, the day Jacob died, I was at your fight," she spoke again, sitting down on the bench. "I didn't even know that you'd started boxing. You didn't tell me anything. I saw an ad on the Internet and couldn't help it. I flew across the country to see it with my own eyes. And I didn't regret it. Back then, in the ring, you were yourself. You were my old Jack. For the first time in ten years, I saw the former you. Determined, ready to go forward no matter what. And I'm not talking about you winning in the beginning. No, I'm talking about you starting to lose. When you fell but got up, when your whole face was covered in blood, but you didn't surrender."

"You..." Jack finally spoke, sitting down next to her. "You were at the fight against Melikov? Were you watching me?"

"Of course, I was watching you. What else should I've been watching? You were fighting in the ring."

"No, no, I'm not talking about the ring. Were you watching me walking toward the ring?"

"Yes, I was," Sophia answered, not understanding why Jack was asking that.

"You were watching very closely. I remember I felt someone watching me very closely as I walked to the ring."

"Maybe closely. I don't remember such details."

"So it was you who shouted for me to get up. It was you who made me recover from that knockdown…"

"I didn't shout."

"Oh yes, you did. When I was lying on the canvas, I passed out for a moment. I didn't understand what was going on and didn't know that I had to get back on my feet. But you shouted for me to get up, and I heard it. I heard it, and that's why I got up. You don't understand, if it weren't for you, I wouldn't have gotten up then, I would've lost that fight and would've lost it by knockout. It's thanks to you that I won. It's unbelievable."

"Jack," Sophia said, taking his hand in hers. "It sure is a very beautiful story, I'd really like it to be true, but it definitely wasn't me. The moment you were on the floor, I wasn't in the arena. I was out in a ladies' room." After a moment of silence, Sophia added, "You know, some drunk chick was sitting in front of me, she had those huge fake boobs falling out of her dress each time she jumped up from her seat. She was the one who shouted a lot. So she was probably the guardian angel that saved your boxing career. Drunk, vulgar angel with fake boobs."

Jack turned his head and looked intently into Sophia's eyes. She smiled back, and the next moment they both started laughing.

..24..

After climbing the stairs and entering the corridor, Jack paused the music playing and took the headphones out of his ears. Ever since Sophia admitted that her song was about him, he could not help but listen to it on repeat again and again. And each time he got a better understanding of the feelings she had for him all these long years, and how difficult it was for her to look at him being with Jacob.

And the more Jack understood that, the more he thought about how much he changed during his marriage. Moreover, now Sullivan was noticing not only good changes. He still refused to acknowledge Jacob's unintentional, yet negative influence, but he remembered a lot of moments when he himself voluntarily abandoned his opinion, his interests, his views.

"Gerard, open up!" Sullivan shouted, coming up to the right door and knocking insistently. "It's Jack!"

There was no answer from the other side. Jack knocked again longer and more insistently.

"It's Jack Sullivan! Open up! I know you're at home! Your truck is at the parking lot, and I stopped by the nearest booze store on my way!"

There was not even the slightest rustle from inside.

"Gerard, I'm not leaving until you get the door! If necessary, I'll force open it!"

Sullivan started knocking using both his hands and feet. All the noise he made finally caused a door to open – not to McKee's apartment though, but to an adjacent one. A little old lady appeared in the corridor.

"I'm sorry, ma'am," Jack said quickly and stopped knocking immediately. "I didn't mean to disturb you, but I really need to get to Gerard McKee's apartment. We're friends. As far as I understand, he's currently having big problems with alcohol and I want to help him. And to do that, I need to get into his apartment."

The old lady shook her head disapprovingly and disappeared through the door. 'Her calling the police on me is the last thing I need right now,' Jack thought to himself but decided to try again anyway. Two kicks on the door were not enough, and as he kicked for the third time, the neighbor's door opened again. This time the old lady came out of the apartment, clutching a hammer in her hands.

Sullivan thought that maybe running away would be a better option than engaging in a fight with the old lady holding a hammer, but McKee's neighbor did not attack him – on the contrary, the old lady handed Jack her weapon.

"Here, try this. It's time someone brought him to reason. He's not bad. He always helps me carry my bags or do jobs around the apartment when I need something. But he drinks too much. My first husband was like this…"

"Thank you," Jack hastened to make an acknowledgment to spare himself the need to listen to the story covering the previous forty years of the old lady's life.

When Sullivan had already raised the hammer, the door to McKee's apartment opened by itself. Jack handed the hammer to the old lady, nodded gratefully, and hurried in. McKee was already walking from the door to an armchair by the window, so that Sullivan could only see his back, covered with an old, yellowed with time, but once white robe, obviously borrowed by the old man in some hotel.

"Gerard, how are you doing?" Jack asked, following the owner of the apartment.

"Doing great," the old man grumbled, sitting down in the armchair and picking up a glass of whiskey from the floor.

It was only when Sullivan saw his face that he

understood the scale of what had happened to McKee in the days since Jacob's funeral. Apparently, since then, the old man had not shaved, combed, or washed his hair, in fact, had not washed at all. Now he looked more like the world's oldest hobo than an owner of a boxing club. McKee's apartment did not look any better either. Empty bottles of whiskey, vodka, beer, and other alcoholic drinks were scattered all over the floor.

At least two of the bottles were shattered. On top of that, Sullivan counted eight stains on the floor from spilled liquids – and it was unlikely that all these liquids had originally been inside the bottles. Not to mention that the apartment had such a smell that Jack immediately went to open the window without even asking for the old man's permission.

"I came to apologize...," Sullivan started speaking, but the old man interrupted him right away.

"For what? You didn't offend me. Everything you said was on point. Sports are shit, athletes don't do anything useful for society, they only feed their ego and make lots of money they don't deserve. Or have you changed your mind about any of this?"

Jack removed two empty whiskey bottles from another armchair and sat down facing the old man.

"I haven't changed my mind, but I still shouldn't have talked to you like that...."

The old man waved his hand and interrupted again, "Come on! Like I've never heard "fuck" in my life? I'm no high society damsel – I can handle a normal manly conversation with no blushing. Don't sweat it, Jack, what you said is true. Serves me right!"

Sullivan was taken aback by such a response. In his head, the meeting with McKee was supposed to go like this: he would apologize, tell the old man that he was ready to go back to the ring, they would immediately make up and together go back to One-Two Boxing the very next day. Now Jack was at a loss as to what to do next. Not having come up with anything better, Sullivan decided to move on to the second part of his so far a failure of a plan.

"I want to return to the ring and I want you to return to One-Two Boxing and continue to train me..."

The old man interrupted Jack for the third time, "Why the hell would you want to do that? What you said was right – that won't bring Jacob back. Even if you could give Ryan a good beating, you'd still hardly call it a just payback. A defeat is not a prison. And for that matter, he can switch to another weight division and become a champion once again. They say the only thing that stopped him from doing that is a big fat contract with IPBU. Should he lose his title, nobody'd object anymore. Where is justice in that? And other than that, there's no need in hell for you to box – you said it yourself, not once. And you were right – you have brains in your head, so put them to work, do something useful, invent stuff, use your fund to help kids. Boxing is only for idiots like me, who'd do even more harm outside of sports. Do you know why I started boxing? Sure thing, I've always liked putting my fists to use, but I never thought of going pro. No one from our block has become an athlete. Criminals – as many as you want. And I thought I'd hustle just like everybody else. Johnny signed me up for this, but I didn't really do it because of him. It's because of my grandma. It was she who told me, 'Take up sports, vent your aggression in the ring, or otherwise you'll kill someone sooner or later because of your bad temper.' And she was right, absolutely right. Even with boxing, I almost got screwed big time not once, and without it, for sure, I'd be long rotting in prison or under the ground somewhere. You see, Jack, boxing is for people like me. Like me and Joe Ryan. It's for complete idiots, the violent ones who can't live like normal people. Our kind should've been euthanized, all of us, but we have a liberal society, so you can't do that. Though it'd be worth it!"

Having spoken up, the old man drained his glass, got up from his chair, and went around the room looking for a bottle in which there was at least something left. Sullivan continued to sit silently in utter bewilderment.

"The guys are worried about you," he finally found at least something to say.

Turning over the third bottle in a row and finding nothing, the old man shrugged his shoulders. "So keep an eye on them, Jack. You're smart, you're obviously gonna be much better at it than I am. The keys to the gym are over there hanging on a nail next to the door. Consider the gym yours. I'm serious, Jack. Kate has all the documents and I remember I signed some piece of paper that gives her the right to sign for me. Take the keys, tomorrow you and Kate can get all the paperwork done and here you go – One-Two's yours. You can open some free classes for children there. Not boxing, of course. Some kind of fitness, pilates, yoga – what other fancy words do they use nowadays? Let them do something useful for health, rather than smashing brains out of each other's heads in the ring. The guys are all there to help you. As their boss, they're definitely gonna like you more than me."

"And you? Are you going to keep drinking until your liver fails and that's it?" It was the only thing Sullivan could find to say in response.

The old man shrugged again. "I'll keep drinking for a while, and then I'll find something to do. Don't worry, this is not my first rodeo. I've taken such vacations more than a few times and it didn't do anything – as you can see, I'm still alive. Haven't killed myself yet, not once."

"There's a first time for everything," Jack said thoughtfully, looking around.

McKee grinned in response. After carefully examining the entire room, Sullivan made a final conclusion for himself that the old man definitely would not get out of this 'rodeo' on his own. But how to persuade McKee to get back to normal life, to One-Two, to boxing, to their team – that he still could not figure out, although he tried his best.

"Why the hell...," Sullivan said even more thoughtfully, almost in a whisper.

"Huh? What are you saying there?" the old man asked,

finally finding a bottle in which there were still two fingers of whiskey left at the bottom.

"You asked me why the hell I would go back to boxing," Jack replied, running his hand through his hair and that way reminding himself again that this haircut, like everything else in his life over the past ten years, had been chosen for him by Jacob. "To prove to myself that I can. To prove it to others. To get back at Ryan," Sullivan just listed his thoughts out loud, until finally he stumbled upon the right one. "To get my old self back. And to do something useful for others, for those who cannot help themselves."

"What are you talking about, Jack? I don't get it. How's boxing gonna help you get yourself back? And what kind of yourself?"

"Sophia. Remember Sophia? I introduced you to each other at the cemetery."

McKee nodded.

"She was my first friend. I didn't have any friends until university. I was weird. I didn't like sports, computer games, fighting, misbehaving – generally, everything that my peers were interested in. I could never get along with boys. They didn't want me in their company. Girls didn't like me either. I wasn't masculine enough for them. But at university, Sophia and I immediately clicked somehow. We were inseparable, although we studied at different faculties. So Sophia opened my eyes to how much I changed after meeting Jacob. I thought that with him I became happy and that's that. But no, it turned out to be much more complicated. And in many ways that change was not for the better. Jacob was an exceptional person. Do you remember when you told me about your grandmother? He also had so much character that it would have been enough for three. I really dissolved in him, as Sophia said. And I finally understood why. Because before him, my whole life was a struggle. I was struggling for survival all the time. At home with my father, who beat my mother and me, at school, where everyone bullied me and also often beat me. Then at university. No one bullied me there anymore, but I desperately needed to prove to everyone that I was worth something. And I studied, grinded, worked on my charity fund. I slept for five hours a day at the time. I didn't work on something and didn't struggle only at those moments when I was together with Sophia. And I got so tired of it all. More than twenty years of struggle... so when Jacob started taking care of me, I instantly let go of everything that had been oppressing me for all those twenty years, everything that'd been making me struggle so desperately. But I didn't notice that with all the worries, with all the hassle that I let go of, I also gave up that part of myself that wanted to go forward, wanted to fight, wanted to achieve things, wanted to do something big and important."

Sullivan got up from the armchair and began to walk around the room, continuing to tell his story, "It was only after Sophia's words that I realized. You see, despite the fact that Jacob made me feel so easy and comfortable as never before in my entire life, despite all his love and care, there was always some anxiety, some lack of confidence that I kept feeling. I always thought it was me. That this was the same lack of confidence that I had at school and university. But no, I was wrong. That anxiety and self-doubt from the past, they've gone. Jacob rid me of them. I remembered that in the first year of our life together I was completely calm. It was the best year of my life. And then what came next – it was something new. New anxiety. It came because I let go of myself. I convinced myself that I wanted to live like that – under Jacob's care so that he'd decide everything for me. But that's not who I really am. Yes, I've always been scared, I've always been a coward. I got cold feet every time it came to any conflict situation, and my insides shrank every time I had to take on some big task. But yet I always stood my ground when people tried to offend me, and I always took on any tasks, no matter how difficult they were. This is who I really am. I'm a resolute coward, this is who I am!"

"Kid, no offense, but," the old man cut into Sullivan's

monolog. "Though it sounds great that you figured something out about yourself, found out what was bothering you in your life, you forgot again that I'm a simple old boxer. I don't get such fancy hang-ups. From everything you just said I couldn't quite grasp what boxing has to do with it."

"Yes, yes, sorry, I got carried away. The thing is that Sophia said... Just imagine, it turns out she was at my fight against Melikov," Jack interrupted himself. "So she saw it all. And she said that there, in the ring, for the first time in the last ten years, I was the same old me, the person I'd been before meeting Jacob. And you know what – she's right! She's absolutely right. There, in the ring, when I won, I felt like I was somehow complete. It was as if I regained what I'd lost, what had been missing in me. It was an amazing feeling. It was a healing feeling. And I want to feel it again. Especially now. After Jacob passed away. I'm not quite myself right now. I yelled at you, I yelled at Charlie. I don't know what's happening to me. I'm falling apart, Gerard, you know? I need to put all the pieces of myself back together again. And I need boxing for that."

Jack paused for a moment, thinking, but then went on, "And not just for myself. When I started all this, I was only thinking about myself. It's not right. I can help others with this after all. Yes, maybe boxing is stupid, maybe sports are stupid. I still think it's crazy that there's such a multibillion-dollar industry out there as sports, which doesn't benefit humanity in any way. But here's the thing – if you and I quit boxing – it won't make any difference. The industry will stay the same. Billions of dollars will still be wasted. And not just wasted, but go to people like Joe Ryan. And he'll be able to buy another Ferrari with this money only to get drunk again and this time run over someone. But if we stay, then we'll be able to make a change. Such things can only be changed from the inside."

"But again, Jack, it sounds really cool, but I still don't understand shit. What kind of change are you talking about?"

"Well, lots of things come to mind. OK, let's start with

the fact that I'm gay. How many gay IPBU champions were there?"

"Not a single one."

"And how many gay champions were there in general?"

The old man thought hard, "Well, seems like there *was* something like that. I guess, Panama Brown was gay. It was a long time ago. But he's in bantamweight. Nobody gives a shit about such light weight divisions. The main stars are always heavyweights. Middleweight, your welterweight get some attention from time to time. Apart from that, nobody gives a shit even about featherweight, not to mention anything lighter than that. There was also Griffith. He's sort of bisexual, though. Also a long time ago, in the sixties, probably. He was a welterweight as well. Oh! I remember he once killed a man for slapping his ass and calling him a faggot. I mean, not in the street, but in the ring. Paret seems to be his name. He died without coming around a few days after the knockout."

"Which means there haven't been any gay champions for at least the last sixty years?" Sullivan hastened to stop the history lesson.

"Yeah, looks like that."

"Gerard, do you realize how much it's going to undermine the position of homophobes if there appears the first IPBU gay champion? How can a faggot beat real men? Can gays be masculine too?"

"Maybe," the old man drawled, still not quite convinced.

"And how about we give all the earnings to charity? And we'll point out each time that it's simply unspeakable to make so much money in sports while children die out there every day! While they're starving, while they have no way of getting an education. And meanwhile, Joe Ryan's cruising around in his Ferrari. Not because he's doing something useful. No, he's just someone who knows how to swing his fists, and that's why he should receive millions that otherwise could go to a good cause. We can make IPBU so ashamed that they'll start transferring part of their proceeds to charity themselves. You know what time we live in – you stir up social media, and companies come running to apologize."

McKee chuckled, "You got that right. Make IPBU ashamed... That would be nice. They're a bunch of jerks. Huckster-bureaucrats. Good idea."

"Well, Gerard, do you agree to go back? Do you agree to change the world together?"

"You're one tough negotiator, I'll give you that, kid," the old man replied with a smile on his lips. "Just like that time you persuaded me to start training you in a serious way. You should go into politics. That's where you'd be able to do a lot of good."

"All right," Jack smiled back. "As soon as I become a champion, I'll immediately go into politics. Not a bad idea, by the way. It'll be a ready-made platform. The hype alone would be enough to become a mayor at the very least. So, Gerard, are you going back to boxing with me?"

Sullivan held out his hand to the old man. McKee shook it firmly. "Yeah. How can you say no to that?"

Without letting go of the coach's hand, Jack asked one more question, "Will you ever forgive me for the things I said then?"

"Are you kidding? I forgave you the very moment you stepped into my apartment."

McKee smiled good-naturedly, then grabbed Jack, and embraced him tightly in his arms. Sullivan, almost crushed by this bearish tenderness, laughed faintly and also embraced the old man in response.

...

Coming back home in the late afternoon, Sullivan went straight to the shower. After taking a shower, Jack examined himself in the mirror and decided to shave as well. When there was no more stubble on his cheeks, Sullivan took a long and intent look at his reflection. And then he took a trimmer and ran it over his head – from forehead to nape.

The line turned out to be terribly crooked, and the trimmer almost broke on its way, and yet Jack was extremely satisfied with the result. Before making a decisive move with the trimmer, he hesitated for a moment. Wouldn't it look like some kind of rebellion against Jacob, who chose his current haircut, and wouldn't it be disrespectful to his memory?

But then Jack told himself that Jacob had always loved him and wanted only the best for him. And Jacob would definitely want his husband to get rid of anxiety and self-doubt once and for all. Having finished, Sullivan ran his hand over his shaved head and laughed. It was his first personal choice in ten years.

And even if it was just hair, one ought to start with something...

..25..

"Now we begin the last, twelfth round of the Jack Sullivan vs. George Robinson fight. The fight turned out to be very intense and very technical. To be honest, I can't even remember the last time I saw both opponents throw such a huge number of punches while still managing to remain on their feet until the last round."

"Yes, Sam, I can't disagree with you. With such frantic action from the very first seconds, I was ready to bet that it would last seven rounds at best, and the fact that we can now see the twelfth round going on is just something incredible."

"Great jab from Sullivan. It's breaking through the opponent's guard, but, of course, at this point, there's not enough strength and speed in it. Sullivan is extremely exhausted."

"And Robinson doesn't look any better. It seems to me that the outcome of today's fight depends not on who's punches will be more frequent, more accurate, and heavier, but rather on who will prove to have more stamina."

"Mike, if both fighters make it to the final bell, who would you award the victory to?"

"Great combination from Robinson! Sullivan's taking way too many hits, but he's not giving up and even manages to counterpunch. As for my preferences – honestly, Sam, I don't know. I can tell you, this is a very rare case, perhaps the only one in my entire commentating career, when I'm ready to support any judges' decision, regardless of whom they rule the winner of this fight."

"It seems to me that there's a great chance of a draw. What would you say if that happened?"

"That's probably where I wouldn't support the judges. I mean, both fighters went all out and they both deserve to win.

The judges must decide what was more important – the aggression, the advantage in the number of thrown punches, and the frenzied courage of Robinson, who almost ended up on the canvas in the third round, or the refined technique, the accuracy of a sniper, and the fearlessness of Sullivan, who's finishing his second fight in a row, covered in his own blood."

"Yes, Sullivan's cut is pretty serious. Which makes me marvel at the job done by his cutman, it's as if he'd cast a spell on the cut."

"Sullivan's executing an excellent combination, but the brave Robinson immediately rushes to counterattack, hitting the opponent with equally serious punches. What a fight! A sight to behold for boxing fans, no matter which one of our tonight's fighters they are rooting for."

"Wow, the fighters are now beating each other recklessly, completely forgetting about defenses. What is it – is it Sullivan's blood on Robinson's face or is it his own cut already?"

"Yes, yes, Sullivan managed to make his opponent bleed too! Are we really going to see a knockout today?"

"Unfortunately not! It's the final bell to stop this frenzied butchery. Both fighters are raising their gloves victoriously. And it's hard to argue with any of them right now – certainly, they both came out victorious in this fight. Even if the judges eventually consider one of them defeated, both the audience and promoters will certainly look forward to the next fight featuring any one of them!"

"What a fight! Just glorious!"

When the final bell rang and Sullivan managed to return to his corner, he had to gather all his remaining strength so as not to immediately collapse into the arms of his cornermen.

"Five more minutes, son, and it'll be over." Noticing at once how tired the fighter was, McKee hurried to support Jack both mentally and physically, picking him up with his huge arm.

The five minutes promised by the old man was a blur

to Sullivan. Previously he thought that there was nothing more exhausting than a fight against Artur Melikov that could actually exist in nature. McKee was right when he suggested that Jack should take his time with the next fight, wait another month, maybe two. But Sullivan thought that he had already managed to fully recover, and most importantly, he wanted to go back to the ring as soon as possible in order to feel capable of something again and at least partially get rid of the overwhelming feeling of helplessness that started haunting him after Jacob's death.

"Do you think we won?" Charlie whispered in Derrick's ear when Sullivan stepped aside to give a traditional hug to his opponent after the fight.

"No clue," the young coach replied, although everything could be understood from his face alone, which expressed an extreme degree of confusion.

After hugging George Robinson and responding to him with some generic words about respect and his qualities as a fighter, Jack glanced over the ropes. One of the seats in the front row was occupied by Sophia. She was the only one of all Sullivan's team members with her whole appearance expressing complete confidence that Jack would become the winner of this fight.

Finally, the ring announcer asked for everyone's attention and proceeded to announce the results of tonight's fight, "Ladies and gentlemen, after 12 rounds of action we go to the scorecards. We have unanimous decision. Judge Kim Broner scores 117 – 116, judges Joshua Hopkins and Adrien Peterik both score 118 – 116. All three in favor of the winner of tonight's fight – Jack Sulivan."

The arena crowd roared – mostly with delight, but the voices of those who supported George Robinson and were left dissatisfied also sounded quite loud. But to Sullivan, the important ones were only the voices of those who were standing behind him at this moment. And all of them – the old man and Derrick, Charlie and Kate, whose services as cornermen, despite McKee's admonitions, Jack had not refused, and even constantly serious Chuck, all unitedly celebrated the victory of their fighter, shouting joyfully and hugging each other.

In a few minutes, journalists ran up to Sullivan with a camera and microphone. After praising his opponent and expressing gratitude to the coach and cornermen, which was standard for such occasions, somehow spontaneously Jack went completely beyond the topic of what was happening in the ring tonight, "I'd like to dedicate tonight's victory to my husband Jacob. He passed away a month ago. Only because of him, only because of what happened to him, did I start boxing. That's why this and all my other victories, previous and future, will always be dedicated to him and only to him. And I want to add that my purse from tonight's victory will be fully transferred to charity fund 'Knowledge for everyone', which provides grants for education to talented children from underprivileged classes. As of today, the fund will bear the name of my husband."

The mentioning of the victorious boxer's husband came as a slight shock to the spectators, journalists, and half of those who were in the ring at that moment. Boxing fans, as well as any other combat sports fans, had never been the ones for holding liberal views in general and tolerance for homosexuality in particular. And the fact that Sullivan's confession was made immediately after the announcement of the winner seemed especially offensive to many of them.

Only a second ago they were excited at the victory of a brave, determined and undaunted fighter, and now it turned out they had been rooting for a damn faggot all the twelve rounds. Many of them did not shy away from booing the winner in a loud manner. Sophia was the first to react to the negative response from the crowd. She turned towards the spectators and started chanting 'Sullivan! Sullivan! Sullivan!', using gestures to make others join her.

Seeing this, Charlie gave Derrick a dig in the side. They

both began to repeat after Sophia. Some spectators followed them, but in response, those booing amped up their pressure too. Sophia did not give up. She started walking along the stands and shouting even harder. More and more spectators sided with Sullivan's team, but the haters did not let up either. Tensions grew stronger by the minute.

The first insults to the winner's sexual orientation started coming from the crowd. It seemed like it would not take long for the verbal altercation to turn into a real brawl. And suddenly, there sounded a yell, amplified by speakers.

"Hey! Shut up!" George Robinson growled menacingly, grabbing the microphone from the ring announcer. "You may not agree with the results of the fight. Hell, I myself think I fought no worse than Jack. But don't you dare boo what he said after the announcement. Did you even hear what he said? He said his whole purse would go to the needs of children from underprivileged classes. I was such a child, and my family also received help from charities at the time. And I will always be grateful for that. Hell, I'll donate my tonight's fight purse to this fund myself! To the fund that bears the proud name of Jack's husband. He lost his loved one just a month ago and still found the strength in himself to get into the ring tonight. And he fought like a real man, not showing weakness for a second. If anybody of you has a problem with something – get into the ring. Everybody get in. Everyone who shouted. Jack and I are barely standing on our feet at this point, but we are ready to stand against all of you. What do you say? Are there any brave ones here? Or maybe shouting from the crowd is the only thing you are brave enough for? And you consider yourselves real men? You think you're better than him?"

Robinson cast a menacing look round the silent stands. When none of the spectators dared to challenge the boxer, he raised his clenched fist and began chanting, "Sullivan! Sullivan! Sullivan!". He was joined by his team, Jack's team, journalists, ring announcer, and finally most of the spectators.

Such ovations had not been heard in this arena even

when everybody's favorite heavyweight boxer Henry Barrera defeated Naseem Wahba in an arduous and extremely bloody fight six months ago, managing to unite all five main championship belts.

When Robinson finally returned the microphone to its rightful owner, Jack approached him and held out his hand. But instead of a handshake, the former opponent hugged Sullivan tightly.

"Thank you, George. You have no idea how much it means to me," Jack said in his ear.

"Don't sweat it, I have two gay cousins. Great guys," Robinson replied and added. "It was a great fight, buddy. Let's repeat it sometime."

After these words, Robinson took Jack's hand, held it up triumphantly, and began to turn around with him, facing all directions, so that all the spectators could see the winner. Halfway around the circle, Sullivan met the gaze of Sophia, who was still chanting his name. Seeing his eyes, his cheerful but shy smile, she thought to herself, "He's back. My Jack's back."

..26..

"I'm coming already," McKee shouted toward the front door and added, grumbling to himself, "Don't piss yourself from impatience over there."

On the other side of the door, there were people whom the old man did not at all expect to see on his doorstep.

"Happy birthday!!!" Kate and Sophia shouted cheerfully in unison.

However, the women did not look festive at all – both were dressed in sports leggings and tops, their hair pulled back. Each clutched a bucket filled with household supplies in one hand and a mop in the other.

"What the hell?" The old man blurted involuntarily but immediately corrected himself. "I'm sorry. Hello, young ladies."

McKee realized he was standing before the women in underpants and an old undershirt and hurried to wrap an equally old and ragged robe around him.

"Come on, Gerard," Kate said cheerfully, slipping inside the apartment without asking. "Do you think we've never seen men in underwear before?"

"Um...," the old man spoke, turning to her. "Can someone explain to me what's going on here?"

"Celebratory intervention!" Sophia answered, also entering the apartment.

"Yeah," Kate picked up her explanation. "We found out that it's your birthday and decided to make you a present. Not a banal one though, like some tie or razor, but a real one that's worth something. By the way, we're not the whole present.

This is only the first part of it. The boys are busy too right now."

"And what exactly is this present?" the old man asked, knowing perfectly well what buckets and mops might be needed for, but still hoping for some other explanation.

"We'll make this place clean and tidy like you've never seen it in your life!" Kate answered with joy, taking a measuring look around the apartment.

"Which way is the bathroom?" Sophia asked.

McKee made an automatic gesture with his hand but quickly changed his mind, blocking Sophia's way.

"No, no, no! No way!" McKee protested, trying to sound as polite as possible, yet insistent. "Girls, thank you so much, I really appreciate all this, but it'd be better if you just left me all these thingies as a gift and that's that. I'll clean up later by myself."

"Yeah," Kate replied. "We could just as well throw it all in the trash right away. Pops, if you're not up to fighting us, there's no chance you can stop us from cleaning this place."

"We can give you five minutes to get rid of a Playboy under the mattress and other boy's staff," Sophia said with a smile, ducked under the old man's arm, and hurried into the bathroom.

The old man did not keep a Playboy under his mattress, but it was not until Sophia mentioned 'boy's staff' that McKee realized he had a lot of other equally shameful things scattered around his apartment. Including a romantic novel with a shirtless dude on its cover, which the old man liked to read during his long sessions on the toilet. With unexpected speed for his age, the old man dashed toward the bathroom, barely managing to get ahead of Sophia, who was already reaching for the doorknob.

"Yes, you know, five minutes – it's a great idea. Not that I have any nasty things around, but just personal stuff that I'd rather not show anybody."

Sophia winked in response, put the bucket on the floor, and went in the opposite direction.

"Come on, let's give our birthday boy time to get ready," she said to Kate, walking past her to the front door.

Kate followed her partner, putting her arm around Sophia's shoulders. Over the two months since they had met each other, the women had already managed to turn into close friends. So when it came to deciding who would go to McKee's place, and who would get busy with preparations in One-Two Boxing, the women offered their services in one voice.

Meanwhile, work was also in full swing in the boxing gym. Jack, Charlie, and Derrick worked hard to bring One-Two Boxing back to its once very presentable appearance. Having finished in the gym itself, Jack opened the door to the old man's office and stopped on the threshold, thinking.

"Charlie, can you come over here for a minute?" he called over his shoulder.

"What?" responded the junior assistant coach, waking up to Jack at once.

"Do you know why the old man's championship belt is in such state?"

Sullivan nodded toward the dirty and dusty belt fixed on the wall above the director's armchair. The words 'IPBU HEAVYWEIGHT WORLD CHAMPION' were barely visible on the belt.

"I've no idea. It's always been like that. I offered to clean it a couple times, but the old man always refused. He even got irritated over it."

"Hmm..." Jack said, rubbed his chin, and added. "What time did the girls say they'd bring him?"

"At about between six and seven," Charlie answered and, not to waste any time, started to wipe the office door.

By six o'clock, Kate and Sophia had managed to dust, wash the floor and windows, clean the entire bathroom to a shine, which seemed a real miracle to McKee, put the kitchen in order, and collect two large bags of garbage. In exchange for their services, the women had the old man tell the story of his childhood and youth.

At first, McKee was reluctant to recall the past, but the guests' genuine interest in his life, regularly confirmed by numerous questions and comments, made him relax and switch to the grandpa mode, telling his grandchildren about his past adventures. When he got to the stories about his high school times, the old man caught himself thinking that in his entire life he had only talked so openly with Johnny Sifaretto and a couple of times with Jack.

Having finished with the cleaning, the women had McKee dress up in a suit, after which the three of them went to One-Two Boxing. A block away from the gym, Kate, despite facing active resistance, still managed to blindfold the old man. When they reached their destination, the women helped McKee to get out, made him stand right in front of One-Two Boxing, and only then removed the blindfold.

"What the hell...," the old man shot out as he realized why Kate insisted on blindfolding him.

Instead of the old signboard, faded in the sun, torn and stained with tags, the wall of One-Two Boxing was now decorated with a new one, on which there was not only Gerard McKee, still young and full of strength, looking at the world around him, his hands clad in boxing gloves, proudly resting on his waist, decorated with a brand-new champion belt, but also Johnny Sifaretto, equally young, with a beaming smile on his face, one hand resting on his side, and the other – on the shoulder of his best friend.

McKee felt the corners of his eyes moisten.

"It's just the beginning, Pops, so stay focused," Kate said vibrantly and nudged the old man toward the front door.

Amazed by the signboard, McKee did not even pay attention to the fact that the old rusty door opened easily and without creaking. Inside the club, the old man was met by semi-darkness, only the outlines of Jack and the other members of the One-Two Boxing team standing out in the middle of the gym. But as soon as the door closed behind the gym's owner, someone flipped the switch, and the whole place became illuminated by the bright light of dozens of new bulbs.

An involuntary exclamation of surprise burst from the old man's lips. The whole gym literally shone with cleanliness – looking no worse than on the day of its opening. Besides, cleanliness and order were not the only changes. McKee began to walk around the room, speechlessly looking at its contents. Punching bags, weights, benches, even the ropes of the ring – almost all of the gym's equipment was replaced with a new one.

It was only after about five minutes that the old man finally managed to gather enough strength to speak. Stopping in the middle of the gym and switching his eyes from one smiling face to another, McKee began, "Guys! Well... you... guys, well, it's just..."

"Wait, Gerard, there's more," Jack interrupted, and then added, "I'm sorry for interrupting you."

The old man waved his hand, making it clear that everything was fine. He was even glad to stop talking, fearing that his thank-you speech would be too emotional. Sullivan continued, "Ever since I first found myself in your office and every time I visited it afterward, one thought has been nagging me. The thought of why your championship belt, the greatest achievement of your career, why is it so dusty and dirty? Of course, when I first came to One-Two, nothing was particularly clean in here..."

The others responded with light smiles.

"... but your championship belt was the only thing that looked as if nobody had touched it since the moment you took it off and hung it on the wall. I think I finally managed to solve this riddle. Gerard, I hope you don't mind me speaking so frankly in front of everybody? Keep in mind that we're all your friends here, and we all came here today on our day off to prepare this surprise for you. And don't think that I'm the only one who paid for all the new equipment. No, we all chipped in. Even Charlie..."

"I'm sure the kid invested the most," the old man tried to

use the joke as a cover for how moved he was.

"Have no doubt, as a percentage of his salary, it is for sure exactly the case," Derrick responded in support of Charlie.

McKee met the boy's eye and nodded to him, making it clear that he indeed deeply appreciated Charlie's contribution. The boy reacted with a blush.

"Like I said," Jack continued. "We're all family here and we all love you, so I'm going to tell you as it is. I think you've never touched the championship belt since then and haven't even let Charlie dust it because you're ashamed of this award. I think you thought you owed your career primarily to Johnny Sifaretto. Both your career and what happened after it ended. I mean, all this..." Sullivan spread his hands, pointing to the gym's surroundings, "...is his achievement. But it's not your fault that Mr. Sifaretto was such a talented manager and businessman. And it's not his fundamental contribution to your career and this gym that you're ashamed of. You're ashamed that you couldn't go on without him. You think you let your friend down when you couldn't manage One-Two as efficiently as he did. Am I close?"

Having become noticeably sad over the course of Jack's speech, the old man exhaled heavily and replied, "No matter how many times I tell you the opposite, Jack, you still stubbornly keep thinking of me as an equal in terms of intelligence. Do you think I've ever analyzed anything so deeply in my life? Hell no! But yes, you're close. Although I'd put it differently."

"How would you put it, Gerard? Don't be shy, we're all here for you and none of us is going to judge you. Isn't that right, guys?"

The others responded with friendly words of approval.

"I'd say that I screwed up my life, screwed up everything that Johnny gave me. And this damn piece of iron on the belt is just a constant reminder that I, unlike absolutely all those with whom I grew up together, except Johnny himself, had not just a real chance of success, I already had a winning ticket in my hand. And even with that, I couldn't do anything without Johnny. You were right, Jack, boxers swing their fists just to boost their ego, but they can't do anything useful."

Jack interrupted the old man's self-condemning speech, "Gerard, all of us here disagree with this. We believe that you have nothing to be ashamed of and nothing to blame yourself for. Just don't interrupt me now, please. Let me finish," Jack said, noticing the old man already opening his mouth to contradict him. "When your best and only friend, your manager, your business partner died, you were left completely alone. Yes, you slipped up, yes, you made a lot of mistakes. But it's not your fault that you couldn't get over the death of a loved one so easily. You know, a very wise man, whose opinion is extremely important to me, recently told me that in such a situation, the only thing a person could be guilty of is that they'd loved the one they'd lost. If you hadn't really loved your friend like a brother, like a person for whom you were ready to die, then you would've been able to take his passing away calmly. There's nothing shameful in showing weakness, normal human weakness, at such a moment, at a moment of great loss and great pain."

Jack turned to Charlie and nodded at him. The boy quickly stepped aside.

"The thing that happened to you and One-Two Boxing is not your fault. It's a tragedy. The tragedy that consists not only in the death of such a remarkable man as Mr. Sifaretto but also in the fact that there were no other people with you who could support you at the time."

Charlie handed Jack something covered with a cloth.

"Gerard, all this long and dramatic speech was needed only to tell you – now you're not alone. We're all together with you now. We're your family. We'll support you no matter what. And we want you to accept this gift with pride, not shame. You deserve it!"

Holding the object that Charlie handed him with one hand, Jack pulled the cloth off of it with the other. Right in front of the old man appeared his old championship belt. Only now it shone as if its plate had been cast just yesterday. Sullivan held out the belt to McKee. The old man, a wet shine in his eyes being already noticeable to everyone, gave at the same time a cheerful, sad, and even a bit thoughtful smile, hesitated for a couple of moments, but still took the belt from Jack's hands.

"Put it on!" Charlie called out.

The old man brushed his suggestion aside with a wave of his hand, but Charlie was immediately joined by everyone else chanting "Put it on! Put it on! Put it on!" and McKee could not but put on his championship belt. The old man even rested his fists on his waist, trying to portray the very pose of his photo counterpart, decorating the face of the gym building. When McKee sucked in his stomach and straightened his shoulders, he really started to look like that proud, powerful, and confident champion.

And this almost magical transformation happened not only and not so much because for the first time in many years the old man put on his championship belt. No, the main reason for this was that at that very moment McKee felt inner strength and confidence, now having the new banner, new equipment, and the polished belt given to him by his team, his friends, his family.

"Guys... This... Well..." the old man tried to speak again, yet his feelings got the best of him, and instead of words, McKee pulled Jack close and hugged him tightly. Following Sullivan, no less strong and emotional hugs were awarded to all the others present. And all of them, even Sophia, who had known the old man for only a couple of months, could not help but show an emotional response, manifested in the shine of their eyes.

Having finished with the hugs and rubbed his eyes, McKee finally found the strength in himself to speak without faltering.

"Guys, all this, Johnny on the poster, the gym, the belt,

the cleaning of my place, the fact that you did it on your day off, the money you spent. All that. You can't even imagine how much it means to me! And, honestly, I've no idea what I've done to deserve all this. For the three of you," the old man pointed in the direction of Charlie, Derrick, and Kate. "I've always been a lousy boss. And, Jack, I acted like a complete bastard when I bullied you. But I'll tell you what – starting today and up until my death, I'll be working hard to pay my dues to you for everything you gave me today. And I'm not talking about money. No, I mean money's also the part of what I'm talking about. I'm gonna make One-Two Boxing prosper! I'm gonna bring it back to its former glory. And all of you. I want all of you to become its co-owners. We're one team. A team may have its captain, but a team can't have its owner. It's our gym, it belongs to all of us, not just me. And as for you, Jack," the old man put his hand on his pupil's shoulder. "I owe you everything. And trust me, now I'll do anything in my power, and even more than that, so that one day you can get the same one." McKee patted the metal plate on his champion belt. "God knows you deserve the title much more than I ever did!"

"Do I absolutely have to get just the same one? How much am I going to have to eat to become a heavyweight?"

Jack's joke was met by the flashing of smiles.

"Well, are you ready for the main part of our celebration?" Charlie asked, walking up to the old man and Jack, putting his hands on their shoulders.

"What? It's not the whole thing yet?" McKee asked in surprise. "You're crazy!"

"Let's go, let's go!" Jack commanded, nudging the old man in the back.

It turned out that the One-Two Boxing team had prepared a whole banquet on the gym's roof. They ate, drank, laughed, had much fun, and even sang songs until the very morning.

When it was already beginning to get light on the

horizon, Jack pulled the old man aside and spoke to him in a quiet, almost conspiratorial voice, "Gerard, I have one more thing that I'd like to discuss with you in private."

"Kid, I am very flattered, and I love you too, but I'm not gay, so it's no use for you trying to ask me out," the old man replied and immediately started laughing at his own joke.

"Very funny. And yes, you're an extremely attractive man, but that's not what I'm talking about. I wanted to talk to you about your drinking problem."

"Listen, Jack...," McKee just started speaking as Sullivan immediately interrupted him.

"In return for everything we've done for you today, you can at least hear me out."

"Fair enough," the old man replied and gestured for Jack to continue.

"Whatever you may think about your strength and longevity, you're no longer young. And the amounts of alcohol you drink would kill even the most inveterate of fraternity members. I hope our reassurances today helped you understand that you have nothing to be ashamed of and so you no longer need to chug booze to make your issues go away, but still I know it's not so easy to quit drinking, even when the problems that made you drink in the first place disappear. You need more assistance with this thing. And I have a solution. I've been interested in hypnosis since I was a child, and I'm quite good at it. At the time, it helped me to make Jacob quit smoking. I think it'll help you too."

"Kid, I don't believe in that sort of stuff..."

Jack interrupted the old man again, "You said it yourself not long ago that you owe me one. Isn't that right? So – as your thanks to me, let me try and hypnotize you."

"Are you sure that in the process you won't mess with my mind in any way which can make me become gay?" McKee tried to hide behind the joke again.

"I'll try my best to resist the incredibly strong temptation of doing so."

"OK, alright. Go ahead. I said it myself that I owed you everything. No one forced me."

Getting the old man's consent, Jack began the process of hypnosis. After the standard preliminary calls to relax and let go of all the thoughts and feelings, Sullivan began to speak about alcohol, and that the old man no longer needed it. And at the end of his session, Jack programmed his mind that with each of his following victories in the ring, the old man would want to drink less and less, and after his title fight win, McKee would once and for all get rid of the desire to even touch a bottle.

Finishing the session, Jack asked the old man to sit with his eyes closed for another five minutes, taking the time to approach Sophia, who had been standing nearby all the while, sipping red wine and gazing thoughtfully at the dawn sky on the horizon.

"I didn't know Jacob had ever smoked," she said, putting her arm around Jack's waist. "I've also never heard of your fascination with hypnosis. Why haven't you ever tried it on me?"

"Are you kidding?" Jack replied. "I made up all this nonsense just half an hour ago when I saw the old man chugging his fifth glass of whiskey."

Sophia laughed merrily and gave Jack a friendly punch on the shoulder.

..27..

Sophia opened her eyes and looked toward the entrance to the arena, from which Jack and his team were soon to appear. Making sure it was still early, the woman closed her eyes again and continued to listen to the music in her headphones. When their old-married-couple "honeymoon" was over and Jack got back to training and working at his charity foundation, Sophia decided to set about her work too.

She finally started doing what she had been dreaming about for so long and what she had been afraid of even longer – working on her first album. Her friend from Philadelphia had already sent her a guitar, synthesizer, and some other necessary equipment, from which Sophia managed to set up quite a good temporary studio.

Losing Jacob, returning to her hometown and to Jack raised a lot of new feelings and emotional experiences in the woman's soul, which laid the most fertile ground for her creativity. One particularly strong motivator to start creating her own music happened to be her conflicting feelings toward Jack, which in recent weeks had been reignited in her to become almost stronger than they had been at university.

Sophia realized that there could be no future for them together and that the longer she stayed with him, the more she would add to her suffering from this completely unrequited love. But hey – doesn't suffering give birth to the best, most poignant, deepest songs?

Engrossed in these thoughts, Sophia did not notice Jack enter the ring. Next came his opponent – black British boxer Josh Smith. Smith had once been the WBC champion with fifteen victories under his belt, but then he had a run of bad luck – first, he lost the title and then lost three more fights in a row. But all that happened a year ago. Since then, in a desperate attempt to regain his former glory, Smith had held five victorious fights, all of which had ended in knockout.

And now Josh Smith was thirsting for the blood of the upstart Jack Sullivan, who had six times fewer fights on his record, but at the same time, he was talked about almost more than all the welterweight representatives combined. With the exception of perhaps only the champion Joe Ryan, who had long proved to be a superstar not only in sports but also in everyday life, constantly appearing on various magazine covers and popular TV shows.

Sophia barely had time to wave to Jack and silently wish him good luck before the boxers were called for the referee's instructions. The fight had begun. Sophia squeezed her eyes shut when she saw Smith lunging at Jack like a fighting dog trying to bite into his face. The opponent's aggression turned out to be so strong that Jack spent the entire first round in deep defense, having thrown no more than five punches at Smith.

"Come on, Jack! You can do it!" was all Sophia could think to herself when the second round almost exactly repeated the first. And then the third and the fourth. Smith was winning by a long shot. But Sophia was still looking at Jack with pride. Any other boxer would have been lying on the canvas a long time ago, but Sullivan moved so fast and blocked so technically that for all four rounds Smith hardly scored even a dozen clean punches.

"You can do it! You can do it! You can do it!" The mantra swirled in Sophia's head. And Jack did it. It turned out that over the first rounds Sullivan was not only dodging and blocking the opponent's blows but also getting familiar with his technique and patterns. And when the bell sounded for the sixth round, instead of going into deep defense as he had done before, Jack first made way for his opponent, taking such a quick step to the side that Smith, carried forward by the momentum of his own blow, almost flew down to the ropes, after which Sullivan landed a powerful hook right in the opponent's nose.

Sophia sprang excitedly to her feet and shouted something cheerful, the meaning of which she did not even understand herself. A stream of blood from Smith's broken nose gushed onto his chest, causing a stormy reaction from the audience. Right after the hook, Jack delivered two more accurate punches to the opponent's face, and then a one-two to the body.

Smith was saved by the bell. During the break, the cornermen patched up the boxer's broken nose, but already in the first seconds of the next round, Jack knocked the blood out of it again. Smith did not give up and acted as aggressively as before, but now that Sullivan had figured out his patterns, it was no longer difficult for him to deliver accurate and powerful punches, most of them falling on the opponent's nose.

As a result, in the middle of the penultimate round, the referee stopped the fight as Smith's nose started bleeding again. The ring doctor stated a broken nose and stopped the fight. Sophia sprang to her feet again and was about to start chanting the winner's name, but she was beaten to it. The woman turned around to see a small, but very actively shouting group of Sullivan's fans, holding rainbow flags and posters over their heads.

Turning back, Sophia met Jack's eye. Sullivan smiled and winked at her. If the previous fights made Sophia realize that her Jack was back, then this victory, this look, and this smile told her that he was back for good.

..28..

Sullivan won his sixth and seventh fights by unanimous decision. McKee remembered that Jack mentioned his IPBU connections and that they would get him to a championship fight with Joe Ryan once he won eight fights. But the old man was still extremely surprised when it happened officially.

The day after Sullivan won his seventh fight, One-Two Boxing was visited by an IPBU representative, offering McKee to arrange a fight, the winner of which would become an official contender for the Welterweight champion title.

And not just a contender, but the last person who could stop Joe Ryan from leaving the ring undefeated, since the current champion, with a perfect record of thirty victories and twenty-seven knockouts, had already announced that this would be his last title defense, after which he would retire. According to rumors, Ryan was to become a Hollywood star bigger than Dwayne Johnson, and he had already been offered the first big role with a seven-figure fee.

McKee was even more surprised when he heard the name of the boxer whom Jack would have to fight to become the title contender. It turned out to be Rick Stanton – the very same fighter whose manager was Mikey Sifaretto, and the one whom Sullivan had floored with the first punch in his first fight, breaking the record for the fastest knockout in history.

Stanton was so enraged by that humiliating knockout that since then not only had he not lost a single fight, but had already held as many as ten fights, all of which ended in knockout no later than the seventh round. Stanton became a real monster, literally tearing all his opponents apart, regardless of their experience and previous achievements.

Actually, Stanton should have already been chosen as a contender for Ryan's title, but IPBU officials could not possibly miss the opportunity to pit the two rising stars against each other in the ring again. There were behind-the-scenes talks in IPBU that this particular fight, and not the championship one following it, could become the highest-grossing fight of the year, or even in decades.

Besides, Stanton himself thirsted for the blood of the one who had humiliated him so cruelly in front of the entire boxing world. The young fighter, just like Sullivan himself in the case of Joe Ryan, wanted not just to defeat his opponent, he dreamed of walking him down, destroying his reputation, making sure that nobody would remember afterward who Jack Sullivan was.

Ever since Sullivan publicly announced his homosexuality, the victory against him became Stanton's obsession, which sometimes even stopped him from sleeping at night. It was one thing to lose to a worthy boxer who had not lost a single fight himself, and it was quite another thing to lose to a pathetic faggot. Such a thing Stanton could never forgive.

McKee himself, who had been a big homophobe not long ago, was quite aware of it all. On the same day when he was visited by an IPBU representative, the old man watched the records of all of Stanton's professional fights and personally made sure that his pupil's former and now future opponent was not only a very angry and aggressive boxer, but also an extremely technical one with a heavy punch.

As compared to his amateur career, Stanton looked at least twice as dangerous in the professional ring. Sometimes, while watching the recordings, it seemed to the old man as if Stanton were possessed by a demon. McKee supposed that this demon had been created by the hands of Jack Sullivan, or rather his right hand, which had thrown that very fatal cross. And as soon as the demon inside Stanton met its creator, the gates of hell would split open right in the ring, turning a regular fight into a massacre of biblical proportions, from which only one would be able to get out alive.

While preparing Sullivan for the fight, McKee doubled down on his work on attack and tripled down on his work on defense. Every day he came up with new ways of training, all of which were supposed to prepare the boxer for the most unexpected turns of the fight. The old man even conducted training sessions with simulations of getting various injuries. Sullivan had to be ready to fight back even if his entire face was cut, his nose damaged, and his eyes half-closed from hematomas.

But the old man kept worrying. He realized that all of that was not enough, because at that very moment Stanton was being trained in the same way, or maybe better. Ever since winning five consecutive fights by knockout and receiving the status of a rising star, Stanton acquired a whole team of coaches, massage and rehabilitation therapists, and even a personal stylist. McKee was not afraid of the latter, but everyone else inspired him with doubts about his own abilities.

Finally, the night had come when there was to be decided the fate of not only Jack Sullivan's boxing career, but also his plan of getting revenge on Joe Ryan, which was the reason he had started all this in the first place.

"Pops, hi! It's been a long time! Who knew we'd meet by the ring again!" Mikey Sifaretto greeted the old man in a deliberately cheerful and laid-back manner.

"Sure, sure, hi, Mikey," McKee replied absently, thinking to himself that the new suit on the son of his late best friend was probably even more expensive than the coolest Sullivan's suit.

"It's Mike," Sifaretto corrected the old man with a slight irritation and added. "Well, let the strongest win?"

"Yeah, take care, Mikey," the old man replied and slapped

the man on the shoulder, making it clear that it was time for him to walk away to his side of the ring, as the bell was about to sound.

As soon as the referee started the fight, Stanton rushed forward so aggressively that if Sullivan had not immediately jumped aside, the opponent would have simply knocked him down.

"Come on, go around him! Spin him!" McKee shouted to his pupil.

Sullivan followed the coach's advice and began to jump aside and immediately take a step forward, while not forgetting to punch the opponent from the side, forcing him to literally spin on the spot. Jack did it so well that soon the coach, who intently followed his pupil with his eyes, started to feel dizzy.

Stanton did not like such tactic at all. Enraged at the opponent so much that he literally began to growl after another spinning trick from Sullivan, he could not stand it any longer and threw a punch after him, which hit Jack in the back of the head.

"What the fuck?!" McKee shouted. "Foul blow! Deduct a point, what are you waiting for?!"

The referee also noticed the foul but decided a warning would be enough. Having sworn under his breath, McKee shouted a new instruction to his pupil, "Jump back. Protect your back!"

Sullivan obeyed that instruction as well and after each attack began to take a quick step back in order to immediately be able to intercept the opponent's punch.

The first round ended in a draw. Stanton was much more active and aggressive, but Sullivan acted smarter and more accurately, putting his opponent in danger several times and that way causing a strong reaction from the audience, traditionally led by Sophia and the LGBT group of Jack's fans, which was becoming bigger, brighter, and more active with each fight.

"Watch him better. Looks like he's completely losing it," McKee called after Jack, squeezing between the ropes to free up the ring space for the second round. Sullivan nodded and readjusted his mouth guard.

Just as the old man feared, Rick Stanton's team really knew what they were doing. His coaches noticed that Sullivan moved much faster and therefore decided to change tactics. In the second round, instead of furious attacks, Stanton started to clinch the opponent at every opportunity, restricting his movement but at the same time continuing to deliver short punches to the body.

"You're dead, you fucking faggot," Stanton whispered in Jack's ear during another clinch.

Instead of a verbal response, Sullivan quickly pushed away from his opponent, simultaneously throwing a left hook into his jaw. The crowd gave a joyful shout and was roaring the very next second, as Stanton, spurred by the blow, desperately rushed at Jack again, punching with both hands.

Sullivan flopped comically backward on the canvas.

"Why the fuck are you counting!?!" McKee yelled. "He pushed him!!! It wasn't a knockdown!!! Look at him – he's right as rain! Knockdown, my ass!!!"

But the referee did not listen this time either. Counting down to five, he gave the green light to continue the fight. In the next two rounds, Stanton and his team tried other tactics, but Sullivan still managed to act faster and more accurately. At the end of the third round, he was close to defeating Stanton by technical knockout, cornering him and throwing punches from all sides. But there intervened the bell.

This attack, which had clearly demonstrated to Stanton that he could lose to Sullivan again, finally made the boxer lose his temper. So, instead of continuing to search for a weak spot in the opponent's technique, Stanton decided to resort to a "technique" that was older than boxing itself – a dirty street fight.

"Below the belt! Below the belt!" McKee yelled at the top

of his voice. "Stop the fight, the hell are you waiting for!?"

But the referee decided to stop the fight only when Sullivan, doubled up with pain due to a missed punch in the balls, got hit by a solid one-two in the face, which caused him to fall backward on the ropes. The referee let that go with a warning again, but at least he gave Sullivan a few seconds to recover. The pain in the scrotum began to recede, but the missed blows to the head took their toll. Jack's vision seemed to blur, and his ears started ringing.

So, when the referee gave the signal to continue the fight, Sullivan could no longer act as effectively as before and during the rest of the round, he got hit by another accurate punch in the face and several punches to the body. Despite the advantage already gained thanks to the foul blow, Stanton decided not to leave the opponent a single chance and continued to box even dirtier.

In the next round, Stanton hit the opponent below the belt again, and also pushed him, strangled him, putting his forearm on the opponent's neck in clinch, stepped on his feet, and even hit him with an elbow several times, pretending it happened accidentally. Despite all the yells from McKee, the referee either wasn't noticing the fouls or only giving a warning, instead of deducting points.

Each dirty trick was followed by a clean, accurate, and very powerful combination. By the end of the fifth round, blood appeared on Sullivan's face again – this time from a damaged nose, and a hematoma formed below his right eye, threatening to soon partially deprive him of vision. But Jack did not give up and even went on the attack himself every now and then. However, it did not affect the scores appearing on the cards after each round.

At times Stanton gained a double advantage on points over his opponent. And McKee could not do anything about it. There was only one thing one could do against dirty boxing – to box even dirtier. But, firstly, the old man never showed Jack such techniques, and secondly, Sullivan stubbornly refused to stoop to the level of his opponent.

After the sixth round, which almost ended in a technical knockout for Jack, the old man could not stand it anymore and approached the opponent's manager.

"Mikey, damn it, what the fuck is your guy doing? Gangbangers on our block fight more honorably than your motherfucker!"

"It's Mike," Sifaretto Jr. corrected McKee with irritation yet again. "It's business, Pops. Nothing personal. Everyone tries to win as best they can. The referee doesn't think anything's wrong, and I agree with him."

Having said that, Mikey turned around and left, pretending that he was in a hurry to do some important business, although in fact, all his business was now in the ring. By the seventh round, Sullivan had already been beaten so badly that Stanton could finally let go of his dirty tricks. Or rather, of the majority of them. He still really liked to step on his opponent's feet and strangle him in clinch.

"Hold on, kid!" the old man instructed his pupil during the break. "Remember how hard it was with Melikov? You were barely standing on your feet – yet still, you did it in the end! You always have a chance for a knockout! The main thing's not to give up!"

Sullivan met the coach's gaze and nodded back. McKee noticed that his pupil's eyes gave no hint that he might give up. "Where did he get such a frenzied willpower from?" the old man thought to himself, diving under a rope. Unfortunately, the eighth round proved to be as difficult for Sullivan as the previous one. Knowing that Jack would never give up and not wanting his pupil to get seriously injured, the old man had already prepared a towel, which, according to the rules, the coach could throw into the ring at any time to stop the fight, announcing the surrender of his fighter.

As if sensing this, Mikey Sifaretto came up to the old man.

"Pops, why haven't you stopped the fight yet? Your guy's

being killed up there. No, of course it's even better for us if Rick beats all the shit out of him, but even I feel sorry for your fighter. He's already beaten black and blue."

McKee responded with a wave of his hand, adding that Mikey should mind his own business. But after the opponent's manager had left, the old man thought to himself that his request was extremely odd, although Mikey tried to appear as laid-back as possible and not interested at all in his own suggestion. The old man's suspicion was reinforced dramatically when Sifaretto Jr. approached him with the same suggestion after the ninth round. This time, he looked less confident.

The tenth and first half of the eleventh round turned into an almost one-sided beating of Sullivan, whose right eye was nearly closed because of a huge hematoma.

"Pops, it's time to stop this!" Mikey approached the old man for the third time.

This time, he sounded extremely worried, which was already impossible to hide.

"What's going on?" McKee hissed into the man's ear, pulling Sifaretto Jr. close to him, not hesitating to grab him by the lapel of his expensive suit jacket. "Don't bullshit me!"

The old man's last words sounded so menacing that Mikey didn't dare to make any excuses.

"Pops, I really need you to stop the fight!" Mikey almost pleaded.

"Come clean or you can go fuck yourself!"

"I need the fight to be ended inside the distance! It's very urgent! I bet ten grand on Rick's early victory."

"Ha," the old man chuckled. "Do you seriously think I'll lift a finger so that you can make money off a bet?"

"It's not *just* about money! It's a matter of life and death! I owe money to very serious people. Tony Morazzone. I'm a dead man if I don't pay it off by the end of next week! Please Pops!!! I'm begging you!!! Do it for me. I'll never ask anything from you again!"

At that moment, there came the sound of the bell. The old man let go of Mikey's lapel and, without answering him, went to the ring to support his pupil for the last time in this fight. Finding himself face to face with Jack, the old man looked into his eyes again, or rather into one eye, since the second one disappeared under the swollen hematoma. Sullivan's gaze remained determined. He would never agree to stop the fight of his own will.

After leaving the ring, the old man thoughtfully clutched a towel in his hand. He knew Tony Morazzone. A long time ago, the latter used to beat him at school, but then McKee grew up and he himself began to beat Morazzone, which surprisingly led to them becoming friends. However, at the age of seventeen, Morazzone went to prison for the first time for stealing, and after that they went different ways. But McKee still knew that now Tony Morazzone, who by the age of fifty had already served three times in prison, had become a big shot gangster with a gang of almost a hundred people.

Morazzone mostly dealt in drugs and guns. Such a person would easily finish off a debtor or, at least, smash their kneecaps with a baseball bat. Meanwhile, the last round started for Sullivan no better than the previous ones. Stanton was ripping him to pieces. McKee really did not want to disappoint his pupil by surrendering early, but he also did not see any point in risking the life of his best friend's only son just to watch Jack being beaten for two more minutes.

The old man already raised his hand holding the towel, but at that very moment Sullivan rushed to attack. An accurate, fast jab, followed by no less fast cross, then two uppercuts, jump back, and a hook. Was Jack going to repeat what he had done at the end of the fight against Melikov?!? The whole arena fell silent, waiting for such an outcome.

But no, this time lightning did not strike twice. Rick Stanton remained standing on his feet and even counterattacked in the last seconds. McKee clutched a towel in his hand nervously. It was over. Jack Sullivan lost for the first time. There was no doubt about it. And he did not just lose – now Rick Stanton took away his right to become the last person to challenge Joe Ryan for the championship title.

And the only good thing McKee could have done in this fight was to let the best friend's son pay off his debt to the gangster who would now, quite possibly, kill him. "What have I done?!? What have I done?!?" a voice shouted in the old man's head. "And he didn't even ask me to throw this fight! Jack was already losing! He lost anyway! What would've changed if I'd finished all this a minute earlier? What have I done?!? I'm sorry, Johnny! I'm so sorry!"

The old man saw Mikey crossing the arena toward the locker rooms. McKee followed him, not even thinking about the fact that he was abandoning his fighter without waiting for the official announcement of the winner.

"Mikey, wait!" the old man said, opening the door to the locker room, which had just been closed behind him by Sifaretto Jr.

"Mike! My name's Mike, not Mikey!" Mikey yelled back at him.

"Yeah, I'm sorry, Mike, I'm sorry. How much do you owe Morazzone? I have some money and I can probably borrow..."

"Why? Why? Why?" Mike interrupted the old man. "Why couldn't you do such a small thing for me? WHY? Why do you keep ruining my life even after I left your fricking gym?!? Your gym! It was my dad's gym! You were just a poster boy, a publicity stunt, and nothing more! It was my father who created everything, and you were just a nuisance! And why was it so necessary for you to make the franchise deal fall apart after his death? I would've gotten millions then, not that miserable pittance for which my mother sold you our share!"

"It was a fair price..."

"Don't you even dare say what's fair!" Sifaretto Jr. interrupted the old man. "Was it fair when my father spent more time with you than with his own child? Why did he have to fuss over an adult man instead of caring for his own son?

Ah!?! You took everything from me! You took my father from me, you took my legacy from me, you took my money, my career, you took my life! My real life, not this crap that I have now!"

At that moment, Derrick was passing by the locker room. He had gone searching for the old man when the latter had not gotten into the ring with the rest of the team.

"Oh, that's where you are," the young coach said, looking inside, but then stopped short.

"It wasn't a stroke that killed him, it was you, you killed him!!!" Mikey kept yelling at the old man. "You've always been a cancer on my father's body, on the body of my whole family! If not for you, my father would still be alive, and I wouldn't have to borrow money from street thugs to finally move up in the world! Don't you have anything to say!?! Answer me!!!"

Since Mikey was demanding an answer to a question he had not asked, McKee kept standing silently at a complete loss. This angered Sifaretto Jr. even more than the old man's words about the fair price. So, instead of another tirade, he made two steps forward, took a swing, and hit the old man in the face with his fist. An accurate hook, once trained to perfection by McKee himself, bumped into his left cheekbone and made his face turn ninety degrees.

"What the fuck?!" Derrick rushed forward to defend the old man as the second blow flew in his direction.

Before the young coach could scoop Mikey up in his arms and pin him against the wall, Sifaretto Jr.'s fist landed right on the bridge of the old man's nose. McKee chose not to defend himself, although his boxing reflexes were still good enough.

"Derrick, don't! Leave him be!" he said to the assistant, pulling him away from Sifaretto Jr. "Don't!"

"But, what the fuck..." Derrick started to speak, but McKee cut him off.

"Wait for me outside. I need to talk to Mike."

"I've nothing more to talk to you about!" Sifaretto Jr. snapped, getting rid of Derrick's grip and examining his hugely expensive jacket to see if it had been damaged.

Having straightened up his suit, Mikey stormed out of the locker room.

"What the hell was that?" Derrick asked the old man, tearing off a piece from a roll of paper towels sitting next to him.

"A family matter," McKee answered, wiping the blood from his damaged nose with a towel provided by his assistant.

"Is he mad because you sort of took away his daddy from him?"

"Yeah, kinda," the old man replied, sitting down in a chair. "He's right, actually."

"Like hell he is. He's lucky he had a dad at all. That's in fact a great luxury. You grew up without a father, right?"

McKee nodded.

"That makes two of us. Charlie's father kicked him out of the house, Jack's beat him all his childhood, and then also kicked him out. Half of my friends either had no fathers at all, or their fathers died a long time ago, or abandoned them, or got stuck in prison. And as for those who had fathers, their fathers either toiled away at three jobs from morning till night or, on the contrary – did not work at all, getting hammered or watching TV all day long and not caring about their children either. Mr. Sifaretto took care of the kid, he left him a decent amount of money and a good house. It's not his fault and certainly not yours that Mikey grew up to be such a jerk."

McKee nodded sadly, far from convinced by the assistant's arguments.

"Come on, Pops, let's go," Derrick said, offering his hand to the old man to help him get up from the chair. "It's Stanton's locker room, he's gonna be here any minute."

"Holy crap!" the old man exclaimed, slapping himself on the forehead. "I left Jack alone! Let's go faster!!!"

In the corridor, they came across Charlie, from whom they learned that Jack had lost with a crushing score.

"Fuck! How could I leave him at such a moment!" the old

man swore and slapped himself on the forehead again.

All three of them walked to the door of Jack's locker room at the same time. Derrick reached for the handle, opened the door, and stood dumbfounded on the threshold when he saw what was happening inside at that moment.

..29..

Sullivan was even relieved when only Charlie and Kate got into the ring after the fight. He absolutely did not need to see pity in the eyes of McKee and Derrick as addition right now. If he could have left now without waiting for the official fight result announcement, he would have definitely done so. But Jack still had to hear the crushing scores from the judges: 117-111, 117-111, 117-111.

Going to the locker room, Sullivan asked his cornermen and cutman to leave him alone. None of them knew about the kind of relationship he had with Joe Ryan and so could not even guess how important this fight really was for him. Sullivan was completely broken and crushed. The last time he felt so helpless and lost was on the day of Jacob's death, half a year ago.

Closing the locker room door behind him, Jack sat down on a bench. He ran his hand over his shaved head, touched the hematoma under his eye, marveling at how in just a couple of minutes Chuck managed to get rid of most of the swelling, so that now the right eye almost came back to its normal vision. Putting his elbows on his hips, Sullivan stared blankly at the black tile floor.

This time he was not going to cry or fly into a rage like when they were watching Joe Ryan vs Carlos Vargas fight. He felt completely emotionless. There was only utter emptiness. He was not even in despair. Just nothing. No thoughts, no feelings, not even a hint that some of that might soon appear.

After Jacob's death, Sophia's return, and the following return to his true self, it began to seem to Jack that the victory over Joe Ryan was no longer so important to him. The desire for revenge devouring him from within seemed to recede before the warmth given to him by Sophia and the real friendship, which helped Jack get rid of the anxiety and self-doubt that had been haunting him all these years.

But now that he lost, all this warmth instantly disappeared. All that was left was oppressive, frightening emptiness. And what if now this emptiness would remain with him forever? What if his unclosed gestalt would work like unclosed doors and windows, because of which all Jack's feelings would now only fly through, like the wind, without lingering inside?

Was it possible that everything he had achieved over the past year eventually led him to exactly the same place from where he started? To the place where he had been destroyed, lost, deprived of faith in himself and faith that some good things were still in store for him in the future. Actually, it *had been* better then. Then he had felt at least something.

Jack's peace was disturbed by the creaking of the door. Sullivan did not look up to see who was entering the locker room, but immediately recognized who it was when Sophia's hand began gently stroking his head. She sat down next to him and took Jack's palm in her hands. Only then did he first look at her. There was no pity, sympathy, or disappointment in her eyes. Instead, they exuded warmth, completely unadorned by any emotion. Jack stared into her eyes and physically felt Sophia's warmth begin to fill him from the inside, driving out the cold, dank emptiness. She moved closer to Sullivan, so that now her shoulder was touching his, and their faces were no more than a dozen inches apart.

For a few minutes they looked into each other's eyes in silence and without blinking, and then Sophia brought her face even closer to Jack and kissed him. Gently and romantically. And Jack kissed her back. The first kiss was followed by the second, and then the third one. Sophia let go of Sullivan's palm and took his face in her hands. Jack put his arm around the woman's waist. With each following kiss, his lips felt warmer and warmer, until Sophia's lips finally burned Sullivan's.

Without breaking the kiss, the woman climbed on top of Jack. His hands began to passionately feel her supple body. Sophia's hands ran over Sullivan's shoulders, arms, then moved to his chest, stomach, and were about to go lower, when suddenly they were disturbed by the opening of the door and an exclamation that accidentally escaped from the old man, "What the hell!?"

Sullivan took his eyes off Sophia and saw McKee, Derrick, and Charlie stand on the threshold. They all looked as if they had seen a ghost inside, or rather a couple of ghosts making out. Sophia turned her head and also met the gaze of the uninvited guests. The woman hurried to get off Jack and, with a quick "Excuse me" slipped between the men standing in the doorway. While McKee, Derrick, and Charlie kept standing motionless, as if afraid that the ghost they had seen in the locker room could lunge at them should they move.

..30..

Not wanting to abandon his team at such a tough moment for each one of them, and, most importantly, being afraid to be left alone with Sophia and figure out what had happened in the locker room, Jack invited everyone to the nearest bar. Everybody but the old man happily agreed, since together it was easier to handle the defeat, which each of them perceived as their own.

McKee said a few kind words to Jack, apologized for not being able to stay any longer, and immediately left. An hour later, the old man was standing at the door of another bar – three blocks away from One-Two Boxing. It was not crowded inside. The old man was not surprised by that. Everybody on the block knew that Tony Morazzone did not like noise and bustle, so the boss's unofficial residence was populated only by those close to him.

Once inside, McKee went straight to the farthest table, where sat a bulky short man about the same age as the coach himself. As soon as the old man was ten steps away from the table, a big man with a shaved head left the bar counter, blocking McKee's path.

"Step aside if you don't wanna see your teeth scattered all over the counter," the old man said in a quiet but very menacing voice.

The boss's guard was about the same size as McKee, but about thirty years younger than him. So, he just laughed in response to the old man's threat.

"He's not joking, Vito," Tony Morazzone's voice came from behind the big man. "He'll beat you up in a minute. Let our guest through."

The guard stepped aside to make way for McKee.

"Hi, Tony," the old man greeted the mafioso, extending his hand to him.

"Hello, Gerard. It's been a while," Tony replied, shaking hands with the old man and pointing to a chair opposite him. "Tell me how you're doing. I feel sorry for your guy. He fought well, even though he's a faggot. Stanton fought dirty. If not for the dirty tricks, your guy would've beaten him."

"Thank you for the sympathy. If you don't mind, I'm gonna cut to the chase first."

"Of course, whatever you say. Friendly conversation, unlike business, does not tolerate haste. What brings you to me?"

Instead of answering, the old man took out a thick yellow envelope from his inside pocket and handed it to Morazzone. Tony did not touch the 'package', but instead nodded to one of his subordinates, who took the envelope, opened it, and showed the boss its contents.

"There's fifteen grand there. As I understand, Mikey Sifaretto owes you twenty? Take fifteen, and, to make up for the rest, you can take away his fancy suit and that gold bling he wears. Just don't harm him. He's Johnny's kid after all. We all grew up together. And please don't let him put any more bets."

"Bets?" Tony asked in surprise. "Did *he* tell you he owed me twenty from bets? By the way, it's actually twenty-three, but since you came to me yourself, out of respect, and in memory of Johnny, I'll agree to your terms. I actually wasn't willing to cripple the kid, but I can't just let him go. You do understand – you let one go, and tomorrow five won't pay off."

"I understand. Thank you, Tony, I knew I could count on you."

"Only there's one problem – if you want Mikey out of the picture, who will take his place? He's one of my best buyers. Without him, I'm up for a serious gap in my budget."

"Buyer? So it wasn't bets he lost money on? Has he been

doing drugs again?"

"Something in between drugs and bets," Tony answered with a grin. "Did you ever think how come Rick Stanton, who'd lost to your guy in the very first fight, knocked out his every single opponent after that? And this despite the fact that less than one third of his amateur fights ended in knockouts."

"Steroids?" McKee took a guess out loud and thought to himself. "So that's the kind of demon he's actually possessed by."

Tony nodded.

"Did Mikey buy twenty grand worth of steroids from you?"

"Thirty-three. First he used up his ten grand. And when his guy started winning, I allowed him to get it on credit. And that was a mistake. The kid spent all the money from the winnings on chicks and parties, instead of paying off his debt."

"Thirty grand for steroids? In my time, prices used to be much lower. Not that I ever used them, but I was in the loop."

"These aren't your simple steroids. New stuff, straight from the Emirates. From what I heard, it was designed for an Arab sheik so that his stallions could gallop faster, and then it turned out that it works much better on people. And most importantly, no modern test can detect it, unless you get tested specifically for it. And nobody's gonna test you for it – I'm the first supplier in the States and no one's taken the stuff before Stanton."

McKee rubbed his chin thoughtfully.

"Listen, Gerard, your kid fought well, he's probably gonna have even bigger fights. How about I switch the deal with Mikey over to you? With my juice, your Sullivan will be undefeatable. You know what – we need to set him up for the third final fight with Stanton. They have one victory each – we need to finally figure out who's tougher. Your guy on my steroids will deal with Stanton with no resupply in less than three rounds. And you can also make great money on sweepstakes. I'll even give you a discount for old time's sake."

Morazzone nodded to another one of his subordinates and a minute later he put a box of ampules with pale blue liquid on the table in front of the boss.

"Here, take this one for free," Tony took out one ampule and handed it to the old man. "Try it on your fighter, see for yourself how well this stuff works."

McKee hesitated for a moment but still took the ampule. After talking business, the old man stayed for a friendly conversation over a glass of whiskey. The former childhood friends sat until three in the morning. When they were done, Morazzone kindly instructed one of his subordinates to take a fairly inebriated McKee back home.

Once at home, McKee momentarily threw off his shoes and pants right at the door and crashed in bed having only his underpants and jacket on. The ampule of steroids rolled out of his pocket onto the sheet. The old man took it in his hand, brought it close to his eyes, turning it over in his hands. Sitting down on the bed, McKee stared intently at the ampule. If he took it to the right people, he could prove that Stanton was using doping. The fighter would be suspended, and all his victories would be held invalid.

In this case, Sullivan would get a chance to face Joe Ryan in the ring. But on the other hand, this same act would forever destroy any kind of career Mikey Sifaretto could have in boxing. If everyone found out that Mikey supplied Stanton with doping, he would lose the right to get anywhere near the ring. And the kid's life would be destroyed forever.

The old man faced an immensely difficult dilemma – on the one hand, he could give Sullivan what the latter had been dreaming of for so long, something that would finally help restore peace and quiet in his heart, on the other hand, he would destroy Mikey Sifaretto's life with this move. He would destroy the son of his best friend. The man to whom McKee owed everything. The man who loved his friend so much that he neglected his own son. The one who left this life so early only because he spent too much energy and killed too many nerve cells solving McKee's problems.

And whatever direction the old man turned the ampule in his hands, he would betray someone one way or another. And not just someone, but his best friend – either former or current.

..31..

Right at the time when McKee and Tony Morazzone finished with their business and started reminiscing about their youth, Sullivan and Sophia were already driving up to the gate of the house. The drive was silent and extremely awkward. It was not until he found himself inside the house that Jack finally decided to speak about what had happened a few hours earlier in the locker room.

"Soph... The thing that happened after the fight... In the locker room... I... I don't want you to feel uncomfortable about this...," Sullivan started speaking, stumbling through the words.

Instead of answering, the woman who had been walking in front of Jack all this time turned around abruptly, wrapped her arms around his neck, and literally sank her lips into his. All of Jack's awkwardness, doubts, and worries disappeared as if by magic. He returned the kiss with an equally strong passion, and then he picked Sophia up in his arms and carried her to the bedroom.

Having more than three years of abstinence between the two of them, Jack and Sophia immediately began to undress each other. And none of them had even the slightest thought that something strange was happening between the two of them now. On the contrary, it seemed to both of them that what was happening now was exactly the thing that should have happened ten years ago. Having unfastened the first four buttons on Jack's shirt, Sophia could not wait any longer and got rid of all the other ones with one sharp tug. The torn buttons flew in all directions.

Jack unzipped Sophia's back, but, having no experience with dresses, he never guessed what to do next, so Sophia had to get rid of her apparel herself. Pulling Sullivan's pants out of the way as well, Sophia brought him down on the bed and climbed on top of him. She started covering Jack's whole body with kisses – from top to bottom.

Finally reaching the cherished spot, the foul blows to which cost Jack the defeat, Sophia was pleasantly surprised to find that neither his former relationships only with men nor Rick Stanton's fists stopped Sullivan from showing the maximum possible enthusiasm for her. Sophia was even more pleasantly surprised by the size of Jack's manhood, which turned out to be disproportionately large compared to his rather modest body size.

Being extremely aroused as it was Sophia now turned into a real sexual warrior goddess, so Sullivan managed to seize the initiative and switch places with her only half an hour later, after Sophia experienced her first orgasm that night and the only one in the last year. Getting on top, Jack pleasantly surprised Sophia for the third time. Unlike the problems with the dress, his lack of experience with women did not stop him from proving himself a first-class lover – gentle, but at the same time passionate and determined.

Three hours, Sophia's three orgasms and Jack's two orgasms later, the couple finally broke their embrace with each other, and both of them fell exhausted side by side on the rumpled and sweat-soaked sheets.

"I think I'm dying," Jack said, still out of breath. "I didn't think you'd wear me out more than Stanton."

"Oh, I'm sorry, what was I thinking! You're all beaten up!" Sophia said and rushed to examine Jack's bruises and grazes.

"Even my testicles seem to suffer more damage from you than Stanton's fists."

Seeing the smile on Jack's lips, Sophia pushed him in the chest playfully, making sure that there was no bruise in that

349

place.

"Oh, come on!" the woman said and kissed Sullivan affectionately on the lips.

After that, Sophia pressed her whole body against Jack, placing her head on his arm. That way they lay for another ten minutes until Sophia decided to disturb the silence again.

"The most important question is this – are you not as gay as you used to think, or am I not as feminine as I thought?"

Jack laughed in response, turned his head in her direction, kissed Sophia on the nose, and added, "I love you, Soph. I've always loved you, I just struggled to realize that I loved you as a woman."

"I love you too. I've always loved you. You know, the day I introduced you to Jacob... at that party... I was going to confess my feelings to you then."

"Why didn't you?" Jack asked and began stroking Sophia's head gently, the way she loved it.

"Because on my way to tell you that, I caught you and Jacob kissing on the porch."

"Yes, it was a very unusual night," Jack replied with a grin. "You know, Jacob was my first and last man. I hadn't even kissed other guys before, and I hadn't even thought about such a thing."

"Really? Are you sure? I hadn't confessed my feelings to you for so long just because I was afraid that you'd really turn out to be gay. Which, in fact, eventually happened..."

"Really turn out to be gay? What's that supposed to mean?"

"Didn't you know? There were rumors about you, right from the first year in the university."

"Rumors? Let me guess, Maria Jackson was the author of those rumors?"

"I think so, although I don't remember exactly," Sophia answered and kissed Jack on the cheek.

"Jacob was my first man, but not my first sexual experience. I'd had it with women. Three women, to be exact.

Maria Jackson was the last of them. You know, I've been laughed at and bullied since I was a child, as long as I can remember. Both by boys and girls. So there was nowhere I could gain confidence from. When it came to sex, all three times, I was so nervous that, well, to put it civilly, I didn't feel particularly firm in the right places. Maria Jackson reacted to that especially emotionally. She started laughing at me and calling me a faggot. And as you've probably already guessed, that wasn't the first time I heard someone call me that. My own father called me a faggot for the first time when I was five years old, when I couldn't catch a ball. I'd never had any interest in men. As well as in women, to be honest. I was too fixated on my own weakness and cowardice. So when Jacob hit on me and immediately started courting me, started telling me how handsome I was, and how interesting my stories were, and then kissed me, I thought that probably it was for a reason that I'd been called a faggot all my life. That I must have truly been one. And when it came to making love, for the first time in my life I wasn't stressed about not looking or acting manly enough. And also, Jacob was very gentle and attentive. It was the first time I got a proper hard-on. I mean, not the very first time, of course, I'd always been good at it by myself. For the first time with someone else. Then I finally convinced myself that I was gay. Although, you know, I peeked down your blouse when you bent over."

Jack smiled and kissed Sophia on the forehead.

"I know! It was because of the way you were staring at my tits and ass that I decided you might not be gay after all, and that was the only reason I was able to gather the courage to confess my feelings to you. But Jacob beat me to it. For many years afterward, I blamed myself for not being able to make up my mind for so long. Imagine what our life would be like now if it hadn't been for Maria Jackson and our shared shyness."

"Yes, and Jacob would probably still be alive," Jack said sadly and to distract himself from sad thoughts immediately added. "Maybe we should send a Terminator to the past to kill

Maria Jackson as a child?"

Sophia smiled. "Although who knows. Maybe if we'd gotten together then, we would've made a lot of foolish mistakes, would've broken up in six months, and would never be able to be together."

"Yes, you're right. Let's not think about the past and how our lives might've turned out under different circumstances. Let's rather enjoy what we have now and what lies ahead."

"Yeah, let's do that," Sophia replied and sank her lips into Jack's.

Breaking off the kiss, Sullivan raised the sheet, looked at what was hidden under it, and, smiling, asked Sophia, "Second round?"

The woman reached her hand where Jack was looking and, with a salacious smile on her lips, rolled over on top of him.

For the next three days Jack and Sophia didn't leave the house. However, this time, instead of spending time like an old married couple, they acted like newlyweds. They were leaving the bed only for food, shower, and to have sex in some other place, like the staircase, the kitchen island, or the pool.

And just like six months ago, the couple's peace was disturbed by Charlie's intrusion. Jack heard the ringing voice of the kid shouting something from behind the gate even before he activated a video call camera on his smartphone. Sullivan opened the gate with his smartphone, put on a bathrobe, and went to meet the guest. He had just come down from the second floor only to find the boy already standing at the bottom of the stairs.

"Stanton... the fight... Ryan... Championship..." Charlie spoke incoherently, gasping for air.

"Did you run here all the way from school?" Jack asked with a smile and motioned the guest to the kitchen.

Only when Sullivan convinced Charlie to drink a glass of water, the kid managed to explain himself clearly, "The result of your fight with Stanton was declared invalid! You're undefeated again! You're now an official contender for the championship title! Jack, YOU CAN FIGHT AGAINST JOE RYAN!!!" Charlie could not help but shout in the end.

"Wait, hold on," Jack said in an uncomprehending voice. "How do you mean invalid? How can I be a contender again? Can such a thing really happen!?"

"It *can* happen! Of course, it can! Stanton's last test revealed some new doping, and then all his previous tests were rechecked, and it turned out he's been on some shit since his second fight. Tributynocadonite, or something like that. The bottom line is, all his professional fights, except for the first one against you, are now officially invalid, and he was banned from boxing for good. They totally Lance-Armstronged him! So your seven zero record's clean again. And YOU CAN BECOME A CHAMPION!!!". Once again, unable to hold back emotions surging over him, Charlie rushed to give Jack a hug.

..32..

"So you're not gay anymore?" the old man asked awkwardly and turned the wheel of the old pickup truck to the left.

"Been holding it back the whole week?" Jack, who was sitting in the passenger seat, replied with a grin. "Tell me the truth, you've probably been dying of curiosity all this time."

"Yeah, right. Like I don't have anything better to do except thinking about your private life. In case you haven't noticed, after your victory against Melikov and especially after your coming out after the fight against Robinson, we have a full gym almost every day. Every second gay in town now wants to become a boxer. I've already had to hire three new coaches."

"But it's great, isn't it!? To take One-Two to the next level is just what you wanted! Oh, by the way, my lawyer has prepared those documents that you requested – which will divide the ownership of the gym between you, me, Charlie, Derrick, and Kate. I'll bring them over to you tomorrow."

"Yeah, thanks. Except you didn't answer my question. Do you seriously think I'm already that old that it's so easy to get me off-topic?"

Jack grinned again.

"No, I didn't even try, actually. Well, yes, it turns out I'm not gay, since I'm with Sophia now. Bisexual, apparently. Or maybe you can call me some other cooler word, like pansexual or queer. I don't care about the terminology right now."

"Kid, I'm very happy for you!" The old man gave Jack a friendly slap on the shoulder and hurried to make himself clear. "No, no, I don't mean that I'm glad you've become a normal man after being gay. Ugh! No, no, you were a normal man even before that! I mean..."

"Yes, I know exactly what you mean," Jack interrupted. "Don't get so spooked, I won't suspect you of homophobia ever again."

"Yeah, thanks. I mean, I'm happy for you and Sophia. She's very nice. And you're very nice. You know, it's so rare. Usually, in a couple, one person must be a dick. At the very least. A lot of times both are dicks. But when both partners are so nice, it's like a miracle. You love her, don't you?"

"I do. I love her very much. I didn't even know that I could love someone so much besides Jacob. Is it okay that I became intimate with her just after six months? It's okay, right? It doesn't mean I've already forgotten Jacob, does it?"

"Kid, don't be silly! I've never seen in my life such love that you had for Jacob. And Justine once also told me that she had seen such devotion as you had only once before, it was some old couple who had lived together for fifty years. Where is she, by the way?"

"Justine? She moved to New York. I added her to Jacob's will. She decided to use the money to go top up her qualifications there. She wants to switch from being a rehabilitation practitioner to theory in order to develop new techniques that will help rehabilitate more patients."

"I'm telling you, Jack, you're a good man! You're too good for us. But you're good enough for Sophia and that's why I'm so happy for you two."

"Thank you, Gerard. I really appreciate your support."

Both men got slightly embarrassed by such a touching moment and fell silent.

"Maybe you should tell me now where we're going after all?" Jack spoke after two minutes.

McKee's truck had just pulled into a quiet suburb consisting of hardly distinguishable white houses with black roofs.

"Just wait a minute, we'll get there soon. Over there, can you see the number on that house? Is it forty-three by any chance? Yeah, that's the one, I can see it now."

The old man parked the truck at the house, which looked a little less kempt than the others. Shutting off the engine, McKee turned to his pupil.

"Jack," the old man began to speak in sort of a solemn voice. "It's only two days left before your championship fight against Joe Ryan. This fight won't be the same as your previous ones. Ryan is a boxer of a whole new level. I share your contempt for him as a person, but you can't deny that he's a great boxer. So, you have to be prepared to meet him not only physically, but also psychologically. Ryan's famous for being able to infuriate his opponents. He never takes any risks himself, carefully studying the opponent, waiting, making him feel nervous, playing possum, provoking. And as his opponent finally loses his temper and starts acting rashly – that's when Ryan goes all out, literally shooting punches at him. The most important thing in dealing with him is to always stay cold-minded. Should you take his bait, consider you've lost already. And you, my friend, unfortunately, have repeatedly had moments when you lost focus and took unnecessary risks. With Melikov, for example, do you remember how he almost had you?" Without waiting for the Jack's answer, McKee continued. "That's what we're here for."

"I still don't get why exactly we're here."

"Considering your history with Ryan, it'll be very difficult for you not to lose your head as it is, even without his 'help'. So, before you face him in the ring, you need to meet face to face with your true great enemy. You need to embrace him. Embrace and let go. It's the only way you can find inner peace, without which you won't be able to do anything in a fight against Ryan. So go already. The thing you need, your great enemy, is behind that door," the old man pointed to the house at which they pulled over.

"Is there a mirror behind the door?"

"Huh? What do you mean?"

"Well, my great enemy, real enemy – isn't it me myself? Isn't that what you were leading up to?"

The old man chuckled, "Kid, how many more times should I tell you – I'm not that smart to invent such things with mirrors and inner enemies. I am an old bo-xer!" the old man spoke in syllables as if talking to an idiot, "Go already! There's no mirror there and no metaphors – there's a person there, an actual one. Go, go!"

McKee literally pushed Jack out of the car. "Who can it be?" the question looped in Sullivan's head as he waited for an answer to the ring at the door indicated by the coach.

"Um..." was all Jack managed to say when the door finally opened.

On the other side stood a short, scrawny woman of about forty-five with a haggard face and tired eyes. Sullivan had no idea who she was and why this completely harmless-looking woman must be his enemy.

"Who's there?" A rough male voice came from another room. "Tell them we're not buying anything and we've already found our god – Mohammed Jesus Buddha Bush Jr."

The sound of this voice seemed to pierce Jack right through – from ears down to heels. He felt every hair on his body move, and a treacherous tremor appeared in his knees. Seeing how much the uninvited guest's face had changed, the woman asked solicitously, "Are you all right?"

"Who the hell is there?" The same rough voice now sounded closer, and the next moment there appeared its owner.

It was a tall man in his sixties. In build he resembled McKee, although he was inferior to him both in height and width. Gray hair stood out on the man's temples. Gray, seemingly lifeless, but at the same time penetrating eyes looked at the stranger so intently, as if they wanted to pierce through his eyes into his skull and come out through the back of his head.

"Jack," the man replied with a bitter, unpleasant grin. "We didn't expect celebrity guests today. Well, go ahead, come on in, since you're already here."

Sullivan kept standing still.

"Come in, I say, you're letting flies in standing there," the man added with a harsh, commanding note in his voice.

This domineering, peremptory tone made Jack's feet step over the threshold as if of their own accord. Even twenty years later, Jack still could not help but obey the will of the man he had been afraid of for as long as he could remember himself – his father.

"You want a beer?" Paul Sullivan asked and looked at the remainder of the beer in the bottle he was clutching in his hand. "Meg, bring us two cold ones."

In the same way, as if against his will, Jack followed his father into the living room.

"Stand up and say hello to our guest," Paul said to a boy of about twelve who was sitting in a chair in front of the TV. "Meet Jack, he's your older brother. This is Paul Jr. Don't just stand there like an idiot – hold out your hand like a man."

The sight of the boy about the same age as Jack was when his father kicked him and his mother out of the house, fear in the boy's eyes that instantly flared up in response to a rough address, and the very phrase "like a man" seemed to throw Jack twenty years into the past, turning him back into the very same intimidated child ashamed of his own weakness, the memories of which Jack tried to get rid of all these years.

The successful charity fund, dozen inventions, and promising projects, millions earned, and even the victories in the ring – all these achievements immediately vanished. He was once again that little boy in whom, according to his father, there was less masculinity than in Paul Sullivan's one single fingernail.

Jack shook his newfound half-brother's hand mechanically. Only a touch of something cold woke him out of his stupor. Sullivan turned his head and saw Meg handing him a bottle of beer.

"Thank you, ma'am. Nice to meet you."

"Yes, yes, you too," the hostess hastened to answer.

Although it was the first time the woman heard about the existence of her husband's another son, she did not even think of inquiring about it. Only Paul asked questions in this house. His wife was only allowed to ask such things as what he wanted for dinner and when to serve it.

Jack looked around. The room was perfectly clean and tidy. This scene suddenly made him feel sick. Jack remembered how his father used to make his mother clean up every day, and each time upon finding at least a single dirty spot, he would start yelling at her so intently that little Jack had to cover his ears with his hands and hide in a closet so as not to wet himself with fear. Because if he had wet his pants again, that would have cost him and his mother already a physical punishment.

"You know, Jack, I did see your fights on TV. It looks like my blood got the better of your mother's defective genes after all," Paul said, pointing with his bottle of beer toward a miniature altar boasting prize cups for victories in charity boxing tournaments among police officers, as well as appreciation letters for honorable service, a lieutenant's chevron placed under glass, and a couple of medals.

The insult to his mother hurt Jack, but he still could not gather the courage to confront his father.

"Meg, what the hell are you doing, standing there?" Paul spoke to his wife in such a tone as if she were a mere servant. "Offer our guest something to eat. It's my son, a famous boxer, not some scumbag relative of yours."

The woman flung her hands up and, despite the objections of the guest, ran into the kitchen. She knew perfectly well that the only law in this house was her husband's words. And the violation of this law was punished without delay.

"Come on, son, take a sit. Tell me all about boxing," Sullivan Sr. pointed to the sofa next to him and then turned to his younger son. "And you listen carefully, maybe you'll learn something. I've had it up to here with him," he added, turning back to Jack. "The kid's even a bigger wussy than you were at his age."

Of course, Sullivan did not expect a warm welcome from his father, but the fact that in just a couple of minutes he managed to insult Jack himself, his mother, as well as his new wife and son, finally started bringing Sullivan gradually back to reality. To that reality in which he was a grown-up, accomplished person who had achieved much more than his father had. Including his achievements in the field of boxing so much loved by Sullivan Sr.

But Jack remembered the coach's words that he needed to embrace and let go of his great enemy. If to defeat Joe Ryan, he had to spend a day with his father, taking his insults every other minute – so be it. Sullivan had come such a long way not just to break down at the very finish line because of his childhood grievances, which should have expired long ago.

That was why, for the next three hours, Jack was silently and diligently taking more and more insults to himself and his mother. Sullivan was even amused by the fact that his father never mentioned his homosexuality, although he could not be unaware of it if he had really watched all his recent fights. Despite all the insults, Sullivan Sr. was clearly proud that his son had become a successful professional boxer, and he absolutely did not want to spoil the party for himself.

However, his out-loud expression of his pride about his son's career was restricted only to giving a few dozen tips and saying phrases like, "If I were in such a situation in the ring, then of course I'd act differently and win faster." Such moments did not annoy Jack, unlike numerous attacks on his younger half-brother. The father turned his every mention of Sullivan's success into an insult to Paul Jr., who was already driven into such a state that he could not look into the eyes of either his father or Jack.

Having finished off his fifth bottle of beer, Sullivan Sr. made a suggestion or rather ordered his sons to go with him to the backyard – to play some ball. This time Jack had already found the strength to stand against his father, but when he saw the fear in his brother's eyes, he realized that he should not do this – not for himself, but for Paul Jr. And Jack understood this fear perfectly well – it was during those infrequent ball games that he most often heard from his father the words faggot, piece of shit, and bastard.

"I see boxing has made you a man after all!" Paul shouted when Jack managed to deftly catch the ball, thrown very inaptly by his father. "You finally learned to catch normally, not like some snotty girl."

Jack said nothing, throwing the ball accurately and carefully to his younger brother. The boy caught the ball and threw it to his father. Despite the throw being executed quite decently, an already far from sober Sullivan Sr. could not catch it and burst out swearing at his son, not forgetting to include his favorite word 'faggot'.

When the ball was in Jack's hands for the second time, he threw it to his father to save the boy from unnecessary risk. But when Paul Jr. could not catch the ball thrown to him by his father, Paul Sr. started yelling at him again. After the boy could not catch the ball for the third time, the father snapped. He walked up to his younger son, grabbed him by the collar, and pulled the boy toward him with such force that the child's head jerked like that of a rag doll.

"Why the hell are you embarrassing me in front of my son! Come on, catch it properly!"

Paul Jr. tried to answer something, but his father slapped him in the face. A palm, almost as big as McKee's, slammed into the child's face, causing him to fall on the grass.

"Leave him alone," Jack hissed through his teeth.

Sullivan Sr. continued to swear at his younger son and so did not make out the words of the older one.

"I said leave him alone," Jack repeated louder this time.

"What did you say there?" his father asked, turning to him, a fierce gleam in his eyes.

"You heard perfectly well what I said," Jack replied harshly. "Leave the boy alone."

"Or what?" Sullivan Sr. said in a mocking tone. "You think you're a match to a heavyweight? Think that since you've smoked a couple of skinnies, you can now raise your voice at your father? I'll show you how to raise your voice at me!"

Sullivan Sr. moved at his older son, taking off his belt at the same time. For a moment it even seemed to Jack that this was the very same belt with which his father used to beat him as a child. The belt that Jack was most afraid of. The belt that left two even, thin scars on his back. But this time Sullivan was not afraid.

"Fight like a man," he challenged his father looking him right in the face. "I'm not a child anymore. You won't scare me with your belt."

"Ha, look at him speaking. Well, come on, you want to do it like a man, I'll show you how a man does it."

Even before he finished his phrase, Sullivan Sr. threw a powerful left hook. If the fist had landed on its target, the fight would have ended before it even started. But Jack expertly ducked under the blow and jumped aside.

"Is that all you've got? Was it office-girls that you boxed with at your police cup?" Jack said mockingly, taking a boxing stance.

"Don't push it, kid, or I won't spare you anymore."

"Spare?" Jack replied, ducking under another blow from his father. "When did you spare me? When you beat me almost every day or when you told me to 'toughen up' after I'd gotten beat up at school yet again?"

Two hooks, jab, and cross did not hit the target and that enraged Sullivan Sr. even more, so he put all his strength and speed into the next blow to the body. Jack jumped back but still not quickly enough. His father's big fist slammed into his stomach, making him gasp for air. Rather than hitting him with another blow, Sullivan Sr. simply pushed him and Jack flew onto the grass.

"I've heard about your hubby. It's a good thing he kicked the bucket. One faggot less!" Paul said and spat on the grass next to Jack.

Jack could tolerate insults to himself and even to his mother, but the disrespect for the memory of his late spouse finally drove him mad. He quickly got to his feet and immediately delivered two fast and accurate punches to his father's solar plexus. Now it was Sullivan Sr.'s turn to gasp for air.

Without waiting for him to recover, Jack attacked his father with an uppercut. Sullivan Sr. tried to counterattack, but Sullivan Jr. jumped aside timely, simultaneously sending a hook into his father's jaw. This blow caused Sullivan Sr. to drop down on one knee. Jack thought for a moment that his father had enough, but then Sullivan Sr. showed himself at his finest.

"What are you staring at, you freak?" he called out in the direction of his younger son, who was standing at a distance, watching the fight closely. "It all started because of you. I'll show you what's what when I'm done with your brother! He'll leave eventually, but you've got nowhere to go."

His father's last words revived in Jack's memory all those hundreds, maybe thousands of times when he would hide from him in the closet, under the bed, in the pantry. But his father would always find him and beat him even harder than when the boy didn't try to run away from him. Knowing that, little Jack still could not find the courage in himself for not trying to hide.

But adult Jack had plenty of courage and rage. Suddenly, he hit his father, who was standing on one knee, with all his might right in the bridge of his nose. Sullivan Sr. fell on the grass, blood flooding from his face.

"Apologize to the boy!" Jack gave a frenzied shout.

"Apologize to him!"

The father did not answer. Then Jack climbed on top of him and began to hit him with short punches in the face. They were not strong enough to cause serious damage, but on the outside they looked very impressive, especially considering that after each such blow, a fresh portion of blood flew out of the victim's nose.

"Apologize! Apologize! Apologize!" Jack yelled in a frenzy.

"Please don't kill him!" Meg's voice came from behind Jack.

Jack stopped. He turned around and looked at the terrified woman clutching the boy to her chest, tears already rolling down his cheeks.

"Hey, Paul," Jack said, turning back to his defeated father.

"What?" Sullivan Sr. asked, spitting blood out of his mouth.

"Tell me, did your father beat you as a child?"

"Eh? What?" Paul repeated uncomprehendingly.

"Did your father beat you when you were a child? Answer me, or I won't stop."

"He did," Sullivan Sr. pushed the words through blood flowing out of his mouth.

Jack got off his father and even offered him his hand. "Here, sit so that the blood does not flow down your throat."

Sullivan Sr. took his son's hand cautiously and sat on the grass. Meg ran up to him, handing him a towel.

"And how did you feel about your father?" Jack asked another question.

"Eh? How did I feel? I... I hated him."

"So why do you treat your own children in the same way? Huh, Paul? Do you want them to hate you too?"

"I, I don't know...," Sullivan Sr. was at a loss whether from the blows suffered, or the unexpected frankness of the question.

"And I do know, Paul. As a child, when your father beat you, you felt small, insignificant, pathetic, and weak. And this feeling has remained in you forever, even as you grew up and became big and strong. Childhood traumas don't go away by themselves. That's why you became a cop and that's why you beat everyone weaker than you. To feel big and strong, while inside you still feel small and pathetic. You still feel like the boy who was beaten by his father. It's a disease that you inherited from your father. And you're spreading it further onto Paul Jr. now. Think about it. You can't fix anything in me anymore, but for him, you can still become at least some semblance of a father. And if you can't, then just leave them alone. I feel sorry for you. Yes, I feel sorry for you, I'm not kidding. It's not your fault that your father made you like this. But when we become adults ourselves, the responsibility is already ours for how we treat other people. I feel sorry for you, but I promise you – if you don't stop abusing them, I'll come back. I'll come back and make you a cripple that will never be able to harm anyone again. Do you understand me?"

"I understand," Sullivan Sr. said quietly in response.

Jack reached into his pocket and pulled out his business card.

"Here, take this," he said, handing the card to his younger brother. "Call me. I'll teach you how to fight back any bullies."

Leaving the backyard and going around the house, Sullivan found that McKee's truck was still in the same place. The old man was dozing peacefully at the wheel.

"Couldn't you find a better place to take a nap?" Jack asked, getting into the passenger seat.

"Huh? What? It's all right," the old man almost jumped from surprise.

"Have you been waiting for me all this time?"

"Yeah," the old man replied, turning the ignition key.

"Why?"

"Just in case. Should something go wrong and you need help. Although, I fell asleep. But I see you're all right."

"I'm fine. Come on, get going already. I don't want to stay

here any longer."

"Yeah, let's go, of course," the old man replied, pulling out onto the main road.

"I'm sorry, Gerard, I failed your task. I couldn't embrace and let go. I did the opposite."

"How's that?"

"I gave him a good beating, maybe even broke his nose."

Jack was surprised to find a sly smile on the coach's face instead of disappointment.

"It was your plan from the beginning, isn't it?" Sullivan guessed. "That's why you brought me here, so that I could punch my father in the face. Right?"

The smile on the old man's face turned into a big grin.

"And what was this exercise all about then? I thought I had to embrace and let go."

"But you did let the emotion go, didn't you? Admit it, Jack, now you feel better after you punched your daddy in the face?"

"I think so," Sullivan admitted grudgingly.

"It was not about embracing, but about learning to face your fears. To turn your weakness into your strength. If you were able to stand against your father, after everything he'd done to you, then you'll certainly be able to deal with Joe Ryan. I'm proud of you, son," the old man said and clapped Jack on the shoulder.

"How did you find my father anyway?"

"It wasn't hard. Last name Sullivan, about my age, a cop, apparently, a hardcore one. I have friends in the police, they identified your daddy right away. Do you know what his nickname is? Dirty Sully!"

Jack did not react to the mention of his father's nickname, but instead asked, "Gerard, can you take me to my mother's now, not my home? I won't stay there for long, half an hour at most."

"Sure, no problem."

An hour later, McKee's pickup stopped near a small but

very neat house in a prestigious area.

"Jack? Did something happen? Is Sophia all right?" Ellen asked worriedly, seeing her son on the threshold.

Jack never visited his mother without giving her a call in advance, and he, generally, rarely came by without her asking him to.

"Hi, mom. No, it's all right. Sophia's doing great, and so am I."

"Would you like some tea?" Ellen suggested out of tradition, letting her son into the house.

"No, thanks. I won't be long. There's a car waiting for me," Jack hesitated for a minute, not knowing how to start a conversation. "Mom, I came to apologize."

"Jack, what are you saying? You couldn't have done anything wrong to me for what you should apologize."

"Mom, please let me speak out. I'm already embarrassed as it is."

Ellen made a gesture as if she were zipping her mouth shut.

"I came to apologize to you. All these years, starting from my very childhood, there was this disconnection between us. From my end, not yours. You did everything right. I felt kind of awkward every time you were around, but I never tried to figure out why it was happening. And today I understood. Just an hour ago. You know, I was at my father's…"

Ellen opened her mouth to say something, but her son stopped her with a gesture.

"I'll tell you about this later. There was nothing special about it. But it wasn't until I met him that I realized why I couldn't love you the way you deserve. Mom, I'm sorry, but I blamed you for what dad did to us. I blamed you for getting together with him, for giving birth to me with him, for not leaving him, for not defending me. Though the last part isn't even true. You were trying to defend me, just how could you possibly do that? He's ten times stronger than you. And then, when that tragedy happened to Jacob, I distanced myself from you even more. At that time I thought I'd just become more reclusive and unsociable in general, but no, now I understand what my deal was. In the way I blamed you for my father, I saw my own reflection. You didn't defend me just the way I didn't defend Jacob. I didn't realize then that you were just a child yourself when you got together with him. A child in a foreign country, all alone, without a roof over your head, without money, without prospects. And then, as he took you in hand, you couldn't do anything anymore. He subdued you, made you believe that you're weak and not capable of anything. He made you believe that without him you would die. And that I would die too. It was because of me that you didn't leave him, isn't that right?"

Ellen nodded in response.

"You can't blame people for not being superheroes, for not being strong and fearless. You've always been a good mother. And that's the main thing. It's not your fault that father is like this. I'm sorry, mom, I'm sorry that all these years, all my life, I've been unfair to you. I feel really ashamed, mom. Please forgive me."

Ellen approached Jack, held him to her chest, and started stroking his head.

"There-there! You've always been the best son anyone could wish for. Yes, maybe there was some awkwardness between us, but you were always kind, you always helped me. If you want me to say it, I'll say it – I forgive you, I forgive you for everything. But you know what, son, promise me one thing – promise me you'll forgive yourself for Jacob, too. What happened to him is just fate, an ill fate, it's not your fault. You must forgive yourself. There's a great and bright future in store for you and Sophia. Don't let the ghosts of the past spoil it. Promise me, Jack."

"I promise, mom, I promise," Jack said, pulling his head away from his mother's chest.

"Good. Would you take some cinnamon buns? Your favorite, I've just baked them."

"Yeah, I'll take them," Jack replied with a smile of relief.

He and McKee ate almost half of the bag of buns on their way. Jack took only two buns with him for Sophia, leaving the rest of them to the old man. It wasn't until Sullivan got out of the car that it finally dawned on him.

"Gerard, how did you know where my mom lives? I didn't give you the address."

Caught off guard, the old man pretended that he could not answer because his mouth was still full with an unchewed bun, and hurried to drive off, waving his hand to Jack.

..33..

Press conference Joe Ryan vs. Jack Sullivan
1 day before the fight

"Joe, how do you feel about defending your title against the boxer who has only seven fights under his belt?" a journalist in a cheap suit addressed the current champion. "Back in the day, you yourself had to hold twice as many fights before you earned the right to a title fight."

"Well, what can I say," Joe Ryan replied with a smirk. "These are the times we are living in now. Even in sports, even in boxing, the hype is more important than the qualities of an athlete. I personally have nothing against Jack. Can I just call you by your first name?" Joe answered rather than asked, turning to Sullivan, who was sitting at another table next to him, and, without waiting for the response, he went on. "I've nothing against Jack, but his strongest qualities are not speed, technique, or the power of his punch, but the hyped biography. Of course, being such a fighter who entered the ring for the first time in his thirties, and what's more who's gay, and what's even more who has just lost his disabled husband, how could you not get a title fight? You all know perfectly well how much hype there was about him on the Internet. Man, his personal life is ten times more discussed than his fights. Again, no offense. But with such a story, he can get anywhere – America's Got Talent, The Voice, or even America's Next Top Model."

Ryan laughed at his own joke, and his laughter was immediately picked up by half of the journalists, who were crammed into the press conference room so tightly that they were almost about to fall out of the door.

"Ignore him, answer only to the point," McKee whispered in Jack's ear, noticing the muscles on his face start moving after the mentioning of his disabled husband. "Whatever you want to say to him, you'll say it in the ring."

Another journalist got up.

"Jack, will we ever learn the answer to the main question – why exactly did you suddenly decide to give up your successful IT career and take up boxing?"

Sullivan took a deep breath, exhaled, and spoke, "As I said earlier, I started boxing because of my husband Jacob Sanders. Almost exactly eight months ago, he passed away as a result of a stroke. This stroke was triggered by a brain injury he had suffered three years earlier as a result of a homophobic attack. All the time that had passed between that attack on him and me starting boxing, I tried to bring the guilty person, the one who had killed my husband, to justice by all legal means. I contacted the police, the prosecutor's office, filed civil lawsuits, resorted to the help of private detectives, tried to gain the support of the press. But the person responsible for this crime has a lot of money and influence. Ten people witnessed his crime, but all of them were bribed or intimidated. The only reason I haven't mentioned the name of this man yet is that his lawyers threatened to sue me for slander and drag me through the court system. I wasn't afraid of the consequences of such a charge for myself personally, but I didn't want to spend in court the last years that my husband still had to live. But now that Jacob's dead, I have no reason to stay silent about it any longer. Do you want to know why I really started boxing?"

Everyone present held their breath in anticipation of a sensational statement. Sullivan recovered his breath and took a sip of water from a glass sitting in front of him.

"I started boxing because I couldn't find another way to get even with the man who had killed my husband. This man's name is Joe Ryan."

A wave of astonished exclamations swept through the

crowd of journalists. But Jack did not stop.

"Three years ago, at eight p.m. on the third of August, in The Franklin Bar at the intersection of the 18th Street and Lincoln, a group of young people led by Joe Ryan began harassing me and my husband. They shouted out homophobic insults and threw food at us. When my husband approached them, politely asking to stop their attacks, Joe Ryan personally dealt him a professionally trained straight blow to the jaw. My husband fainted and hit his head on the stone floor as he fell. This hit caused him brain herniation which required decompressive craniectomy. Jacob fell into a coma. As a result of the injury, his brain suffered irreparable changes, causing Jacob to spend the last two years of his life in a wheelchair, forget how to read and write, lose most of his memories, and stoop to the intelligence level of a seven-year-old. I have all the necessary medical reports stating that all of this, including the stroke that eventually killed my husband, all this was the result of the injury Jacob sustained due to the blow inflicted on him by Joe Ryan."

Sullivan got to his feet so abruptly that his chair flew back and overturned.

"This man is a criminal, a murderer!" he said, pointing at the champion at the next table. "He should be in prison, not here joking and laughing in front of you!"

"Wow," Ryan spoke for the first time since Jack was asked the question. "I told you, the guy is a real marketing genius! With such drama talent, he's also going to get an Oscar!"

Ryan leaned back in his chair and began to applaud mockingly. Sullivan charged at him, but the coach, already prepared for such a development, grabbed him with his huge hand and quickly dragged him back.

"I'm gonna kill you! I'm gonna kill you!" Jack yelled in a frenzy.

"Okay, okay, of course! Take away this hysterical fairy already," Ryan feigned a laugh, calling out after the Sullivan's team dragging their fighter away into the next room.

Journalists immediately vied with each other, demanding a comment from the champion concerning the accusations thrown at him.

"Well, guys, I can tell you this much – perhaps, if I'd knocked out someone's husband, I'd remember it. And that knockout would definitely appear in my record."

Ryan laughed, and half of the journalists supported him again.

"And in fact, I'm even glad about all this buffoonery Jack has played out. Just imagine the revenue that will be generated by our fights' pay-per-view after such a completely insane statement. I'll make at least a dozen extra millions off of it. And Jack, too. Probably, that was the idea behind him inventing all this nonsense in the first place."

..34..

For the title fight *Joe Ryan vs. Jack Sullivan* there was chosen the legendary MGM Grand Garden Arena on the Las Vegas Strip. It was here that Mike Tyson bit off part of Evander Holyfield's ear, and it was here that another great undefeated Welterweight boxer Floyd Mayweather Jr. held his legendary fights against Oscar De La Hoya, Canelo Álvarez, and Manny Pacquiao.

The arena was packed to the brim, and almost five million viewers gathered before TV screens. Many analysts claimed that, thanks to this fight, Joe Ryan would be able to break another record of his eternal rival Floyd Mayweather Jr. and become the highest-paid boxer in history.

Jack Sullivan tried very hard not to think about it. Not to think that even if Ryan lost the fight, he would still become richer by at least a hundred million dollars. Jack himself was owed only five million under the contract, all of which he had already promised to his charity.

Sullivan tried not to think about Joe Ryan at all. Losing his temper during the press conference already jeopardized the whole fighting spirit that the coach had been building in him for the last two months. McKee repeated over and over that with Ryan, one should never give in to emotions. It was exactly what the champion was waiting for, and it was exactly the thing Ryan was good at like no other boxer.

The whole evening after the scandalous press conference and the whole today's morning Jack had spent in meditation together with Sophia. So, now, walking toward the ring, he looked completely calm and even peaceful. At one point, there was even a slight smile slipping through his lips, caused by the ring walk song.

It was the song that Sophia wrote especially for this occasion. The first song of her own to be heard by someone outside her family and friends. Sophia made a point of not revealing the song to Jack before the fight, and now it became a very pleasant surprise to him. Sullivan thought to himself that it was hard to imagine a song better suited for this occasion. It contained both proper fighting spirit and heartwarming lyrics, through which Sophia managed to capture Jack's complex, multi-faceted personality.

Sullivan listened to the song with such delight that he almost forgot to greet his LGBT support group, which this time looked especially numerous and bright. "My personal Pride parade," Jack thought to himself and gave the fans a wave of his hand and a wide smile. Sophia, who was sitting in the front row, and Ellen, who came to her son's fight for the first time, received a less wide, but very tender smile.

"How are you, Kid?" McKee asked after they finally entered the ring. "Cool as a cucumber or is it just an appearance?"

"Cool, inside and out," Sullivan replied, but the next second his face altered so much that the old man wondered for a moment whether a ghost had appeared right behind him.

And a ghost did appear at that very moment in the ring, only Jack did not see it, but heard it.

She packed my bags last night pre-flight
Zero hour 9:00 a.m.
And I'm gonna be high
As a kite by then

Sullivan's lips tightened, his jaw muscles moved under his skin, and his left eye started twitching involuntarily.

I miss the Earth so much I miss my wife

It's lonely out in space
On such a timeless flight

A vein throbbed on Jack's forehead, and his fists rose by themselves, as if ready to start the fight right away.

"Jack! Jack! What's happening? What's wrong with you?" McKee spoke anxiously, taking his pupil by the shoulders. "Talk to me!"

"The song," Sullivan said through his teeth barely making any sound.

"What's wrong with the song? Do you know this song?"

"Rocket Man," Jack said a little more clearly.

"What's wrong with it?"

"This is the song Jacob and I danced to in that bar. The song they started bullying us to. This is our song. The song that got him killed. He remembers. The bastard remembers everything. He even remembered this song…"

At that moment Joe Ryan was already approaching the ring. McKee realized that once the champion stepped over the ropes, Jack would lunge at him without waiting for the bell to sound. And then, probably, biting off Holyfield's ear would no longer be the most bizarre thing the walls of MGM Grand had ever seen. The old man quickly figured that he would not be able to calm down his fighter timely himself, so he decided to call in the big guns.

"Sophia, come over here! Quickly!" He shouted from behind the ropes.

Seeing first the terrified face of the coach and then the face of her man distorted with rage, Sophia instantly realized what was happening and immediately ran up to the ring.

"Jack, Jack, look at me!" she shouted, touching his shoulder with her hand.

McKee lifted Jack a bit as if he were a child and turned him around to Sophia.

The woman took Sullivan's face in her hands, pulled him closer to her, and began whispering something in his ear that was meant only for him. The words of his beloved affected the boxer like real magic. Making sure that Jack's eye was no longer twitching and there was no more teeth grinding, Sophia leaned over the ropes to kiss Sullivan on the forehead, saying, "I love you" and hurried back to her seat, as the referee had already invited both fighters to the center of the ring for the final instructions.

"Whatever she whispered to him, it definitely worked," McKee thought to himself, seeing how after the sound of the bell Jack did not lunge furiously at the opponent, but went forward slowly, measuring his every step and every move – doing exactly what the coach advised him to do.

The first round was spent in keeping with the best traditions of title fights – neither the current champion nor the contender rushed to attack, preferring to exchange a punch at a time from a safe distance, feeling each other out for breaches in defense.

"Jack Sullivan has definitely done his homework. Now he's acting exactly the way Joe Ryan's acting himself – prudently, methodically, without haste and unnecessary emotions. If there's a recipe for defeating a champion, this is definitely it."

The second round started with a fast attack by the champion, resulting in a clinch.

"So what do you think of my entrance?" Ryan hissed in his opponent's ear. "Did you like the song?"

Sullivan got rid of the opponent's hold, sending a quick punch to the head. The champion dodged and immediately countered with a punch to the body. Jack responded with a block. Then Ryan feigned another attack but actually closed in on the opponent only to lean on him in the clinch again.

"I remember that night, Jack. We all had so much fun then," the champion hissed again.

This time Jack did not come out of the clinch but instead delivered two quick punches to the body. Of course, they could not do much harm to the opponent, but in the long run they had the potential to 'prepare' his ribs and liver for a full-fledged blow.

"Joe Ryan's traditionally checking the opponent's defense in the clinch in the second round, as he always does. If the champion's already managed to find breaches in the opponent's defense, then in the next round we can expect Ryan to deliver fast and accurate single punches aimed at throwing the opponent out of his game."

"Dan, look at how confident the champion is – he's clearly talking about something with his opponent right now. It's amazing how Ryan manages to both feel his opponent out and make a small talk at the same time."

"Whoa! I didn't expect this coming! Sullivan literally exploded, rushing at his opponent as if he were up against some amateur, not the champion."

"A great combination from the contender, but you can't just mess with the champion. All the punches landed on the guard."

"You just look at that – Ryan's laughing! Yes, yes, there's no doubt he's laughing right in the face of his opponent."

"Bam! The thing we mistakenly predicted only for the fourth or fifth round has already happened. Joe Ryan caught his opponent with a counterblow. A fast and accurate jab in the jaw, and Sullivan's dropping on the canvas!"

"Fortunately for the contender, the knockdown wasn't heavy. Sullivan's getting up on the count of three. The referee's giving the signal for the fighters to come closer. Unbelievable! Ryan's immediately knocking the opponent down for the second time! What a technique, what a skill! And who knows, maybe this fight would end right now, but the bell's ringing, allowing Sullivan to recover during the break."

"What happened, Jack!?! You're doing the opposite of what we've talked about!" McKee said irritably when Jack took his place on a chair and got rid of the mouth guard.

"He called Jacob a pathetic faggot and said he deserved to

die," Jack said through his teeth.

"Jack, this is exactly what Ryan does! This is his main strength, not his fists! Don't fall for it! Don't listen to him! Think about something else. You can go over a nursery rhyme in your head – Solomon Grundy born on a Monday or something like that. But don't let him get in your head!"

A signal from the referee interrupted the coach's instructions.

"It looks like Jack Sullivan has learned a lesson from the previous round, which almost cost him defeat. Now the contender doesn't take risks anymore."

"What's more, Dan, apparently Sullivan decided to play the champion's game. Now he's mimicking Ryan's manner of acting defensive and forcing the opponent to go forward and make mistakes."

"Right, right! Not bad! Ryan managed to dodge, but Sullivan's hook still grazed his face. Now Ryan's returning to his favorite position again, and we can see a rather rare situation for a title fight when both fighters act defensively, neither of them willing to go forward and take risks."

"Well done, Jack!" the coach spoke during the break. "Keep doing that! Even if you have to dance around passively until the twelfth round. The main thing is for Ryan to snap first. And he'll definitely snap and go on the attack sooner or later. He's a champion, he can't have people saying later on that he got scared of you. This is his last fight! He'll definitely make a move, and that's when you catch him with a punch. The main thing is to hold out, to wait for the right moment. Don't let him provoke you into attacking!"

The fourth and fifth rounds were just as passive as the third, and the crowd was beginning to express dissatisfaction. It was the negative response from the crowd that had always hit Joe Ryan much stronger than the punches of his opponents. The fighter, who could represent the gold standard of egocentrism, simply could not allow anyone to doubt his greatness. So, during the next break, he beckoned to his entourage and gave them some kind of order.

"The first half of the fight is almost over, and we still don't see any action taken by either side. The spectators are beginning to express their indignation louder and louder."

"Dan, I think it's not indignation. They're chanting something."

"Yes, yes, indeed. Now that the voices got louder, I can hear it too. They're chanting the words 'Rocket Man'."

"It must be Joe Ryan's support group repeating the name of the song to which he entered the ring today."

"Yes, yes. By the way, such a great choice of a song for the farewell fight. Very poetic."

"But what do we have here, it looks like the active support of the champion infuriated the contender! Sullivan rushed at Ryan like crazy. I've never seen such a barrage of blows against the champion. Will Sullivan really manage to break through Ryan's legendary guard now?"

"Boom! And that's exactly what the fans of the champion were waiting for. Once again Ryan did something he's always been famous for – despite the barrage of blows from his opponent, he managed to choose the right moment to deliver an accurate cross."

"Sullivan's in big trouble now! The champion's cross has clearly done its job. The contender's attack stalled, and now Ryan's unleashing his blows."

"A great combination to the body and here it is – a right uppercut forcing Sullivan back. What is it – did the contender just slip or is it his third knockdown already?"

"This is definitely not an accidental fall! The referee's counted to seven, and Sullivan still can't get up!"

"Is that really it?"

"No, it's too early to write Sullivan off. The contender's getting up informing the referee that he's ready to continue."

"That's dangerous! Pretty dangerous! And we've got the first blood! Sullivan's unfortunate right eyebrow is split again. The contender is hurt and hurt badly. And the champion still won't ease up."

"The bell! Sullivan's saved by the bell. And if not for the bell, we could quite possibly witness a knockout right now."

Sullivan did not know what hurt him the most: the numerous hits he took or the flooding memories of the night Joe Ryan killed Jacob. But he knew for sure that it was the latter that hindered him from going on much more than the physical pain. Instead of watching the opponent's hands and feet, the images of that night kept popping up before Jack's eyes over and over again. He kept hearing Elton John's voice over and over.

Several times, when he was ready to punch his opponent in the face, instead of Joe Ryan, for some reason there was Jacob appearing in front of him, and his fists went down by themselves. And as they went down, Joe Ryan, who had been Jacob just a moment ago, did not miss the opportunity to hit him with accurate, fast, and very powerful blows.

Besides the split eyebrow, the seventh round brought a damaged nose and a hematoma under the right eye. For all the seven rounds, Jack himself, never scored a single worthwhile punch against his opponent, so Joe Ryan was fresh and full of energy.

"Things are looking very bad for Sullivan. The right eye has already begun to close, the split eyebrow and the damaged nose started bleeding again. I'd say that the contender's team should consider ending the fight inside the distance."

"Yes, Dan, I totally agree with you. The current situation reminds me very much of The Dream Match De La Hoya versus Manny Pacquiao. Ryan's dominating the fight now just as strongly as Pacquiao dominated that fight. In fact, starting from the fifth round, we've been witnessing just a one-sided beating of Jack

Sullivan."

"But I'd like to point out that the contender has a lot of guts. I can hardly recall such fortitude in any of Joe Ryan's former opponents."

"Yes, we should give Sullivan lots of credit for the strength of his character, especially considering his life story, specifically that he started boxing just a year ago, and before that he was a programmer, which is almost the furthest thing from boxing."

"Sullivan's getting hit with a strong one-two to the body. To be honest, it even hurts me to look at it. I'm almost tempted to shout to his coach, former heavyweight champion Gerard McKee, that it's high time to throw in the towel."

There was no need for the commentators to shout anything to the old man. He himself was already thinking that it was time to stop the fight, so when Sullivan took his place in the corner at the break, the coach spoke frankly to him, "Jack, he's killing you. This needs to stop. We should stop the fight. Believe me, I know what you're capable of, and I remember all your victories in the last seconds, but that's not what's happening here."

Jack gave the coach such a look that the old man immediately felt uneasy.

"No. Don't you dare. I won't lose. Not that way. Even if I don't win, there's no way I'm going to give up before it's over. Not after what he's done here. He must know he failed to break me."

"Jack, son, but he's killing you!" the old man pleaded.

"I'd rather die here in the ring than give up. Do you understand me? Gerard, look me in the eye and say you understand me! Don't you dare throw in the towel!"

"I understand, Jack, I understand," the old man breathed out heavily.

The eighth round was a blur for Jack. A jab and sharp pain in the chin. A cross and the split eyebrow started stinging again. Two jabs to the body, and the ribs started aching as if they and everything under them cramped. "Just don't fall, just don't fall!" Jack kept telling himself, but the very next blow floored him.

"Get up! Get up! Get up!" It was only by sheer willpower that Sullivan managed to get to his feet. The referee should have denied him the right to continue the fight, but Jack gave him the same look that had confused the coach, and the referee didn't dare to object to him. At that moment, Sullivan, half of his face covered in blood, looked like he would have attacked the referee as well if the latter had stopped the fight.

Unable to take it anymore, McKee called Sophia to the corner so that she could persuade Jack to stop the fight. But even his beloved woman could not make him change his mind. Sullivan said he loved her, but added that if he gave up now, he would lose himself forever. And leaning over to the coach, he added that if the old man threw in the towel, he would curse him and do everything to destroy both McKee and One-Two Boxing.

The old man knew Jack as the kindest and noblest man he had ever met, but at that moment he believed his words. Sullivan was now fighting not with Joe Ryan, but with his own demons, with all the humiliations and insults that he had endured throughout his life from his father, classmates, homophobes, including Gerard McKee himself. And if Jack lost this fight now, then he would lose not to Ryan, he would lose to his demons. He would lose and forever stay in that dark place where Jack Sullivan was a weak and helpless little boy, afraid of his own shadow and wetting his pants from the sound of the thundering voice of his drunken father.

Nobody, not McKee, not the commentators, not Joe Ryan, not even Jack Sullivan himself, understood how he was able to stay on his feet until the end of the tenth round. Jack literally turned into a zombie. A slow, half-rotted, but still steadily advancing zombie that could only be stopped by cutting his head off. He was getting hit with punch after punch but continued to go at his opponent. Senselessly and mercilessly.

Sullivan's mother was deliriously whispering the words of an old Russian prayer, clutching a cross with her fingers white from tension. Sophia was biting her lower lip so that it bled. Kate could not stand it and turned away from the ring. Charlie was trembling all over, and even Derrick lowered his gaze from time to time, unable to watch what was happening in the ring anymore.

Finally, the old man could not stand it either. With tears in his eyes, cursing himself for not having done it earlier, McKee threw the towel in the ring and immediately followed it, rushing in between the fighters along with the referee. Sullivan tried to protest, but there were mostly blood clots coming out of his mouth rather than words. When the coach tried to take him to the corner, Jack pushed the old man aside and left the ring himself, shouting over his shoulder for the others not to even think of following him.

The fight was over, and there was only Joe Ryan with his team remaining in the ring, celebrating the victory with such emotion as if it were not another champion title defense, but a fight for his first belt.

..35..

"Let me patch you up, son."

Sullivan looked up to see an elderly man standing in front of him.

"Don't worry, I'm a professional, not some local lunatic," the stranger added, taking cutman tools out of his pockets.

Jack only shrugged. He did not want to talk to anyone at all, but his face hurt terribly, so he had no objection whatsoever to getting professional help. The stranger handled Jack's injuries surprisingly quickly.

"Thanks," Jack muttered.

"Just because you lost in the ring doesn't mean you lost outside of it," the stranger said and went on about his business.

It was only when the old cutman left that Sullivan noticed a small TV in the corner of the locker room, which had previously been blocked from view behind the man's back. There was a live broadcast of what was happening three hundred feet away from him in the ring. Jack turned up the volume.

Joe Ryan, already with the championship belt on, acted as if he had just defeated not an ordinary opponent but the global economic crisis. Only after five minutes of his triumphant dancing, he finally decided to leave the ring. The journalists followed him down the aisle.

"What can you say about your opponent's performance?"

"Well, what can I say. The ring has cleared things up. Jack Sullivan has been a hyped- up boxer since his very first fight. He pulled it off exclusively because of his story, not skill.

At first, it was dumb luck for him. Then his opponents made stupid mistakes, and then he got lucky again. On top of that, he was purposefully matched up against not the strongest of opponents. And I wouldn't be surprised to learn that at least a few of his fights were fixed. Sullivan's just a publicity stunt, a clown whose performances disgraced the glorious sport. Even if everybody gangs up on me after that, I'll say it anyway: the ring is a place suited only for real men. The real ones, you get what I'm talking about? It's no place for pampered princesses. And even more so for those who use their dead husband and made-up stories to attract more attention to themselves."

The champion's words were met with approval by half of the crowd, but Sullivan's LGBT fan club did not lose courage and started chanting anti-homophobic slogans while approaching the aisle, in the middle of which the champion stopped surrounded by cameras and microphones.

If Joe Ryan had not been so egocentric and after these words had peacefully disappeared under the stands, most likely nothing of what followed would have happened. But Ryan could not resist seizing yet another opportunity to show off in front of the cameras. Waving his arms like a conductor, he started egging on his fans, who began to chant the name of their idol in response to the slogans of Sullivan's support group.

Ryan did not know that he had made a fatal mistake of insulting Jacob's memory again by mentioning him. Hearing these words, Jack Sullivan got so enraged that he immediately forgot about the ringing in his ears, his still slightly bleeding face, and aching ribs. He forgot about everything except one thing – that he needed to destroy Joe Ryan.

Kicking the locker room door open, Sullivan rushed out into the corridor.

"Hey, Ryan!" a sharp and ringing shout came from the corridor leading to the rooms under the stands.

The spectators and cameras in the arena turned in the direction of the shout as if on cue. Framed in the bright light,

Jack Sullivan was standing there. And now he looked like he was two heads taller than usual.

"Fight with me like a real man!"

"Pfft..," the champion grinned in response. "Calm down already, will you? Enough of these theatrical tricks! Don't embarrass yourself!"

"Fight with me like a real man!" Jack repeated even more sternly.

"Did I hit you so hard that you forgot I'd just smashed you all over the ring?!?"

"I said, fight with me like a real man! No gloves, no referee, no judges. One on one. Or you can't do that? Huh, pussy?"

The champion did not want at all to put up with the insults, but he also did not want to deal with Sullivan, who had clearly lost his mind.

"Don't you have anything to say, fucking champion? Or the only thing you can do is to sneak attack gays outside the ring, right? How about attacking a gay who's ready to fight back?"

Joe Ryan would be happy to beat Jack again, but he did not forget for a second that more than a dozen cameras were directed at him now, and all this would look very bad on the screen. They would say that he beat a poor man who had run mad because of the loss in the ring and the loss of his gay spouse. But the problem was that Ryan needed to go to the locker room, the way to which was blocked by Jack. If he tried to go the other way, they would later call it a cowardly escape.

So Ryan chose to go toward Jack, but at the same time, he raised his hands in a conciliatory manner and spoke loudly enough for his words to be clearly audible to the viewers.

"Man, I'm not going to fight with you. It's clear to everyone that you're out of your mind. You need to see a doctor. A brain one."

"Not enough balls to go against me face to face without a referee or your cronies around?"

"Say what you will, I'm not going to fall for your tricks anyway, crazy princess," Ryan said when he was no more than three steps away from Sullivan.

"I now realized why you hate gays so much and why you assaulted my husband," Jack finally found something to really hurt his opponent with when Ryan had just caught up with him. "It's because you're a closeted gay yourself, and you liked Jacob." Leaning over to the champion, Sullivan added almost in his ear. "Admit that you wanted to put my husband's big and juicy cock into your mouth."

The response came even sooner than Jack expected. Turning to Sullivan, Ryan simultaneously punched him with his fist, which was no longer covered with a glove, directly into Jack's mouth, now also damaging his lips.

"Thank you," Jack said with a frightening, bloody grin of a madman. "What I do now will be considered self-defense."

Saying the last words, he threw a straight punch, hitting Ryan in the nose. The security guards and the champion's numerous entourage immediately rushed to his aid, but the bright crowd decorated with rainbow flags suddenly rushed to cut in front of them.

Mostly, quite slender and intelligent-looking men and several women from Jack's LGBT fan club stepped so fiercely in between the fighters and those who hurried to separate them that much more powerful and seemingly much more courageous security guards and the champion's entourage got hesitant. And when they became aware of dozens of cameras broadcasting all of this live, their fervor finally faded. None of them wanted their face to be shown later in the news with a bar saying "thugs attacking a peaceful LGBT demonstration."

Meanwhile, as Sullivan's rainbow fan club pushed the others aside, clearing space for some sort of a ring in the aisle for the fighters, a real massacre broke out between Sullivan and Ryan. Without gloves, the fists were smashing noses, lips, and eyebrows much faster. Sullivan's entire face was already covered in blood from his newly disturbed injuries, but Ryan's first own blood also started running from his lips.

"Fucking stop it!" the champion hissed. "I don't want to kill you in front of the cameras!"

"Only when you admit that you attacked Jacob! Say it!"

"No way," Ryan spat out with a fresh portion of blood.

The champion tried to cheat. Clinching the opponent, he began to deliver forbidden blows to the back of the head and kidneys, but he did not take into account the fact that Sullivan was no longer bound by the rules either. Jack hit the opponent with his head. His forehead crashed into Ryan's nose, knocking blood out of it as well.

As soon as Ryan hesitated for a moment and reached for his nose to check if it was broken, Jack immediately struck a short, lashing jab in his jaw, and then a hook in his ear. For a moment, Ryan's vision went dark, and in order not to allow the opponent to gain further advantage, he plainly tried to kick Sullivan between the legs. Jack blocked the opponent's kick with one hand, hitting him in the solar plexus with the other.

"Say it! Admit that you attacked my husband!"

This time, the cameras caught Sullivan's words clearly.

"I didn't attack anybody!" the champion cried out, counting on the very same cameras. "You're insane!"

Joe Ryan charged forward and tried to tackle the opponent. Jack met him with a crushingly chopping blow, which once again landed on the champion's nose. Ryan got knocked off to the side.

"Admit that you attacked him!" Jack shouted again, letting his opponent get to his feet.

The champion's entire chest was covered in blood, which was running heavily from his now broken nose.

"You're insane!" Ryan barely managed to force the words out, already thinking to himself, whether or not he should just run away.

But camera flashes brought him back to his former state of a champion obsessed with his own greatness, who would never back down and never give up. Ryan charged at Sullivan again, this time striking him successfully first with a cross and then with an uppercut. Despite the terrible pain, as if his skin had been ripped off his whole face, Jack did not even blink, immediately throwing a fast one-two to the opponent's head.

Ryan staggered. Sullivan momentarily proceeded with a hook to his left ear. The champion fell.

"Admit that you attacked him! Say it!" Jack yelled again.

Ryan shook his head negatively. Then Sullivan sat on top of him and started pummeling him with punch after punch, shouting over and over again, "Say it! Say it! Say it!" Seeing that the champion was defeated, the security guards and his entourage made another attempt to rush to his aid, but Sullivan's LGBT fans, who were inspired by the indomitable fortitude of their blood-soaked idol, responded to them with furious roars and even raised fists.

"Say it! Say it! Say it!" Jack repeated over and over again.

The champion remained silent, trying to throw his opponent off of himself. Sullivan's gaze focused on the bridge of Ryan's nose. He suddenly remembered something he had not thought about since the moment he and Sophia confessed their love to each other. Something he had been preparing for so hard by himself and what he had been thoroughly hiding from McKee. The very same fatal blow with which he had originally been going to end the fight against Joe Ryan.

"Say it! Say that you attacked him!" Jack yelled again and raised his fist to deliver that very blow. Just one blow and the world champion would head from the ring straight to the grave – where he had previously sent Jacob. Just the right place for Joe Ryan to be in.

Ryan just shook his head in response. With a cry of rage, pain, and despair, Jack sent down the blow he had practiced for more than a year. Not to the face of the champion though, but to the floor next to him. Jack did not even notice breaking two fingers from the blow. He grabbed Ryan's head with his hands, brought his face close to his, and yelled with all his might, like a cornered wild beast gathering all its strength for the last, suicidally desperate jump at its adversary.

And Joe Ryan broke down. The narcissistic champion who had left the ring victorious almost a hundred times, the undefeated boxer whom no one had ever been able to even press to the ropes, the man who had never doubted his own superiority for a second in his entire life. The one who had always attacked first, the one who had made a routine out of humiliating and insulting other people, the one who had never caved in, and the one who had never found himself in the role of a victim. Now he was lying on the floor, choking on his own blood, and looking into the furious, maddened face of someone who was not afraid of him, someone who did not give up against all the odds, someone who went on even after he had lost.

It was someone who was ready for anything. And Joe Ryan got scared. For the first time in his life, he was paralyzed with fear. He saw in Jack Sullivan's eyes that he would never back down, never give up, never leave him alone. Joe Ryan realized that neither money nor fame, connections, expensive lawyers and fixers, numerous hangers-on, and a dozen guards – nothing could protect him from Jack Sullivan. The champion realized that there was only one way to get rid of this most fearsome opponent in his life.

"I attacked him! It was me!" in a barely audible voice the defeated champion said or rather spat the words out through the blood that filled his mouth.

"Louder!" Jack shouted. "So that everyone can hear!"

"I attacked your husband. I hit him. It was me!" Ryan started crying out hysterically. "I'll admit to everything! Just leave me alone! Please!" the champion begged and suddenly began to cry, sobbing like a child.

Shocked by what had happened, Sullivan's fans loosened their tight ranks, and the journalists rushed to the fighters, almost knocking down Jack, who was already getting up from his knees.

"Do you admit to attacking Jacob Sanders? Do you admit

that you inflicted a fatal injury on him?" journalists vied with each other.

Joe Ryan admitted to everything through tears, repeating over and over again that it was him. He was afraid that if he stopped talking, Jack would come back.

"Make way, you fricking paparazzi!" McKee barked, having just managed to get close to his pupil.

The old man was leading Sophia behind him. Together they grabbed Jack by the arms, his strength leaving him along with rage.

"Pops," Sullivan addressed the old man by this name for the first time. "I did it! I beat him! For real." Each word was followed by a new portion of blood running out of Jack's mouth. "I got justice, didn't I, Pops?"

"Of course, son! You beat him! You avenged Jacob," the old man said, barely holding back tears. "You're the real champion!"

Jack smiled wearily, saying, "I love you guys," and fainted.

... AFTERWORD ...

One month later

Joe Ryan's live confession attracted the attention of the entire country's press to the case of the assault on Jacob. Seeking sensation, journalists quickly found all the witnesses who were in the bar at that time. Each of them admitted that Joe Ryan and his people put pressure on them, and half also had to admit to receiving large sums of cash.

Getting ahead of everyone, TMZ managed to find even the video record of what had happened, the existence of which had been denied three years earlier by the bartender who worked there at the time. According to rumors, it was he who sold the recording to journalists for five million dollars. Joe Ryan and the entourage who was with him in that bar were immediately arrested. And that was just the beginning of the champion's downfall.

His cronies, realizing that they were facing real prison terms for complicity and concealment of the crime, and not enjoying the protection of such cool lawyers as Ryan himself, immediately began to reveal other crimes of the boxer in hopes that their testimonies would help them avoid prison.

So, in just two weeks the public learned about three rapes, the seduction of a minor, seven DUI cases that had led to accidents, including one with a fatal outcome, tax evasion, and numerous death threats, including those involving illegal firearms.

The same TMZ also unearthed the fact that in the course of his ten-year boxing career, Joe Ryan had spent at least twelve million dollars to buy the silence of his victims and witnesses of his numerous crimes. Taking into account all these circumstances, the judge denied Ryan bail and sent the boxer to await trial along with ordinary murderers and rapists.

Meanwhile, Sullivan's team was on the rise. It was now possible to sign up for One-Two Boxing classes no earlier than next year, so Kate, who unexpectedly proved herself to be a hardcore business shark, was now negotiating the opening of three new branches of the gym at once. Inspired by his friend's adamancy, Charlie began to study three times harder and had already managed to make it to the top five students of the academy.

Derrick, who like everyone else had now become an official co-owner of the gym, had taken over the One-Two Boxing charity program helping teenagers from disadvantaged families. In the gym, they were not just taught boxing but also instilled character and the idea that force can and should only be used to stand up for the weak.

The ring walk song, written by Sophia, attracted the attention of a large label. She was immediately offered a six-figure record deal. Of course, the whole sum was transferred to Sullivan's charity fund, which was now co-chaired by the newly-minted singer.

And most importantly, Jack and Sophia got engaged, and to celebrate the engagement all the other members of the team gathered in their home on this day. McKee and Ellen were working magic on the grill. Kate and Derrick were running around the garden together with Leo and Yara – Derrick's children, whose existence no one at One-Two Boxing had suspected before. Charlie made himself comfortable in the living room in front of the TV, waiting for the IPBU press conference to start, which had been announced the day before.

Jack and Sophia stood aside and could not stop being close to each other, as if they had not seen each other for at least ten years until this very day. Sullivan's injuries healed. Only there remained a scar in place where his eyebrow had been split. Sophia said that the scar made Jack look even more masculine.

"JACK! JACK! JACK!" Charlie shouted as he ran as if a war had broken out. "OVER THERE! ON TV! THEY JUST SAID!!!"

"Whoa, whoa, stop," Jack responded to the boy's shouts with a smile. "Where's the fire?"

"IPBU, Jack!!! They just said!!! It turns out that Joe Ryan fixed fights at the beginning of his career! They found evidence! He was stripped of his title and all his victories were canceled! Just like in Stanton's case, only even better! The title is vacant, Jack! They just said it themselves, they themselves said that you, Jack, you can get a shot at it!!! JACK, YOU CAN BECOME A CHAMPION!!!!!"

Printed in Great Britain
by Amazon

30488597R00218